SECRET SPEAKERS

and the Search for Selador's Gate

WITHDRAWN

SECRET SPEAKERS

and the Search for Selador's Gate

K.S.R. Kingworth

RAWLE & WINDSOR

First Edition

Library of Congress Cataloging-in-Publication Data
ISBN: 978-0-9801303-5-5   2010922277
Manufactured in Canada
Published April 6, 2010

FSC

Mixed Sources
Product group from well-managed
forests, controlled sources and
recycled wood or fiber

Cert no. SW-COC-000952
www.fsc.org
© 1996 Forest Stewardship Council

This
book is dedicated
to God who gave me breath.
For Dwight, Sadie and Quinn.

Then you will be brought low;
From the earth you will speak,
and from the dust where you are prostrate
your words will come.
Your voice will also be like that of a spirit
from the ground,
and your speech will whisper
from the dust.

ISAIAH TWENTY-NINE
VERSE FOUR

Chapters

Of the Gods there be but two who live in Airen-Or.
From great intelligence their wisdom grew
and thus was born a plan, a door
through which their hoomin of light would pass
and bid farewell to Thelras, to Cael;
then through the law of Arbiter Will amass
glory or condemnation, a consequence, still.

And so the Secret Speakers tell
the tales of those who choose
to return through the door in splendor or blight,
bearing marks of those who win or lose.

Prologue

 y name is Liver. You are not alone in this world. The time has come to tell you a story—a story that has been kept secret for ages in the Eternal Book of Time. If you believe it then it will change who you are. There will be no going back and no way for you to know what that change might mean.

Just know that you've been duly warned. If you don't want to risk the change then shut this book now. Tear out its pages. Burn it. Throw it away.

I reveal this story to you at a great sacrifice: You see, once my story is told I will be destroyed. So please, read carefully. It's possible that those who are powerless will find power. And those who are alone will be alone no more. The silent voices of those who are crying out might, just possibly, be heard.

Listen. Learn. Pass the knowledge on. That is, if you choose to continue. Just know this: I cannot lie for I am made of light.

Before you are allowed to open the sacred pages let me give you an explanation of things. I'll start here in the center of endless space, where I sit in the palm of the gods.

In the center of space there is a room. The room is a room of smooth stone floor surrounded by numberless stars. In the center of the room there is an enormous glowing orb that slowly spins and hovers above the glossy floor. The orb is an orb of blinding white-hot immortality. It is called the Mysterielle, for it is endless. Within the Mysterielle countless smaller orbs tumble and roll. Each one resembles the Mysterielle in luster and luminosity. Each is filled on the inside with a Luminamen: It is the soul's star, woven with shimmering threads from the Aurora Borealis.

These orbs of light in miniature, filled with a rotating Luminamen, are called Secret Speakers. I am one of them. Most are assigned to tell the truthful story of the creature to which they are singularly born, each at its appointed moment.

Some, however, known as era-born Secret Speakers are born to tell the story of an era. And so, these Secret Speakers are born to many. We are called Secret Speakers, not because we expose your secrets or the secrets of the misdeeds of man as you might imagine, but because we know your inmost heart where secrets, most sacred, live.

I am about to tell you something that has never been revealed before. So, listen carefully and consider its meaning. You were born with a glowing Secret Speaker nestled behind that bump in your throat: the one that goes up and down when you swallow. Touch it with your fingertips. Can you imagine a small ball of light hiding in there? When you lie awake at night perhaps you have seen the movement of its light and particular color behind your closed eyelids. Or, perhaps when you stare at something—say, a left-over grape sitting on your plate—and close your eyes, you see its image. Its shape and shadow. Your spinning star inside it. What you are seeing is just a snippet of what we Secret Speakers are recording of your life in its fractional triviality.

We Secret Speakers are put there for one purpose and one purpose only: We are note-takers of sorts. We record your life, its every moment, every memory, and every choice you make. Then, when you are dead and gone—or 'lightened' as we say (for the body is, indeed, heavy)—the gods place us in the golden cover of the Eternal Book of Time. It is in their constant possession, where it rests on one or the other's lap. We then re-tell all the smallest details of your life while they listen. As we speak, the words—and images—write themselves into the Book, filling up leaf after leaf in page-flipping fury. All those details, no matter how meaningless they may seem, add up to something wonderfully important, as you shall see.

I must give one word of final warning: If you do not choose the thoughts and actions of your life wisely, your Secret Speaker will not return to recount your story, and it will go untold. Not because your story isn't important, but because you haven't *made* it important. There's a difference.

Our number is known only to those who sit with the Mysterielle without beginning of days or end of time. And those who sit, who wait for the Secret Speakers to be born, one by one, consist of two gods most holy.

I'd like to tell you a story that is mostly mine and mine to tell. Not because I am possessive of it but because the gods have asked me to make it known to you at long last. I narrated it for the Eternal Book of Time long ago, but it is worth re-telling to you here because it has everything to do with you, as you shall come to learn. To state it more plainly, this particular narration touches every soul that has ever lived, or will live.

There was, you see, a small event that took place long ago in Cloven Grave. To the hoomin of Cloven Grave it happened ages ago, but a hundred years in Cloven Grave is a mere year in man's reckoning of time. And so, the event happened sometime last week, most likely while you were blowing your nose or eating supper.

Today—just as it was then—Cloven Grave is a mild-weathered valley nestled within what the folk there refer to as the Lands of Ice. If it could be found, the land would be mapped out near the North Pole. As I said, you are not alone on this planet. From my vantage point here in Airen-Or, Cloven Grave looks like one of several small, green emeralds scattered on the fur of a polar bear—as do a smattering of other green and fertile countries surrounded by snow and ice.

From where I sit, I see a strand of pale blue water that winds through the emerald of Cloven Grave. It curls like a necklace out to the north seas. To the untrained, earthly eye looking down from a plane, there is only white to be seen. No green. The gods have kept these lands invisible from the world.

The folk of Cloven Grave called (and still call) themselves hoomin. The term isn't too far different from the English word human. For the hoomin, however, the word means "people that are hidden." This is true, for they are land-loving folk who are hidden away from the world of man. They know nothing of trains, electricity, running water, or airplanes, though they hear the drone of airplanes in the sky above them, from time to time.

Their language is a conglomeration of the many languages of man. And they are very fond of songs and words that rhyme. This conglomeration of tongues came from a time when the hoomin sent ships along that strand of blue river which is warmed by a volcanic crack beneath it. These ships were sent out into the world to bring back spices and citrus fruits, particularly in the dead of winter. During the Shortlightren Dons, the days were short, and the hoomin's bodies craved flavorful things.

Even the way the hoomin dress shows an outside influence from their unseen travels. The men hoomin dress in kilts and high wool stockings similar to the kilts and stockings worn by men in Greece or Scotland.

Once a wee hoomin, or a child, reaches the age of hoomin-hood, knee-length pants are exchanged for the much longed-for kilt. No hoomin would ever be seen wearing pants. They are considered childish.

The hoomin are normally pleasantly plump as far as earth-dwelling creatures go. During the time of this story, however, they were deprived of having enough to eat. There is one characteristic of the hoomin that neither hunger—nor the ruling impostor, Harrold King—could not erase. The cheeks on the faces of the hoomin are rounded and slightly pink, as though covered with the skin of an apple.

As for the ever-present hunger, the hoomin folk were required to take all that they grew, milked or sewed to the temple of Osden Shorn once every seven days. It was then handed back to them in small, sad-looking portions. Law-making Harrold King hoarded the rest within the walls of the temple, where it often turned to rot and pig fodder—except for what made its way into his belly.

And so, nearly everyone (except those that hid what food they could) felt keen hunger nearly every day. During the chilly Shortlightren Dons, the nights were colder than they should have been because they didn't have enough blankets to keep them warm. It was difficult to sleep the whole night through without waking up in a shiver. As I mentioned, Cloven Grave has a mild climate, but the evenings do get cool at certain times of the year.

The hoomin have always had a particular fondness for sheep. The grass-munching creatures dot the hillsides and valleys at every turn. The hoomin also find great pleasure in planting and tending to orchards and vineyards. So, where sheep are not seen grazing, or where there isn't a stone cottage thatched with grass on the roof, there is most likely an orchard. Or vineyards. Or woods. The land is thick with furry green trees and woodlands. Near the rivers, the bark of trees is covered with thick green moss. The horses of Cloven Grave are enormous. They have a blanket of thick hair that swishes around their hooves when they move at an ambling gait.

Beneath the feet of the hoomin, the fertile land is rich with jewels, gems and gold. They are cultivated by the small and spritely Impissh Nissen. These winged creatures are no taller than the length of your hand. They call the jewels "moss blossoms," for they sprout out of the moss, almost like flowers. The roots of the moss blossoms have no end. No one knows where their reaching, feathery fingers go.

The moss blossoms are used as currency by the hoomin, except that they are called shackles. You humans use coins and paper money to pay for what you want (as well as what you have to pay for, even if you don't want to). The hoomin call them shackles, because that's exactly what they represent to them: bondage to Harrold King.

The hoomin's cottages are situated between the road and the lake where the hillsides slope more gently. The hillsides slope around Lakinren Bae, a lake that glistens like a jewel in the center. Due to some force of nature, mountains rise sharply skywards to the east. On both sides of the lake the mountains give way to hillsides, where the hoomin of Cloven Grave live. To the west lie the lowlands that are marked by winding canals, naturally called Low Grave.

The hoomin mark time according to the eras—or periods of time—that shape their existence. At the time of the story I am about to repeat to you, they were living in the midst of the Fallow Era. The year was F.E. 797.

There was one among them at that time who prophesied that the Fallow Era was coming to an end. And so, of course, stories were being told of what might come. The legend of the Planter Era was on their lips amidst whirls of pipe smoke during quiet evenings in front of the glowing embers of their fireplaces. The hoomin wondered, as they fell asleep, what would happen to them when the old era passed away to make room for the new.

There is one more thing I would like to mention about the hoomin folk. They have an almost uncanny ability to sense the spirits that dwell in the rocks and trees around them. It's not that they are superstitious. I think perhaps it is due to the fact that the valley of the Graves is surrounded by ice. Like a funnel, the very stuff of life gets poured into that spot of earth. The air pulses with a vibrancy unknown on other continents where life can be spread, well, rather thinly. The grasses grow greener and more lush, the vines and flowers more vibrant and colorful.

They teach from the Scrolls of Truth that all things have a light, or spirit, that existed before they were created in physical form. (Whether rock, bird, twig, cloud—or hoomin.)

I wish I could describe what we Secret Speakers see when we look down on earth and all that dwells upon it. As Secret Speakers, we are able to see particles of light. We are, you see, made up of nothing more than light ourselves (being as we are, pure intelligence). And so, we see the earth as a moving, shifting ball of burning brilliance and smoky darkness. We are able to see the light—and shadows—of man tread upon its skin. Everything you touch, and all that has been created, is made up of light in varying degrees. Suffice it to say, you are absolutely brilliant to behold. So is this book in your hands.

There are those whose light is more refined, and, for lack of a better word, shimmery. Why you don't see it, only the gods know. But it is there just the same. There are those (such as a hoomin I shall soon tell of) whose light is so diminished that they are nearly as dense as lead metal. There are many varying degrees in between. This diminishing light is the cause of much suffering in the world of hoomin and man alike.

I mentioned that my story began with an incident. It was a birthday, but it was all that was needed to get the ball rolling.

Let me explain. Just before my host left home to celebrate the event, there was a small *pop!* An opening appeared on the Mysterielle. As with the birth of all Secret Speakers, I emerged like a luminescent, blue marble and rolled onto the floor. Inside me, a glowing Luminamen had already begun to spin. It was the soul star of The Great Deliverance: the story I had waited so long to reveal.

I was one of the few Secret Speakers of which I told earlier. I was not assigned to a person, but to an era that was to shape the destiny of all things living. To be more precise, I am Secret Speaker number 538,336,628,696. I am era-born Secret Speaker No. 3.

In other words, 538,336,628,695 Secret Speakers needed to be born, until it was my turn. Two of them were era-born Secret Speakers. They needed to record the events of their assigned eras. Then, it was my turn.

I tumbled out and rolled across the floor; whereupon, the delicate hand of Thelras, Mother Queen of Light, reached down and picked me up. She turned me over in her hands and whispered,

Mysterielle nah brah steerrohn.

The sound filled the air like the rushing of great waters. It was a sound that would make you want to sit and imagine what you hear in its music—much like when you sit by a fire at night and imagine what pictures you see in the dancing flames.

Then Cael, Father King of Light, reached out and took me in his hands. He looked into my ocean-blue depths. His deep, thunderous roar pierced my heart, and I trembled.

Yes, dear one, it is time for the change.
The great plan unfolds. Let the story begin—
and end—according to the law of Arbiter Will.

One final thing might be worth explanation: The gods never interfere in the lives of their offspring. That is the meaning of the law of Arbiter Will. Their offspring must act for themselves in all things. Cael looked at me once again and nodded. It was time. I rose in the air and hovered.

"I should like to hear your report once it is finished," he said to me.

"And you shall," I said. No sooner had I spoken, when I disappeared from his hand.

In the next instant (and miles below the realm of Airen-Or), I hovered above the neck of Fair O'Nelli. She lay motionless in a wooden box, as though she were dead. Scarcely breathing.

Oh, what a gentle face. A crack of moonlight pierced in between the planks above her. In that moment the darkness was transformed into a dusty glow, and her face appeared to be the sun! I rested upon her forehead and spoke these words,

So nice, so kind, polite and loyal.
So clean, so humble, valiant, royal.
You, dear one, have a journey to make.
You will not be alone, though much is at stake.

That accomplished, I lay upon her neck. My excitement caused me to be somewhat more dense than usual. It took me a moment to calm myself, so that I could return to my permeable state. I nestled beneath the bump in her throat, in what you call the Adam's Apple. My presence there would give her the feeling, for the rest of this story, that she had just the hint of a lump in her throat.

You must remember that I was not born to her as her personal speaker. She was *already* born with one. I am an *era-born* Secret Speaker. The events of the era to which I was born could not take place without her actions. So it was with her (and her personal Secret Speaker) that I resided to tell the tale.

Know that if there are moments when Fair and I are not present in the story, I shall call upon the Secret Speaker of the hoomin who is. They shall fill in for me. And now, to press on with the telling of the tale.

The sound of a sharp trumpet blast awoke the hillsides of Cloven Grave like a rooster announcing the coming of dawn. In the dark wooden box, Fair opened her eyes and saw nothing but more darkness. Her pale, blue eyes glowed faintly like watery ponds. Such a simple moment, yet, it is all woven into this story, which makes this moment—and every moment of her life—great indeed. You shall learn in due time whether or not she survives. That is, if you choose to keep reading and risk possible change.

One final note before you open the Eternal Book of Time

Through the expanse of space, Thelras and Cael saw me nestle into Fair's throat just before she woke up. I heard Thelras say, "Perhaps we should have chosen her brother for the task, Cael. Fair is so wide-eyed and unsuspecting."

"Yes, but her dog will be a comfort to her. And it couldn't be helped about her brother. It was not our place to interfere, nor has it ever been, nor will be."

"Of course, but as a mother . . ."

"I know, dear. I know."

I recorded every sound. I recorded every word spoken. I recorded every event that seemed important to the story. When The Great Deliverance was accomplished, I returned to Airen-Or. Thelras placed me into a hollow area, carved into the thick, gold cover of the Eternal Book of Time. The story I held within me melted into its pages, never to be erased, never to be forgotten.

The time has now come to open the pages of this story for the first time, where it has lain untold for hoomin ages. For reasons unknown to me, the gods of Airen-Or have chosen to make it known to you now. Perhaps you will come to understand the reason by story's end. Perhaps not. The pages are opening. You are almost there.

This is the story of a
compassionate heart.

You are about to open
the Eternal Book of Time.

The Eternal
Book of Time

The Story of The Great Deliverance
as told by Era-born Secret Speaker No. 3
(otherwise known as Liver)
Color: Sky Blue
Filled with a glowing white Luminamen
Year: F.E. 797

1 : Released

he hoomin lay completely still inside a closed wooden box. It was dark, shallow, and wide. Although she had been dead to the world for nine years, she had learned much about life during her cold, extinguished childhood.

A loud horn blast sounded in the distance. Fair O'Nelli awoke and opened her eyes. The two round pools of silver blue hovered in the coffin-like space, blinking. She began to hum a little tune to herself, almost silently.

It was early morning and still dark from a moonless night. Fair was in the back of her mother's wagon. She had been there all night, counting her heartbeats between waking and sleeping to pass the time. She had waited like a butterfly in its cocoon for dawn to come.

She had dreamt of this moment. She was officially, as of that morning, thirteen. She was headed for Lamb's Tavern to receive her apron of maidenhood. After this day all would know that she was officially of age.

A maiden.

No more darkness. No more hiding. No more cold.

Fair was sandwiched uncomfortably between a wooden floor beneath her (which her head found to be particularly hard) and a false, wooden floor above her (which her nose felt to be painfully close). This was a necessary discomfort. The reason was simple: the space she lay between needed to be as shallow as possible so no one would suspect it wasn't an ordinary old wagon pulled by a horse and driver. To make the journey more tolerable, her mother had spread out a thin, woolen blanket that softened the bumps. It prevented Fair from getting too many splinters.

Her dog, Sauveren, lay above her surrounded by sacks full of old, fragrant apples. He had whimpered all night inches above Fair's prostrate body, staying close by. Just in case. She had felt helpless to reach out and cradle his head in her hands, to soothe him. The thin wooden floor was the first barrier she and her dog had known in nine years. Not feeling him wrapped around her like a blanket was almost painful. Even worse, she'd had to keep silent. She had to swallow the gust of words that flew constantly from her mouth. She had to gulp down the need to share everything with her dog that entered her mind.

His damp muskiness fell through the cracks like loose soil along with the fragrance of apples and straw. She took a deep breath in. His warmth seeped through the planks and surrounded her in familiar comfort. She knew this would have to be good enough for a while longer. Fair placed both palms against the wood above her and ventured a whisper, "I know you're there, Sauveren."

At the sound of her whisper, her dog desperately whimpered and sniffed at a crack through the floor, just above her face. He scratched desperately at the wood with his claws, as though he were trying to dig a hole in it. Just to lick her hand. Fair put her fingers to the spot and whispered, "Won't be long now." Her reassurance seemed to settle him. He stopped scratching and cocked his head to one side. His throat warbled a melody of questions, beginning high in his throat and working its way downward until it was low and hesitant. Then he was quiet. The wood groaned and creaked as he lay back down and rested his chin on his paws.

In the darkness her mother approached the wagon like a drifting cloud, outlined by the faint light of the coming morning. Her name was Lariel. Their neighbor sat in the wagon seat. He was called Gibber Will. He held the reins. He had built the false floor for the wagon. It lifted up like a door on hinges if you knew where to pull up on which edge.

"This is as good a time as any," said her mother.

Gibber Will said, "The light's changin'. Folks are startin' to head for Osden Shorn. Better be off."

Fair realized she could faintly hear the sound of wagon wheels on dirt in the distance. *Good,* she thought. *We'll be lost in the crowd.* She felt a bump and her nose almost touched the rough wood above. Her head came down, *ouch!* on the thin blanket beneath her. Dust from above filtered down through the cracks of the wagon and swam in the air around Fair. She held her breath until she couldn't hold it any longer. She felt it settle on her face and arms. On her nose. Without warning, the yelp of a sneeze escaped. Lariel and Gibber Will's eyes both grew round with fright when they heard it.

Instinctively, Gibber Will tried to cover up the sound with a series of high-pitched coughs and snorts.

Lariel looked straight ahead while she walked alongside the wagon and whispered as loudly as she dared, "Fair. Keep silent. Please. You've come too far to ruin it now."

"I couldn't help it," Fair whispered.

Lariel casually placed her hand on the side of the wagon. She continued to look ahead. She said, "I'm sorry I won't be there to see you. You know, in daylight." To anyone who might be watching, it looked as though she were simply muttering to herself.

Fair whispered reassuringly, "I know."

Lariel absent-mindedly adjusted a red scarf tied around her long brown hair. It was the only hint of color she wore. Her ankle-length dress was woven from drab brown cloth. Her apron was a dull cream color. Her eyes were large and round. To look at her for the first time, the light of knowing told strangers that she was a good, kind hoomin.

"You'll come back to me, Fair?"

"You don't need to worry, Mother. Besides, I packed a basket." Fair had filled her basket with a few soft apples, a leather flask of water, a pot of salve in case she got slivers during the ride, and a chunk of coarse brown bread. It sat at Gibber Will's feet, nice and tidy.

Sauveren got up and went to the side of the wagon. He panted and stared at Lariel through a curtain of mist that hung in the darkness. She reached out and dug her fingers around his ears. He bowed his head so she could give him a really good scratch.

"And Fair . . . ?" she paused, while she searched for something else—something final, yet hopeful—to say. She nodded when it announced itself.

She simply said, "Emerge."

Fair thought that was an odd word for a farewell. *Emerge?*

Gibber Will ignored Lariel's last comment. "She's right, Lariel. No need to worry." Lariel shook off a small laugh.

She smiled and said, "You're a fine one, neighbor, the way you're shivering and shaking like a rabbit."

"Can't help it." Gibber Will wiggled his nose and sniffed. His two front teeth poked out over his bottom lip. "She's just like one of my lammies. Precious, like. And now she's grown up. Feel like I'm losin' her." He pulled a wad of cloth from a white fur-covered purse that hung from a belt below his belly. He dabbed at his forehead. He had known Fair since she was a baby. In recent years he had felt very protective of her.

"I'll be fine!" Fair whispered. She was giddy with the thought that she'd be able to come and go as she pleased now. She reached out to her side for Sauveren, a habit born from many years of solitude. She startled when her hand felt nothing but air. *That's right. He's just above me.*

"Goodbye, Mother."

Lariel looked around nervously, in case there were unseen ears listening nearby. She said a little more loudly, and rather stiffly, "Thank you for taking in my apples, Gibber Will. It's all I have to give this time."

She swatted the horse on the rump and the horse quickened its pace. Then she whispered a final word to him, "Keep your ears open for me, will you?"

"I can't never say no. T's not in my nature," he said. He tipped his cap with a shaky hand. He felt the tremble and took a deep breath in to steady himself. He whispered out of the corner of his mouth, "I got the ears to hear anything that don't seem right." He clucked and made his ears wiggle. This brought a faint smile to Lariel's face. He looked at the changing morning sky and blew a gust of air out with billowed cheeks.

"Hyap!" he ordered, giving the reins a jiggle.

Fair felt the wagon lurch with life. She knew she was on her way. Darkness would be her companion for just a while longer.

She gently bit the end of her tongue, determined to keep it squished between her teeth for the rest of the bumpy ride, in case she had the urge to speak. She hadn't lived a life of darkness, damp, and cold only to ruin her chance to see daylight now.

Gibber Will gave a cough and looked both ways before passing out of O'Nelli Gate onto Cloven Grave Road. It followed the curve of the lake. His was one wagon in a long line of wagons headed for Osden Shorn.

Cloven Grave was laid out thusly: Most cottages were situated between the road and the lake. Every cottage was surrounded by a stone fence. Every stone fence was surrounded by a field or an orchard. Every entrance onto the property was guarded by a brightly painted gate, and a hoomin's cottage was referred to by its gate. For instance, Gibber Will's home was called Will's Gate. Harrold King's gate was called, of course, King's Gate.

Harrold King, the venomous impostor of Cloven Grave, required that every hoomin who stopped to visit a neighbor must pay an entrance fee at the gate. He had spies placed everywhere to ensure that no one got away with selfish hoarding. He told himself that no hoomin under his royal thumb was going to deprive him of his wealth. If it meant they had to use their precious shackles just to visit friends, then so be it.

The consequence of non-payment was having your own cottage carted away, stone by stone until you were left with the echo of nothing, hovering in front of you.

The hillsides on the upside of the road were dotted with sheep. The road was edged on both sides with low stone walls covered on top and in every crack with thick cushions of moss.

As the furry-hoofed horse and wagon bumped along, the blackness around Fair changed into dim gray fuzz. Her heart skipped a beat when she saw a crack of light in between the wooden planks. Daylight. Freedom. Walking the roads as she pleased. She could hardly imagine it.

The smell of grass wafted into the space around her. She fought the urge to hum. *Today is my becoming day,* she smiled to herself. *I am no longer a wee hoomin.* Fair tugged at her dress, her first dress of color. It felt too tight at the waist and shoulders. Compared to the loose woolen smock and pants she'd worn for so many years, it just didn't feel right.

Contrary to the law, her mother had not turned everything she made over to Harrold King. She kept one length of pale peach-colored cloth and painstakingly stitched it into a dress for this very day. Fair wondered what her apron would look like. She had never seen one on a girl wee hoomin. She hadn't seen a girl, or boy, wee hoomin for that matter, for nine years.

The wagon bumped along Cloven Grave Road for a long while. Fair could hear the thud of a water jug against the side of the wagon. Gibber Will had fashioned it out of leather that he'd soaked in water and oak bark. He had pounded it for an entire day then stitched it into the shape of a pot with a handle on top, with two spouts at each end. Once it dried, it was as hard as rock.

Fair licked her dry lips and swallowed. *The water's so close I can hear it sloshing*, she thought. She hadn't had a drink since the afternoon before, a precaution against having to empty herself while in her coffin of liberation. This was an enormous sacrifice, for she was always thirsty. She wouldn't be able to have a drink until she was safe within the walls of Lamb's Tavern.

The ride seemed to go on forever. Bump, bump, bump. *Ouch, ouch, ouch.* Fair was accustomed to darkness and waiting. She began to content herself, as usual, with the thoughts in her head. She bit her tongue and pretended that she was sharing them with her dog.

Memories of light.

Memories of laughter.

A father.

A brother.

The memory of her mother's face—pale and frozen stiff with fear—the day she moved Fair down into the cellar. The sound of her mother's voice was frantic as she gripped the door with white knuckles. The words replayed in Fair's mind: "Please, trust me. Know that I love you, so very much." At the time, Fair felt frightened and had no idea what her mother was talking about.

"I know you don't understand. But you will, someday. It will all become clear." She kissed Fair with a yelp of apology and slowly closed the door as lovingly as she could. *Thud.*

Memories of darkness.

Before she learned to gather light.

There were always two words that popped into her mind when the daydreams started: *Little Sparrow.* They always came with a luminous face: her father's face, framed with dark hair, gentle and kind. A wide, toothy smile.

Remembering the shape of his mouth as he said those words—Little Sparrow—and pulled her close.

They always came with a feeling: warmth and being surrounded. His large warm hand wrapped around her small and slender one as they walked to the barn.

They always came with a smell: a smell she couldn't quite remember, but it was right there, just beyond the end of her nose.

Warm.

Teasing her.

Little Sparrow.

After some time, Gibber Will relaxed and began to talk to his horse. *Click, click,* went his tongue and cheek. "Atta girl. Won't be long now." He looked as though he had good reason to go into town. The wagon was filled with sacks of last seasons' apples and lots of straw to keep them from bruising. Anyone would assume he and his dog were headed for Osden Shorn with the rest of the hoomin folk.

It was the day of rendering, when all the folks in Cloven Grave were required to bring all that they had grown, milked, raised, plucked, or weaved to Harrold

King. Harrold King was the governing lender of lodging, the lender of the very pillow you saw when you got in bed and wondered—oh, silly thought—that it might not be there by the time you laid your head down, because some unseen hand had snatched it away. Harrold King was the lender of the spoonful of porridge poised outside your mouth. The lender of life and breath itself. You knew it didn't belong to you until you swallowed it.

Once it all came into his ownership, he then filled his own belly with it or let it go to rot for pig fodder. Osden Shorn used to be a temple before he took over the rule of Cloven Grave. Now it could be smelled long before you got to it. No one knew what he did with anything that wasn't edible.

Fair froze when she heard Gibber Will say, "Woah." The wagon lurched to a stop. She slid forward like a corpse, head first. She clapped her hand over her mouth and resisted the urge to ask what was happening.

Fair swallowed. Her wide eyes blinked and searched through the muddy air as she tilted her head this way and that. She used her ears to hear the slightest hint of an answer. She heard someone swallow, and it wasn't Gibber Will. Her hearing was exceptional, since she had spent so many years in darkness. Fair felt a mouse scurry onto her dress and sit on her thigh. She was used to mice and liked them quite much. They had kept her company in the cellar all those years.

A voice said, "Have you eaten today, Gibber Will?"

"Yes, thank you. Have you eaten?"

"I don't believe you, hoomin. You look weak. You're shaking."

"It's nothin' . . ." Gibber Will coughed.

Inquiring after someone's health in Cloven Grave never consisted of, "How are you?" but more importantly, whether or not you had eaten that day. The hoomin folk of Cloven Grave were usually hungry. You wouldn't necessarily know it by the look of their slightly rounded, ruddy cheeks.

Fair heard the voice say, "Just wanted to let you know . . ." There was a pause while the voice looked up and down the road and into the woods, ". . . that the Harrold had himself a dream last night. Dreamt someone was sitting on his throne and it weren't him."

Gibber Will whistled through his two front teeth. With his palms, he smoothed back the clouds of whiskers that grew above his cheeks. They popped out instantly like rebellious tufts of sheep's wool that refused to lie flat.

"Again? Ach, his dreams don't mean nothin'. Pray there won't be another whisking."

Fair's heart caught in her throat: the whisking. It was a word and a memory she had locked up tightly in a far off place in her heart. But now, there it was again. Spoken.

The Whisking.

The lock instantly shattered.

She bit her bottom lip to keep it from quivering.

Where did Harrold King take my brother? Her only memory, nine years old and faded, was of a four year-old wee hoomin with a head full of golden curls. She remembered a freckle on his neck beneath his ear. The shape of a sword, long and dark—a swipe of brown that sometimes frightened her. Her twin brother. The sound of his lisp when he talked.

He was taken because he couldn't reach over his head and touch his ear on the opposite side. She could. So the Protectors assumed she was too old, because—as she heard one of them say—she was growing into her head.

Fair swallowed a lump in her throat and pressed her hand against a rough wooden plank above her. Sauveren pawed and licked the planks as though he knew what she was feeling. *He knows*, Fair thought. *He knows what I'm thinking.* She could smell his furry fragrance and it gave her comfort.

"Nah," said the voice. "It weren't a wee hoomin like that other dream. Says this time he'll know who it is when he sees 'em. He ain't telling how. He's posted a law on the Cries Unia to have everyone come to Clock Tower Square. Have yourself a look-see."

Gibber Will looked at the trees that lined Cloven Grave Road to find a tree trunk with a Cries Unia, a plaque, hanging from it. He read:

All hoomin shall come to
Clock Tower Square at midden meal,
after the clock finishes striking twelve.
All latecomers will be laughed at
on the platform of punishment.

By order of his royal eminency and majesty,
Harrold King.

Gibber Will sounded disgusted. "Him an his dreams. Ach. It ain't even the Harrold's throne. You and I both know who's supposed to be sittin' on it."

"Tell *him* that!"

Fair heard the two men laugh. She felt movement on her leg. She felt the mouse's small claws tickle her skin as it crept along the fabric of her dress, almost as if it were inspecting it. Then she felt the claws moving in a line along her body towards her head. It crawled onto her neck and sat there for a moment. Its body and tiny feet felt cold on her skin, not warm—a sensation that surprised Fair.

Oh please, she begged silently. *No. Not now.* She didn't dare raise her arm to brush it away in case she made a noise. She felt a slight, cold pressure as it prepared to move again. *Why is it so cold?* She gulped as she felt it crawl up her chin, across her mouth, and onto her upper lip. Fair could hear the two hoomin talking outside. She desperately wished Gibber Will would move along quickly.

Just then, she felt an icy tail tickle the tip of her nose. She moved her lips around frantically, hoping to make it fall off. It dug its claws into her skin and held on. She felt the tip of the tail touch the edge of her nostril. Then, to her horror the tail slid inside. Then—*no*—she felt it tickle the edge of her other nostril. Almost as though it were daring her not to sneeze. Almost as if it knew.

"Oh, I almost forgot. Payment for passing," said the voice. "Two blue shackles."

Fair could feel a sneeze coming. Without thinking she swung her arm up in a sideways arc and grabbed the mouse with a firm grip. But it was too late.

A high-pitched sneeze shot out of her mouth. The force of it slammed her forehead against the ceiling of the wagon. Her hand squeezed down on the mouse. She threw it to the side and heard it splat against the side of the wagon box. It began to make a scratching sound almost like sandpaper. The only thought in Fair's mind was why the mouse felt so cold. A shock of realization hit her: It was hairless. The thought made her shudder.

All this happened in an instant. Gibber Will began a series of high-pitched sneezes in case Fair made any more noise. He noticed out of the corner of his eye that the Protector was watching the dog growl and paw at the wagon floor, sniffing around.

The Protector looked at Gibber Will, "Found himself a mouse, I reckon."

Gibber Will breathed a silent sigh of relief, snapped open the silver rim of his belly bag and rummaged around for a couple of shackles. Blue ones, the size of his small fingernail. He dropped them in the Protector's hand and teased, "My, but you're a mean one!"

The voice laughed, "A Protector's gotta do his job."

When Harrold King made himself ruler over Cloven Grave many years earlier he promptly surrounded himself with 400 hoomin. He gave them the title of Protector. Some of them were local hoomin; others were called in from Low Grave. This one was nice. They all wore burgundy-colored kilts, black caps, and capes that hung over one shoulder.

Fair felt the wagon lurch again. *Ouch.* She knew they'd made it and she wanted to feel relieved, but a shovelful of fear sat in her stomach. *What was that thing?* She wanted to have a look so she did something she had done for years: she held her breath until the tip of her first finger began to tingle, then glow.

When the yellow light it cast was bright enough for her to see by, she slid her head to one side, careful not to scrape her ear against the wood above it. She pulled her chin down to her shoulder to see what the creature was. She heard it scuttle down to her feet where it hid from view. She let her breath out with a frustrated sigh, and her finger stopped glowing. The darkness returned.

Over the years, Fair had practiced holding her breath to pass the time. She got to the point where she could hold it for minutes on end. At first, the activity had seemed harmless. But as time went on she felt something begin to change. Soon, she began to feel tiny prickles course through her body. With time she noticed the prickles direct themselves to her first finger, and not just the finger, but the tip of it. It tingled.

One day (which was really night for the rest of Cloven Grave), Fair was holding her breath and waiting for the tingling to start. To her surprise she began to see faint shapes: the outline of her blanket, the glimmer of water dripping down the stones of the cellar wall. Mice. At first she didn't believe it. Then she saw the glint of her dog's eyes staring at her. He licked his chops. She actually saw it happen.

She could see! In the darkness. Without a candle.

Her fingertip tingled so intensely that she looked at it and discovered with shock, surprise, and fear—all at the same time—that it was glowing like a candle and vibrating. The skin was a warm, illuminated, yellowish pink, which showed the outline around her fingernail. She shook it quickly, hoping to extinguish it, but wherever her finger passed through the air it left trails of light.

As the days, months, and years went on Fair occupied herself with drawing intricate landscapes in the air, where they hovered for several minutes.

In the wagon, Fair's mind wandered to what Harrold King was going to do about his dream this time. Nine years earlier his first dream had cost her the only brother she had. It had cost her a father. A father she would never see again, she feared. It had cost her sunshine, freedom, and friends. But, she consoled herself, he had not been able to steal her light or stop her from gathering more. Her mother told everyone Fair was dead. She gave her daughter the protection of death to save her life.

Fair slept in the cold, damp cellar by day. She went out to play with her dog in the death of night when there was no moon to make shadows. Her mother taught her to read from the Scrolls of Truth near a window when the moon was full and bright enough to read by.

No candles.
Ever.

Fair understood. Mostly. She was waiting for this day. Mother. Moonlight. Stars. Her mother's voice. The tinkling sound of her father's music box, painted with the snow-capped mountains of Mount Rilmorrey. Listening to it while they read from the Scrolls of Truth,

> *Knowledge is truth.*
> *Truth is light.*
> *Light is power.*

Light invites more light
and banishes that which is dark.
Darkness is another power altogether.
Use your power wisely and well.

She watched particles of light leap from the sheepskin pages as she read. She felt them pass through her face, her hands, her arms, her chest—where she felt everything that beat and lived within her absorb it thirstily. She was gathering light. She could feel it when it happened. She knew—somehow—it was the same light that tingled and buzzed inside her when she held her breath to see through the darkness.

Neither Fair nor her mother knew when the rays of light would jump from the pages. When they did, her mother quickly closed the curtains and covered Fair with a dark blanket. She knew her daughter would have enough light to read by from the pages alone.

Fair sensed her mother's pleasure during those times, knowing that her daughter, if just for a moment, could see. The fact that Fair could use her fingerlight to see by in the cellar was a secret she kept just for herself. It was like a treasured belonging that felt more treasured by the very fact it was hers and hers alone.

Fair woke from her daydreams of fingerlit landscapes and reading from the Scrolls. The wagon had stopped again.

"Oh no," Gibber Will groaned.

Fair bit her tongue so hard it hurt. She wanted to ask what the matter was but knew she had to stay silent. Then she heard a strange, groaning sound.

The wagon came to a stop.

Gibber Will whistled through his teeth and muttered, "Ach, we're surrounded front and back by a whole flock of the wee bleating creatures." He was thoughtful for a moment. He craned his neck to look up the road. He looked over his shoulder.

He reached under his seat and moved Fair's basket aside. He pulled a small string that opened a tiny square door into the space behind his feet. Fair felt a rush of cool air hit her face. She sucked it in gratefully.

Gibber Will spoke, "It's all clear now, Fair. You alright back there?"

Fair swallowed and quietly said, "I don't think I'd better speak."

"It's alright. It's only sheep in front and behind what don't plan on going nowheres. So?"

Fair did have something that was bothering her. She began to speak. Haltingly. "There's something crawling around me. I don't want it in here."

"Can't help you there, much as I'd like. Hasn't bit you, has it?"

"No. I'm alright." She thought about how it tickled her nose, almost knowingly.

"Fine, then. Anything else?"

Fair knew he liked to hear stories, and better yet about her dreams. She said, "I had a dream last night while I slept here in the wagon."

"You did, did you? Good or bad, pray tell?"

"Good mostly. And I remember every part of it, too."

"How about telling ole Gibber Will a story then? I'll warn you when you gotta bite yer tongue. You don't need to worry. Not a bit."

2 : Through the Sinky Down

 air licked her dry lips. She craned her neck to see out of the small door and saw the heels of Gibber Will's boots. Nothing more. She trusted he would keep his word and warn her if anyone came close enough to hear her speak.

She put her mouth as close to the opening as she could and began. In one long breath she said, "In my dream I was lying in this same wagon and a glowing, squishy glob called a Glommer squeezed in through a crack and lay next to me. Then, these eyes sprouted out of the glob and inspected me from head to toe."

"How do you know it was called a Glommer?" Gibber Will asked.

"I just do."

"Go on."

"Well, its arms just sort of pushed out of his round rubbery shape and dragged me from my body out of the wagon, all the way down to Lakinren Bae. I could see the water glistening in the moonlight." She paused and asked, "Do you remember that smelly place next to the shore?"

"That I do. The Sinky Down. You went there when you were a wee, wee hoomin with your father and . . . well . . ." He wanted to mention her brother, Hale, but thought better of it.

"That's it."

The Sinky Down was a shallow bog that smelled of rotten eggs. It bubbled near the edge of the lake and was no bigger than a kitchen. Years earlier, her father had taken Fair and Hale to look for frogs in the reeds. He pushed his oar into the shallow, soft sediment of decay that covered the bottom of the bog. It was so soft that it took no effort at all to push the oar all the way in. They all crinkled their noses and exclaimed, *ewww!* when they discovered there seemed to be no bottom.

"So tell me what happened. Were you afraid?"

"Not at all. That's what's so strange. I asked the Glommer where he was taking me, but he didn't answer. He just kept a hold of my wrist—well, my not real wrist, since my real body was back in the wagon. But he took my spirit wrist and dove into the smelly water. I sailed in behind him, flapping like a white tablecloth on a windy night.

"He took me down through the feathery, floating muck. It was dark but the water was warm, and I could breathe. Then all the muck was gone and I could see that we were in a smooth, brown tunnel made of clay that went straight down."

Gibber Will's eyes went wide, "This is a good one. What then?"

"Then I knew, because it was a dream, that the Glommer was pulling me into the center of misery and woe. Mother has told me stories of such a place. Just then, I saw an opening carved into the side of the shaft. We were coming up to it, and I knew if I was going to get away from the Glommer I'd have to do it soon.

"When we got close to the opening, I wrenched my wrist free and swam for safety. Right away, the eyes bulged out from the Glommer's shapeless body. Each eye looked in different directions to try and find me. I knew I didn't have much time.

"The opening was a cave of sorts, filled with what looked like piles of garden tools. I crawled over the first pole, but I felt it move."

Gibber Will said, "Moved? That gives me the shivers. What then?" He paused. "Wait, Fair. I hear something."

Fair bit her lip and froze.

"Never you mind. The shepherd's comin', but he's a long ways off. So go on. The pole moved."

"Well, when my eyes got used to the murky light— you know, sort of like how a cloud in front of the moon takes on a shape if you look at it—I saw that the sticks and poles were the shadows of hoomin instead. They were just skin and bones, leaning up against both sides of the cave. None of them spoke, but they weren't sleeping. It's like hope was just gone from them."

"No hope at all, you say?"

"It felt dreadful. I quickly clambered over them and felt the Glommer grab at my toes."

"Did he get you?"

"He got my big toe, but I yanked it free."

"And you got away?"

Fair told how she crawled over all the branchy arms and legs and felt her head hit some metal bars. They were part of a gate. She pushed against the gate, which swung open into a room that was lit up and bright as daylight.

Gibber Will said, "Now that's the sort of dream you'd like. Lots of light."

Fair smiled. She said, "It was a very large place with floors made of white, smooth stone and walls. The room was filled with rows and rows of stone boxes with stone people standing on them."

"Those would be statues on pedestals, I'm thinkin'," Gibber Will suggested.

"The strange thing is, from where I peeked in, the water in the cave stopped right at the opening into the room. It wobbled like it was soft glass. I stuck my head through it and the room smelled inviting and wonderful. I pulled my head back into the cave and asked the tangled bunch of hoomin if they wanted to come with me."

"And?" prodded Gibber Will.

"One of the hoomin looked at me with large sunken eyes. He reached his hand towards me with one finger and held it there. Pointing at me. Then he said, 'Ahhhh.'"

"Ahhhh? That was it?"

"It took all the strength he had. I crawled over to him and took his hand, but he let it drop and looked back at his knees. I asked him, 'Please sir, don't you want to come?' but he just closed his eyes. Then I thought of the Glommer. I looked up and saw that it had spotted me with one of its eyes and was coming towards me. I hung from the opening in the cave and dropped to the floor. When I looked up, I saw the Glommer looking down at me with its sprouted eyes, but it couldn't get through the watery wall."

"That's quite a dream, Fair."

"Oh, but it just started, Gibber Will. There's more. I gave a shake to dry myself off and realized that my dress was dry. I looked around me and saw that at the far end of the statues, there were wide steps that led up to a deep red-colored curtain made of this thick, furry cloth."

Gibber Will said with a snort, "That would be velvet. That's just for the richest folks in High Grave. Or Harrold King, himself."

"Velvet," Fair said, thoughtfully. She told Gibber Will that in the dream she'd seen a sign hanging above the curtains for the Rall Kindaria Museum. Painted in smaller letters the sign had read: Do Not Touch the Artwork. Donations Kindly Accepted.

"I felt sad because I couldn't pay," Fair said. "But then I heard a voice say, 'You've already made your donation, Tharin.'"

"He did now, did he? Called you Tharin?"

"I told him he had me by the wrong name, because my name was Fair. Fair O'Nelli."

"Who was it?" asked Gibber Will, rubbing his nose with a slide of his finger.

"Can you guess?"

"Well I wouldn't know, now." Gibber Will wondered aloud, "Just a voice from nowhere, maybe?"

Fair said, "I couldn't see who it could have been, so I asked, 'Who said that?' and a voice nearby said, 'I did.' There was a statue close to me. When I looked at it, his eyes blinked."

"I'll be," said Gibber Will.

"He took a cap off his head and bowed to me. He said, 'I'm so very glad you've finally come.'

"'Finally come?' I asked."

"Oh me, oh my," Gibber Will muttered to himself.

Fair continued, "That's what he said. Then he said, 'Oh, we all know who you are. And, as a matter of fact, we know who everyone else is on the hillsides of Cloven Grave and the world beyond the Lands of Ice. I even know your great-great-great-great grandpapa, and grandmama.'

"'Over here!' Two voices called, many rows away. 'Yoo hoo, Tharin, we're over here!'

"I saw two hoomin wearing crowns, waving their arms at me, calling me by that name."

"Crowns?" Gibber Will asked.

"Yes. Odd, isn't it?"

Gibber Will didn't say anything.

"I remembered my manners and called out, 'Pleased to meet you both!' Then I said to the statue, 'And pleased to meet you, too.'

"'Oh, but we've all met before,' they all said at the same time.

"'Met before?' I asked, but they didn't answer. So I said to the statue, 'I think you've got the wrong person. I'm not Tharin. And besides, they don't look like my many-great-grandparents. They're not even old.'

"He said to me, 'Oh, we've got you by the right name, to be sure.'

"It was all so confusing, Gibber Will. Then something occurred to me. So I said, 'Why, I don't even know your name.'

"'Oh, you don't need to know my name. I'm just supposed to get you from here to there. And no, they don't look like what you might call old. They're in their prime, just like the rest of us.'

"I told him it must be quite dull just standing there all the time, so I asked him, 'Do you ever get hungry? Or sleepy? Can you lie down when you're tired?'

"'No, no, and no. But it's all as it should be. For now, that is. The air has simply been all a-buzz with anticipation for the last few years. Thirteen to be exact.'

"'And I'm thirteen years old!' I said. 'This very day!'

"'Precisely,' said the statue.

"I told him it was my becoming day—you know, my day of maidenhood. He nodded and quietly said, 'Yes. I know,' almost like he was being reverent."

Gibber Will listened intently, without saying a word now.

Fair continued, "I said to him, 'I don't understand. You all know who I am. And you knew I was coming, right on my birthday, even. And no one looks old here, and . . .'

"'. . . and I know where you're going,' the statue said.

"So I asked, 'Where am I going?'

"'Back to Rall Kindaria, kind maiden, armed with the knowledge of home.'

"'But isn't this Rall Kindaria?'

"'This is just the edge of it. Here, let's go sit where you can have a story.' He jumped off the . . .'" Fair couldn't remember the new word and Gibber Will helped her.

"Pedestal."

"'Pedestal . . . and took my hand. He led me to the steps of the stage and said, 'Shall we go?'

"I didn't understand what he meant, so he said, 'What I mean to say is, would you like to go to Rall Kindaria, to the Land of Light?'

"'Oh! Very much!'

"The steps in front of us were quite high and very deep. There were seven of them.

"He looked down at me and waited. I gave his hand a squeeze to let him know I was ready. He smiled and lifted one knee to take the first step. So I did, too."

Fair paused.

"And?" begged Gibber Will.

"There's no more. That was my dream."

"That's a fine thing, to leave me hangin' like that, Fair O'Nelli."

"I'd tell you more if there was more. If you like, I can make something up."

The sheep began to move with prodding from the shepherd, who was coming within hearing range. Fair could hear the sound of his bagpipe music getting closer.

Gibber Will coughed and bent over to close the little door under his seat. He slid the basket in front of it with his boot.

Fair understood and was silent.

Soon, they were on their way again.

The wagon took a turn here, a turn there, with much water sloshing. Fair licked her dry lips. *Water, water.* She wouldn't say another word until they got where they were going.

Fair heard the sound of the wheels change. They no longer ground into dirt and rocks. Just rock. Her head bumped up and down so quickly that it made her teeth chatter. They were in the village now, riding over cobblestones. She could hear the clatter of other wagon wheels and horse hooves. She heard the sound of voices calling out. She heard the sound of squawking chickens. Life. Movement. Freedom.

The village roads were teeming with the bustling and noise of a town market: wagons, horses, pigs being pulled by ropes, chickens in their cages—only nothing was to be sold. It was all destined for Harrold King.

Fair couldn't hum, so she let her mind turn again to the comfort of her daydreams. This time it was a feeling of cool bumpy metal beneath her fingertips.

The dark shadow of an open doorway.

Her front door.

The sound of words.

The same words leaving her lips, night after night when dawn painted the doorway with pale, gray light, just before she became invisible to the world and hurried away to the cellar.

Do what is right, let consequence follow.
Follow your heart, come joy or come sorrow.

Those words were one of the constants in her life. They were written on a brass plaque that hung by her front door. Over the years, she had learned to use her fingers like mouse whiskers to detect shape. Movement. Change. Her fingertips were able to read the plaque just before she went to sleep every morning, just as people were waking up. Backwards days where day was night, and night was day.

It was family tradition—or so her mother told her—to kiss your fingertips before touching the plaque and to repeat the words written upon it. In fact, it was the last thing Fair did before leaving her home to crawl into the wagon the night before. Well, it was almost the last thing she did. Just before getting in to the wagon, Fair traced her mothers' forehead, eyes, and cheeks with her mouse whisker fingertips before giving her a kiss.

In her daydream, she kissed her fingers, reached blindly for the letters and let them trace their shape. As her mind passed over the words of her daydream she whispered, "Do what is right, let consequence follow. Follow your heart, come joy or come sorrow."

For some reason, her daydream ended. Something was different.

No movement.

Silence.

The wagon stopped this time without the sound of a *woah*.

Fair heard some muffled speech. Keys jangled. A door hinge creaked. Or maybe it was two sets of hinges? She heard Sauveren sniff at her through a crack in the planks and shuffle off. She heard the words "alley way." Then she heard the creak of another hinge.

Suddenly, Fair was blinded by bright light. She thrust her pale arms up to shield her eyes from the pain.

"Up you come, wee Fair," said Gibber Will.

She hesitantly pulled her pale lanky arms away from her face. She blinked as though her eyes were full of sand. "It hurts. I didn't know light was so painful," she said.

"You'll adjust real soon."

I can't. I can't keep them open. Fair squinted her eyes tightly. She opened them as slowly as she could to let the light in. Soon she felt the pain ease up. She tried again. *A little longer this time.* She blinked deliberately, one last time, almost as though she were bidding farewell to darkness. She opened her moon eyes as widely as she could.

Like a dream, the gray shape of Gibber Will's face swam into colorful focus. Soon Fair saw his eyes looking down on her. His mouth was in the shape of a smile. Flesh-colored with a bit of red. A pronounced overbite. She could see it clearly.

She thought of her mother's face: a shape she remembered only as a shadow. It had no color, but she knew its contours perfectly.

He held the wagon floor up with one hand. His other hand reached for her. When he did so, a flash of red color shot out of the wagon with the sound of small scratching claws. Sauveren pawed at it and missed. Then it was gone. He followed it with his eyes as though he wanted to have a chase, but Fair whispered, "Stay with me," and he settled.

"There went your friend, Fair. Take my hand, now," said Gibber Will. "But be quick, like. I've got jelly for legs."

After a bit of effort Fair licked her cracked lips and hoarsely said, "Where's my dog? . . ." She looked around. "I can hardly move. I'm so thirsty. More than usual."

In a flash, Gibber Will whipped the water flask off the side of the wagon. She felt him wrap his arm behind her back. He held her up and gave her a drink. She felt its coolness course through her body while she lay back in Gibber Will's arms.

Sauveren stood up and put his paws over the edge of the wagon. Fair saw him out of the corner of her eye. She smiled while she drank. They gazed at one another for what felt like forever. She reached out and rubbed his nose. When she did so, an iridescent, blue butterfly fluttered into view and lighted on her finger.

"Look Gibber Will . . . on my finger," Fair whispered. "A tiny, tiny bird."

"It's a butterfly, wee Fair. I'm thinkin' it's a good omen."

"A good omen?"

"Time will tell," he wiggled his nose and sniffed.

He handed her an apple. She bit into it and chewed with relish. Its sweetness gave her strength. In a moment, Fair got herself up into a sitting position. She heard the sound of something knocking.

A voice spoke, "You gotta get going. A Protector's coming this way. I gotta move the wagon out. Close up the doors."

Fair looked around and noticed two enormous doors. They were attached to the corners of two gray, stone buildings. The doors had been built for two purposes. When they were closed they blocked the alley way from view. When they were open, they hid whatever was between them. Right now, the wagon was between both open doors, mostly hidden.

On the other side of one of the doors, a Protector ambled along in their direction, looking with mild curiosity at the door blocking his way. He was dressed in a burgundy wool jacket, kilt, black cap. His high leather boots made a loud knocking sound on the stone. He casually swung the bully stick in his hand.

Gibber Will's friend stepped out onto the street and called, "Just making a delivery, sir. You'll have to step around. Won't be long." He stepped back into the safe protection of the doors and looked intently at Fair and Gibber Will. He swished his hands as if to say, "Get out of here!" Beads of perspiration popped onto his forehead.

In one swift motion, Gibber Will scooped Fair up and out of the wagon with one arm. He let the floor down quietly with the other and rearranged the apple sacks into the middle of the wagon. They had slid to one side. He realized he had better let his friend know what he was "delivering."

He whispered, "Apples."

Fair, her dog, and Gibber Will took off running down the alley.

Just in time.

The Protector asked, "What you got there?"

The hoomin poked his head out beyond the door. "Apples."

The Protector cocked his head to one side and narrowed his eyes, "Apples? The season for apples hasn't started, hoomin." He smacked the bully stick into his palm.

"Last seasons' apples, but the owner of Lamb's Tavern says they got a use for 'em anyways."

By now, Fair, her dog, and Gibber Will were far down the alley. They turned the corner just as the Protector peered in and saw that nothing seemed amiss.

He untied the twine at the top of one of the woven sacks and took a look inside. "If he likes mushy apples, I guess that's his business. Why don't you pull the wagon down the alley?"

"Too hard to back out. Just going to carry 'em."

"Alright then. I'm glad it's you and not me doing all that hefting." He shook his head.

Gibber Will knocked at the back door of Lamb's Tavern. In a moment, a curtain was pushed aside. Fair saw a nose. No more. Just shadows. Again, more shadows.

The door swung open and a big belly greeted her. There was a smile with rosy cheeks. A melodious voice boomed, "We've waited a long time for this day! Come on in, Fair."

She felt a large hand on her wispy shoulder, and she was pulled in with what she could only describe as love.

Her nose, mouth, and throat filled with the smell of food. It was a warm smell. Yeasty. Meaty. Humid and soupy. Her mouth filled with saliva and she swallowed.

She and Gibber Will were ushered down a hallway towards the sound of laughing, clinking, and chairs scraping on a wooden floor. Sauveren lumbered along behind them like a big bear.

Fair's heart pounded. She felt on the verge of what she thought might be joy.

I can't believe it, she thought. *I'm here. And it's not nighttime. I can see.*

When they turned and entered in through the doorway, she saw round tables surrounded with hoomin. She also saw what she assumed was a family. Two of the wee hoomin looked close to her age. A bit older, maybe. They were all laughing and talking with each other.

Fair had waited for this day, this moment, for nine years. Full of anticipation. Yet, what she felt at that moment was something completely unexpected:

She had never
felt more

alone.

I am Fair's Secret Speaker, Liver.
Lariel's Secret Speaker, Blue Toe,
will narrate the next chapter.
Since Fair isn't in the room
and I can only see what she sees, I would
only be giving you second-hand information.
I'd much rather you had it right from
Blue Toe's mouth.

3 : A Knock at the Door

ariel sat eating at her small table just after the sun came up. She heard a loud pounding at the door. She finished a bite of gruel and wiped her mouth.

As she approached the door, her hand went to the red scarf on her head. She took a deep breath in to steady herself and lifted the latch. So far, the morning was playing out just as she had expected.

"Yes?"

A tall Protector stood in front of her. His look was not the least bit forgiving. "Just checking on you, lady. You wouldn't be going anywheres today, would you?"

A gravelly voice boomed from the direction of the fireplace in the next room. "That, she would not."

Lariel quickly looked over her shoulder towards the sound of the voice, and back again. She said, "No, I don't need to go into town today. The neighbor's taken my offering in for the rendering, like always. I'm not breaking any law."

"That's not what I mean. Today would be your daughter's thirteenth birthday. You'd be preparing for a little celebration, I'm thinking." He looked over Lariel's shoulder and tried to get a peek into the house.

Lariel held on to the doorpost for support. She needed it. She also hoped she would be convincing. *The gods give me strength*, she thought. She looked over the

Protector's head and paused as though she were counting the days.

She looked into his eyes for a moment. She said, "Ah yes. That's right. It would have been today."

All the years that she kept her daughter hidden flooded into her mind. The nights she had stayed awake to read with her daughter had taken a toll on her. The nights blended into day. She usually came up out of the cellar once the sun came up, to keep her house in order. So little sleep.

The thing that pulled at her most was knowing how hard it had been for her wee daughter. And where was her son?

But Fair was alive. Harrold King had not taken her. Now he never could. Fair no longer belonged to just her. She now belonged to the hoomin. The day of her maidenhood, therefore, needed to be public.

That's the way things were in Cloven Grave. Once Fair belonged to the hoomin Harrold King wouldn't dare incur the wrath of a mob. *Or would he?* Lariel had wondered. He was so unpredictable.

Her eyes brimmed with tears. They were real tears from years of worry. "Now if you'll please be on your way. I'd like to be left alone." She began to close the door.

"Not so fast, lady." The Protector shouldered his way past her and said, "I'll be having myself a wee look around the place, I will." He strode from room to room.

When he saw only one bed, Lariel's bed, he seemed satisfied. As he prepared to leave, he had a thought and stopped. He strode into the kitchen. He saw two bowls with steaming gruel in them. He saw two mugs.

He tipped his cap to the second Protector who sat near the crackling fireplace and said, "I see you beat me to it. You're the woman's brother, ain'tcha."

Lariel's brother nodded in greeting, "Been here since last night in case I might catch her. Strange thing. Thought my sister was lyin' all them years."

He leaned back in a chair by the morning fire with his fingers laced across his belly. His legs were stretched out in such a way as to suggest that he didn't plan on doing the slightest bit of work that day. Small bushes of red hair sprouted from his bulbous nose, which was covered with a map of purple veins.

Her brother sat and pondered the fire. "There's a nice price for being an informer, there is. You disappointed me, Lariel." He fished in his ear for a good-sized piece of earwax. Upon finding the object of his desire, with a well-aimed flick of his finger and thumb, he sent it sailing into the fire, where it popped and sizzled.

Lariel quietly said, "You are no brother of mine." She'd had enough. She picked up a broom. She started swinging it in the air as though she were trying to scare a fox away from her chickens. She said, "Get out of here. Both of you. I want to be left alone."

The broom came so close to her brother's nose with the next swing that he had to cross eyes when it flew past. He pulled his chin in. The movement made him lose his balance. He grabbed uselessly at the air and leaned forward, just as the chair went backwards. He landed with a grunt. Lariel tried not to smile. Her brother got up with a huff and kicked the chair. "We're done here."

The other Protector slapped his comrade on the back. "You ain't fit to keep watch. The Harrold shoulda hired yer sister instead."

Lariel's brother shot him a wicked glance to shush him.

The Protector grew serious, "You ain't seen no signs of her wee hoomin girl? Ever?"

"Not a one."

Lariel breathed a silent sigh of relief. Her brother had arrived just after Fair scrambled into the back of the wagon.

The Protector said, "No matter. I'll be keeping my eye on the place the rest of the day, you know. I've got my suspicions."

He paused and looked at Lariel with a penetrating gaze, "We never saw the body."

Then they were both gone.

Once the door was closed, Lariel leaned back against it. She slid down against the wood and slumped over her knees. Completely numb. Her body felt drained. After a bit of time she crawled over to a striped rug in the pantry and lay down. She chuckled to herself when she remembered seeing her brother topple over: his legs and boots waving upside down in the air. And swinging a broom . . . she didn't know she had it in her. She pressed her cheek against the rug and closed her eyes.

She fell into the first restful sleep she had known in years. Beneath her, beneath the striped rug, lay the secret door to the cellar where Fair had been dead to the world for the last nine years. The grave was empty. Her daughter was alive.

I've told my part of the story, Liver.
Let me know if you need me again.

I will, Blue Toe.

4 : The Presentation

round, short woman toddled over to the windows of the tavern. She closed the curtains that looked out onto the street. The room grew instantly dim with brownish light.

"No one can see in now," she muttered. Fair felt a fleshy hand lead her into the dimly lit space. The owner sat her down at a small table.

With a room full of hoomin watching her, Fair devoured her first warm meal in nine years. She struggled to eat with the strange utensils and finally gave up, pulling the food apart and stuffing it in her mouth. Drinking soup right from the rim of the bowl.

It might sound cruel, but her mother didn't dare keep a fire going during the night and risk the smell of food cooking. She didn't dare risk having a Protector pay her a surprise visit, only to discover her keeping food for two warm in the coals.

His question would likely be, "Who you keeping that warm for?"

And so, Fair ate simply. Very simply, but consistently and well. But now, here at the tavern, Fair felt like her belly was going to burst.

She looked around the room, amazed by the cracks of light that pierced through the closed curtains, flecked with stars of dust. She was startled by the hints of color she saw on hoomin cheeks. She felt soothed by the warmth that passed over her tongue and down her throat. Delight filled her when she saw movement.

The hint of someone's eyes.

The shape of a nose.

The sound of laughter.

Although the room should have smelled like porridge cooking for breakfast, it smelled more like dinner. The tavern owner—and cook—had asked what Fair would want to eat.

Lariel guessed that it would be poppenballs (those warm little pastries topped with butter that melts into succulent pools), roast leg of lamb (as there was no shortage of lamb to be found at the tavern), vegetable soup made with fiddleheads (Fair used to call them baby fern curls when she was small and foraged for them in the woods with her father), and a big cow's-horn mug of glug made from the juice of mashed strawberries and honey.

Drinking out of a cow's horn was stinky business. They never seemed to lose their smell. So Fair pinched her nose while she took a sip and moved the mug away from her face. She unplugged her nose, which allowed her to taste what lay in her mouth. *Oh, that tasted good.* Fair pinched her nose and finished off the entire mug in one breath. She licked butter, lamb's fat, and other tastes off her fingers, and licked her lips over and over to get every last bit of flavor she could.

A burp rose from her belly and made itself heard. She knew she was forgetting manners for eating, but couldn't remember them. She thought her mother had told her something about burping. What was it?

She felt a hand patting her on the back. It was the cook. "I see you enjoyed your meal!" She looked around, and everyone was smiling at her, giggling. Fair smiled apologetically. "I burped." Everyone laughed. Fair joined them.

A wrinkled smile grew on the round woman's shining dark face. "It's time for cake!" she announced. Lariel had hoped Fair would like a swizzlenut torte with brownsen glaze for her birthday cake. She had asked the owner to make one.

The owner went from table to table, pouring grape juice into everyone's mug. He poured one for himself and turned one of the chairs around with a loud scrape. He laughed and straddled it cheerfully with his stocky legs and lifted his mug to each one of the hoomin there. They lifted their mugs back to him. He looked around the room and hollered, "Everybody!"

Everyone in the tavern turned to look and, seeing the mugs held up, did the same. He bellowed, "Here is to Fair's day of maidenhood! Drink water bound!" Fair felt a warm stream of comfort wash through her.

The whole room resounded with a hearty repeat of his toast, "Drink water bound!" They all put their mugs to their lips and gulped the contents until they were gone. They slammed the mugs down on the table with gusto, *clack, clack, clack!* Polished horn hit wood with a percussive melody.

The toast had been spoken for as many years as anyone could remember. It was made any time a hoomin held a mug and wished to say it. Where it came from, no one knew, but they assumed it meant to fill your stomach with drink, as though it were bound to go somewhere: drink water bound.

When it came time to eat the cake, Fair relished every bite of it. *It's just how I remember it,* she thought. *Chewy and nutty. It's just perfect.* She wiped her mouth with her hand and licked her fingers again. She looked around and people were using the edge of their tablecloths to wipe their mouths. She stopped licking and put the edge of the tablecloth to her mouth and wiped her fingers.

"Come, Fair. It's time," said the woman.

One more bite. Pop it in the mouth. Chew. Lick.

She led Fair to a low table in the middle of the room. "Stand on the table, if you will."

Fair stepped onto the table. Her dog, Sauveren, climbed up and sat next to her on his haunches. His weight made the table creak beneath him. Everyone in the room laughed. Fair looked around, wondering why everyone was laughing. She was used to always having him with her. She tugged at her dress, which felt too tight around her waist.

"And your dog, too," the owner laughed.

Fair took a moment to look around, "You all seem to know me, but I don't know you." The feeling reminded her of her dream, but this was real.

Fair watched with wonder as they scooted out their chairs and lined up to greet her. They didn't seem afraid of anything or anyone. *Amazing*, she thought.

The beautiful round woman moved towards her. She moved like a rolling boulder beneath a long dress and apron. Her shoulders were covered with a dark purple cape flecked with silver. It was clasped beneath her neck with a locking silver circle. The woman slid along the floor, coming towards Fair. Fair wondered if this woman had feet. She cocked her head to see if she could have a peek at the tips of her shoes. Nothing.

Her face, neck and hands were the color of freshly turned fragrant soil. A rich, deep brown. Her skin glowed as though the thinnest bit of copper lay just beneath the surface. Her hair was frizzled with gray. It hung in a wiry braid as wide as her shoulders and fell down to the back of her knees. Fair thought she knew who the woman was.

Fair remembered having seen her as a child. Her name was Azanamer. Fair's mother told her that Azanamer's skin was dark because she had absorbed so much of the sun. It had darkened her skin to show that she was filled inside with nothing but light.

She took both of Fair's hands in hers. Fair remembered how she used to smell sweet, like ripe peaches. She still smelled the same. Fair noticed Azanamer's hands were warm. Fleshy. Her voice was barely audible, like a soft wind. Fair had to lean in to hear her.

"I am Azanamer. I was with your mother the day you were born. I brought you into the world and named you. I wove your soul star—your Luminamen."

"Yes, Mother told me."

Fair's mother once told her that when Azanamer held a weeborn hoomin in her arms, she was able to see the shape of its soul's light and purpose revolving within its Secret Speaker. She was always present at a birthing to give the weeborn hoomin a name to match its soul.

At nightfall, Azanamer then pulled threads of colored light from the aurora borealis, which danced every night above Cloven Grave. With those threads she wove the complex, geometric shape of the Luminamen— the shape of the soul's light and purpose. Each one was unique, as was each weeborn hoomin.

Fair used to stare at her Luminamen for hours, imagining that the light she was made of—if she could only see it—looked the same. *This is who I am . . . even in the darkness*, she often thought. *It surrounds me.*

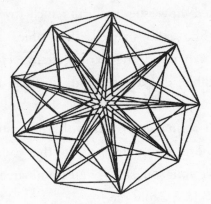

Azanamer moved aside. Next, a hand thrust out and took Fair's hand. "Apparently your father wanted us to be here. I'm one of your mother's brothers. That makes me your uncle." He paused and looked at his wife and wee hoomin. "We're family. I . . . I didn't know you were alive . . . until this morning. We just found out. It's a wonderful surprise," he said. He pulled his daughter close to him. She was about Fair's age.

Fair felt her heart lurch into her throat. The girl snuggled into her father's arm. A yelp jumped like a frog of longing to the edge of Fair's mouth. She swallowed it down.

I missed all that.

The light and the love of family.

My father's arm around my shoulder.

All those years in darkness.

The lump in her throat felt as if it would choke her. *I feel so alone.* Sauveren gave her hand a nudge, and Fair ran her fingers through the fur on his shoulder. She looked at him and thought about how he'd been with her all those years. So had her mother, when she could. *But still*, she thought.

Right then, Fair felt a desire sprout violently within her from seed to tree. *I've got to find my father and brother.* It was a feeling that was so strong that she could have burst out of the room right then. Into the streets. Running wildly from place to place until she found them. Words from the Scrolls of Truth entered her mind:

> *You have something big to do here, now.*
> *Not doing it will feel like a burden.*
> *Not doing it will make you feel like you*
> *aren't doing what you came here to do.*
> *Not doing it will leave you feeling empty.*

Was that it? Finding them? She wondered. Fair felt her heart pound so hard that she thought her chest was going to burst. Her face flushed for an instant and she felt out of breath. She heard her mother's voice in the darkness of her cellar days. She often spoke while the music box played, "Pay attention to the signals, Fair. Your body lets you know what your heart is trying to tell you."

My heart is beating fiercely. Finding them must be "it," that "something big."

A boy hoomin, her cousin, stood next to his father. Her uncle. He looked up at Fair through beady eyes. He narrowed them, cocked his head to one side and asked, "Who are you anyway? You're so pale."

It was true. Fair looked completely different than the rest of the hoomin in the room. Although she had the rounded cheeks of a hoomin, they weren't rosy. Her skin was so translucent that it gave her round face a moon-like quality. The only bit of color came from her full pink lips beneath her slightly upturned nose. Her eyes, too, were a clear, silver blue.

Fair felt confused. She wrapped her arms around Sauveren's neck. She looked around the room and back at the boy hoomin, "I . . . I don't . . . know. I've . . . I've been in a very dark place for a long time." She stood close to Sauveren and dug her fingers into his thick fur. "This is my dog. He was my blanket and kept me warm."

"Why? Didn't your parents care about you enough to keep a fire going?"

Fair said, "It's not like that." She didn't want to have to explain, so she left it at that. "You can pet him if you like."

She noticed a dreadful-looking hoomin sitting at a small table in one corner. He had black matted hair that fell over his face and down his back. He had not introduced himself to her. He didn't seem to be paying any attention to what was going on in the room.

Fair watched as he poured honey into a big bowl of milk, stirred it up with his finger, and sucked the liquid off the end of it with a pop. As he drank, the honey milk poured out over the rim and dripped down his beard. He put down the bowl and tore apart a poppenball. He tapped the crumb against his beard.

What's he doing? Fair thought.

Immediately a small mouse peeked out. The hoomin put the crumb in front of the mouse, who took it in its paws. Fair stood and watched. Astonished. It nibbled the morsel and darted back into the hoomin's beard. *What an odd creature*, she thought, not thinking about the mouse.

As far as bowls of milk go, it is all he was ever seen eating—or drinking, actually. Some said that except for the warm sweet milk the tavern provided him, he lived off the bugs he dug up under fallen logs. Why Harrold King hadn't put him away was anyone's guess.

For no reason at all he sang and dribbled,

> *A mighty hoomin, he is, he is*
> *A mighty hoomin he is.*
> *No hoomin is worthy to tie his shoes*
> *He'll dunk below the fizz.*

Fair couldn't take her eyes off him. *He doesn't make any sense.*

Now, the owner of the tavern stood next to her. He looked at the hoomin sitting around the tables. Fair realized in some far off way that he was speaking just to her. She felt fuzzy and just heard snippets of words. "We know how long you've waited . . . loss of your father and brother . . . so sorry . . . didn't find you . . . thanks to your mother." She saw heads nodding.

She felt like everything was moving in slow motion. His voice sounded far away, as if she were in a bubble. While he spoke, Fair surveyed the whitewashed room.

Thick windowsills, just like at home.

Geraniums in the windows, just like at home. Only these had a hint of red in the dim light, not dark grey silhouettes in the moonlight when she sat reading with her mother.

But the hoomin. There were so many of them. She counted nine in all. Nine hoomin with flesh and blood! Not daydreams. They were real. How strange to be surrounded by life.

So confusing, she thought. *They all look at me like they know and care about me, and I've no idea who they are, except for Gibber Will.* He was enjoying himself tremendously. He nibbled at his cake with a toothy grin.

She reached out and found Sauveren. She feathered her fingers into the soft, glossy fur on his black head. She looked at him and felt the hint of a smile draw itself on her face. "I think it's time," she whispered to him. His head was as high as her chest. The girl and her dog regarded one another for a brief moment of knowing.

Azanamer looked at the tall clock in the corner. Not much more time left before they all had to leave for Clock Tower Square. Fair felt Azanamer's hand on her shoulder. "So the time has come," she said.

A chill ran through Fair and she felt a tide of tears beneath her eyes. She gulped and looked over at her dog. All her years of darkness flashed in her mind in an instant. She thought, *I'm here. Finally.*

"In a few moments you will be known as a maiden, no longer a wee hoomin."

Fair pulled Sauveren close to her. She wished her family were there, but she tried to brush the longing feeling away. The room became dead silent.

"You were born thirteen years ago today. In keeping with tradition, the Woolly will present you with your apron of maidenhood in the presence of witnesses. Even though we are small in number this time, those in this room are your witnesses." Fair tugged at her dress, which was already uncomfortable enough without an apron tied around her waist.

She had no way of knowing how fun the celebration would have been at her home, if things had been different. Fireworks, crowds of hoomin, food and frolic.

Fair looked around for who the Woolly might be. Everything was so still. She hadn't met the hoomin yet.

She pulled at the neck of her dress and looked at the back doorway, expecting to see someone walk through.

She saw a movement in the corner. Heads were turning that direction. Her eyes grew round. *The mouse-beard hoomin? Him?* "Oh my . . . ," she muttered.

The Woolly stood up. His chair fell over with a clatter. He gave a loud growl, showing lots of teeth. He scratched his chest and belly, clearly satisfied by his favorite drink. His elbows flapped wildly. He wiped his beard dry with his sleeve.

Fair realized her fingers had gone up to the scarf her mother had tied around her head the night before. She could feel her long, brown hair pressing on her shoulders. It rippled down her back in wild, dripping rivulets. *This is my becoming. Here I am. In front of these hoomin I don't know. In front of this strange hoomin.* For the first time in her life she wondered how she looked.

The Woolly walked up to Fair. He held a folded piece of cloth on his upturned palms, like a pillow. He silently unfolded the apron and put it over Fair's head, then walked behind her and tied it around her waist. She moved her shoulders around to get comfortable. She looked down and saw that the apron was white. *Not a spot on it. Not a shadow. Nothing but white. Light. Freedom.*

At last he spoke, "Your full name is . . ."

Azanamer stopped him. "Not now. If Fair doesn't know, she can't tell. It's her last protection."

The Woolly followed by saying something remarkably coherent, "You are your parents inheritance. A great gift."

Fair knit her eyebrows together for a brief moment. *Mother says that every time she says good night: "You are my inheritance from the gods, my great gift." Do all parents say that to their wee hoomin when they tuck them in at night?*

Then she heard the Woolly say, "And you are to bring a miracle to Cloven Grave."

Hold on. What? Fair was stunned. Her stomach became a heavy stone.

"A miracle? Me? What do you mean?"

"Just that." He made a move to leave, then stopped. He stopped to scratch Sauveren's head. The two furry creatures looked remarkably similar if it weren't for the fact that one of them stood on two legs. The Woolly's demeanor changed then, and he walked back to his chair, muttering,

Tie your shoes, I can't, I can't
Tie your shoes I can't.

The night before, as she lay in the wagon dreaming of this moment, she imagined that it would feel wonderful just to be a part of the world outside her cottage. Outside her cellar. But to *do* something she knew nothing about? This didn't feel wonderful.

She hadn't planned on her new world being a world of so many unknowns. She had traded darkness, daydreams and comfort for light, sight and unexpected responsibility. It was a complete shock.

Fair looked around at everyone in the room. They were all looking back at her. Full of expectance. They were used to the Woolly's gibberish, but he had never pronounced anything like this before.

A miracle! *The* miracle, perhaps?

For some time now, mysterious writings had been appearing along roadside trees. Every time Harrold King had the frequent whim to post another law on the Cries Unia that hung from the roadside trees, the following night, words were burned into the leather parchment, completely replacing what he had decreed as law.

There had been quite a few tree writings, as they had come to be called. They prophesied that a miracle was coming, and that a new law would do away with the Laws of Memory. This made him furious. Harrold King had taken the Laws of Memory to the extreme, and so the hoomin of Cloven Grave had looked forward for a long time now, and with great expectancy, for the coming of this "miracle."

Now the Woolly was telling them that Fair was going to bring them a miracle.

Fair noticed movement in the room. Some of the hoomin were beginning to stand up. Her uncle was encouraging his wee hoomin to stand. *They're standing because of me.* Fair felt like she wanted to hide. *I have no idea what I'm supposed to do. How do you bring a miracle?*

She said in a barely audible voice, "Not me. Please. I, I just want to know my father and brother again. . . . I want, I want to know who I am. . . . I want to know why everything has been such a secret all my life."

Azanamer glided up to Fair. She held her hands together as though she were praying. "Some things just are."

"I don't understand, Azanamer."

"You may call me Grandmother. Everyone else does."

Fair took her cue and said, "I don't understand, Grandmother."

She paused. "Why . . . ?"

"You will find out in due time," Azanamer answered. "I wanted to take this moment to tell you a story. It's the story of the beginning of the hoomin—and your beginning, Fair. But we don't have time."

"I'd really like to hear it . . . Azanam . . . that is, Grandmother."

"And you shall, but not now. We must be quick if we're to make it to Clock Tower Square. I'll simply announce this: You are now, as of this moment, a maiden. She turned to the hoomin in the room and said, "Fair now belongs to us. Accept her gladly."

A shock of light filled the room, and everything became brilliant and white.

The owner of Lamb's Tavern had yanked open the curtains. He threw open the windows, held onto the windowsill, did a little jig, and shouted, "Hallelujah!" into the street.

The silence in the room erupted into laughter and talking. Fair felt kisses on her cheeks and her hand being shaken, over and over.

She was free.

Fair was jostled to the front door with a lot of laughter. She looked behind her and noticed she was first in line to leave Lamb's Tavern. The door opened.

Two rows of pipers in kilts and tall bearskin hats formed a path into the street. Music began to drone like a sick cow, then surge and swell majestically until it filled the air with chilling beauty. Fair looked at her arms and saw goose bumps.

Everyone was laughing, but all she heard was the melody. It filled her from the inside out.

She looked to Azanamer with a surprised look on her face, "What's all this?"

"This is the usual way to end the celebration of maidenhood, Fair. This one is a modest procession . . . but nonetheless. You go first, dear maiden."

Fair smiled. Now she felt the joy she had hoped for. She was on the edge of walking freely into daylight for the first time in nine years. She and her dog walked past the pipers, through the door, and into the wide, wide world.

Hidden inside a crack in a wall, two red eyes watched her leave. And there was the faintest sound of something scratching.

Like sandpaper.

5 : Something Unexpected

air sat on the wagon seat in full daylight. She smoothed her apron and looked at her lap. *I blink my eyes, and I can see,* she thought. *White apron. Peach dress. My hands.*

She looked up and down the street. *I can't believe I'm awake,* she thought. All the buildings were made of thick, gray stone. The street was paved with cobblestones. *That's why my head was bumping when I rode here.*

Gibber Will said, "We need to head straight for Clock Tower Square, Fair. Then we'll get you on home." He paused and added with a twinkle in is eye, "I know someone who's going to want to see what you look like when the sun's shinin'." Fair knew he was talking about her mother.

He smiled at her and said, "You look every bit the maiden." He kept his playful eye on her round face, winked, clucked, and whistled for the horse to get a move on. He gave the reins a jiggle with a lift of one shoulder. "A true maiden," he smiled.

He looked at the horse, tilted his head forward and said, "Get on there missy!" He was such a surprising sight that Fair laughed.

"Did you hear me? I laughed!"

Gibber Will said, "Now that's a sound I've been waiting to hear for a long time."

Azanamer sat silent and gentle on the other side of Fair.

The Woolly sat in the back with Sauveren, the straw, and all the unloaded apples. One of the creatures had a mouse for a friend. The other creature had Fair.

The wagon and its passengers rattled down the street, followed by the sound of laughter and bagpipe music coming out of Lamb's Tavern. As soon as the place was empty, the music moaned to a stop. The pipers packed up and ran to Clock Tower Square.

Can't be late. Can't be late!

Gibber Will guided the horse into a wide-open space surrounded by more gray stone buildings. In the center, a tower jutted up from the ground. It had a clock at the top with large, black hands. Both hands were at the top of the clock. The larger one clicked over one notch. It landed exactly on top of the other hand.

Dong . . . dong . . . dong . . . dong . . .

The tower was surrounded by a water fountain. The water fountain was surrounded by a circle of stairs. The square was full of hoomin. They pressed against each other, craning their necks. They were trying to get a glimpse of something on a wide wooden platform. Fair felt something that didn't feel quite right.

"What's happening?" Fair asked. She wondered if this was what Gibber Will had been talking about earlier.

"It's a shame is what it is," Gibber Will said between dongs. *Dong.* "It's the place where the Harrold does his public punishments. Got so many laws he has . . . "

Dong.

". . . that you can't sneeze without breaking one of 'em and getting in trouble for it. He's called everyone in Cloven Grave here by order of one of them laws."

Dong.

"Big shame if you get here late."

"I want to get down from the wagon, Gibber Will." She wanted to see this for herself, in her own way.

He shook his head, "Ehm, we're fine right where we are, in truth. But I wouldn't begrudge a maiden her first request, now."

He hesitantly helped Fair get down from the wagon. She started walking ahead of it. Fair had been counting. *Twelve. Twelve bells.*

All was silent.

But only for a moment.

Loud clattering exploded into the square. Echoing. Rumbling from all the streets that led into it. Everyone looked around to find where the noise came from. It was impossible to tell.

A closed carriage pulled by four black, snorting stallions careened around a corner and came barreling into the square. It was a dark gray-green color, trimmed in burgundy and gold. It came straight toward Fair in a dreadful explosion of wheels and hooves on stone.

Gibber Will stood up and shouted, "Fair, watch out!" His eyes were frozen open with shock.

Fair couldn't move. She stared blankly at the carriage bearing down on her. In one motion, Sauveren leapt off the wagon and stood in front of her.

The carriage driver heard barking. He looked down and saw a large wall of fur in front of him. He immediately seized up on the reins. The whole bundle of wood, wheels and hooves came to a crashing halt.

Then he saw Fair. His face paled because he realized he could have hit her.

A voice inside the carriage pounded fists against the door, "Not here! Don't stop here! This isn't close enough."

"Something is in the way, your eminent and royal highness," said the driver.

The door of the carriage burst open from the inside. Immediately, two legs poked straight out and stayed poking out, almost as though there was an invisible footrest beneath them.

How odd. Fair cocked her head and wondered what the legs were waiting for.

The shoes on the end of the legs were black, long and pointed. They would make easy work of squishing a cockroach in the corner of a room.

"Carry me," said a voice. Fair assumed it belonged to the legs. "It's time for the show."

Fair looked up at Gibber Will. "What show?" she asked.

Gibber Will started to talk then checked himself. He didn't want to be heard. He spoke as quietly as he could, "What's going to happen to them what's late. Except for him. He's above the law, the crusty scab."

Two men pulled a flat table top off the back of the wagon and slid two poles into the length of it. They opened the door on the other side of the carriage and hefted out a large chair. They fastened it upon the table top. Next, they carried the two legs, pointed shoes, and the hefty hoomin that came with them out of the carriage. They deposited his green velvet-robed bulk onto the chair.

Harrold King sized up the crowd beneath heavy eyelids that formed a straight line, as though they were curtains ready to fall. His eyelashes were dark and short, giving the impression that he had smudged the thinnest line of charcoal in a severe swipe across the straight, heavy lids.

They matched the equally severe, slightly upward swipe of his straight black eyebrows. His lower lids hung like fleshy garlands beneath his dark, piercing eyes.

His face was thick and jowly, and his long wavy hair grew in a thin rim from one ear to the other, leaving a bald head bulging above it.

A Protector hurriedly placed a white curly wig over his head. "You forgot this," he muttered.

Harrold King let the Protector adjust his wig, sniffed proudly and slipped his gloves off his hands. He flipped them against his hand. "Am I late?" He snorted. "Ah well. No matter." His mouth shouted, "My foot stool! My foot stool!"

Like his eyelids and eyebrows, his lips were black. His face was powdered a ghostly white, and his cheeks were painted to look rosy. They gave the effect, instead, of a wee hoomin who had forgotten to take off the make up after playing dress ups.

Fair felt sick to her stomach just looking at him. She pulled her dog close. "Look at that mean hoomin, Sauveren. Bossing everyone around like that."

A wigged servant dressed in white satin said, "We forgot it, your royal and eminent majesty the king."

"Forgot it? But my feet *hurt!* In fact, they *burn!* Do you know what it's like to be on fire? Well? . . . Do you?"

"No, your majesty."

"Well, I do. You'll be punished for this." The one thing Harrold King disliked more than anything was pain.

His feet really did hurt him. Enormously. His legs were swollen and red beneath his stockings. His ankles bulged with boiling ferocity over of the edge of his shoes.

He jabbed a finger straight in front of him like an arrow and spoke to his Protectors, "Now get me up on that platform!"

Six hoomin lined up, grabbed the poles, three on each side of the dais. Together now. Heft. Grunt. They carried Harrold King aloft through the parting crowd, kilts swaying, to the steps of the platform. The Protectors set the dais down in front of the steps with no small effort, wiping perspiration from their faces and necks.

Two hoomin, roughly sixteen years old or so, stepped off the footrests at the back of the carriage. One was tanned and had curly blonde hair that sprouted from his head like a bush of golden autumn grass. The other had a glossy head of brown hair that fell around his angular face. They were the sons of Harrold King.

"You, Fella Doon," he ordered, "help me up . . . and follow me, sons." His two sons got in line. The blond one was first.

One of the Protectors stepped onto the dais and offered his arm to Harrold King, who hooked his elbows over the proffered arm.

"What would I do without you, Fella Doon? I'm going to pull against you now."

"And I'll pull up at the same time. One, two, three."

At three, the two of them worked together to bring Harrold King to a grimacing, but standing position. Fella Doon helped him up the steps and positioned him in front of a purple, velvet chair that had been placed in the middle of the platform.

"Humph!" grunted Harrold King. He landed with a gelatinous sounding jiggle and the creak of stunned wood. He glanced quickly at several wooden stocks held closed with black chains and enormous locks. The platform was made of old, graying wood and appeared to have seen many years of use.

He looked over the crowd, "No latecomers, I see. I praise you for your obedience and love for me. I praise you for honoring my kind request that you be here. You may applaud now."

The crowd burst into applause.

How strange, Fair thought. She held her hands together quietly and looked closely. She saw a terrible emptiness behind his eyes that all the applause in the world could never fill.

Harrold King looked around, soaking in the attention. To Fair's horror, his gaze stopped when he saw her. He narrowed his eyes and stared at her for a very long time. Then, his focus slid greasily to her dog.

His suspicious gaze turned into a quick smile. He poked his nose in the air.

"Good day, kind maiden," he said to Fair.

How unexpected. Harrold King, whom she had hid from for the last nine years, had just greeted her with a measure of kindness.

He looked at her a bit longer, then his eyes slowly wandered to Sauveren.

To the wagon.

Gibber Will.

Azanamer.

And finally, to the Woolly.

Fair gulped and wondered why he had chosen to speak to her when there were so many hoomin there.

Soon, a hush moved like a wave from the outside of the crowd and rolled towards the platform. All heads turned to look. A woman had just walked into the square. She held a baby in her arms. A line of wee hoomin followed her like ducklings. Their pudgy little fists held onto a rope tied around her waist.

Harrold King followed the hush to its source, "Aha! Miss Tilly. Tried to sneak in late, did you? Come up here and be found accountable for your crime."

She looked at the ground and kept moving forward.

Miss Tilly was the local caretaker of wee hoomin whose parents were busy in the fields.

Like Lariel and all the women in Cloven Grave, Miss Tilly wore a long heavy skirt covered with a drab apron. Hers, a pale blue, had several deep, squarish pockets sewn on the front, which were places .of safekeeping for the many trinkets she gave to the wee hoomin. She loved shiny, tinkling treasures. She delighted in the wee hoomin's glee at what she produced from her pockets.

There was one pocket, however, that no one had ever seen her dip into. It was a leather pouch, actually, that hung from a belt around her waist. It made tinkling sounds as she moved, giving one the feeling that they were in the presence of an Impissh Nissen without knowing why. Wee hoomin sometimes asked her in wide-eyed wonder if she herself were an Impissh Nissen. She would just press her ear to her lifted shoulder and shyly laugh while she looked at the ground.

She kept her dark hair pulled back in a bun under her scarf, and when she smiled she had a mouthful of crooked teeth that were situated just so, giving an impression of imperfect goodness. She wasn't overly thin, nor overly plump.

In fact, one didn't take notice of her proportions, only her softness. Her rightness. She did, however, have an ample bosom, a welcome pillow of tenderness when little ones came to her needing a lap to cry on or when another fell asleep in her arms. The one remarkable thing about Miss Tilly was that she never spoke to grown-ups. Only wee hoomin. If a parent addressed her, she spoke to the parent through the wee hoomin.

When Harrold King ordered her to go to the platform, she looked up, startled. "Oh! Look what I've done, wee ones. Come," she said to her little brood. "I've put you in harm's way."

Harrold King waved his fleshy hands and ordered the crowd, "Somebody take the vermin from her. Make way! Make way, now."

Miss Tilly said, "Hurry to these kind folks. You'll be alright."

Several hoomin in the crowd rushed to take the wee hoomin in order to be helpful to her—or perhaps they were afraid of Harrold King.

Two Protectors stepped in front of her and two more followed behind, holding wooden poles close to their chests at a diagonal. The poles were tipped with shiny metal lances. Pointy and sharp. The crowd moved aside as Miss Tilly made her way to the platform with her head bowed. She was trembling. The Protectors' boots were noisy reminders of who was who as they stomped across the cobblestones.

"How fortunate that I'm in a good mood today," said Harrold King.

Before Fair realized what was happening, a Protector locked Miss Tilly's hands and feet between hinged wooden planks. She sat on a thin board, a few feet above the platform. She didn't say a word. Fair felt horrified.

Harrold King then said, "You may now laugh at her, citizens. Go ahead. Laugh. Be glad you've been so obedient to the law. You, at least, are clean. She, on the other hand . . . is nothing but filth. A lawbreaker."

Complete silence.

"Laugh, I said! It is the only way she can be cleansed of her crime."

The silence was broken by a few nervous laughs that stopped and started in the crowd. They knew and loved Miss Tilly.

Soon something strange began to happen: As the hoomin realized how grateful they were not to be in the stocks, they began to laugh with relief.

Soon, their relief turned into brave derision, since they were down on the ground, safe from harm for the moment, and Miss Tilly—who in other circumstances was their friend—was not.

Hoomin nature is a surprising and disappointing curse at times. Many hearts were torn with shame as they laughed at their friend.

Fair's mind flashed to her years of study with her mother near the moonlit windowsill. Memories of their conversations about what it meant to be truly hoomin. This was not part of anything they had ever talked about as they read from the Scrolls of Truth, while the music box played.

Fair reached out. Fur. Friend. Confidant. She pulled Sauveren to her again and said, "Oh, he's so mean. This isn't right."

Sauveren looked at her and licked his chops. He followed her gaze and looked at the platform. He barked, as if he were saying, "So true."

Tomatoes and old cabbages began to fly through the air. Fair looked. *What in the world? Where did they come from?* She was puzzled. Soon she realized that hoomin in the crowd were throwing them at Miss Tilly. They must have brought them to give at the Rendering.

Above the roars of laughter and flying food, above the buried shame, Fair shouted, "Stop it!" before she realized what she was doing. She looked around nervously and pressed her lips between her teeth. She held her breath. *What have I done?*

It was too late.

A few hoomin nearby stopped and looked at her. Back in the wagon, Gibber Will started to tell Fair to be quiet, but Azanamer held his arm and shook her head.

Fair knew she had to finish what she had started: Do what is right, let consequence follow. Follow your heart, come joy or come sorrow. *It's our family way,* she thought. *Let consequence follow . . .*

"I said stop it!"

More heads turned. Again, a wave of hushed fear made its way up to the platform. They seemed shocked that a young maiden had spoken up. They moved away from her.

Harrold King spotted her easily, "You dare defy me, maiden? Come up here. And bring your dog with you."

Fair looked around and stared into the eyes of the fearful crowd. She couldn't move.

A memory came to her just then. It was her father. In a flash, she saw him in the garden behind their cottage. He was showing her how to make scary things feel safer. She had been staring at an ominous black cloud in the sky. Fair remembered the knot of fear in her stomach that she'd felt. He sat down next to her and showed her how she could pinch the cloud with her finger and thumb. When she looked at the cloud between her finger and thumb, it looked tiny and harmless. She pinched it. He laughed and said, "Poofs!"

Fair did this now. She looked at Harrold King through her finger and thumb. He looked very small. She almost wanted to giggle. She pretended to squash him—not to be unkind, for she knew that all things living had a spark of goodness in them—but to feel safe. She said, *Poofs!* in her mind and felt better.

Harrold King demanded, "Come here, I said!"

She adjusted her apron and said, "Come Sauveren." Harrold King had looked no bigger than a potato bug. And she'd squashed him with a poof.

With every step she took, Fair felt a surge of strength fill her from the earth beneath her feet. She felt held up. A few stray leaves from the cold season swirled and chatted in doorway corners.

Soon, she and Sauveren were at the top of the steps.

"Come closer, maiden."

Fair stepped forward a few steps.

"No, not that close. Take two steps back."

Fair stepped backwards. One step. Two steps.

Harrold King seemed satisfied. He said, "Did I hear you say something down there, in the crowd?"

Fair felt strength continue to fill her in a way she didn't understand. It was as though the wood beneath her feet was breathing courage in to her, as if the air itself had solidified in order to hold her up. She took two steps forward. The crowd gasped.

He stared at her feet, the feet that had dared to take two steps. He looked at her face through narrowed eyes. "Well, did I hear you say something?" He was just a potato bug sitting all alone on a very large chair. At least, to her.

"Yes, you did. You're a mean one, picking on Miss Tilly, just because she was late. You were late, too. Why aren't you locked up in those things? You should be ashamed of yourself." It poured out all at once and she had to force herself to hold her tongue.

Harrold King stayed silent for some time in powdery thinking. He looked at Fair beneath his straight black lids. "You know, no one has ever dared stand up to me until now. I . . ." he paused. "I admire that."

Fair didn't know quite what to think and looked at her dog. Sauveren stared at her and panted. They were nearly eye-to-eye. He pressed his furry shoulder against her waist and she caressed his head.

"That's quite a . . . what is it, a dog? . . . that you have with you. He looks more like a bear."

"Yes, sir, I mean your majesty. He never leaves my side."

"What a loyal creature." Harrold King moaned in a way that seemed a little forced. Then he said, "You know, my feet hurt me terribly. Do you think he might lie down beneath them so I can prop them up for a moment? He'd make a nice footrest."

Fair was bewildered that he hadn't seemed offended by what she'd said to him about being mean. She said, "Why of course he would. And he's so nice and soft. It might make them feel better." She said, "Go over and lie down beneath his feet, Sauveren."

Her dog lumbered over and lay down.

"Fella Doon," Harrold King said, "help me get my feet up on this good dog. I've never seen anything like him. He's a giant."

In a moment, and with a bit of honestly painful grunting, Harrold King had his feet propped up on Sauveren's back. He sat back in his chair, took a hold of his armrests and sighed, "Marvelous. Such soft and gentle support for my weary feet."

Fair felt pleased, and confused—all at the same time.

He looked over to the wagon, "Are those your friends?"

Fair nodded. "And very good ones, too."

A look seemed to cross Harrold Kings face like a gathering storm. He moved his feet surprisingly quickly and kicked Sauveren to get him to move.

"That's enough, now. I've decided to keep the beast for myself," he said.

The words didn't register in Fair's mind. Just a moment before, he'd seemed quite friendly.

Sauveren was enormous as far as dogs go, but he moved aside quickly to keep from getting kicked again. Harrold King snapped his fingers and called to his carriage driver, "Have the Rooter come get this animal."

Then it hit her.

Sauveren? Keep him for himself?

Fair felt that she was face to face with a monster. He had tricked her. Horrid white face. Black lips. Painted cheeks. The Loathsome Hoomin. "What do you mean, keep him for yourself? You can't do that. He's my dog!"

"Oh I can't, can't I? Look there," he pointed.

Fair saw something dash out from behind Harrold King's dark carriage. It was a small black wagon topped with a square black cage made of iron bars, pulled by two shiny black stallions. Their manes and tails flowed like ribbons of dark clouds in front of a midnight moon.

A sunken-faced man with a long pointed nose, big ears and beady eyes stood at the front of the wagon, cracking a whip. His hair was pumpkin orange, but dry and straight as straw. It poked out beneath the rim of a tall black hat. Fair thought she could see the hint of a sneer on his pale face.

The Rooter hobbled onto the platform where he stood, hunched over and skinny. He took off his hat and held the rim of it in his pale, bony hands. His eyes darted back and forth for a moment then narrowed in on Sauveren. In a nasal voice he beckoned, "Come here, little doggy. I have a bone for you."

Sauveren stayed where he was.

The Rooter's purple lips formed a glorious shape as he sniveled, "Little squirrels count their nuts but don't know where they hide them." He giggled and looked at Fair. "My nose, it smells a missing one. That means it's mine. Good-bye."

He pulled so hard at Sauveren's collar and neck pouch adorned with small bells that the clasp broke and sent the Rooter flying backwards. His arms and legs did a lanky dance to keep him from falling, and he finally landed in Harrold King's lap.

Harrold King shouted, "Get off me, you fool!"

The Rooter stepped on Harrold King's feet when he got off and the pressure made Harrold King howl in pain.

"They're under . . . !" He couldn't finish what he wanted to say.

The Rooter said, "Under where?"

"Your foot! Auugh! My feet . . . you're standing . . ."

The Rooter looked down and scuttled off before he got in more trouble. He retrieved a long hook from the carriage. He twitched up the stairs of the platform like a stick with moving parts, hooked it around Sauveren's neck and pulled. The dog didn't budge.

Fair ran up to the horrible hoomin and tried to pull the hook away. "But you can't do that!" He gave the dog a strong knee in the ribs and Sauveren winced. He took a step, and the Rooter began to pull him along.

"As you can see, I'm doing it," he smiled. He picked up the collar and pulled Sauveren along with the hook. He led him down the stairs.

She tried to follow him but Fella Doon stopped her. He held her shoulders and whispered, "I'm sorry."

Fair realized by the look on his face that Harrold King must have given him a silent order to stop her. Fella Doon looked at the ground. Fair looked out at the crowd and pleaded with her eyes that someone stop the Rooter.

Nothing.

She cried out, "But he's my dog! He's the only thing . . ." She tried to pry Fella Doon's fingers off her shoulder. She tried to twist away from his grasp. She attempted to kick him, but he moved too quickly. Finally, she looked into Fella Doon's eyes and simply said, "Please?" He stared at his feet and shook his head.

From the bottom of the steps, the Rooter narrowed his eyes and looked Fair up and down. "I still smell something—something mousey. I've caught one rat, but there is still one more to catch."

Fair watched with horror as Sauveren walked up a plank into the iron cage. When she heard the lock clink shut, she put her fingers to her mouth and screamed, "Sauveren!"

With much effort, Sauveren slowly turned around in the cramped cage, then looked at Fair with longing eyes. He barked. He poked his shiny nose between the bars.

Just a hint of his pink tongue showed. Fair could hear him whimpering and it tore at her.

The Rooter walked back to the platform, up the stairs and stopped in front of Fair. He put his nose close to hers and stared into her eyes. He smelled of dampness and rot. Fair stood her ground and stared back at him in equal measure.

He said, "What's your name, maiden?" His eyes darted quickly to Harrold King, who sat forward in his seat.

"Fair. Fair O'Nelli." Harrold King growled and sat back. Fair wondered why the subject of her name had come up again. Why did it matter?

The Rooter wasn't satisfied. He peered at Fair even more closely, as though he were inspecting a bug. He gave the side of his nose a tap and said, "My nose . . . ," he paused for dramatic effect, "it usually never fails me. Next time I won't be so kind." He and Harrold King exchanged glances again.

As they passed through the crowd, some of the hoomin spit on Fair's dog. Others threw food at him. She had enraged the Harrold's wrath, surely. Who knew what pain might follow? And so her dog became the brunt of their fear. One Secret Speaker heard his host think a thought that was quite unusual, just as he let a rotten tomato fly: *Why do I do things I can't believe I'm doing, even while I'm doing them?*

The Rooter hopped onto the wagon seat. He cracked the whip. The sound of Sauveren's fading whimper was soon replaced by the rumbling of wheels on cobblestone. In a moment the dog was gone.

Fair automatically reached out to find reassurance, even though she knew he wasn't there. *He kept me warm for nine years.*

Her feelings of loss were interrupted by the faraway sound of Harrold King's voice, "So now, what was that you were saying about me being . . . what was it . . . mean? By the way, tell me who you really are."

Fair's mind went instantly to her dream. *What was that name? What if the dream wasn't a dream, and my real name isn't Fair?* The Woolly had said something about her "real" name, but Azanamer had stopped him for some reason.

Fair could still feel the grip of Fella Doon's hand on her shoulder. She wriggled out from under his grasp. Not having her dog with her to touch, to listen to her, left a hole of emptiness in her chest. But tears were something she would not show. Not here. Not now. This was not right, and it needed righting. She faced Harrold King squarely and set her jaw. Even though she didn't know the answer, she said, "I'll tell you when you return my dog to me."

"Why would I do that?" Harrold King laughed.

"Then I'll get him back myself," Fair said with great insistence. She took a step towards the edge of the platform and looked for her wagon beyond the edge of the crowd.

Something felt strangely odd.

So much light.

So much fresh air.

So much had happened today.

Wonderful things.

Terrible things.

So many years of being locked away.

My legs, she thought.

The darkness was returning.

Fair felt her knees buckle.

The wood beneath her feet began to swell. The faces in front of her began to swirl in a slow smudge of gray and color.

"Father," she called out, weakly.

Why . . . did I . . . say that? she thought as she felt her strength leave her. *Do I . . . smell . . . honey?*

The crowd surged forwards. Fella Doon lurched to stop her fall and missed.

Fair went down in a twisting flurry of peach and white cloth, flowing hair and sparkled light.

The back of her head hit the platform first.

Then nothing.

She lay at Harrold King's feet. The silence was deafening. Her long hair rippled around her face.

"It's her, isn't it? . . ." Harrold King spoke, as if into the air. He gave her body a nudge with his ponderous foot,and let her flop back. "The maiden from my dream."

A little red lizard scurried out from beneath Harrold King's wig and onto his shoulder. There was the faintest sound of sandpaper scratching.

The lizard hissed in Harrold King's ear, "The very one. You'll keep your throne, yet."

Gibber Will saw the lizard and was stunned. It was the same creature he'd seen jump out of the wagon.

Harrold King reached up and took the red lizard from his shoulder. He petted it in his hand. He addressed the crowd, "As you know, I called you all here because I had a dream that an impostor intended to take over my throne. She lies here at my feet. You must avoid her. She is bedeviled and unclean."

Everyone in the crowd backed away a few steps. But Fair's mother edged her way near the front of the crowd, keeping herself carefully hidden behind the hoomin in front of her.

Fair lay as still as though she were dead; yet, in her motionless slumber she went to a place very, very far away.

6 : The Battle of Rall Kindaria

 air found herself standing at the base of the steps she had seen in her dream.

She looked around her and was shocked to discover that the platform of punishment, the crowds, Clock Tower Square—and Harrold King—were nowhere to be seen.

"Do you know where you're going, Fair O'Nelli?" said a voice. It wasn't the voice of the statue, but a quieter, softer one.

Just then, a warm, soft hand wrapped itself around Fair's fingers.

Fair looked up. She expected to see a different statue, but it was Azanamer. Her beautiful, black skin glowed. Fair was surprised.

She said, "What are we doing here?"

"Do you ever have dreams, Fair?"

"Why, I had one last night, and I was right here. Only . . ." she looked around for the statue, and saw him standing on his pedestal. He gave her a wink. She looked up at Azanamer, bewildered.

Fair said, "It wasn't a dream, was it."

Azanamer shook her head. "Did you go to Rall Kindaria . . . the Land of Light?"

"Just to the edge of it." *Wait. How did she know?*

"Did you see the battle?"

"Battle?" Fair asked. "No."

"Then your vision was incomplete. It's time you knew the story of the beginning of the hoomin—and your beginning, Fair. This is what I wanted to tell you back in the tavern."

"My beginning?" *I can't remember much besides darkness and daydreams*, she thought.

Azanamer raised her foot and moved onto the first step.

Fair did the same. Fair thought Azanamer would take another step, but she just stood there. Fair didn't move.

At once, the step rose miles into the air, taking all the stairs—and the stage—with it. Azanamer and Fair took another step. Then another. They soared miles higher with each step they took. The air around them grew finer and brighter with lightening shades of golden light. When they arrived at the curtain, Fair was surprised to see that they were surrounded by stars.

Azanamer whispered, "And now we shall enter the land of Rall Kindaria, my dear Fair. I am to tell you a story, and you will see it exactly as it happened." She said, "Harparat Ofarat." The curtains opened ever so slightly, like an eye that was just waking up.

A brilliant light erupted behind the curtains and bathed them with illumination so intense it looked as if they were on fire.

Azanamer squeezed Fair's hand and said, "Look."

Fair peeked through the curtain.

Everything was so bright.

"I can't see a thing."

Azanamer began to speak, "Oh so long ago, in a land far, far away—long before Cloven Grave was a place, or a had a name—there was a great battle that took place between two prince brothers in Rall Kindaria, the Land of Light. Their names were Rithel and Selador.

"No one ever slept, because time was as a continuous day. No one ever ate, because they were not made of meat and bones. They were wee hoomin of Light. To look at them was like looking through a sheer curtain rippling at an open window on a Longlightren's Don.

"Their Mother Queen and Father King of Light had many, many transparent wee hoomin that were more numerous than the sands of the sea. All of them princes and princesses.

"Selador was the oldest son and then came Rithel. After many ages of time in light had passed, the time came when this father and mother gathered all their glowing wee hoomin before them on a vast and grassy hillside. The blades of grass looked as if they were made of gold and yellow light. They were soft and wide, thick as chewy taffy, and bent over with dewdrops. They were beautiful enough to eat.

"To look at this sea of wee hoomin on this field of gold was like witnessing a scene so beautiful in its splendor that you could not gaze upon it without withering and falling to the ground in a heap. If you look closely, you will see them."

Fair's eyes had adjusted to the light by now, and she exclaimed, "I see them, Grandmother. I see them."

"This is good, Fair. This is good."

She paused and continued her narration. "Spreading his arms wide this Father of Light proclaimed, "As birds must fall from the nest in order to fly, two birds have chosen to leave our nest, so to speak, and your mother and I need each one of you to follow them."

"The look on the faces of these wee hoomin of Light was one of shock and disbelief."

Fair quietly said, "Mother has told me the story of Nestfallen."

"Yes," said Azanamer, "But that's another story."

"So then what did Father say?"

Azanamer pointed and said, "See for yourself."

A scene began to play out in front of Fair. She saw everything just as Azanamer had described it. Father King said, "You will all return, but you are to go to a school so many mountains and seas away, that you won't be able to return for a holiday. It is there you will learn all your mother and I hope to teach you through the very best teacher we can find. It is there you will taste of Life. You will be solid. You will get hungry. Sometimes very hungry. And you will get hurt.'"

A pit of grief opened in Fair's stomach as she thought of her darkness and hunger in the cellar.

"But you will also know how food tastes, with all its textures and flavors. You will know how pleasant it is to have a full stomach."

Fair thought of her birthday lunch earlier that day and smiled. It was especially good because of all the years she hadn't had anything closely resembling it.

"And you will know how nice it feels to get better after having a terribly stuffy nose or after getting scratched. You will also know disappointment. Betrayal perhaps. Fear and grief. All difficult things."

Father of Light needed a volunteer to lead all the rest back to their nest, one by one upon graduation. Graduating with highest honors meant that those dedicated students would become Father Kings or Mother Queens of Light in the endless land of Rall Kindaria.

At this news, many of the wee hoomin raised their hands and shouted, "Ooh, ooooh! Pick me!"

A frown appeared on the face of Thelras, Mother Queen of Light, and Father lifted his hands again to quiet the clamoring wee hoomin.

"My wee hoomin," he whispered, "It is no easy task to do what I am asking. You have tasted of Light, but you must taste of Life. In simply going away to school you will know a change such as you have never known.

You see, you are creatures of Light. This voyage means you must take on flesh and bones."

A few hands went down. They didn't know what flesh and bones were.

Mother chimed in, "Wee hoomin, this must happen gradually. And so, I will take each one of you, as your turn arrives, and guide you towards your entrance into Life. Your all-knowing minds and light will enter into a very small, soft shape. It is a thing of beauty and yet a thing of complete simplicity. When you are born into this school and take your first breath, you shall breathe in a mist of forgetting. You will not remember Father. You will not remember me."

At that, a cry of tears resounded like steady rain upon the field. Then, pausing to look over his vast family, Fair noticed that all the hands had gone down.

"Finally, when you leave this home of yours, there is no way back in, except one. The way was etched in The Eternal Book of Time long ago and I cannot change it. The way is this: He who is chosen to lead must find the Door of Reunion found in Cloven Grave—then open it—but to turn the key brings certain death."

Fair gasped and sat up again. "Death?"

Azanamer continued, "And so Father gently said, 'Whom shall I send?' Look."

Fair looked. Without a pause, the two prince brothers stepped forward. Rithel edged ahead of his older brother and nudged Selador behind him with his shoulder. His father looked at him.

Rithel said, "Father, I shall go." Rithel was large and strong, competitive and handsome.

"And what do you expect in return, Rithel my son?"

"Since I shall lead them, I shall tell them how to get back and make sure they do what I say. No one will be lost. No one." He took a deep breath and filled his lungs. "I want the glory of bringing every last one home. I want nothing more." His nostrils flared and he smiled, so that the edges of his closed mouth turned down.

"And you, Selador?" his father asked.

Rithel thrust up his chin, folded his arms, and turned towards his brother.

Selador said, "The greatest gift of the ages is the eternal law of Arbiter Will."

Fair turned to Azanamer, hoping to get an explanation.

"And so Father said, 'What do you mean, son?'"

Selador said, "This is our home and we must leave you. The only way to be with you again is to come home through the Door of Reunion. I am the oldest brother. If I must die to open it, so be it. These are my brothers and sisters. I know them like I know my own heart and will do all in my power to lead the way."

Father King of Light looked silently pleased. Selador continued, "My brothers and sisters must be free to choose for themselves. I will show them the way to the

Door of Reunion, Father. But I can only show the way. They are free to follow me or not, for Arbiter Will is the law of the ages, and I cannot deny its power."

"And what do you expect in return my son?"

"Only to bring my brothers and sisters home to you and mother, if they will come."

"And the glory, Selador?"

"The glory is yours, Father." Selador said no more. He had nothing more to say. So Father asked him to explain.

"You and Mother are the parents of us all. We are because of you. What greater glory can be given than to those who gave us life?"

"But son, you shall be a stranger to them, because they will not know you as you are now known."

Selador remained silent and simply looked at his father.

Mother Queen of Light—this glorious mother of so many—kept her head down but glanced upwards at Selador with her eyes. Her frown disappeared. A look of peace took its place and spread slowly across her countenance.

This father of so many said, "I see." He took a moment to sit beside her. He lifted her quiet chin with his finger. Those closest to them heard him say, "Mother?" and they took counsel in private whispers. They both nodded their heads.

A look of resolve sat upon Father King's regal brow, whereupon he sat up and beckoned to Selador. Selador stepped forward.

"My son, you are our oldest wee hoomin. It is fitting and proper that you have offered to open the Door of Reunion. We expected nothing less of you. Your brother, Rithel, has promised to bring each wee hoomin home, as you know. However, yours is a desire void of greed and glory, filled with love for your brothers and sisters. This is as it should be.

"Selador, you shall go, but know that it will not be easy. Some of them may not find their way, but you have offered to give them the ability to choose—to use their Arbiter Will. This is a wise thing, for they must be responsible for themselves, with no one else to blame but themselves if they fail."

He continued to speak but was interrupted by Rithel, who threw himself upon the ground. He began to cry like a baby and kick his feet.

"Pay no attention to him, Father," said Mother. "That's just Rithel being Rithel."

After a space of several moments, he froze. Rithel had made a very public spectacle of himself. All eyes were fixed upon him in round-eyed wonder.

In one swift movement, he flipped onto all fours like an animal ready to attack. He narrowed his eyes. He began to creep forward, his breath heaving in and out the sides of his mouth like fire. He paced back and forth rapidly. His gaze was fixed upon his father.

Fair recognized him instantly. It was the red lizard who had jumped out of the wagon that morning. She shuddered. It was the lizard that had been in the wagon with her. Scratching. Breathing. All night.

In a voice that seethed, rather than spoke, he fumed, "Oh I see. This is as it *should* be? And me?" He took the crown off his father's head and placed it upon his own like an insolent brat. "Am I not fitting and proper because I was not first *born?*"

Flames shot out of his mouth with fury when he said the word born. He stood, turning to the endless sea of faces that shone like the sun upon the golden hillside. As he did so his frame grew and grew. His skin turned redder and redder until it burst into flames that sent out an unbearable heat that would have scorched the grass around him had it possessed the matter and substance of the physical world. His eyes were a yellow glow. Fangs and spit took the place of his once beguiling smile. He reached and groped into the air in a wild, fruitless gesture, searching the faces before him.

A wave of fear crashed through the wee hoomin of Light. The first few rows scooted back like the ebb of a yellow sea. Looks of confusion covered their wide-eyed faces; however, some were intrigued and sat forward. Entranced.

Six bulges appeared to sprout and lengthen out of his neck like seedling plants. His own neck lengthened out to match the other wormlike growths. They soon began to swerve and dance. The ends of them took on the shape of Rithel's own crowned head. Soon, all six heads began to speak, clamoring to wear the crown Rithel had claimed. He spit in the face of each one. At once a crown appeared.

With a screeching yowl, all seven heads bellowed, "Who shall be lost?" Pointing a finger he began to jab it towards different faces in the golden sea of wee hoomin. "Will it be you? . . . Or you? . . . Or you, perhaps?" He paused for a long moment, looking over his brothers and sisters. He began to laugh and shrink in size until he assumed his familiar handsome shape. There was movement among the wee hoomin of Light. They seemed to be weighing the consequences.

As if nothing out of the ordinary had just taken place, Rithel smiled, "Oh, I'm sorry." He smiled again and looked at the ground in front of him. "Really, if anyone wants to come with me so that you're sure not to get lost, I'll be more than happy to lead the way . . . I . . . I wouldn't allow you to fail."

At that, Father began to stand. Mother put her hand on his arm and shushed him. "Let him be, Father."

He patted her hand. "Yes, divine companion."

Ignoring Rithel, the Father King of Light continued to speak. Rithel was silenced because he was ignored.

"Selador, you will suffer more pain than your wise mind can even comprehend. You will be spit upon and beaten, whipped and left alone by some who are here with us. But you will not forget your mother or me. You will remember. You will know each one of your brothers and sisters. You will know Rithel."

At that, Rithel smiled.

"This is not all. I am asking you to suffer for them. Oh, they shall suffer in knowing life and what it is to have a body and need sleep and food, and what it is to go *without* sleep and food. They shall suffer from hurting each other and themselves, both heart and body. But you, you shall suffer *everything* they suffer. Every suffering of every wee hoomin will have a moment and a memory, and you will live and know each one."

"So Father," Selador quietly interrupted, "Everything is to be suffered twice."

"Yes and no, my son. The life of hoomin is like a dangling rope full of knots. Each knot belongs to a hoomin. Each hoomin grips their knot tightly, hoping they're strong enough to hold on. You will climb that long, endless rope, hand over hand, passing through each living creature one by one, born and unborn, feeling everything they have felt, feel, or will feel. You will know them better than they know themselves, because you will see them from the inside out. You will be their one true friend.

"You will live and know their every pain. They can choose to blend into you and let you share and bear the pain. This is called the One Suffering. Or, they can hold on alone. This is called the Suffered Twice."

He continued, "Here is the importance of going away to school. Your brothers and sisters will be taught to correct their mistakes on frequent examinations. They can always turn them in to their teacher for a better mark. They have the opportunity to learn the wisdom of feeling sorry, the wisdom of making right what they have done wrong, the wisdom of blaming no one if their life is not as they would wish.

"You see, if they come to you, *all things* are possible for them no matter what sufferings they bear, because you shall bear their sufferings for them to keep them free, if they will so choose."

"All things?" Selador asked.

"All things. And they will learn the wisdom of turning away from that which brings darkness and doubt. But most importantly, the wisdom of coming to you to ask that the Light return to their hearts and minds when they have done that which would send it away through wrong action or thought. It is the only way to be guided."

"Guided, Father?"

"Now I must speak," joined in Thelras, Mother Queen of Light. Looking at Selador and her vast posterity she spoke in a whisper that could be heard for miles. "I will go with you wherever you go. I will be with you wherever you are, but only, only if you are good and kind, virtuous and pure. If you darken your hearts with heavy thoughts and deeds, I cannot stay, for I am Light. You will not see me, but you will feel me, for I will be there to comfort and protect you, guide and give you help in choosing between Selador and the whisperings of Rithel."

"And how do I turn the key, Mother? Father?" asked Selador.

Thelras answered, "To turn the key means that in suffering you shall know the misery, the cruelty of hoomin-kind and suffer for it. You shall know the most bitter wickedness and deepest greed of your brothers and sisters. You shall feel the binding chains of blame, selfishness and false need. You shall hear and feel the pain of words spoken that pierce the heart as daggers. You shall know each one of your brothers and sisters by name. You shall see them in your mind and know every detail of their life in your heart. Then, my son, you will be killed by some of the very brothers and sisters that sit beside you now." The children of Light gasped and shook their heads. It couldn't be.

"But, to turn that key also means that when you die, in falling you shall push open the door that leads home. In that instant, you shall be filled with life and light once more. You will rise to your feet once again and come to your Father and me. Your death will be only a memory."

Turning to the sea of wee hoomin before him, Cael, Father King of Light, placed his arm around Thelras and said, "Know that the mountains are treacherous and the seas deep and wild. Many of you will be lost, as yours is the choice to follow your older brother wherever he may lead you. It is easy to take a wrong step if your eyes are not on him at all times. All he asks of you is to trust him.

"Believe that he will show you the way home. Ask that his suffering erase your own. Turn away from that which is wrong. Many of you will choose to bear your own suffering alone, and so Selador's suffering for you will be all for nothing."

To Selador he said, "This will cause you pain as well, but know that it is not your fault, for the greatest gift your mother and I have given each one of you is the freedom to choose for yourselves in all things, as you said so well yourself."

A cry rose from the front of the sea of wee hoomin. It started small, and grew into a thunderous whine, "But what about me? I could do what you're asking."

It was Rithel. Turning to his brothers and sisters he shouted, "Who will follow me?"

At Rithel's invitation, one wee hoomin stood up and shouted, "I'm going with Rithel. He promised we won't get lost." Heads turned this way and that to look at Selador and Rithel, weighing the consequences. The wee hoomin looked at his brothers and sisters and said, "Who wants to come with me?"

Soon, a wild commotion ensued. The wee hoomin began to take sides to join Rithel or Selador. Shields appeared on their forearms because they simply willed it. Swords appeared in their hands because they wished it so. As if fed by greed and the thirst for glory, Rithel resumed his gargantuan proportions. The seven crowned heads pierced the air with their yellow gaze. They narrowed their eyes and silently dared the wee hoomin of Light to follow Selador. Rithel's tail swished along the ground like a beckoning finger.

And so the great battle began. It was a battle of will, not of flesh.

None were lost in death for none could die. None were wounded or harmed, because wounds were inflicted and sealed without pain. But the fighting was fierce, and the battle long. From afar it looked like a heaving sea, seething with shards of light.

Fair said, "I've never seen hoomin fight. It's terrible."

"It was terrible," Azanamer corrected. "You are only watching a memory. They felt no pain, only the shift of will. You felt no pain. Not in Rall Kindaria."

Fair wasn't sure she'd heard correctly. "Me? I felt no pain? What do you mean?"

"Look," said Azanamer. "At the battle front. Next to Selador."

Fair looked into the boiling movement on the field of light. She saw swords flashing. Shields clashing. Faces. Arms.

And then she saw.

"I was there. Standing beside Selador." Fair felt something surge within her throat. It was a feeling of disbelief and hope mixed together, combined with a longing so deep that an ocean of tears fought to find an escape.

"But I look so . . . so glorious and shining." As she stared at her memory, she took a breath in. "There is my brother, Hale. I. . . I see my mother and father, too."

"Yes, you all chose to fight for Selador. You fought valiantly." Fair was shocked to see a certain hoomin fighting near the front of the battle.

"Is that Harrold King?"

"Yes. He fought valiantly, too. Everyone in Cloven Grave did. Would you like to see more of the story?"

"Oh yes. Please."

"Look."

Fair looked and saw that Selador seemed small compared to Rithel, yet his fighting was steady and fierce. They each fought with silver swords.

Mother and Father sat and watched, dismayed to see that Rithel delighted in the following of wee hoomin that chose to side with him. Yet still, they took comfort in the fact that most of their wee hoomin remained with Selador.

The battle continued for a space of great length. At long last Father stood and said, "Enough."

Father's voice pierced the deafening sound of shouting and metal clashing upon metal. The clanging cacophony stopped. All eyes turned to him. Rithel drew his tail around all those who had joined him and pulled them close. His scales fell off. The seven heads shriveled, leaving Rithel looking as he had before: a red lizard.

"Sit down, my wee hoomin," said Father.

There was an enormous shuffle in the air as all the transparent wee hoomin sat upon the golden grass. It was still untrampled, even after such a long and horrid battle. No battle in the history of all things living has been fought since.

"You have chosen whom you will follow. It is your right through the eternal law of Arbiter Will; however, there is only one way to return, and that way is through Selador. It has been decreed.

"To Rithel and his followers, each one of you our dear wee hoomin," he said as he swept his arm towards their mother, "We must tell you this: you shall never taste of death, for you shall never taste of life. You shall look upon it and thirst for it, but never drink. You shall reach and grab for it, but shall never feel it in your veins. You shall be able to look in through the schoolroom windows, but never enter through its doors."

He passed his hand over the followers of Rithel, and they were changed from wee hoomin of Light into the serpent-like shape of lizards.

"And Rithel, you and yours shall be felt as confusion and seen as a shadow. You shall influence, but you shall not force. You shall whisper in the ears of your brothers and sisters, but you shall not always be clearly heard. You will be shadow, for your light is now diminished. You are fallen, dear Son of the Dawning Day. As there is good, so must there be evil. Otherwise there is no other way for our wee hoomin to choose. You, dear Rithel my son, will provide a balance. So be it. The battle is finished. You have chosen."

Turning to Selador and his followers, Cael, Father King of Light, said, "I ask that each one of you, our dear wee hoomin, come to me before you depart for school. I shall leave you with my blessing. Your mother will grace you with her embrace before she leads you through the Door of Separation, away from the nest. May you study from the best books of learning. May you learn truth and goodness. May you learn that you alone are responsible for the greatness of your life. May you choose wisely and well. Rithel will, as you have seen, do all he can to turn you away from Selador. I hope . . ."

Rithel narrowed his eyes, rose to his feet and whirled around in a flash. "You will be mine!" he bellowed, finishing Father's words with words of his own.

Rithel looked at their father and then back at his brother. He thrust his sword towards Selador. Rather than injure him, he began to scratch the tip of his sword into the side of Selador's sword, making shapes as though he were writing something. White lightning shot out from the tip of his sword as he wrote. When he was finished two words could be seen, "Falling Go."

Selador responded by doing the same. When he was done, the words, "Risen Low" could be seen glowing like white hot embers.

Rithel shouted, "If you go with him you will all fail. I laugh at you! Ha!" He jabbed the sword at the sea of living light. Those who had chosen to follow him, however terrifying, looked smug in the knowledge they would not be lost.

Father's voice trailed as he spoke to his wee hoomin, "I hope you will simply laugh in his face."

Rithel looked at his father. He clenched his fists so tightly that it shot a red fire of anger into his face.

"Sit down, Rithel," motioned Father with a brush of his hand.

"I will not!" Rithel snarled at his mother, then his father, who both ignored him. They folded their arms and watched. This infuriated him and he looked back and forth at them in an attempt to figure out just how he might prolong his dismissal. He clenched his fists into tight little balls at the sides of his legs, and as he did so, he began to shrink. Holes formed in the side of his head where his ears had been. His eyes took on a red hue, and a slender yellow tongue began to dart in and out of his mouth, which no longer had any teeth.

He continued to look back and forth at his parents until he was crouched on all fours. A tail swished behind him. Fiery scales flew off his skin. As only a lizard can, he scampered to the hem of his father's robe and circled up his clothing like a squirrel climbs up a tree. Small and swift, he found himself perched on his Father's shoulder, where he could whisper in his ear.

From afar, it was difficult to hear what Rithel whispered, but at this Father King took Rithel by the neck and simply said, "Be off with you, Rithel."

He gently dropped him and sadly shooed him away. He had lost not one wee hoomin, but many, and his heart wept.

Rithel scurried off towards the seated crowd of transparent wee hoomin and disappeared into the mass. It was easy to tell where Rithel was, because one wee hoomin, then another would hop up with a startled exclamation of one sort or another.

A wee hoomin on the front row began to cry as he looked over his shoulder to see his hopping brothers and sisters. They each inevitably said, "Oh!" and this trail of surprised exclamations, *Oh! Oh! Oh,* formed a wandering line deep into the sea of wee hoomin. It looked like shifting, breathing ice in a state of melting, leaving puddles of color from the reflection of the sun. The wee hoomin next to him began to laugh, and soon the laughter spread and developed into a chorus of bell-like mirth and surprise.

At one point, far in the distance, Rithel appeared on one of the wee hoomin's shoulders, and a very small sound could be heard: *Shwipwish*. It was a hiss. Another laugh erupted near Rithel, and like a pebble being dropped into a pond, it began to ripple out and spread, until it merged with the next laugh and the next, like a melody being woven into the laugh already in concert.

This King put his arm around his Queen and they watched the spectacle with a bemused look on their ageless faces. When Rithel finally disappeared and was gone, the father looked once more over his posterity. He motioned for Selador to come stand beside him.

Selador came to his father's side. His father grasped him by the shoulders with the gentle firmness of a loving father, beaming with pride, and turned him to face his brothers and sisters. "This, my wee hoomin," he paused, "is your teacher." A reverent hush fell upon the endless field covered by the wee hoomin of Light.

The moment was interrupted by the appearance of a scaly tail that shot up from the distant horizon. It was Rithel's tail. Within moments, it reached those he had gathered aside earlier. It swept them into its grasp, keeping them for himself. In one violent, upward sweep, it carried the tongue-flitting crowd of serpents high into the air. After a pause, it flung them through the darkness of space and time, to the land of the Graves, where they would swim as shadows: waiting, wishing they had chosen differently, reaching out and grabbing at the lives of the living, but never knowing what life feels like. But Rithel didn't know that then. Neither did his followers.

At that, this Mother and Father wept. Father wiped his nose with a handkerchief that Thelras gave him and said, "Rithel and his own have place no more among us. They shall seek to have place in your mind and soul, in your feelings and thoughts. Be diligent students and Selador will fill your mind and soul with light to overflowing so that Rithel and his darkness will have no place to dwell. Your mother and I want you to come home. We want you to inherit all that we have and dwell among us once again with hearts and souls rejoicing. That is, if you so choose."

Then, the vision was gone. Fair saw nothing but an empty field.

"And then what?" Fair said to Azanamer.

"That's enough of your story for now. Just know that the land of Cloven Grave is the school of which he spoke. The school has no rooms, nor windows, because the lives of the hoomin are its walls. Its windows are the eyes with which you choose to see the world."

Fair was thoughtful for a time, then she said, "Selador's already in Cloven Grave, isn't he."

"Yes. Are you ready, Fair?"

"Ready for what?"

"You are descended from royalty and shall return to claim your throne. But first, you must find what seeks to be found."

7 : Fair Wakes Up

nly seconds had passed since Fair tripped and hit her head.

She moaned awake.

"Drinkwater . . . ," she whispered. Fella Doon leaned close to have a listen. "I think she said something, your majesty."

Fair moaned and said it again, "Drinkwater."

He stood up. "I believe she's thirsty, your majesty."

"And what if she is? She has defied me and needs to be punished," said Harrold King.

He was full of so much rage that he bolted to his feet without help and took a toddling step towards the spot where she lay helpless, using his scepter like a cane to support himself. He was clearly in pain.

The top of the scepter had a clear, crystal ball held in place with four rounded strips of gold that came together like a cage around it. At the very top a transparent, ruby-colored stone glinted in the sunlight. It was in the shape of a heart rimmed with gold, including a lightning bolt of gold that shot down the middle.

Since Harrold King had taken over Cloven Grave, the hoomin had come to call it the Heart Breaker, because he took it with him wherever he went and his every action seemed bent on breaking the hearts of the hoomin.

Rithel was on his shoulder and said, "Quickly! You must do it now."

As Harrold King lifted his arm to strike Fair and do her harm, a gust of wind blasted through the square. He and everyone present looked around. Rithel looked around frantically, stood up on his hind legs, and hissed.

A melodious voice filled the air, "You shall not touch her, Harrold King."

He held his scepter more tightly and looked around to find where the voice came from.

Rithel's yellow tongue shot in and out.

Fair stirred.

A bright light filled the sky directly above the platform. Every hoomin in the square looked upwards and gasped. Music, ever so quiet, chimed in the air and filled the space with an immediate hush.

Harrold King looked up with the rest of the crowd, transfixed. What he saw filled him with red-faced anger. He gripped his scepter until his knuckles were white.

A figure descended like a cloud from the sky in long rippling wisps of the palest yellow. Her hair was bright white. Her face glowed so intensely that it was almost painful to look at. Her tall silver crown appeared to sprout narrowly from the top of her head, where it then grew into a spread of lush, glittering leaves of the palest green, far above its base.

Harrold King looked around to see if anyone else saw what he was seeing. The entire crowd was staring at her. This was no apparition.

"I'll do what I please," he bragged, "even if she is a maiden. This insolent brat has broken the law and spoken up to me. She must make a sacrifice. It's the law."

"Who says?" the figure asked.

Harrold King grit his teeth together. He hated to be defied. "The Laws of Memory say so!" He was seething. "And, who are you? Why are you here?"

Rithel sat on Harrold King's shoulder, swishing his sandpaper tail.

The figure turned to the crowd and spoke, "I am Thelras, the mother of all who have ever lived or will live." She turned to look at Harrold King and said, "Even you."

He spit on the ground. "Not mine, you're not. I never had a mother."

He began to toddle painfully towards Fair. Thelras ordered, "Stay where you are, impostor."

Gibber Will turned around to see how Azanamer was reacting to such a sight, but she was nowhere to be seen.

"And if I don't?" Harrold King laughed, his belly all a-jiggle.

"She is a maiden. A maiden is not to be harmed. Especially this one." She held her palm out to stop

Harrold King, turned to the crowd and said, "You have all been waiting for a miracle, have you not?"

A few heads nodded. Barely.

"Be quiet, stranger," Harrold King ventured, in a trembling voice.

Thelras ignored him and continued, "For some time now I have watched you all talk about the tree writings in quiet tones by your fires at night. And you all know the legend of the Planter Era."

A few heads nodded and exchanged knowing glances.

To Fair, Thelras said, "Arise."

Much to her surprise, Fair felt herself pulled to her feet in swift and misty movement. She rubbed the bump on the back of her head and felt a slight burning in her eyes. She winced and rubbed them.

Fair faced Thelras, not knowing quite what to expect. She reached out to pet Sauveren, but he wasn't there. She gulped.

Thelras looked at Fair and said, "We have all been waiting for this day. Happy birthday, Tharin . . . Tharin Zothiker."

Before Fair even had time to have a thought fill her head, Thelras raised her arms and sent a gust of wind whirling through the square. As she did so, she spoke with words that left her mouth like a windstorm. The words blew themselves around every hoomin there, whispering remembrance into their ears:

From underneath the mighty foot
Ones stepped upon shall rise,
to open the door and lance the bull
amidst his anguished cries.

The seeds of law lie fallow now,
yet root and stem shall form.
The Planter then shall gather all
at the sounding of the horn.

The crowd gasped. Hands went to mouths in amazement. Lariel's brother who had waited all night at her cottage clenched his jaw and looked around for his sister. Lariel put her hand to her mouth to stop herself from screaming. After all her years of trying so hard to keep her daughters' existence—and her name—a secret, she wasn't able to stop what was meant to be.

Fair looked at Thelras. She thought, *That was the name in my dream.* Yet, her head, and years of experience told her otherwise. So she said, "No I'm not. I can't be."

Thelras said, "Oh, but you are. Who you believe yourself to be and who you really are, are often two very different things." A few hoomin looked at each other with knowing glances. Then at Harrold King.

Harrold King's face paled beneath its powdered layer. His eyes glazed over and flashed red for a moment as his mind whirled. He shouted, "Impossible! I've taken every measure to . . ."

"To what, Harrold King? To rid Cloven Grave of the Zothikers?"

Harrold King's son with the blonde bushy hair turned to his brother and looked as though he were trying to say, "What did he say? Who is she?" He asked with his eyes, with his knitted brows. His brother shrugged his shoulders and turned his back to him, not wanting to be bothered.

Fella Doon walked up to the blonde-headed son and took his hand. He opened it with the palm facing upwards. Fair watched him as he spelled the letters T.H.A.R.I. and N. on his hand. The young hoomin looked at Fella Doon, who mouthed the word, "Tharin."

"Terrin?" he asked. Fella Doon nodded and smiled. Harrold King's oldest son was deaf. Fella Doon spelled out the name "Zothiker" on his hand. The young hoomin's eyes went wide, and he looked at her. Fair quickly looked away when she caught her gaze, then looked at him again, out of the corner of her eye. Just for a moment. He was still looking at her.

Harrold King shot a glance at Fella Doon. "Be quiet, I tell you!"

Thelras continued speaking to the hoomin in the square. "Harrold King has changed the Laws of Memory, your laws of sacrifice. You are no longer sacrificing your sheep, your wool, your milk, your cloth and all you have in thanks for life, or to be clean.

"This monster, this . . ." she turned and faced Harrold King. "This impostor asks for your sacrifices at the Rendering for one reason and one reason only: to fill his belly." She continued speaking to the crowd in a gentle voice. "Do you think it was right that you had to give up your wee hoomin all those years ago?"

The hands of many women went to the red scarves on their heads. Scarves of remembrance. Lariel Zothiker was one of them. She had watched all this in horrified silence. If she spoke up, or if Harrold King saw her, she might not ever return home where Fair would need her.

Thelras looked into Fair's eyes until she was certain Fair was returning her gaze in equal measure. "Your Father King and I have something to give you."

"Me?"

Thelras nodded. "Do you see the heart at the top of the scepter?"

Fair looked and noticed the heart-shaped stone. She also noticed that Harrold King held the scepter close to his chest. Thelras pointed her hand to Harrold King's scepter, to the Heart Breaker. Then, she placed her palm against Fair's forehead and kept it pressed there, gently.

Her hand feels so hot, Fair thought. *How strange.* Soon the heat condensed into a single spot on her forehead.

The air began to buzz.

Nothing more than that seemed to happen.

At first.

Thelras kept her hand there a moment longer. She said, "Are you ready, Fair?"

"I don't know what to be ready for." She remembered how Azanamer had asked her the same thing.

Right then she felt something deeper, something peaceful, like a river that flowed deep within her soul. She was right where she was supposed to be at that very moment.

She nodded.

Thelras continued, "You have been gathering light even in your darkness, Fair. You are ready to see." Fair thought of the Scrolls of Truth, surprised that Thelras knew. Thelras pulled her hand off Fair's forehead and looked quickly at the Heart Breaker.

Harrold King followed her piercing gaze and shouted, "The heart! What have you done with it?"

Fair looked at the scepter and noticed that the stone was gone. Where was it?

"Give it back to me!" he cried. He stepped towards Fair with painful difficulty, gouging frantically at Fair's face.

Fair panicked. *What is he doing? He's trying to scratch my face.* She put her hands up to shield her face, turned her head, and heard him scream, "Ach! My hands!"

When Harrold King reached out to touch her, he felt a crackling shock go through him that sizzled and burned like fire.

Fair hesitantly peeked through her fingers and saw Harrold King recoiling in pain. His hands were smoking. *Hold on.* Her middle finger felt something beneath the tip of it. *What's that small lump under my finger?*

She rubbed the spot, right in the middle of her forehead, just above her eyebrows. *What is it? A smooth, glossy shape.* Her finger traced its outline. Her mouth dropped open.

It was the stone.

The red heart.

It had shrunk in size and was now a little smaller than her fingernail.

"Give it back to me," growled Harrold King.

"But I . . ." Fair didn't know what to do. Surely she could give it back to him. She tried to peel it off, but she couldn't even get a fingernail beneath the edge of it.

Thelras said, "You will not be able to take it off, Tharin. It will protect you from harm and guide you on your journey."

"My journey? And please call me Fair."

"If you *will* go, that is—Fair. It is time for the departed wee hoomin of Light to return to our waiting arms." She looked at the crowd of hoomin one by one, even Harrold King. She said, "You are, each one of you, our departed wee hoomin. We want you to come home."

Harrold King's jowls jiggled with fury.

She turned to Fair and said, "Your Father, Cael, and I would like to make a bargain with you."

Fair said, "A bargain? With me?"

"You will find your dog and all that you seek if you will agree to find the Door of Reunion at Selador's Gate. When you find the gate, you will find Selador there. Will you agree to it?"

All these words, and names, and places, Fair thought. She nodded. Then she thoughtfully asked, "How will I find what I'm looking for if I don't know *what* I'm looking for?"

Thelras said, "You're the only one who can find what needs to be found. And you have everything you need to help you find it."

"Everything I need? What do you mean?"

"You will see, in time. Here is my instruction: You have until the day after the Blood Moon rises to find Selador's Gate. You will know the time is drawing near when the air grows cool and fields have ripened for the Harvestaren Shoomin. In the meantime, you will pass through seven gates along the way. You have passed through two of them so far."

"Have I?" Fair asked. "What gates?"

Thelras snapped her fingers, and a stream of flossy light swam between the onlookers in the crowd. It swam up the steps of the platform. When the light grew still around Fair, it became clear that it was made up of a dozen or so Impissh Nissen with small pointed noses, phosphorescent wings and long legs. Their wings brushed against her skin.

"Who are *they*?" asked Fair.

Thelras said, "These are the Impissh Nissen: They grew the Ruby Eye from the soils of Cloven Grave long ago. And these words were born with it . . ." Thelras signaled with her hand.

They swirled around Fair and sang,

> *Purity of heart, strength of mind,*
> *They who seek shall also find.*
> *Eyes to see, ears to hear,*
> *Look through me and to me*
> *and all will be clear.*

Fair was bewildered, "How do I look to it and through it? I mean . . . it's a stone."

Thelras answered, "The truth will reveal itself to you, if you look closely."

This is all so new, Fair thought. *It's all so confusing.* She put her fingers to her forehead and felt the middle of the Ruby Eye. She said something that had been troubling her about the jagged line of gold that split it apart. "The heart . . . it's cracked."

"Ahh . . . but you can only see through a broken heart."

"Broken?"

"A tree grows only from the seed that splits apart."

Thelras placed her hand upon Fair's cheek. She continued, "Remember to look through your broken heart. That way you will see what is real and true."

Maybe it will help me know what happened to my father and brother.

Thelras read her thoughts and said, "You will find your brother along the way, Fair. And your father . . . ," she paused.

The cold fish of fear shuddered inside her. *All these years I thought it was my fault that Hale died. But he isn't dead. And my father? . . . is he even alive?* She didn't dare ask it out loud.

Thelras said, "Know that it won't be easy. You'll be tested in every way."

Words entered Fair's mind like a whisper, words from years of studying the Scrolls of Truth by the blue glow of moonlight near her mother's window. Words that were etched into her soul while the music box played:

You are powerful.
You will always have strength given to you
when you need it most.

In a panic, Rithel scurried down Harrold King's robe. He positioned himself at Fair's feet, capturing her curious gaze. His scales began to shrink and fade as he grew in size and shape. He held Fair's eyes in his until he became a tall muscular hoomin with a well-shaped jawline. His hair was a glossy, wavy brown. Fair realized he was the sort of hoomin she could easily talk to. *How absolutely sickening,* she thought. She looked away. He stood inches from Fair's face and kindly said, "If you want to give the Ruby Eye to me . . . I'll just . . . ," He lightly reached out to touch Fair on the forehead, but recoiled in pain.

"Ahhh! What have you done to her, Mother?" he cried.

"You will not be able to touch her either, Rithel. You have no power to destroy her, as long as she bears the mark of the broken heart."

"We'll find a way," he seethed. A slow smile slithered across his face and he looked at Harrold King, who straightened his stance.

Thelras said, "Possibly." Then she ordered, "As you were." He shrunk back down to his decreed size and shape. Red. Scaly. His yellow tongue shot in and out.

"Go away, Rithel," Thelras ordered.

"Oh, I'll go away, but I won't be far," he hissed. "The Blood Moon rises at the end of the Longlightren Dons. We have until then to get rid of the maiden." He looked at Harrold King. "We'll destroy her yet."

Then he was gone.

8 : The Journey Begins

arrold King leaned on his scepter. "Fella Doon, help me up. Put this, this threat—this demon—into my carriage."

Perhaps Harrold King thought if he couldn't touch her, Fella Doon could. Harrold King looked into the crowd. If eyes were daggers and stares were thorns, he wielded them now. "And bring her friends, too."

It wasn't going to happen quite that easily.

"More to say. More to say," called out the Woolly.

Harrold King looked over to the wagon. "What, words from a madman?" he scoffed.

The Woolly looked at those with him on the wagon, then at Harrold King. "If you are going to take us away, these are my parting words, Harrold King: By Harvestaren Shoomin when bonfires light the fields at night, when frost begins to form on the withering leaves and the harvest is brought in, know this: when the three days of darkness descend, the walls of Osden Shorn will crumble and you will rule no more.

"I would curse you . . ." he spit upon the ground in front him. "But no curse is needed. It is decreed."

Harrold King had been silenced with the slap of prophecy. It was something he could not argue with. He pulled his scepter close to his chest, shook his wobbly chin and growled, "You're mad!"

The Woolly ran up to the platform in a flurry of tattered clothing and dirty bare feet. Much to Harrold King's dismay, the Woolly put his arm around Fair's shoulder and said, "Open the door and lance the bull!"

Soon, the crowd was shouting as one, "Open the door! . . . Open the door!"

In a noisy spectacle of wood-creaking fury, Harrold King walked on his own two feet back down to his carriage, crying, "Ahhh, my feet! They're burning! Get me out of here. Immediately!" He snapped his fingers. "Come with me, sons."

His feet had nothing to do with why he left. Hurt pride is often best covered with an excuse of some sort. Feet that hurt works quite well.

"And Fella Doon?" growled Harrold King, "I want you to get in that wagon—and bring everyone in it to Osden Shorn." Azanamer and Gibber Will looked at each other. The Woolly seemed oblivious.

Fella Doon nodded. "Right away, your majesty."

Harrold King's carriage drove away with the unstoppable sound of horse hooves clacking wildly on cobblestones. Whip slicing air.

After they left, Fella Doon didn't move. He looked like he planned on taking his time following orders.

Now, the only hoomin remaining on the platform were Fair, the Woolly, Fella Doon, and Miss Tilly, who was still locked up. The crowd didn't seem to know what to do.

Everything went silent for a moment. Everyone waited for Fair to speak. She looked around and wondered what she could say. *Nine years of darkness and loneliness, and now these faces are looking at me. So many of them.*

Fair felt the Ruby Eye grow warm on her forehead. *How strange.* A thought came to her from the Scrolls of Truth:

> *You come into this life with a bundle of wisdom*
> *that you are supposed to unpack and give away.*
> *If you don't give it away,*
> *it will get heavier and heavier,*
> *until the only option is to drag it behind you.*

She looked at Fella Doon, who looked the other way, as though he intended to let her do what she pleased.

So she asked the Woolly, "Would you please do something for me?"

The Woolly looked at Fella Doon, who gave a slight nod of his head as he looked off into the distance.

The Woolly took this as a signal that all was clear.

"Of course," he said. "Anything."

"I need you to bring me my basket . . . and my blanket. Would you?"

The Woolly ran to the wagon. Gibber Will pulled the basket out from beneath his feet and handed it to the

Woolly. He lifted the false floor of the wagon and pulled out the blanket. He rolled it up, tied a rope to both ends and gave it to the Woolly.

In a moment, the Woolly was by Fair's side.

"Here you are."

Fair took the basket and blanket. She put the rope over her head so the blanket hung down her back. She turned around and looked at Miss Tilly, who had watched everything from her place in the stocks. Fair walked up and sat down beside her on the thin wooden plank. It hurt to sit on it, because it was so narrow.

Some of hoomin moved from one foot to the other, uncertain of what might happen. This had been an unusual day.

Fair opened the basket. "Here. You can have my midden meal. I've eaten well today."

Miss Tilly looked ashamed and turned her head.

"When did you eat last?" Fair asked.

Miss Tilly kept her head turned away. She looked down. As Fair looked at her, she saw something that made her pull away in shock.

Miss Tilly disappeared.

What was even more strange, Sauveren sat in her place. Fair reached out to pet him by force of old habit, but before her hand could even touch him, Miss Tilly was there again just like before. *Oh my*, Fair thought. *I'm seeing things.* Her eyes stung, so she rubbed them with the heel of her hand.

Fair said, "Did you eat morning meal?"

Miss Tilly shook her head. Fair felt sorry for her.

"Last night's even meal, then? Surely . . ."

Again, she shook her head.

"Yesterday's midden meal?"

She shook her head again. Fair was amazed. Miss Tilly hadn't eaten for a whole day.

Fair untied a knot of sky blue cloth that held a chunk of bread, an old apple, a jar of balm and a leather flask of water. She reached in and pulled out the chunk of bread, then broke it into pieces. Miss Tilly looked at Fella Doon. He turned his head the other way.

Fair said, "It's alright. He won't say anything." She uncorked the flask and gave her a sip of water. Then she put a piece of bread in Miss Tilly's mouth, who chewed it ravenously. Fair fed her, one piece at a time, until the bread was gone.

She carefully put the apple to Miss Tilly's lips and said, "Here, have a bite."

Miss Tilly bit into the crisp flesh. When its sweetness passed over her taste buds, a slow smile crept across her lips. She stole a shy look at Fella Doon.

After she finished chewing her bite of apple, Miss Tilly looked shyly at Fair's flask of water. Fair uncorked the end of it again and put it to Miss Tilly's mouth. Miss Tilly drank until the flask was empty.

Fair grew thoughtful. "Can I ask you a question?"

Miss Tilly nodded.

Fair stood up and went to the front of the wooden stocks. Miss Tilly's hands dangled from the locks. Fair took ahold of her hands and leaned over to whisper, "Do you know where Selador's Gate is?"

Miss Tilly shook her head.

"Are you quite sure?" Fair felt disappointed.

Miss Tilly nodded, looking sad that she couldn't help. She slowly said, "I hope . . . you find what you're looking for . . . and . . . thank you."

The air stood still.

The crowd was silent.

Miss Tilly had spoken.

Someone muttered in disbelief, "She spoke to a hoomin. It's a miracle." Everyone looked at each other. "She spoke," they repeated. They cheered.

Fair didn't pay attention to the noise coming from the crowd. She hardly heard it. She said to Miss Tilly, "I know what it's like . . . to be stuck. And hungry. I wish I could do more for you."

"You've . . . done plenty, Fair. Before you go, there is something I want to give you . . . please . . ." She looked down at her lap, "My apron pocket. The small one."

Fair found the pocket and reached in. She pulled out a small, drawstring bag made of rough brown cloth.

Miss Tilly nodded, "Take it with you wherever you are going. Payment for entry."

"Payment for entry?" Fair asked.

Miss Tilly nodded. "Everyone has gates here. If you're looking for someone, you'll need to pay to enter."

"You mean, I just can't walk up to someone's door?" Fair realized her mother hadn't told her, because she hadn't needed to know.

"Harrold King has Protectors posted at every gate to make sure you pay."

Fair opened the bag and poured the contents into her hand. She counted seven shackles, each one a different color: red, orange, yellow, green, blue, indigo, and purple. She let them fall back into the bag, pulled on the cords to cinch it closed and slipped them around her wrist.

"Thank you, Miss Tilly. I need to say good-bye now. I have something I need to do."

When Fair turned around she announced, "I need to go now." She touched the Ruby Eye on her forehead absent-mindedly. She had no idea how to find the Door of Reunion at Selador's Gate, let alone Selador.

The Woolly held out his arm for her to take. "I haven't got my head on straight, but you can't do whatever it is you have to do alone. Can I come along?" He looked at Fella Doon to see if he'd let him get away with it.

Fella Doon had a family that expected him to be home at the end of the day. He knew if he didn't do Harrold King's bidding, he'd be punished. He reached into the neck of his shirt and carefully untucked a red scarf that he had loosely knotted around his neck.

Everyone realized he was one of them. He had lost a wee hoomin in the whisking. He quickly tucked it back out of sight. "I'm sorry, but I've got to take you in to Osden Shorn. You," he pointed with his nose, "and your friends. As much as I don't want to."

The sight of the scarf made Fair think of her mother. Her red scarf. She wondered how she could leave her, and if she'd ever make it back home to her. Her mother had already lost a son. Fair felt the stone of guilt drop into her stomach with a shuddering thud. But the thought of going home made all the darkness of the past nine years pour through her head like rocks. They clattered down to her toes and slowly filled her up, until she couldn't move. She knew she couldn't go home. She couldn't bear the weight of it again. She looked into the crowd to see if she could find her mother. Waiting. Silent. Yearning.

Lariel was there. She had stepped back into the crowd, not wanting to draw any attention to herself. She wasn't sure she could fully trust Fella Doon, even though he seemed like one of the kind ones. She needed to make sure she was home if and when Fair returned.

"I know," said the Woolly. "It's enough to make any hoomin crazy."

How does he know? Fair thought. There was a certain knowing in his voice and she knew he understood. She put the flask in the basket and picked up the blanket roll. The Woolly held out his arm. She took it and gave him an understanding kiss on his cheek, just above the edge of his beard.

"I want to say good-bye to my friends," she said.

"Fair enough."

The crowd parted for them like a slice of warm bread peeling off the loaf as Fair and the Woolly walked towards the wagon.

Fair looked up at Gibber Will and Azanamer, who sat beside him, once again.

Gibber Will was shaking his head. He told Fair she wasn't strong enough for a job like that after being in the cellar all those years.

"I'll be alright."

"No you won't. I saw you faint up there. It almost made me pass out just lookin' at ya. Just come on home, now. Your mother'll be 'spectin ya."

"I just can't."

He dabbed his forehead and told her he'd been as scared as a rabbit she wouldn't be coming home. He also admitted he couldn't stop her, since he had a hard time saying no.

Fair felt herself take an invisible step from a scary place of not knowing, to a sure place, where not knowing didn't matter.

"I made a promise, Gibber Will . . . you know . . . to do what is right."

"I know. But you gotta be brave to do that," he said.

Azanamer put her hand on Gibber Will's trembling arm. "Shush now, Gibber Will." She looked at Fair and told her to look through her heart. It would keep her on solid ground. Rock solid.

"Then, tell me what to do. Where do I start?" Fair asked. "How do I find someone when I don't even know where to look?"

Azanamer pointed down one of the several cobblestone streets that led out of the square. Sunlight glinted on the stones and the south-facing shops. She told Fair the street would take her out into a lesser known part of Cloven Grave where she might find what and who she was looking for.

Gibber Will's eyes grew larger. "You mean the grassy path?" He turned to Fair and tried to talk her out of it. He told her no one used that path because no one knew where it went and that he wouldn't be going that-a-way if he were her.

Fella Doon walked over to the wagon and said, "Time to say good-bye, Fair."

"What are you going to say when Harrold King sees you didn't bring me with you, Fella Doon?" He told her not to worry.

Azanamer said, "Just follow the grassy path."

Fair felt something comforting surround her, and she knew Azanamer was right. With a firm look of resolve mixed with excitement, Fair took the Woolly's arm. She wanted to ask him a question but wasn't sure if she should. *Yes*, she decided. "Are you really crazy or do you just pretend?"

"I feel like I'm going crazy every day," he answered. "But I have a job to do."

"What job?" Fair asked.

"Perhaps you will find out one day."

They turned on their heels and headed for the sunlit street, glinting with the promise of an awaiting destiny. At the entrance to the side street Fair turned around and waved good-bye to her friends. Sunlight glowed in a haze behind them.

I'm not in close enough proximity to Harrold King
to know this part of the story, Gasper.
We need your help to tell it.

I've been looking forward to
telling the tale of my host.

So you'll do it?

I'm meant to do it.
When do you want me to begin?

Now.

9 : The Chamber of Mirrors

arrold King lay on his back in a large rectangular pool, floating like a glistening, unpoppable bubble. Steam rose from the surface of the water and swirled around him in the air. There were no windows in the room. Torches burned in sconces along the walls, casting an eerie glow through the steam.

The room smelled like rotten eggs. Sulphur. The scepter lay across his greasy belly. A look of pure bliss slept on his flushed face. He felt no pain when he was in his mineral bath. It was fed by a natural hot spring that bubbled deep beneath the floors of Osden Shorn.

Right then, however, the bliss on his face had nothing to do with the absence of pain. It bloomed from the rotten soil of his heart. Like a cow chewing its cud, over and over, the thought kept repeating itself in his mind: *She's almost out of the way. She's almost out of the way.*

A knock sounded. He snorted. *Oh bother. I want to be left alone.*

He opened his dark, heavy-lidded eyes.

He yawned. "Enter."

A solid wood door creaked open on its damp iron hinges. Fella Doon stepped into the dim yellow glow and said, "I was told I'd find you here, your majesty." He had come down a long winding staircase made of stone.

Harrold King looked at the ceiling. It was in fact, an enormous polished mirror. It was flecked with dull patches of black beneath its surface, due to years of damp and heat. The surface wasn't completely smooth, since it was made from large tiles of handblown glass that extended from wall to wall. He could see Fella Doon's rippled reflection in the ceiling. He lazily pointed his scepter right at him. The mirror was quite clear, since steam evaporated long before it arrived at its surface.

With a loose upwards jab of the scepter at Fella Doon's reflection he asked, "Have you got the hoomin with you?"

"They're just outside the door."

"Bring them in."

Fella Doon disappeared out of the doorway and reappeared with a noisy clanking: Gibber Will, Azanamer, and the Woolly wore chains around their wrists.

Harrold King felt a chortle of satisfaction rumble inside his throat as he watched their muted and wavy reflections clink and clatter in through the doorway. He licked his lips and waited for Fair to walk in. *My prize, my pride, and my prisoner. At last,* he thought. She never came.

"Where is the maiden? The Zothiker?" he bellowed, bobbing with bulbous ferocity. His movement sent waves of ripples onto the black tile floor.

She was the one he wanted.

Fella Doon calmly lied, "When I tried to bring her in, I got the same painful shock you did. None of us could touch her."

"Humph," Harrold King grunted. "Bah, I see." He struggled to calm the fury that rose behind his eyes. He sighed, "Such a shame."

He lay in silence for some time. Fella Doon finally said, "What do you want me to do with the prisoners?"

Harrold King twiddled the fingers of his free hand on his chin. "Give me time to *think*, will you?" He jabbed his scepter at the reflections in the ceiling. "You—rabbit face, round woman, and the madman. Come stand near the edge of the pool where I can see you better." *Something will come to me. Something good.*

They walked over to the edge of the pool.

Gibber Will shook like a leaf.

Azanamer stared straight ahead, with cool surety.

The Woolly said, "Tie his shoes, I can't I can't."

Then it came. Harrold King had an idea. A plan. *This IS a good one!* he told himself. He felt giddy and giggled, "Unlock them, Fella Doon. No further need for their chains."

"But . . ."

"But what? Do as I say."

Fella Doon fished a key out from beneath his shirt and twisted it in the locks around each of their wrists. Three sets of chains. Three loud clatters as the chains fell to the ground.

"Very good," Harrold King said with a loud snort. He reached over to a bowl that was floating next to him and grabbed a piece of meat. He dropped it in his gaping mouth and swallowed it, *galumph*, without chewing.

Then he said, "There is one thing you need to know about me, you three. I'm a lonely man. I like it that way. I have plenty of company that floats around me. Company that doesn't eat my food or threaten to take away my throne. Pity you can't see them. Truth is, I don't really have a use for you or have any desire to lock you up. Not with chains anyway."

Fella Doon's face went pale. He looked as though he feared what was coming.

"Fella Doon, I'd like you to close the door."

Fella Doon walked silently over to the heavy door and closed it with a creak and thud. He turned around and stood there in his kilt, cape, and boots. He adjusted his cap and assumed his usual standing position. Feet spread apart. Hands held behind his back.

"Very good," said Harrold King. "Let's see now. Who's first, I wonder." *What fun*, he thought, as he looked at the rippled and firelit reflections of his prisoners in the ceiling.

He pointed his scepter at it and began to draw circles in the air. He spoke lazily. No one really paid attention to what he was saying until they noticed that the ceiling began to cast a greenish glow in the room.

Three times around, and three times again,
give me power and give me gain.
Darkness come and darkness stay
while the mirror casts its evil sway.

By now, the newcomers were looking at the ceiling in drop-jawed horror as green and yellow light swirled together like a gathering hurricane.

Gibber Will saw Harrold King's scepter pointing straight at his reflection in the mirror. He jumped and quickly grabbed ahold of the Woolly. Harrold King said, "Such a scared little fellow. I'll bet you can't ever say the word, "no." Let me make life a little easier for you."

He jabbed his scepter at Gibber Will's reflection in the ceiling. A bolt of light shot out, ricocheted off its surface, and sailed straight for Gibber Will.

He was hit with an explosion of light.

Once the smoke subsided, Gibber Will was nowhere to be seen. In his place, a small light brown rabbit trembled and wiggled its nose. It had furry white tufts above its cheeks.

Azanamer and the Woolly looked down at the rabbit then over to Harrold King. By the looks on their faces, it was clear they realized they were next. They looked up at the ceiling and saw their own reflections, as well as Harrold King's shining, bloated belly glowing in the torchlight.

Fella Doon wanted to shout and tell him to stop, but he knew he might never go home to his family if he did.

"There," said Harrold King. "Big ears and whiskers suit you much better. As for you, old woman, you seem to feel and know everything." He jabbed his scepter at her reflection. "Do you know what it's like not to feel?"

A bolt of light shot out from the scepter at her reflection. It bounced off the ceiling towards her. She was surrounded by a flash that smoldered after it disappeared. When the smoke wafted away, a boulder, large and brown, sat where Azanamer had stood.

The rabbit—Gibber Will—immediately hid behind the stone and peeked out from behind it. His furry ribs swept in and out with rapid, panicked breaths.

Azanamer's world went dark. She could think, but she couldn't feel a thing. Not even in her heart. She couldn't even feel a heartbeat. Harrold King watched her struggle to open two spots on the surface of her stony self.

"Ha!" Harrold King laughed. "I see you, and you see me! Such a happy family!" He began to laugh uncontrollably, and it took him some time to contain himself.

"So let's see here . . . we have a rabbit, a stone, and a . . ." he jabbed his scepter at the Woolly's reflection. The Woolly was changed into a big brown monkey in a flash of more light and smoke. He blinked his large, shining-black eyes in surprise.

"A crazy monkey. Now I'm satisfied." What he didn't say was that he wasn't satisfied. Only mollified. Vengeance on the maiden's friends merely brought him a temporary, surface pleasure. *I want that maiden.*

The Woolly looked at his arms and touched his face. His tail whipped around and brushed his face. He began to protest, and the room echoed with the sounds of *Ooo, ooo, ooo, ooo, ooo!*

"Quiet!" said Harrold King.

The Woolly stopped making his monkey sounds.

"I'm going to be brief so you can get out of here and leave me alone. You're still my prisoners, since you are all friends and accomplices of the brat. You obviously don't need chains, though!" He laughed heartily.

Little furry Gibber Will and the Woolly, who had an out-of-control brown tail, looked at each other.

Fella Doon said, "Begging your pardon, your eminent, royal majesty the king."

Harrold King's eyes darted to Fella Doon's reflection, "What is it?" he demanded.

"How am I supposed to get that boulder out of here?"

"Ahhh . . . hmmmm, yes. Good question."

Harrold King sent another streak of light at Azanamer's stony reflection. He said, "Now she can roll uphill, downhill and any which way she chooses. If she prefers to be a pebble, that's fine, too. Now get out of here. All of you."

Soon, there was a loud thundering. The stone, who was Azanamer, had begun to slowly rock back and forth, gaining tediously slow momentum. The room shook as she rolled towards the door.

Gibber Will sniffed at his front paws. He tried to hop, but since he had never hopped before, his hind legs pushed too hard and sent him head over heels. After several wild, floppy attempts he began to hop towards the door in a forwards, backwards, and sideways direction.

The Woolly didn't seem to have any trouble at all with his new body. Perhaps it was all his years of living in the woods, but he scooted over to the door using his feet and the knuckles of his hands. He clambered up onto Fella Doon's shoulder. He looked at Fella Doon's torchlit face through his round black eyes, then grabbed the cap off Fella Doon's head. He put it on his own.

Fella Doon grabbed his cap back and put it on. He opened the door with a loud creak. Azanamer rumbled through the doorway and Gibber Will followed clumsily behind.

"Fella Doon," Harrold King bellowed.

Fella Doon looked over his shoulder, "Yes, your Highness?"

"You're getting too soft for my liking. Your behavior on the platform of punishment was pathetic." Harrold King had noticed how protective Fella Doon felt towards Fair. "I'm sending you down to the caves. You'll be much more useful to me there."

Fella Doon looked panicked. The caves beneath Osden Shorn were for the lowest of the low. Every Protector dreaded being sent there to keep watch.

He nodded, "Yes, your royal eminency. I'll go straight away." The Woolly pulled at Fella Doon's ear.

Before the strange crew left Harrold King alone with his unseen friends, Fella Doon turned around and asked, "Will they always be like this?"

"What do you think, softy?" snapped Harrold King. "There is no way to undo what is done, unless there is someone who knows as much as I do about such things, and that's impossible."

Then he closed his eyes and began to snore as though he were asleep, in a very unconvincing way. He clearly wanted to be left alone.

"I see," said Fella Doon. The motley group went ahead of Azanamer, who bumped, rolled, and pounded—stone against stone—up the long, circling flight of dismally lit stairs, while Harrold King watched them leave, with one eye open.

Dimbelly, it is time to speak for your host.
Mine is not present in this part
of the story, as you know.

Yes dear Liver, and I'm glad she's not.
I have known I would need to do my part
in telling the tale of The Great Deliverance.
But I must confess, it brings me pain to do so.

Look for the joy in it, Dimbelly. It is there.
And now, breathe. The time has come.

10 : Sauveren's New Home

he Rooter sat at a small wooden table and leaned back on the legs of his chair.

On the table, a single candle cast its glow on a large, black leather-bound book, a pot of ink, a quill pen, and another pot of something or other.

Although Harrold King had nicknamed him the Rooter, he was known as Pewgen Flype. He pressed the tips of his bony fingers and thumbs, against each other. Pull together, spread. Pull together, spread. With only the light from the candle, they looked like a pale spider doing push ups against a mirror. His thin lips formed a slight, curved smile as he told himself, *All mine. Something of my very own. All mine.*

He sat in a long dark cave carved out of the gray stone, deep beneath Osden Shorn. Thin straw mats lined both sides of the long walls. A thin, scraggly hoomin lay curled up on each mat, chained by the ankles to large metal links attached to heavy wooden beams above them. There were hundreds of them.

Fella Doon sat on a low stool with his back against a thick wooden beam. A torch burned in its sconce above his head. He stared at Pewgen Flype with a twinkle in his eye.

Just a few minutes earlier, Harrold King told Pewgen Flype to take Sauveren down to the caves, where he could keep him for a pet if he wished. Harrold King had never intended to use the dog for a footrest. Pewgen Flype felt a tingling in his hands and feet at the thought. His parents had never let him have a pet, or anything for that matter. Their favorite word was spoken slowly and deliberately on a daily basis: deprivation. Ever since then, he'd always wanted something to own. Something to grab. Something to kick.

"I have just the place for him," smiled Pewgen Flype.

He pulled Sauveren by the neck with the long hook he had used earlier: down long corridors. Down stairways. A jangle of keys. The twist of a lock. The creak of a door.

Pewgen Flype pushed it open.

Sauveren began to sniff the air in front of him. His nose was hit with the smell of dampness and dirt, metal and filth. He stepped back and sat on his haunches. He pricked his ears and turned them this way and that—to the sound of grating. The sound of something scratching. Something very dark. Something that was everywhere.

When Pewgen Flype tried to pull him in, Sauveren growled. Pewgen let go and took a step back. He twiddled his fingers in the air with wanting reaches towards the dog, then pulled his hands to his chest, not quite sure how to be master of such an enormous beast. *Patience now, Pewgen my boy. A bit of patience is all.* He called out through the doorway, "I've got a surprise for you all!"

Sauveren moved his ears towards the sound of rustling inside the room.

Pewgen Flype peeked his head into the room and pointed at a young hoomin. "You. Lisper! Get over here and help me. We've got company."

A young hoomin with a head of blonde hair (whose true name was Hale) ran up to him in filthy tattered rags for clothes. He was Pewgen Flype's trusted gopher boy. Pewgen Flype gave him jobs to do that he didn't want. He had even trusted the boy to keep watch while he'd gone to Clock Tower Square.

Hale lisped, "Yeth thir," and took ahold of the handle.

"Did they give you any trouble? The matternots?"

Hale shook his head. He was one of *them*, so no, they hadn't given him any trouble. If they had, Pewgen Flype would make Hale pay for it, and they didn't wish that on their friend. Matternots is the name Harrold King gave to the wee hoomin he whisked away from their parents when they were small. The parents never knew what happened to them. But Harrold King knew. He knew very well. They were his slaves.

"Not even a little bit?" He hoped they had so their punishment could occupy him after he'd dealt with the dog. Hale shook his head.

Pewgen Flype said, "Well then, come take ahold of this." He wasn't in the mood to trouble himself with an uncooperative animal, so he said, "I'll unlock the cage. You bring him over to me. You can do that, can't you?"

The young hoomin inched his hands along the handle until his hands were close to the wide metal hook. He tentatively put the back of his hand beneath Sauveren's nose. The dog pulled back quickly, then changed his mind and began to sniff at the boy's fingers.

Hale gave his muzzle a pet. The dog didn't bite him. When he realized the dog would be friendly towards him, he began to pet him between the ears.

"I had me a dog like you wunth when I wuth little. But not ath big ath you."

"Isn't that touching," Pewgen Flype teased. "Now pull him in here before I change my mind and lock you up instead."

Hale took Sauveren by the collar and pulled. The dog got up off his haunches. The boy startled when he saw how enormous the dog was. He led him through the doorway and noticed a jingling sound. He looked underneath Sauveren's neck and saw a pouch hanging from the collar. It was made of leather that was dyed sky blue. Bells were sewn along the flap that covered the opening.

Pewgen Flype slammed the door, *thunk*, behind Sauveren and, *clink*, turned the key in a large black lock.

He felt a pillow of importance fill his chest in a comforting way. He had a pet. He was master.

He turned around to face the room and announced, "The Harrold gave me an award today for being the best Protector he's got. He gave me this dog as a token of his appreciation. He's mine, so don't any of you go thinking you can even take a liking to him."

He walked over to a square opening in the long stone wall, directly behind his small table. Hale had kept the candle burning. Iron bars covered the hole.

More jangling of keys. The twist of a lock. Pewgen Flype opened the cage door and motioned to Hale, who led him up to the opening in the wall. Sauveren sat down and wouldn't move.

This irked Pewgen Flype. "We'll have none of that," he fumed. "Get the dog to lie down, Lisper." Hale looked confused, but knew he'd better do as Pewgen Flype said.

Pewgen Flype looked around the room in a flood of panic. If the matternots saw that he couldn't control a dog, they might not obey his orders as easily as they always did.

His eyes landed on the single chain that zig-zagged up and down through all the ceiling links then ankle bands of the hoomin on his side of the wall.

He ran past the rows of hoomin lying on their mats until he got to the far end of the wall. He unlocked the end of the chain, ran back to the hoomin that lay closest to his table and unlocked the chain where it was secured to a link on the wall.

He gave the chain a yank and kept pulling until he had a sufficient amount to work with. Hale had succeeded in getting the dog to lie down. Next, Pewgen Flype pulled a length of coiled rope off a hook hanging from a beam next to the table and wrapped it around the dog's feet while he muttered, "Lock him up, lock him up, kick him well, and hang him."

Before anyone realized what was happening, Pewgen Flype threaded the chain through the dog's bound legs and began to pull while he whistled a tuneless melody, thinking to himself,

> *My pretty little pet.*
> *My very, very own.*
> *I can do what I like.*
> *You'll get no bone.*

He wasn't strong enough to pull the dog off the floor, so he ordered the newly unchained matternots to help him.

The boys grabbed the chain and pulled back in what looked like a tug-of-war. Soon, the dog was hanging upside down from the ceiling. Pewgen Flype secured the chain and locked it.

He said, "There! Who's the master around here?"

"You are, Pewgen Flype," the matternots answered mechanically.

He gave the dog a push with his foot. The dog began to sway back and forth, upside down. Pewgen Flype filled his nostrils with the air of pride.

A voice came from a far corner of the room. "Are you so sure?"

Pewgen Flype coughed on a bit of spittle, narrowed his beady eyes and pulled off his tall black hat. He felt threatened that someone else was down there. He held the rim in his hands and looked from side to side, out of the corner of his eyes. "Who said that?"

Fella Doon stepped out of the shadows. "The Harrold ordered me to help keep watch down here . . . and congratulations, Pewgen Flype. That dog is quite a reward for being the best Protector he's got."

Pewgen Flype said, "I don't need any help." He ignored the comment about the dog being a reward, since he knew Fella Doon understood it was a lie.

"Don't worry. I'll stay out of your way. This is your territory down here."

Pewgen Flype relaxed when he heard that and put his tall hat back on his orange-haired head. He said, "Find a stool and sit down." *What in the world is he doing down here? I'm Harrold King's head protector.* The days were going to be very long with the Not Knowing of things.

Fella Doon found a stool and contented himself to lean his back against a supporting beam.

Pewgen Flype ignored his new comrade and announced, "Back to your mats—all of you." Once the matternots were back in their places, he reached behind his back and said, "I stopped at the sweetie shop on my way back here. I brought you all a little something."

He pulled out two lollipops. A huge cheer went up from both sides of the room. He handed a lollipop to a matternot at each end of the two rows alongside the opposite stone walls. Four rows altogether.

He chuckled to himself. *Loyalty can be a great motivator.*

They each had a lick then passed it along to the next matternot, who had a lick, until the lollie made it to the end of the row.

Having grown slightly smaller, it was passed back in the other direction, then back again—as many times as it took—until only the stick remained.

Pewgen Flype didn't bring them the lollies because he cared about them. He figured that they would work all the harder for him the next day if they thought he loved them.

By the time the lollies were licked down to nothing, Pewgen Flype ordered that the matternots help him get the dog down.

This time, Pewgen Flype easily led Sauveren into the cage and locked him up with a smug dusting of his hands. He sat down on his chair and leaned back.

He pressed his fingers together. Back and forth. Back and forth. *Lock him up, lock him up, kick him well and hang him.*

After several minutes of inflated self-admiration, he whipped his hand with a small thin cane and called out, "Time for your lessons, my little insects!"

When he stood up, the chair stayed stuck to his bottom. Little did he know that Fella Doon had covered the seat of his chair with glue he'd found in the other pot on the table.

11 : Follow the Grassy Path

air was far beyond the edge of the village. The further she walked and stared at her feet, the more the cobblestones started to show signs of ill use. Moss started to fill in the cracks. The further she went, the more it filled them in, eventually covering the stones entirely with green.

Finally, the mossy cobblestones ended and gave way to a dirt road, which eventually petered out altogether, leaving the narrow grassy path Azanamer told her about.

At home in her cellar, there were always answers to Fair's questions of what to do next and where to go:

> *don't leave the cellar during daytime*
> *cuddle up to Sauveren to stay warm*
> *daydream*
> *eat cold hard-boiled eggs and old apples*
> *sleep when it's light*
> *wake up when it's dark outside*
> *study the Scrolls of Truth*
> *you will be filled with light*
> *stay invisible*

But ever since Fair left her friends behind and took her first thrilling steps on the grassy path, she was flooded with the jagged, disorienting feeling that she had no idea

what to do next,

or where to go.

She didn't know the answers.

She wished she could reach out and wrap her arms around Sauveren's warm fur.

"Sauveren," she said into the air, "I'm not sure I can do this. There's so much dirt and grass. The sky goes on forever, and I'm all alone."

Wait, he isn't here. How silly of me, she thought.

She decided right then that she was going to set out to find her dog. She could look for him as well as Selador at the same time. Why not?

Just then, Fair saw a brown rabbit dash, somewhat clumsily, along the path. It stopped, then headed back in the direction it had come from before disappearing into the grass.

She had taken no more than a dozen steps or so when the path divided. The path on the left was a bit wider and more worn with use. The one on the right was narrow and clearly unused.

Which path led where she needed to go? And more importantly, where was where?

"Oh, Sauveren, I don't know which way to go. I'm afraid if I go left, I should have gone right. And I'm afraid if I go right, I should have gone left." Sauveren had been her lifelong companion and confidante when she needed to talk. Even though he wasn't there now, she spoke out of habit. While she stood there staring at the fork in the grassy path, she noticed movement in the ground, right where the path divided.

She saw something shiny and black move inside a small hole in the ground. She jumped back when a furry face appeared.

"Oh! . . . You frightened me!"

"Well I should say *you* frightened *me*, Fair. You're so much bigger, now that I'm so much smaller."

He spoke. At this realization, Fair felt a drum of confusion start to beat and pound in her head. She waited a moment for it to slow down. She tapped her head with the palm of her hand. Maybe she'd been imagining things. But maybe not.

So she asked, "So much smaller?" *This is just like being in Rall Kindaria*, she thought.

"Don't you recognize me at all, at all, at all?" asked the rabbit, licking his paws.

Fair knelt down and put her face close to the creature. She thought there was something vaguely familiar about the tufts of fur above his cheeks. The longer she looked, the more she realized this rabbit was awfully funny looking.

He had big front teeth.

Then it hit her.

It couldn't be.

"Gibber Will?"

"That's me, alright. He turned me into a rabbit, the big turd. He's evil, I tell you. Evil."

"Harrold King?"

Gibber Will sniffed as loud as it's possible for a rabbit to sniff. "Evil, I tell you. I ain't never known the meaning of being afeared 'til now. Everything is so, so, so enormous," he stuttered.

"Oh, Gibber Will. What a horrible thing to for him to do! Why don't you come along with me?"

"Can't do that, can't do that," he said, wiggling his whiskers. "This hole is nice and s . . . s . . . s . . . safe," he stuttered.

Fair thought for a moment, "But wouldn't you like to do something brave and help me find Selador? You were so brave when you took me to Lamb's Tavern in broad daylight. Really brave."

"I was, wasn't I?" said Gibber Will. "And besides, Harrold King said that if I find someone who knows how to undo what he did, that I could be me old self again, or something of that sort."

Fair thought about all that she had seen in Rall Kindaria. Maybe Selador could help him. She said, "Let's ask Selador, when we find him. Perhaps he can undo what was done."

Gibber Will came out of the hole in the ground and stood up on his hind legs for a brief moment. "Truth be told, I'd much rather be big about being afeared than small about it. Hiding is small."

"Well said," Fair smiled. But she wasn't sure if that meant he was coming. She waited for his decision.

"I suppose, I suppose I'll go with you. As long as we're together, I ain't gonna be the least bit afeared . . . except of getting eaten, eaten, eaten." He looked at the sky to make sure there weren't any hungry birds around. He hopped over to Fair's feet.

"I'll protect you," she said. "Now, which way should we go?" She kept her wish to find her dog to herself.

"I wouldn't know, but why not keep going in the direction you're headed?"

"But there are two paths here."

Gibber Will looked at the sky nervously again, then at Fair. "It seems to me that if you're trying to find someone you don't know, you might, might, might want to take the path that no one uses very much."

"I believe you're right, Gibber Will." Fair headed down the less traveled of the two grassy paths.

Gibber Will darted in and out between her feet, until he realized it was much safer, for the time being, to hop along behind her.

Gasper, can you fill in this part of the story?

I'm ready, Liver.

12 : Watched

 arrold King stood on a balcony, overlooking the waters of Lakinren Bae. Rithel scurried out of his hiding place in Harrold King's crown, settled down on his shoulder, and whispered, "We have a small problem." Harrold King jerked his head and glared at Rithel. "What sort of problem?"

"I would suggest you see it for yourself in the Chamber of Mirrors." Harrold King snapped his fingers. A Protector was standing near a wide, open doorway. Harrold King ordered, "Take me down to my hot spring! My feet are on fire."

Fella Doon's replacement, a Protector with jet black hair and sharp, angular cheekbones said, "Right away, your majesty."

His name was Salloroc. He led Harrold King to his portable chair.

Within minutes, Harrold King was positioned inside a long hallway that could be closed off from both sides by double doors. Once he was set down, he ordered all of the Protectors to leave. All except for Salloroc. He was the only one who knew about the secret passageway. He locked both sets of doors.

Salloroc slid aside a painting of Harrold King, revealing a wooden door. He opened it and helped Harrold King into an elevator. He closed the door, slid the painting back into place, then let Harrold King down to the Chamber of Mirrors by means of a smoothly oiled crank and rope.

The elevator plunked into place. Harrold King undressed down to his shorts and toddled painfully down the stairs into the pool, using his scepter for a cane. He turned around and let himself fall onto his back into the warm, odiferous water. When the waves subsided, he bobbed up to the surface.

When his eyes were free of water, he looked at the mirror and said,

> *Three times around, and three times again,*
> *give me power and give me gain.*
> *Darkness come and darkness stay*
> *while the mirror casts its evil sway.*

The mirror filled the room with green, swirling light. Harrold King saw the maiden in the mirror. And the rabbit.

⌒ ⚜ ⌒

Back in his room, Harrold King lumbered back and forth, running his hand through his unkempt hair and across the stubble on his cheeks. The floor creaked and groaned with the weight.

"You've failed me, Rithel."

"He's just a small rabbit," Rithel said, smoothly.

Harrold King muttered the words over and over, "But I want to find her alone . . . a Zothiker. Unbelievable. I thought I'd done away with them all."

He allowed his bloated mass to drop into a chair with a gurgling grunt, whereupon a terribly forceful, gaseous wind erupted that shook the very floor beneath him.

He felt terribly alone, and the thought of it made him tremble. There are many ways to be alone, and some of them are almost divine. There is a feeling that comes from being at peace in such a solitary moment, sensing in a very deep way that the space you occupy is important and fulfills the measure of its creation by simply being.

Your sleep is untroubled because you have a clear conscience towards all, for you have made right that which you have done wrong as best you can.

Harrold King knew a feeling of being alone that resulted from a different reason altogether. Simply put, he detested all, and he was detested by all. He could never have enough. Enough power. Enough land. Enough hoomin to rule. As a father with two sons, one would think he had a certain understanding of how to act grown up. But he was and had always been an irritation, beginning with his parents in Low Grave. After they died he was a bother to his sister, Queen Graeshara. He thought he knew better than she did in all matters of authority.

When Graeshara hurriedly sent him to Cloven Grave to get rid of him, he became just as bossy there, and he hurriedly did away with Bander Zothiker, king of Cloven Grave. Harrold King sent him out on a boat used for public sport, called the Joust and Dangle. He sent his most trusted nobles and servants to put him in a suit of armor, and tied the usual cord around his ankle.

Usually after a good joust and thrust overboard, the losing opponent was hoisted up with a crane by his ankle rope. In Bander Zothiker's case, there was no crowd to witness the Joust and Dangle. The king was simply pulled out of bed in the middle of the night, rowed out in the middle of Lakinren Bae wearing a cold suit of uncomfortable armor, and pushed overboard. Harrold King ordered that the ankle rope be cut.

And that was that.

It took no time for the hoomin of Cloven Grave to despise and fear him. The more they cowered, the more he detested them—and required more from them as a result.

As the hoomin grew thin (but not too thin) from working for and sacrificing nearly all for this hoomin, he grew fatter and fatter from the gluttony and greed that fueled his very being.

He knew he could not have the hoomin's affection, but he could fill himself with the fruits of their labor. He knew he could not have the hoomin's respect, but he could have them suffer in shoes that were so small that they pinched, or so very small that some hoomin were forced to wear no shoes at all.

By now he had four hundred personal Protectors. His sister sent most of them from Low Grave when he complained that the hoomin of Cloven Grave had attempted to kill him, which wasn't true in the very least. Some of the Protectors were hoomin he had already ordered into service. Once he had organized this army, he promptly put them all to work. The first thing he ordered them to do was to build a high stone wall around the temple.

And so, Harrold King was a horror to all who knew him. But in the guilty conscience that simmered somewhere far beneath his pea-sized heart that had no beat, he was a terror to himself. This is what it means to be truly alone.

No amount of food could fill that void. No amount of destruction could satisfy his attempt to be the only hoomin left who could stand and say he was a ruler to be respected. Instead, this glutton lived, and moved, and expressed his being as a swollen, bloated, and futile attempt to fill the void he had created.

The pallor of his jowly face destroyed any notion of possible joviality. It was ashen white, as though he had dumped his head into a bucket of flour. Even this he dusted with powder.

Upon close inspection, his eyes appeared to have nothing behind them. His large nose spoke of his ability to smell out all sorts of things, the fine smell of money, for instance, found in the rich smell of earth that he loved to crumble in his large heavy hands. And of course, the constantly emerging growth of food that flowed from the kitchen, where his many cooks scurried, whipped and stirred.

His face was the very picture of a cancerous boil on the flesh of a giant that appeared ready to burst. His legs had open sores that crawled with small, wriggling worms that his servants plucked out when he went to bed at night. His bed creaked and groaned under the weight and was replaced—cracked and shattered—every few shoomin.

He knew, more keenly than anyone, that no one would shed a tear for him when he died. And so he ordered in the Cries Unia that at the moment of his death, the nobles whom he had selected to attend him be executed immediately so that there would be universal mourning. At the very least, he thought, *that way hoomin will mourn when I die. If it is not for me, then it will be because of me.*

These were not the thoughts that troubled his mind this morning, however. There was one thing—two things actually—that niggled in the back of his hard little brain at that very moment. One was knowing that even though he could be as bossy as he pleased in Cloven Grave, he was merely a monarch and not a king and never would be. He let out a growl as he realized that someone could replace him. Another Zothiker, at that.

The second little niggling thought was more of a constant jab that seared the back of Harrold King's mind like a red hot poker, and had done so for a very long time. This caused him a great deal of pain, which he took out on everyone around him in the form of smoking fury.

This niggle was something that Mannem Esseren made known to Harrold King's parents, who eventually told it to him when he was grown. Mannem Esseren was the seer of the Esseren Tribe (from which the King family descended).

The day Harrold King was born, old and grizzled Mannem Esseren had seen a flock of birds dipping and falling, rising and rounding in the air. Since he understood the language of flight, he knew that Harrold King would live longer than thirty years, but no longer than forty, because a king would come to take his place.

I'm almost forty, he thought.

He had to act fast.

Thank you, Gasper. I'll continue from here.

My pleasure.

13 : Back on the Grassy Path

ibber Will and Fair came upon a wide field. Fair stopped to pick some flowers. The feel of the stems felt wonderful between her fingers. The color of the blue blossoms was a feast for her eyes. Gibber Will hopped and bounded ahead in floppy, uncoordinated excitement.

"Hold on, Gibber Will!" Fair called.

He stopped and turned around. The grass was low to the ground all around him in that particular spot. He saw Fair off in the distance, pulling at something in the ground.

To pass the time, he did a few somersaults, testing out his newfound abilities. Before long, he was giggling and snorting. He'd never had this much fun as a hoomin. He stopped and called out, using his ear for a megaphone. When he discovered that it actually made his voice louder, he giggled all the more.

"Fair, come see what I can do, do, do!"

She looked over at Gibber Will, who was doing lazy flops and somersaults further up the path. She picked a final flower and added it to her bouquet.

"Oh Sauveren," she said to herself. "I wish you could see these flowers." Then, she called down the path, "I'm coming, Gibber Will!"

She heard a quiet voice, "Run for cover."

Who said that? The sun was shining. She sniffed her fragrant bouquet. All was well as she walked towards her furry friend.

She heard it again, "Run for cover."

Fair looked around. She was sure she was imagining things.

Then it happened. A loud screech sliced through the air high above her. Gibber Will stopped hopping and flopping. He looked around. There it was again.

Screeeeech!

He looked up.

An eagle circled above him, going higher and higher. The higher it went, the faster it could dive. It was a bald-headed eagle with an odd-looking rim of long black feathers that circled around the back of its head. Its eyes were rimmed on top with a dark black strip of coloring that went straight across, and a garland of black coloring that dipped underneath its piercing, wild eyes.

From high above, the eagle heard Fair call out, "Run for cover!"

Gibber Will was just a small speck, but the eagle tucked in his wings and felt its clear, protective eyelids slide over his eyes.

He dove.

He dropped like a feathered stone, aimed by some unseen hand.

Fair and Gibber Will ran towards an enormous tree.

The eagle shot towards them like a swerving arrow.

Soon they heard a loud drumming sound.

Gibber Will hopped in a side-to-side, forward fashion, in a clumsy attempt to head for the tree.

"My heart!" he cried. "Oh, my little heart!" He had never been so afraid in his life.

The eagle came down on him with its legs straight out. His razor-sharp talons were spread wide open. For grabbing.

Gibber Will hopped to the side when he meant to hop forward. His clumsiness saved him from two open talons: four dagger-shaped talons on each foot. Three in front, and one in back, like a thumb. They grabbed at Gibber Will but got air instead, barely missing pale brown fur and tall ears.

Fair screamed.

The eagle spread his wings and swooped up and around, looking for his prey.

Fair and the rabbit were almost to the tree.

"Just a little farther!" Fair cried, out of breath. "We're almost there!"

The eagle couldn't get either of them now, so he circled around the clearing. Fair and Gibber Will dashed into the shade of the tree and looked back. They could see the eagle swooping and circling around the grassy field. He looked over his shoulder and flew towards them.

The eagle came straight for the tree and called out, "I'll get you! Just you wait!"

At the last moment, looking as though he was going to fly straight into the branches, he spread his wings wide and swooped up and over the edge of the woods.

It was Harrold King.

"Good gracious," said Fair, from the safety of the dark shadows. She held onto a mossy tree trunk and looked at the rabbit.

"Crumbs!" said Gibber Will, panting rapidly.

Just then, it began to rain.

14 : A Tree Is a Safe Place to Be

air leaned back against the furry green tree trunk. She watched the rain fall for a moment. "Almost got me," she panted. All she knew was they had been chased. She never looked back.

Gibber Will hopped excitedly. "Don't you remember, 'member, 'member? He can't touch you. The Harrold wasn't after you. He was after me."

Fair wiped her face with her hands and felt the Ruby Eye on her forehead. She'd forgotten all about it. So much had happened that day. It was all so new and hard to digest in her mind. Darkness and daydreams seemed so far away.

Gibber Will was trembling. She picked him up to soothe him, then sat down on a large stone next to the trunk of the tree. The rain came down in long sheets of gray all around them. She put her chin on Gibber Will's head and sighed while she stroked his ears. Mist began to swirl around her feet.

A voice came from nowhere, "Do you know the story of your beginning, Fair O'Nelli?"

Fair sat up and looked around. *I know that voice. I know those words.* Fair couldn't see anyone, so she got up and walked around the trunk of the tree. No one there. She looked up into the leaves. Nothing. So she sat down again, wondering if she were imagining things—or not. "Azanamer . . . is that you?"

"I thought I might find you here. Or that you might find me."

Fair looked around again. "Where are you?"

"Harrold King has turned me into a stone."

"Stone?" The only rock she saw was the one she was sitting on. She jumped off and stared at it, holding Gibber Will close to her chest. There was a crack in its side that opened and closed. It was Azanamer's mouth.

"Good gracious!"

"Sit down, please."

Fair knelt down next to the stone and put her hands on the rock, "Oh, how horrible. How dreadful, Grandmother."

Azanamer spoke, "Often we hear only what we want to hear, when we think we're hearing everything. So really, we come away having learned nothing at all. Just pieces."

"What do you mean?"

Azanamer asked Fair to tell what happened in the field. She asked her if she'd heard any sort of warning.

"No. None at all. He just came out of the sky so fast. It was dreadful!" Fair said.

"Dreadful!" echoed Gibber Will.

Azanamer quizzed her again, "No warning at all?"

Fair thought for a moment. "I did hear a sort of whisper, actually. Twice, in fact. It said, 'Run for cover.'"

Then something dawned in her mind. "How did you know, Azanamer . . . about the warning?"

"I might not have a heart anymore, but I knew. No harm is going to come to you if I can help it. You must listen for my voice, quiet though it may be."

Fair sighed, "I will. Oh, I will."

She leaned back against Azanamer and pulled an apple out of her basket. She felt much safer now that her two friends were with her. She took a bite and began to hum to herself while she chewed.

Off in the distance black clouds began to roll and tumble in. Birds that had been chattering and singing in the trees went silent. The shuffling of small paws and hooves in nearby thickets grew still.

Suddenly, a gust of wind whipped at Fair's dress. The leaves in the tree above her waved and shook for a moment, then stopped. She stood up and scooped Gibber Will up into her arms. "I think a storm's coming. We need to hurry."

Azanamer said, "You might want to sit down. This is going to be a bad one."

"But . . . ," Fair began.

"It's better to wait for storms to pass instead of trying to struggle through them."

Fair heard a branch come crashing down and realized Azanamer was right. She adjusted the blanket strapped over her back and sat down on Azanamer to wait out the storm.

Soon, the sky was dark as night. The wind whipped at Fair's apron and threatened to pull the basket off her lap. Out of her hands. Fair looked at the trees swaying around her. She shouted above the howl of the wind, "Azanamer . . . I'm scared."

Azanamer spoke slowly and clearly so Fair could hear her above the sound of cracking branches and wind. "This . . . is no ordinary . . . storm. Do you . . . trust . . . me?"

Fair nodded. The wind whipped at her hair. *Something's very wrong. Something's very wrong.*

Azanamer shouted, "Kneel. Put . . . your hands . . . on . . . me. Quick! You too . . . Gibber . . . Will."

Fair slipped the basket over her arm. She knelt on the ground. As soon as she put her hands on Azanamer, two cracks formed on the surface of the stone and swallowed her hands like bread dough, up to her elbows. The stone hardened. It felt cold around her fingers and arms. She couldn't move them at all. She felt more afraid than she had before. Gibber Will had been hopping towards Azanamer, but the wind was too strong. For every determined hop he made, the wind blew him back to the place he started.

Fair felt something pull at her from behind. She looked over her shoulder and saw a swirl of wind forming on the path where she had been, just minutes before. It grew higher and higher, wider and wider. It was so strong that it sucked Gibber Will right into its spinning mass, along with bushes and branches, squirrels, and foxes. The outer edge of the whirlwind had a smooth, greenish glow to it.

Soon, the pull was so strong that Fair was pulled off her knees. If it weren't for Azanamer, who held her hands fast in a stony grip, Fair would have been sucked into the glowing, spinning whirlwind. The basket was horizontal, and its bottom faced the storm, which kept the contents plastered firmly inside.

A green face began to form in the side of the whirlwind. It was Harrold King. Every few seconds, Fair saw Gibber Will swirl past Harrold King's face, shouting, "Fair!" along with other objects in various tumbling, tossing positions. Harrold King's voice rose above the screeching of the wind and said, "Give me the Ruby Eye."

Fair felt so scared that she couldn't answer.

He ordered, "Old woman, let go of her hands."

Azanamer said, "You shall not harm the maiden, Harrold King. Be gone."

"I'll do as I please, you heartless piece of conglomerated soil."

"And so will I," she said. "Heartless as I am."

Harrold King roared and gnashed his teeth. His black-lidded eyes bored into Fair and she gulped. The whirlwind sucked the shoes off her feet and swallowed them instantly. The wind pulled at her so hard that it hurt.

"Please!" Fair called out.

"Please!" mocked Harrold King. He grew instantly serious and said, "Give it to me."

"I won't," Fair hollered.

A bolt of lightning shot from the sky and struck the tree that sheltered Fair and her friends. The sound was deafening. Fair felt the hair on her arms and head stand on end. The light was blinding and left her momentarily unable to see.

The tree split open. It fell to the ground on both sides of Azanamer. The whirlwind spit out Fair's shoes along with Gibber Will and everything else it had swallowed.

Then it was gone.

Fair dropped back down to her knees and laid her cheek on Azanamer. Raindrops began to fall as the clouds gave way to lighter-colored tufts.

The sun came out.

Azanamer disappeared beneath Fair's arms. Fair went sprawling onto her belly. She felt relieved to feel dirt and grass beneath her hands. A muffled sound struggled to make itself heard beneath her. She got up and discovered a small, round pebble sitting where the large rock had been. Fair picked it up and noticed two black, glinting eyes peering at her from cracks in the stony surface.

"I'd like to come with you, if you don't mind," Azanamer said through a crack that split open beneath her eyes.

"I'd like that," Fair whispered, realizing for the first time that Azanamer could change her size. She pulled the cloth pouch that Miss Tilly had given her out of the basket and said, "Do you mind if I put you in here?"

"Not at all."

Fair heard the sound of someone moaning. It wasn't Azanamer, or Gibber Will. She let Azanamer drop onto the shackles, who woke up and clattered aside to make room.

15 : A Spy

air followed the moaning sound. She stepped over and under the branches of the furry green tree and stopped when she saw a hoomin foot. She startled and cried, "Oh my! Someone's under these branches, Azanamer . . . Gibber Will, hurry!"

Fair pulled Azanamer out of the pouch on her wrist and held her up for a look. Fair didn't know if the foot belonged to someone kind, or otherwise. "What should we do?"

Soon, she and Gibber Will were pulling back leaves and branches to discover if the foot, and everything that belonged to it, was alright.

They found the other foot. The legs were scratched and bloodied. They could see the bottom edge of a torn kilt. Fair felt a sense of urgency. She said, "Pull these branches out of the way! He might be dying. He's gasping!"

Fair pushed aside as many branches as she could, while Gibber Will nibbled through tiny branches in an effort to be helpful. They came to a branch that was big around and much too heavy to lift. It was crushing the chest of a young hoomin with a head of blonde curly hair. Gibber Will hopped back when he saw who it was. "Oh my, my, my. Oh my."

Fair looked at him and said, "What's the matter?"

"It's the son of Harrold King, it is. How, now how did he get here? Or more importantly, what does he think, think, think he's doing here in the first place?" Fair peered at the strange boy through the branches. She recognized his face from the platform, earlier that day. She looked away, then back again.

Tooli looked into Fair's eyes and studied her face. His mouth was contorted with pain, and he gasped for breath. "Hepp me!"

Fair wrung her hands together. She bent over and tried to lift the branch off him once more. She grunted, "I don't know what to do. I can't lift it. And Gibber Will, you're too small." She felt frantic, because the branch seemed to be crushing the bones and breath out of the young hoomin. Gibber Will hopped up and down, helplessly. Then he had a thought.

"Put Azanamer underneath the branch, Fair."

Fair brightened at the suggestion. She hurried and positioned the pebble in a good spot.

She said, "There. Can you lift this branch, Azanamer?"

Silently, Azanamer grew bigger, and bigger, and bigger, lifting the branch higher, and higher, and higher. The higher it went, the more easily its victim breathed and relaxed.

When Azanamer had lifted the branch completely off Harrold King's son, Fair got her hands under his shoulders and pulled him out far enough to be safe from danger. She collapsed on the ground and sat back against a branch, panting.

Azanamer shrunk back down to the size of a pebble. She rolled over and under scattered branches and torn leaves until she found Fair's hand. She rolled onto the soft, bleeding flesh of her palm. Fair weakly clasped her fingers around the stone.

Everyone lay there for a moment, quite stunned from the dramatic encounter. Slowly thoughts began to fill each of their minds. *What's Harrold King's son doing here?*

He looked embarrassed to have been found out.

Gibber Will asked him, "What do you mean, meany, mean, spying on a maiden like that? Did your father send you?"

Tooli rolled over weakly and didn't respond. Azanamer said, "He can't hear, Gibber Will."

"Right. Oh yes. Right."

Fair looked at the injured hoomin and felt afraid. This day had been a succession of moving from one scary place of not knowing to the next. What would this scary place be like? She leaned further into the branch behind her. She would have stood up to leave, but she was too worn out from exertion.

The longer she stared at the young hoomin, the more she noticed scratches all over his arms and legs. What was worse, a pool of blood was widening in the dirt around his head. The Ruby Eye in her forehead began to fill her with gentle warmth. Fair brushed the emerging thoughts away from her mind with this thought, *He might mean me harm.* Still, he was bleeding, and she couldn't stand to see him suffer.

"Dear me, he's bleeding horribly from his head, Grandmother. What should I do? I mean, he's Harrold King's son."

"I have no feeling to know what my heart would tell me, Fair. You'll have to decide for yourself."

She muttered, "Oh Sauveren, I wish you were here." She rubbed the Ruby Eye on her forehead and took a deep breath.

She looked at the hoomin and tried to look through him, somehow, while he stared at her chin. When she looked at his eyes, she felt something fill her soul with an understanding and knowing she couldn't explain.

The Ruby Eye began to open up in her mind's eye. She saw a scene in her mind of a misunderstood and unwanted child whose father and brother ignored him. Then it happened again, right in front of her eyes: He disappeared. Her dog lay there, in his place. It only lasted a second, but it made Fair's heart pound. *What's going on? I don't know what's real sometimes.* Then, Sauveren was gone.

Fair licked her lips and said, "Oh my, I think something's wrong with my eyes. Ever since I fell on the platform of punishment, I . . . well . . . I've been seeing things." She shook her head. "Never mind."

When Fair was sure the hoomin was lying there in front of her and not a vision of her dog, she quickly crawled over to Tooli, who lay there groaning. She didn't have any time to lose. She patted him on the forearm. When he looked up, she touched his ear. It was her way of asking him if he could hear. He shook his head.

"What do you want?" she said, being careful to let him see what she was saying. She hoped he could tell her how to help him.

"Ah wan do beat my bruddah."

What an odd answer. Did he say "beat his brother?"

"You want to beat your brother?" He didn't look like the kind of hoomin who would do that sort of thing.

He nodded and said, "Duh Joust an Dangle."

Fair understood. The two brothers were going to compete.

She looked at him intently. She sat up and tore a strip of cloth off the bottom of her apron. Then another. And another. She said, "It just has to be done, no matter who you are." She would help him get well.

Fair gathered up the strips in her hand and pushed his hair aside to find out where the head wound was. It was just above his left ear. The wound wasn't large, but a steady stream of blood made its way onto the leaves beneath his head. They were stained a bright, shining red.

Fair pressed one of the wads of cloth against the wound. She said, "Gibber Will, come hold this in place and press it firmly." He did as she instructed with his small paws, without saying a word.

Fair tore another strip off her apron and tied several strips together. She wound them around his head and over the bandage Gibber Will held in place. The bleeding stopped. Gibber Will pulled his little red paw away and licked it. Fair squirted a stream of water from the leather flask into the rabbit's mouth. He quickly cleaned himself with two busy paws.

Without thinking, she placed her palms on Tooli's ears. "There we are. You should be . . . ," she began to say. She saw something else. It gave her a strange feeling. The hoomin was looking at her. She looked at Gibber Will for help. He didn't seem to notice anything out of the ordinary.

Tooli screamed out in pain just then. Fair pulled her hands away and crawled down towards Tooli's feet so she wouldn't have to look at his face. I must be silly in the head, she thought. She began to hum. He kept his eyes on her while she busied herself. His brow was furrowed in confusion.

"Watt did oo do to me?"

She ignored him and quickly opened the cloth bundle in her basket. She pulled out the pot of salve she had brought along with her. She popped the cork top off with her teeth and spit it away. She swallowed and hurriedly dipped into it with a grubby finger. She dabbed salve on every scrape she came across, wiping it clean first with her apron. She moved from his feet and legs all the way to his shoulder, where his shirt was torn. She couldn't stop swallowing down the feeling that she was being watched.

Fair arrived at the wound in his shoulder, where she gently rubbed salve into the scrape. It stopped bleeding immediately. The hoomin was still watching her quietly.

She had noticed a cut on his cheek but didn't know if she dared look into his face again. Her heart began to pound. But she felt confused. She didn't feel afraid. She felt a wave of warmth creep across her cheeks, as though a candle flame were passing in front of them and hovering there. She willed herself not to look at him.

What is that feeling? Is he looking at me? But he's cut and bleeding. I can't leave him like that. I've got to look.

Fair forced her stare to move from his shoulder wound, up along the tear of his shirt, along the dirty cloth of his collar, where her gaze followed the contour of his neck and jawline.

He was breathing more peacefully now, and she felt glad. Right then, she wanted more than anything to know his name. She wanted to know what to call him.

Then, she felt a hand on her arm. It was his hand.

Her ears numbly heard, "Dank oo." *Dank oo?* she thought. *Does that mean he's glad? He talks so strangely.*

She hurriedly pulled her arm back, dipped her finger into the pot and cared for the wound on his cheek. *I've got to know your name.*

"What's . . . what's your name?" she asked.

He didn't answer. She felt her face grow hot. Then Gibber Will said: "He can't hear you, Fair O'Nelli. He's deaf."

"Deaf?" She hadn't understood what Azanamer meant when she said he couldn't hear.

"What I mean is, his ears don't work. They can't hear sounds."

Although Tooli couldn't understand the sound of the words since he had only known language as the shapes made by a mouth, he slowly repeated, "Watt did oo do to me?" He touched his ears.

"I don't know." Fair felt the Ruby Eye grow hot on her forehead and she looked right into his eyes. All of a sudden, she didn't care if he was staring at her or not. And she decided she'd think about those strange feelings later. "I'm sorry if I hurt you." He looked at her mouth as she spoke and nodded his head.

She patted her chest. "You know my name, don't you."

He nodded. "Terrin."

She shook her head. She didn't want to be called by that name. "Fair," she corrected. "What is your name?"

"Tooli Keen," he said. She knew he was trying to say "King."

Fair had so many questions she wanted to ask him. She wanted him to put his hand on her arm again, but instead she said, "Will you be alright here? Can you sit up?"

He found that he could sit up. By the time he looked up to thank her, Fair was nowhere to be seen.

She had run away.

16 : The Dark and Fearsome Woods

nce inside the dark safety of the woods, Fair reached in her pocket. She found Azanamer and pulled her out.

Gibber Will caught up to her, after she ran away from the lightning-struck tree . . . and Tooli.

He looked around at the trees. Long vines hung from them and he could hear animals scurrying and screeching. He began to tremble.

"Oh my," he said. "Look at these vines and roots and black scratchy trees. I have to say I don't, don't, don't like the looks of things in these woods, but I like them an awful lot better, better, better than having a big blue sky over my little furry head."

Fair said, "But I like the big blue sky a lot more than I like it in here. These woods are such a scary place. Maybe I could hold you."

It was all Gibber Will could do to say, "no." He stuttered and stammered, "Th . . . th . . . this my answer, wee Fair, N . . . n . . . no." Just saying the word gave him courage. He stood up on his hind legs and said, "In fact, a very emphatic *no!* I don't, don't, don't want to get eaten, and it would be worse for you if I was taken right from your arms."

Fair said, "Then we'll stay in the woods."

Azanamer quietly said, "That was an awfully quick answer, Fair. Are you sure? I may not have a heart, but you do. What does your heart tell you?"

Fair sat silent for a moment. She touched the heart on her forehead. It grew warm in a comforting sort of way. She nodded, "Yes. Things will be alright, even though my skin has goose bumps all over." She rubbed her hands on her arms to warm herself.

"Just have courage, Fair," said Gibber Will. "Not that I'd know what that means, but just have courage. You've got us here to help you, if we can."

"So I do!" Fair smiled. "A brave little rabbit and a stone with a big heart."

Fair looked around. She spotted a narrow path that shone between the black and ominous trees. "Look! There's the grassy path. We would have had to come into the woods, anyway."

"I've got to put you back in my pouch, now, Azanamer. Do you mind?"

"Not at all."

Fair put Azanamer in the pouch and slipped it in her apron pocket. She picked up Gibber Will and said, "We're on our way. We'll find him, I just know it!" To herself, she quietly said, *Oh, Sauveren. I wish you were here. I'm so afraid.*

Gibber Will cried, "Let's go find Selador!"

Once she was on the shining path, she put Gibber Will down to hop on his own. She patted her pocket and felt Azanamer there, safe and sound. The three of them walked, hopped and rode deep into the woods.

Fair dodged vines that hung across her way. Gibber Will hopped over roots. Azanamer listened to the sound of screeching and rustling all around.

"It's so dark in here," Fair said.

"Not if you keep your eyes on the path in front of you and under your feet," said Gibber Will.

"It's easy for you, Gibber Will. But I have to dodge these vines and branches."

"Then how about keeping a watch out for what might hurt you. Just make sure you keep your eyes on the path. Look up and look down."

Fair kept her eyes on the narrow path, looking in front of her. The grass on the sides of it was a bright, glistening green, and the soil beneath her feet was a sandy, golden yellow. She looked up every once in a while to see what dangers might be in front of her.

Black vines.

Creatures scuttling about her in the trees.

The hoomin are very fond of rhymes and are able to speak in rhyme when they wish. It comes easily to them. Fair began to hum a tune and sing.

Soon, Gibber Will and Azanamer joined in,

> *Deep and dark though woods may be,*
> *beneath my feet this path leads me*
> *to the one I know, the one so kind*

who I once knew and now must find.
So guide me to his hiding place
and I will see his shining face.
Then hand in hand we'll find the door
that opens to the other shore.

Before she knew it, Fair was running and laughing with Gibber Will, who hopped speedily in front of her. She reached up to move a vine out of the way and ran under it.

While she was in the middle of truly enjoying herself, with her life of darkness and cold so far behind her in such a short amount of time, she felt something jump onto her arm and grab ahold. She screamed, "Get off me! Get off me!" She danced around blindly, shaking her arm, "Oh, Gibber Will, what is it?"

Gibber Will stopped and turned around. A monkey was holding on for dear life to Fair's wildly flailing arm.

"Get off, off, off, I tell you!" ordered Gibber Will.

The monkey did a flying leap back onto the vine and hung there, eye-level with Fair.

"You sure scared us all," said Gibber Will.

"I didn't mean to," said Fair.

"Not you, wee Fair." He pointed to the monkey. "He did."

Fair held her fists close to her chest and stepped back. Wide-eyed. *He's talking to the monkey,* she thought. She looked down at her pocket, then at Gibber Will. It couldn't be. But then, of course maybe it could.

"Woolly? Is it you?"

"I'm sorry I scared you, Fair. It's just that I'm losing my mind in these woods. I keep seeing things that aren't there. At least that's what the other animals are telling me."

Fair's heart stopped pounding a bit. She breathed sigh of relief and said, "You're not going crazy. The woods are a scary place and I can't wait to leave here. Whatever is frightening you, I'm sure it's real. Don't you think so, Gibber Will?"

The Woolly added, "I'm quite sure of what I see, but perhaps it's nothing at all. I really don't know. And they tell me I'm doing strange things like stealing their food, but I don't remember doing it. When I saw you running by, I thought I'd hop on and go with you wherever you're going. I want to get out of here."

Gibber Will looked around him, then up in the trees. He said, "Just what sort, sort, sort of things are you seeing? I don't want to know, now that I think about it."

The Woolly didn't seem to hear Gibber Will's last comment and he said, "The snakes . . ."

"Snakes?" screamed Gibber Will, who hopped up into Fair's arms. She held him close and said, "Go on."

"The snakes spell things."

"Spell things?" Fair repeated.

"Spell things. They get together and make letters to spell out words with their bodies. Words like, "nuts." When I tell them that I see what they're spelling out—at least I think I do—they tell me they don't know what I'm talking about."

"Oh, I'm sure you do, Woolly," said Faïr.

"Yes, but what if I am making it up? Oh, please take me with you. This is a scary, scary place. I can't make things right if I'm here like this. Please let me come." He was talking all in a panic.

"Of course you can come. With the three of us. You can put things right yourself."

"The three of you? I only see two, oooo! Ooooo!" screeched the Woolly. "See? My brains are falling out of my head."

Fair pulled him off the vine and put him on her shoulder. "Now, now," she consoled him. "What if I told you Azanamer was a pebble and she was in this pouch?" She held up her wrist. "Would you believe me?"

The Woolly wiped his eyes with his tail and said, "I remember now. Yes. Harrold King turned her into a stone and said she could be a pebble if she wanted. Yes, I believe you!"

"And that's why you saw only two of us, even though there were three."

The Woolly kissed Fair on the cheek and said, "So I'm not . . .?"

"No, you're not," finished Fair.

Gibber Will added, "Even if you are a monkey."

The Woolly grabbed at his heart and said, "I just knew it. I just knew it."

Fair said, "Gibber Will and Azanamer are coming along with me to find Selador's gate. If we find his gate, then we'll find him. Maybe he can undo that nasty spell Harrold King placed on them."

"Do you think he might do the same thing for me? Selador, I mean?"

"It can't hurt to find out," Fair said. She thought of her bargain with Thelras and Cael: that her dog would come to her if she helped Selador find the Door of Reunion. *If I can just find Selador*, she thought.

"What are we waiting for, then?" laughed the Woolly.

"You," Fair smiled.

"Let's go, then," he said. He began to swing in long loping arcs on the vines in front of them above the shining, grassy path.

17 : The Clearing

he Woolly swung from vine to vine. He spotted a clearing in the woods up ahead. His excited howling could be heard throughout the woods, "Oooo, oooo, oooo! There's a clearing up ahead, Fair. You'll see it in a minute. You can actually see the sky."

Fair gave him a wave and said, "We won't be long! Wait for us, will you?"

The Woolly was already there by now, so he hung upside down from his tail and swung back and forth, waiting patiently.

Fair heard a voice just up ahead. It came out of the shadows off the side of the path. "Not so fast, young maiden. Not so fast."

When Fair got close to the voice, she noticed an old wrinkled woman sitting on a log, looking intently at something on her lap. Fair walked up to her and said, "Hello. I'm looking for . . ."

"Go back," the woman said without looking up. "Go back where you came from." She held the blue head of a boy hoomin on her lap. His eyes were emerald green.

The blue head's eyes looked up at Fair when she spoke. His head was the color of cobalt, and his face was covered with a map that changed size and shape every few moments. Fair saw shapes of places she had never been to before. At the top of one map, she saw a land of white. She figured that must be the Lands of Ice, where she lived. In a moment, she saw the grassy path form on his face, and she saw that the woods came to an end.

He smiled gently at her, knowingly, and winked.

Fair and Gibber Will looked at each other, then down the grassy path where they could see the Woolly swinging lazily from his tail, upside down.

The old woman continued speaking, "You've made a mistake in coming down this path. It doesn't go anywhere."

Fair said, "But have you gone . . ." She paused and looked at the beautifully strange, living head. "Have you gone where the map tells you to go?"

The old woman looked up at Fair and her friends. Her eyes were completely white. "What map? There's nothing but darkness and doom in this place."

Fair told the old woman there was a map on the blue head's face that showed where the woods came to an end.

The old woman held the blue head close to her and scoffed. "You want my precious head, don't you? A map on his face, my eye. *Bah!* Go back where you came from." She held the head closer and shivered.

Fair realized the old woman couldn't see the map on the blue head, even though it was right in front of her. "But I've got to find someone, and we have something very important to do." She felt the Ruby Eye grow warm on her head. It happened again. She saw Sauveren sitting there, not the old woman. *I must be the one that's going crazy*, she thought.

She pulled the blanket roll over her head by its rope. She slipped it out of the knots at both ends and unrolled it. "Here. Let me put this around you. It doesn't look like you plan on going anywhere."

"I don't." The white-eyed woman pulled the blanket around her and stuck out her hand. "If you're not going to heed my advice and turn back, then you'll be paying me to pass."

Not a smile. Not a word of thanks.

"But I don't see a gate," said Gibber Will. "Don't pay this woman, Fair."

Fair said, "Yes, I don't see a gate. I thought only Protectors required payment for passing."

"Not in these woods, they don't. You're at Woods Gate, you are. It's all around you."

"I see," Fair said. She slipped the bag of shackles off her wrist and opened it. She fished out a yellow shackle and placed it in the woman's bony, wrinkled hand.

"I'm not sure what you'd be needing shackles for in here, but there you go."

The woman began to rock back and forth. "Turn back. It's my last warning."

Fair looked down the path and saw the Woolly looking at her. She looked at the woman and thought what a lost, sad soul she was. *The answer is right in front of her.* Fair gathered her courage and headed for the Woolly. Whatever *could* go wrong couldn't be that bad if she had her friends with her.

"Come on, Gibber Will." She reached in her pocket and pulled out Azanamer. It made her feel better to hold her for a minute.

"What took you so long?" called the Woolly. He swung in a circle from vine to vine around the clearing. "This is the best I've felt since the Harrold turned me into a monkey." He started to make sounds that echoed through the trees. *Oooo! Oooo! Oooo!*

The sound was so loud that it drowned out Azanamer's tiny voice. She said, "Stop. Don't take another step."

Fair thought she heard something, or · felt something. A feeling like she should stop. But the Woolly was just ahead. The grassy path continued on the other side of the flat sandy clearing. Everything was fine.

"Did you hear something, Gibber Will?"

"The only thing I can hear is the Woolly."

Fair took a step into the clearing and looked up. The sun shone on her hair, her face, her dress. "I could stay here all day," she said.

She took another step and immediately dropped. She screamed as something heavy pressed against her legs. It grabbed at her and pulled her down.

Quicksand.

She flung her arms out, reaching for anything she could find. "Help me!"

Azanamer flew out of her hand into the edge of the woods.

Gibber Will hopped around the edge of the quicksand and kept muttering, "What to do, to do, to do? What can I do? Oh, she's doing down. Quick, quick, quicksand! She's up to her waist in it!"

"I can't climb out!" Fair screamed. She clawed at the sand. It closed around and sucked her into its gritty stomach.

Gibber Will snapped his furry paws and said, "Got it!" He looked up at the Woolly who had the same thought at the exact same time.

The Woolly yelled, "I've got a crazy idea, but it just might work!"

Fair said, "Oh please, how will I . . ." just before she took a deep breath and went completely under. She felt cold sand scratch against her legs, arms, and face, as she fell through it. It filled her nose and ears. It pressed against her eyes.

Her world went silent.

"Azanamer, where are you?" the Woolly cried.

A loud crashing came from the edge of the woods, as a huge boulder rolled into the clearing. A mouth formed in the side of the boulder. "Here I am."

The Woolly found a loose vine and pulled it. One end of it fell to the ground near the grassy path on the far side of the clearing. He called down, "Roll onto the end of it, Azanamer. Make sure it can't move. Can you bite it?"

Azanamer understood and rolled around the edge of the clearing where it was safe. She rolled onto the end of the vine. She bit it and swallowed. It wasn't going anywhere.

"Gibber Will, I need you hold onto the vine. When you feel me give a tug, tell Azanamer to start rolling down the grassy path. Is that clear?"

"Clear as a bell." He hopped around the edge of the clearing, grabbed the vine with his small paws and looked into the empty space where Fair had been standing, just seconds before.

Deep within the cool, gritty pit, Fair's mind whirled back to the day before when she had lain on her bed in her cellar, dreaming of her becoming day.

It wasn't supposed to be like this.

She felt as though she were being crushed on every side. Everything was so black and cold. Again.

I've got to remember the things I've seen.

She was deaf to the Woolly's loud yell, "Here I come!" He held onto his end of the vine and dove into the quicksand. It swallowed him immediately.

Gibber Will looked at the spot where the vine disappeared into the sand.

He waited.

And waited.

"Oh me. Oh my, my, my," he mourned. "I'm afraid we've lost them both." His trembling little paws held to the vine. He became more and more distraught. His words turned into whimpering gibberish. "So be, so be, lah, lah, lost . . ."

Fair held her breath until she couldn't not breathe. When her lungs struggled to fill with air, nothing came. She began to panic, but couldn't even move. Her mind searched wildly for something, anything to hold on to.

The music box.

Her father's music box.

Think of the music, she told herself.

As the tune began to play across her mind, she heard her mother's voice as she read from the scrolls, "Strength will be given to you when you need it most."

She felt something grab onto her hair. It grabbed at her arm, then her waist. Even in her desperation, she found that she was thinking about the last blue flower she picked. It was beautiful.

The vine moved slightly. Gibber Will felt a tug. He hopped up and down and cried, "He tugged, Azanamer! Roll, roll, roll! Hurry!" With a loud thundering she began to roll slowly down the grassy path. The vine wound itself around her the further she went.

Fair felt something wrap around her waist and stay there. She knew it had to be the Woolly. *But how?* The sand was so thick everywhere. Before she knew it, she felt herself being ripped up, even as the quicksand tried to pull her back.

Fair and the Woolly exploded through the surface of the sand: *Gasp!* Azanamer kept rolling and dragged them to the far edge of the clearing. They gasped for breath and spit out sand. Their chests heaved in and out. Two hands made of sand emerged from the pit. They reached for Fair and the Woolly, trying to pull them back.

Gibber Will cried, "Keep rolling, Azanamer. It's grabbing for them! It's alive. The sand's alive!"

Soon, Fair and the Woolly lay safely on the grassy path, looking like sandy creatures in the shape of themselves. The hands of sand, finding nothing, collapsed into fingered piles.

"My eyes," Fair said. "They burn." She didn't dare rub them, so she kept them closed. "Thank you, Woolly. You saved my life."

She felt a furry tail wrap around her hand and stay there.

18 : Selador's Gate

 eep beneath the earth, the mirrors went dim. Harrold King growled. He was still floating and bobbing deep in the Chamber of Mirrors. His fingers and toes had become very wrinkly.

Rithel scurried along the ceiling until he was just above Harrold King and dropped—*plop!*—onto Harrold King's oily belly.

"She was supposed to die!" said Harrold King. He breathed heavily through his large humid nostrils. In and out. In and out. Fuming.

"We didn't know the monkey would save her," said Rithel.

"You should have known. You're my advisor in these matters. You disgust me."

Harrold King felt around the missing place at the top of the scepter where the Ruby Eye had been. He said, "I want the Ruby Eye returned to its place. I have no intention of giving up the throne."

"Yessss," hissed Rithel. "But the prophecy is real. The Blood Moon will rise when the weather cools—unless Fair O'Nelli is destroyed." He thought of the great battle of Rall Kindaria. If Fair could be destroyed, perhaps Selador would not find the Door of Reunion. The great plan would be ruined. Rithel's imagination surged with a rush of greed and glory. "All will be mine," he muttered.

"What did you say?" asked Harrold King.

"All will be *fine*, your majesty," he lied. "I have thought of another plan."

Fair and her friends approached the edge of the noisy, fearsome woods. Before them, a vast field of goldenrod spread out for miles all around. The sky was clear blue and dotted with white fluffy clouds. The grassy path seemed to point like an arrow, right through the middle of it.

"We did it, did it, did it!" cried Gibber Will. "We're out of the woods!"

He dashed ahead of Fair and the Woolly, who rode on Fair's shoulder. He hopped as high as he could to see over the goldenrod as he went along. His head popped up above the height of the yellow flowers.

"This is glorious!"

He disappeared again when he dropped earthwards for another good leap, then instantly reappeared.

"Magnificent!"

He disappeared and reappeared with a zesty shout.

"Pure sunshine on the ground!"

Fair skipped behind him in wide-eyed wonder. "And the sky, it's so blue. But where do we go from here?"

"I don't know very much, you know, you know," said Gibber Will. "But my guess is there ain't nowheres to go but straight ahead, Fair. We're on the grassy path, and there's only one."

"And this might sound crazy," began the Woolly. He shyly grabbed his tail and didn't finish what he wanted to say.

"Come on now, I'm sure you have a great idea, Woolly," prodded Fair.

"Well, I have a clear notion that you're about to find who you're looking for, Fair. Very soon."

Fair turned to look the Woolly in the eye, just inches away. She reached up to pet him. "Selador? Oh do you, really? Wouldn't that be wonderful? We've come such a long way. And I might get my dog back."

She paused and looked at the pouch hanging from her wrist. She opened it and took out Azanamer. "What are your feelings on the matter, Azanamer?"

Azanamer said, "I wouldn't know, because I still can't feel a heart beat in all this stone. So, let me ask you, Fair, what does your heart tell you? You know better than anyone what you're supposed to do."

"Oh no, not me. Really, I don't."

"Listen, Fair," Azanamer whispered.

"For what, Azanamer?"

"Not *for*, but *to*."

"To?" asked Fair.

"To your heart."

"Oh, I almost forgot," said Fair, touching the Ruby Eye on her forehead. "How silly of me." She looked at the field of golden rod from one end to the other and then at the path. "I really don't know how to listen, but I'll try."

Fair closed her eyes and stayed silent for a while, long enough to feel the wordless knowing that filled her soul. Something felt really clear inside, in a way she couldn't explain—even to her dog, had he been with her. It was sweet, like sugar that had been painted onto the underside of her skin with hundreds of little wet brushes. It was cool, like the water that dripped down her cellar walls and filled her waiting cup so she could drink. She just knew she was on the right path.

So, she made a decision. She would keep moving forward. Soon, the Ruby Eye began to grow warm on her forehead. Fair noticed for the first time that her own heart felt warm. At the same time she got goose bumps all over.

She took it as a good sign.

She opened her eyes.

"Straight ahead," she said.

"Are you sure, Fair?" everyone asked.

"Yes, I'm sure!" Fair laughed.

Soon she was walking waist-high through the field of bright yellow golden rod. Gibber Will's ears and head could be seen bopping up above the flowers every time he jumped and had a look around.

After several hours the Woolly said, "I don't believe my eyes, but I think I see something shining up ahead, off in the distance."

"Do you really?" Fair said. She pulled her hands to her chest and hardly dared to hope. She was thirsty and tried hard not to think about it.

She stopped walking and looked. Nothing.

Gibber Will hopped up and down to have a look. "I can't see anything," he complained. He flopped on the ground and went limp. "I'm tired of being so small."

"Here," said Fair. "Let me pick you up." As she reached down to pick him up, she thought she saw Sauveren lying there. It lasted just a moment, but it was so clear to her that she shook her head and thought to herself, There it is again. I'm seeing things.

She picked up Gibber Will, pulled Azanamer out of the pouch, and together they all looked off into the distance. They squinted their eyes to see what they could see.

"Where?" said Gibber Will.

"There," pointed the Woolly. "Just to the side of the grassy path."

The sun came out from behind a cloud just then. Off to the left of the path, far in the distance, a castle revealed itself in a glorious shape against the sky. It reflected the sun like a golden mirror. It was so bright that everyone looked away.

They opened and closed their mouths in silence. Compared with the dark and fearsome woods, this was a change for the better indeed. Then, they all began to talk at once, in a flurry of exclamations and excitement.

"Could it be?"

"That must be Selador's Gate. I just knew it!"

"It's so beautiful!"

"How come no one knew about this place?"

19 : There at Last

air skipped and ran along the grassy path towards the shining golden castle. Her braids escaped beneath her scarf and played with the wind as she ran. A breeze played at her peach-colored dress that billowed around her legs.

"We're almost there," she panted, smiling, and out of breath.

By now Gibber Will had insisted that she put him down so she could run, unencumbered. The Woolly ran and clambered along using his front knuckles and legs.

Oh Sauveren, Fair said to herself, *I wish you could see all this.*

The path began to widen, and soon it gave way to a long tree-lined road that led straight up to the front gate. Fair and her friends stopped where the road began.

Gibber Will pointed at the gate and said, "We're almost there, Fair. If this is the place I think it is—and I'm starting to believe I'm seldom wrong—then you are about to meet who you've been looking for."

"I can't believe my eyes," said the Woolly. "I'm not imagining things?"

"No, Woolly," said Fair, "It's really real. A golden castle. I'm sure Selador is in there." She pulled the round pebble that was Azanamer out of the pouch and held her up to have a look.

"I see," said Azanamer. A line formed beneath the small dents that must have been her eyes. It looked like a frown. She said no more.

"So, so, so what are we waiting for?" hopped Gibber Will. "Let's go!" He began to hop down the tree-lined drive, straight for the golden gate. Soon, the rest followed.

As they got closer and closer to the gate, a sign came into view. The Woolly said, "I don't believe it. The sign says Selador's Gate. We made it!"

"I hope they've got a whole pile of carrots in there," said Gibber Will. "I could eat a whole plate of them."

"Even better," said Fair, "Perhaps Selador can undo what Harrold King did to you, and you can eat the sort of food you like. That goes for the rest of you." She didn't mention her desire to find Sauveren and the rest of her family.

They walked up to the wide golden gate. It was as wide as a cottage. There was a booth made of gold walls, and gold tiles on the roof, off to the left.

Fair picked up Gibber Will. The Woolly scrambled up Fair's leg and settled on her shoulder. Azanamer was snug in the pouch on Fair's wrist.

Fair walked up to the booth and said, "Is anybody in there?"

A head popped up and appeared at the window. It was Fair's uncle, though she didn't know it. He'd been napping and had a big sleep wrinkle across his whiskered cheek.

He smudged his hands across his face and tried to push his smashed purple nose into place. He searched for his cap and put it back on his head and snorted, "Mmm, why yes. It's been a slow day. You're the first ones to pass by."

He looked at the maiden in front of him and realized it was Fair, whom he had seen for the first time just hours earlier, at Clock Tower Square. He sleepily stuck out his hand and sneered, "Payment for passing."

Fair put down her friends and reached into the pouch. Her uncle eyed her and thought how rotten it was that she had been under his nose all those years—in the cellar of all places. He hadn't even known there was a cellar—and he'd missed claiming a reward for informing Harrold King.

Fair fished for a green shackle and placed it in his open palm in a very deliberate, cheery way, "There you are, my good hoomin."

"Nah. That ain't enough," he said. He wanted some shackles for himself, a belated reward of sorts, so he said, "The rest of what you've got. This one's an expensive gate." He spit at the ground in front of Fair's feet.

"I see," said Fair. She crinkled her nose and hunted around in the pouch. She put the rest of her shackles in his hand.

He eyed the pouch suspiciously, "Don't I see another bump in that pouch?"

Fair pulled out Azanamer. "This is a pebble I found."

He brushed his hand as if to say he wasn't interested in a brown rock. He disappeared from the window and stepped out of the booth. He walked over to a very large hinge on the gate. There was an enormous set of silver gears fixed to a golden plate. The whole contraption was fixed to the end of a stone wall. He began to turn a crank that set the gate to opening. Slowly.

While Fair and her friends waited for it to swing open, Fair asked, "So have you seen Selador?"

"Selador? I don't even know who the hoomin is," he grumbled. "All I know is this is my post for the day. Didn't even know this place existed. But I do know you're supposed to get the royal treatment inside."

"What does that mean?" Fair asked, looking at her friends expectantly.

He spit and answered, "Don't know." The gears came to a smooth, well-oiled stop. "There you are. Gate's wide open."

"Thank you." She looked at him closely. There was something very familiar about his face. She leaned over and instinctively gave him a kiss on the cheek.

He felt himself blush. He looked at the ground and adjusted his cap. Then he kicked a rock and sent it sailing.

"Off you go now," he blustered. "Three knocks on the door."

Fair said, "There's hope for you." Then she and her friends ran through the gate and up wide gold stairs to the door. As they ran up the curved stairs, they saw their reflections on the smooth yellowish surface beneath them.

"I can see myself," said Fair. "Look," she pointed at the stairs. "They're as shiny as mirrors." Everyone looked with amazement as they watched themselves run, hop and clamber up the stairs.

Soon they were at the door. It was as wide as the gate and endlessly taller. Fair looked at both ends of the entrance. Large gold pots of enormous red geraniums with luscious green leaves bloomed on both sides.

"Just like at home," Fair announced. "My mother loves geraniums." She stopped to look up. The front of the castle seemed to go on forever, nearly touching the sky. She saw clouds floating by in the sky behind her, reflected on its surface.

Blue sky.

Birds chirping. Somewhere.

Fair felt all her cares and worries melt out of her. Everything was light here.

No darkness.

No cold.

Just warmth and a gentle breeze.

She reached for the round gold ring on the door in front of her. It was larger around than her head.

"My this is heavy!" she said. She lifted it and let it thunder back onto the door, with a metallic *gonnnngggg* that lasted for a long, long time. Everyone looked at each other. "That sounded important," she added. Everyone nodded.

Gibber Will's nose wiggled up and down, "I smell something cooking, something cooking, something cooking, I do." He began to preen his whiskers with his paws, then he stood up. He pulled his shoulders back. "I'm ready."

The Woolly scrambled up on to Fair's shoulder and said, "I've waited a long time to see this, Fair."

She smiled and said, "Haven't we all!" He patted her on the head in a knowing sort of way.

Fair hefted the knocker and let it drop two more times: *gonnnngggg, gonnnngggg!*

The door opened inwards in what Fair thought to be a welcoming sort of way. Pure light burst out of the doorway. Fair looked down and saw white flower petals strewn on the ground in front of her. She breathed in and held their sweet, fragrant air in her lungs. A gentle breeze gusted through the door behind her. It sent some of the flower petals swirling.

She squinted her eyes at the glorious entrance into Selador's castle. There was a long hallway with a circular space at the end with a square gold door at the far end of the round room.

A voice echoed, "Welcome."

Fair looked around. She didn't see anybody, so she asked, "Who said that?"

She felt something tug at the hem of her apron. She looked down and noticed a luminous small hoomin, no taller than her knees. His face shone as if it was made of sparkled light. His white hair and beard were as long as he was. It fell to his feet in brilliant waves. His fingers were long, and his silver shoes curled up at the toes. He wore a shimmering silver robe that went down to his feet.

"Welcome to Selador's Gate. You've finally arrived. Come with me, all of you."

He turned around and said, "To your posts! Everyone!"

Fair looked down the hallway. Dozens of small shining hoomin darted here and there, finally standing in place in two long lines. Fair thought of the moment when, just that morning (could it have been just that morning?) she left Lamb's Tavern in between a row of hoomin playing majestic music on their bagpipes.

She felt a tug at her apron again. "No time to waste," the small hoomin said.

Fair and her friends entered Selador's Gate. The small hoomin showered them with flower petals as they walked down the long hallway towards the circular space.

Small crystals hung from invisible strands from the endlessly high ceiling and cast rainbows of light everywhere.

Fair asked her guide, "Where are you taking us?"

"You'll see—soon enough," he said.

It wasn't long before they arrived at the circular space. Fair stopped and looked up. The others bumped into her. The ceiling was a dome with golden curved panels. Light poured through the windows between them.

Doors lined the wall of the round room. There was one square door, different from the rest. It was same one she had seen from a distance when they first entered the castle.

"What's that square door for?" Fair asked.

"So many questions," the hoomin smiled. "First, it's time you were all taken care of. You've come a long way. I understand you've suffered quite a few unpleasant adventures."

Before they knew what was happening, Fair and her friends were feasting at long tables full of food. Fair was served whatever she requested. Gibber Will got platefuls of all the carrots and cabbages he wanted. The Woolly had piles of bananas placed in front of him. Azanamer was washed and polished until she shone like a wet rock. Fair got to take a long steamy bath and put on her freshly washed and dried clothes.

It was glorious.

Soon, the light coming in through the domed windows began to fade. Night was falling.

Fair felt surprisingly weary. She thought back on the long journey that day. The man looked at her and said, "A comfy bed awaits you, Fair . . . . You each have your own bed and your own bath."

"But I already had a bath," Fair said.

"That's alright. You can have two." Fair had never been treated so regally, and she blushed.

"Let's start with the monkey, here."

Fair said, "Why of course. Let's see where you'll be staying, Woolly."

The little hoomin led the Woolly to one of the doors in the circular room. Everyone followed along. When the small hoomin opened the door, everyone saw a room strung with vines. A waterfall fell from an unknown source off to one side of the room, and parrots flew from tree to tree. Green leaves were piled invitingly in the center of the room.

"This looks like home," the Woolly smiled, "if ever there was a home for a monkey."

The luminous hoomin said, "This is where you'll be sleeping, Woolly. Goodnight."

The Woolly turned to everyone and said, "Goodnight." Then, he clambered into the room and ran to the waterfall for a quick bath, before settling off to sleep in his pile of leaves.

Next, Gibber Will was led to a door that opened into an earthy tunnel. It smelled of dirt and roots. A wide, thick bed of freshly carded rabbits fur lay in front of him.

"Say, say no more," Gibber Will sniffed and preened. He went into the tunnel, looked back and said with a toothy smile, "We'll be seeing each other in the morning, we will, we will."

Fair was taken to another door. The small hoomin looked up at Fair and said, "This room is for Azanamer." He turned the handle and opened the door. Before them, there was just a smooth, clay wall with a spherical space carved into it.

Fair smiled, "I think I know what to do." She let Azanamer drop out of the pouch onto her palm and placed the round rock in the half-sphere. It, or she, fit perfectly.

A mouth formed on the side of the round stone and Azanamer said, "Listen to your heart, Fair. Goodnight." Then she yawned.

The small hoomin closed the door and said, "That does it. We're done."

Fair felt her heart drop. "But what about me? You said we each had a room."

"So I did!" he smiled. "So I did!"

He passed several doors and Fair ran to catch up. Her arms and legs were heavy with sleep. She imagined a tall bed like the kind her mother had told her about, covered with a thick white duvet filled with soft down feathers.

They passed one door after another. Fair expected the little hoomin to stop and turn the handle at every door they came to. She kept asking, "Is it this one? . . . Perhaps it's this one . . . I'm sure this door goes to my room."

The hoomin just kept walking ahead of her without answering. He stopped. He turned around and said, "This room is worth waiting for." He smiled and reached up for her. She bent down and he caressed her cheek. She looked at the door. It was the square one she had seen earlier.

She yawned, "So this is my room." The bottom of the door was as high as her knees. "I saw this door when we walked in. Thank you," she yawned again. "So much."

"Nothing at all. Now close your eyes for a big surprise. When I open the door you'll find what awaits you."

Fair closed her eyes. She clasped her hands together in sleepy anticipation. The Ruby Eye felt heavy and cold in her forehead, but she was so sleepy that she ignored it. She heard a muffled voice call out, "Run." She sleepily thought, *How strange. That sounds like Azanamer.*

She heard the door open.

"Goodnight, Fair. Sweet dreams."

She reached in and tapped around inside. The floor was level with the doorway. She crawled in and was surprised to feel rough wood beneath her hands and knees. *Just a bit further*, she assured herself. She opened her eyes to look for her bed and discovered that the wood beneath her hands was greasy and black. She felt confused and looked around, dismayed to discover that she was surrounded by black iron bars. *Please, no.*

That iron cage. That thin, darkly clad man. Fair heard the echo of Sauveren whimpering in her mind.

Fair whirled around and looked at the luminous hoomin. She said, "But this isn't . . ."

"Isn't what?" Shards of light shattered off him and clattered to the floor like falling tiles.

It was Rithel.

He slammed the door shut.

Fair pounded her hands on the splintery wood and shouted, "I know who you are, Rithel . . . I know who you are!" She began to shout and hit on the door even harder, "Help me, Azanamer! Woolly! Gibber Will! Help me!" She knew they couldn't hear her. *My friends*, she thought. She gulped down a lump of fear. *What will become of them?*

Inside the golden castle, the three friends were settling down to sleep. Azanamer didn't move. The Woolly pulled leaves around him and nestled in. Gibber Will wriggled down into his thick bed of downy fur.

While Fair repeatedly slammed her fists against the door, she heard the grating of metal above her. She looked up and pulled her hands away just as an iron door slid down and sealed her inside the cage. She felt a chill.

Fair noticed it wasn't completely dark inside. She felt a cool gust of air brush her skin. She looked around and saw lights twinkling in the distance. She crawled over and held the bars. They were cold and rough. She looked at the darkened space around her.

Those are stars. Glittering. In the sky. But how?

A voice filled the air and entered Fair's ears. "Hello Fair. I thought I smelled a rat."

She looked over her shoulder and narrowed her eyes to see better. She was able to make out the slender silhouette of a hoomin wearing a tall black hat. He turned his head to face her, and for an instant she saw the shadow of a long nose.

It was the Rooter.

She was in the cage on the back of his wagon. She felt it move. Fair instinctively put out her hands to balance herself. She looked more closely at the Rooter. He was sitting on a bench. She could hear the sound of wheels parting grass. She could hear breathing, snorting horses.

I am not going to be invisible, she cried inside. "Let me go!" She tried to lift up the iron door, but it wouldn't budge. "I've got to get back to my friends."

"Oh, I'll let you go, maiden, shmaiden . . . as soon as I take you to Harrold King. He has a special room for you . . . with lots of friends."

I, Gasper, shall speak for my host.
Other Secret Speakers will share the thoughts
of their hosts to help fill things in.

20 : Fair's Special Room

y now, Harrold King was dressed
and in his throne room. He looked
annoyed. Even though he had
lain in his bath for hours, his feet
had begun to burn again.

Rithel sat on his shoulder. He
hissed, caressing his clawed hands. "She should be
here any moment."

"You surprise me, Rithel. Your imagination is a
marvel." Harrold King had witnessed the entire scene at
the golden castle from the Chamber of Mirrors. He
laughed to himself. *All an illusion.*

The lizard's tongue shot out and he hissed, "The
imagination is not a marvel. The marvel lies in the
motive that gives birth to imagination."

Harrold King ignored Rithel and said, "I'm growing
impatient. She should be here by now."

There was a knock at the door.

"Enter!" Harrold King shouted.

The door opened at the far end of the hall. Fella
Doon walked in.

A shadow appeared in the doorway and plodded
into the room. It was Sauveren.

"You," frowned Harrold King, "What are you doing
here?"

"You called for the dog, your royal eminency," said Fella Doon.

"I did nothing of the sort."

Fella Doon stayed silent. He knew Harrold King was right. But when he saw Pewgen Flype put on his black hat and say he had a rat to catch, Fella Doon realized what was about to happen. He couldn't let Fair be alone.

"Well, as long as you've brought him. You might as well both stay to watch the fun. By the way, who's keeping an eye on the matternots?"

"Lisper is standing watch."

"That piece of drivel? Well, we shouldn't be long, so . . ."

An echoey noise came from the hallway on the other side of the doors. Pewgen Flype's voice was unmistakeable. He had Fair with him and was trying to get her to move.

" . . . even if I have to drag you," Fella Doon overheard. He grabbed Sauveren's collar and they both stepped aside, just inside the entrance.

"Just try it," Fair said, knowing Pewgen Flype would get shocked if he did.

Fair felt a shove. She shot into the room and fell on all fours. Pewgen Flype had used the end of his long hook to push her.

Harrold King heard the noise. He grunted and didn't look up. He was eating. He was going to take his time about it, now that the time had come. *I will not show my impatience in front of the maggot. She has been the menace of my waking dreams.*

He sat on pillows and yards of red velvet that covered his hard throne of stone. He looked up while he was in the middle of biting into a greasy turkey leg. He growled like a bear, and a piece tore off in his teeth. A long strip of torn meat hung from his mouth.

"Grrrum—what?" He chewed a bit. "Can't you see I'm busy?" He chewed the greasy meat furiously and his cheeks sloshed with the effort. While he looked at Fair, his mind flashed to his own sister, Graeshara, Queen of High Grave.

Years earlier he had dreamt that a wee hoomin would come to rule in Cloven Grave. But not just rule. This wee hoomin would reign supreme over Cloven Grave and Low Grave as the one and only king. In this dream, a wee hoomin stood on his lap holding the scepter. Harrold King wasn't able to see around the wee hoomin. He had to crane his neck to look at the crowd before him—or her. He thought it had been a boy hoomin, but wasn't sure, exactly.

To make doubly sure his dream would never come to pass, Graeshara immediately sent Harrold to Cloven

Grave. She was secretly quite pleased to be rid of him, because if he was there, she knew he could be as bossy as he pleased. He had the annoying habit of telling her what to do and when to do it.

The first thing he did when he arrived was to whisk all wee hoomin in Cloven Grave away—those who were the same age as the one in his dream. "Boy ones and girl ones alike," he'd said. "Just to make sure."

As for Harrold King, he didn't mind being sent away. High Grave was full of older, pompous lawmakers and bookkeepers. Tedious. Boring. He knew Cloven Grave well. He had gone there frequently as a wee hoomin to play with other wee hoomin. Cloven Grave was at that time a contented and happy hamlet that spread its arms wide in welcome like a lily pad upon the waters of time.

Pewgen Flype said, "Move."

Fair said, "I will not."

Harrold King's thought was interrupted. *What was that noise? The maiden's voice.*

He looked at Pewgen Flype, snapped his oily fingers at Fair, and said, "Come here, you."

Fair didn't move.

Pewgen Flype was about to jab her with the end of his hook, when Fella Doon spoke up, "You'd best be doin' as the Harrold says."

Fair's heart jumped. *A familiar voice!* She looked over her shoulder and spotted Fella Doon. Then, out of the corner of her eye, she saw a mass of black fur. *No. Could it be?* she thought. She ran over to Sauveren and wrapped her arms around his neck. The bells on his collar tinkled. "Oh, Sauveren, they promised me I'd find you. I didn't know it would be this hard."

Fella Doon needed to sound tough. He said, "No time for that. Now go."

Fair looked up at him. He winked. She turned around. *So much good with so much bad. How do I swallow it all?* She slowly made her way past the many marble columns that held up the ceiling of the voluminous hall.

Fella Doon and the dog followed at a distance. Once Fair reached the stairs below the throne, he stood off to the side. He stood at attention as a captain should do. He stood tall and stiff, looking straight ahead.

Pewgen Flype stayed near the exit, just in case Fair tried to escape. He held his hook at the ready.

At Fair's approach, Harrold King held out his arm with an upturned hand, as though he were used to having things put on the plumply padded flesh of his palm. "Give it here, maiden." He snapped his fingers again. "I want the Ruby Eye. It belongs to me." He looked her over and sneered at how filthy she appeared.

Fair remained silent.

"I'll give you a chicken for it. You know . . . to take home. I bet you haven't eaten chicken in some time."

Fair still didn't speak.

"Are you deaf?"

"I hear perfectly well," Fair answered. "How do you expect me to give you the Ruby Eye when it can't be removed? And you can't touch me." She turned around and began to head for the door. "I'm going home."

"Fair!" he shouted.

She turned around.

"Where do you think you're going?" He leaned forward and fumed, "No Zothiker enters this place and leaves alive. Now wash my feet. They burn."

Fair stood there as though she hadn't understood. *Did he ask me to wash his feet?* She looked at his stockinged feet. Liquid oozed through the white cloth.

"I said, *wash my feet!*"

Fair realized that she had heard correctly the first time. A stench wafted up to her nose and she felt sick to her stomach. Then, she felt the Ruby Eye begin to grow warm on her forehead. She looked at Harrold King and saw Sauveren sitting there on the throne. She shook her head and looked over at her dog. He was sitting on his haunches next to Fella Doon. *My eyes. Something is wrong with my eyes.*

I'm so confused, she thought. *He is the whole reason I've been so miserable for the last nine years. I can't do it.* She gritted her teeth together. The muscles on her jaw made a clear outline. Then, words from her dark remembering entered her mind:

> *Some things are just wrong*
> *and don't merit a reward.*

She looked Harrold King squarely in the eye and quietly answered, "I will wash your feet, but first you must start over."

"Start over?" he yelled. "How dare you tell *me* what to do."

Fair stood silent. Unmoving.

Harrold King knew he wouldn't find any relief unless he found a way to get her to do it, so he asked, "Start over?"

"Ask me. Don't tell me."

Harrold King wanted to strike the maiden, but the pain of touching her earlier was clear in his mind. He swallowed. His feet burned so terribly that his eyes were wet with pain.

"My feet. Please." He struggled to utter the request. "Wash them?"

Fair answered kindly, "Yes, your majesty the king. Where is the water to wash them with?" Inside, she felt like vinegar had taken the place of the blood in her veins. It hurt to be kind right then. But she knew she had not rewarded his rudeness, and that was some small comfort.

A servant returned with a shallow bowl of water which sloshed as he walked.

"There," Harrold King groaned. "There is your water. And a cloth. Dry them when you're done."

Fair sat back on her heels and folded her arms. She looked at him and raised an eyebrow, waiting.

He growled and said, " . . . Please?"

The servant turned and walked away, leaving Fair in the presence of a hoomin who would have made any other maiden tremble if she had known what he was capable of. But she was not an ordinary maiden.

Fella Doon and Sauveren both had their ears cocked for trouble.

In Airen-Or, Thelras asked Cael:

Shall we let Fair know what happens to her friends?

No, my heart, she'll find out soon enough.

21 : The Foot Bath

 t was difficult, but Fair managed to pull off a sticky stocking from Harrold King's red and scaly foot. It was smelly in a putrid sort of way, and a milky yellow liquid oozed out of cracks that formed small canyons in its flesh.

"You said they burn, your Lordship," shuddered Fair. When the words left her mouth, she felt something shift inside her. The Ruby Eye felt warm—yes, that was no longer a surprise—but it seemed to pour a soothing liquid through her soul. She could do this. What was more, she *wanted* to do this.

"What's it to you?" Harrold King scoffed. "Just wash them, you vomitous mass of filth."

Fair felt strangely sorry for him and felt no insult. She only said, "I'm sorry they hurt you so much."

He grunted.

And so, Fair lifted the heavy hot foot and tried to place it as gently as she could in the cool water. Harrold King rolled back his eyes and let out a gurgley sigh. He laid his head against the back of the throne and took ahold of the armrests in a moment of brief satisfaction and relief. His fingers hung like sausages off the end of the armrest.

He lazily said, "Do you know what happened to your grandfather, Bander Zothiker?"

"My grandfather? I don't know anything about him."

"You poor little thing. Your father's father. I sent him out on a Joust and Dangle and had the cord cut when he went overboard."

Fair looked up at him in disbelief. "A Joust and Dangle? What's that?"

"Nothing but a silly game."

He killed my grandfather . . . in a game? . . . I am washing his feet. Everything began to swirl around in her mind, but the Ruby Eye continued to glow warmly on her forehead. *Focus on his feet,* she told herself. *Focus.*

Scoop water. Fat red foot. Armrests carved into the shape of a bull's head, with well-worn horns. Harrold King absent-mindedly polishing them. The Ruby Eye shocked Fair and it hurt for just an instant. A wash of understanding flowed through her and she was surprised to hear herself say, "You don't think you deserve to be loved, do you." The words came to her like an echo, out of the pages of the Scrolls of Truth.

He growled and said, "Why do you say that, you little putrescence?"

She quoted from memory: "Because 'we only accept the love we believe we deserve. No more, no less.' You don't let anyone love you. So you must not believe you deserve it. And you don't let anyone else have friends. You must be very lonely to be so bossy and mean." She couldn't stop the flow of words and bit her tongue to stop herself from saying more.

Harrold King flared his nostrils and glanced out the window without moving his head. He wasn't used to being spoken to with such honesty. A faint smile curved on a corner of his mouth, then disappeared.

"Do you always say what you think?" he growled.

Fair thought of telling him that the Planter was coming to change the Laws of Memory. He wouldn't be able to make any of his own silly laws any more. But when she looked out of the corner of her eye at him and saw how nasty he looked, she knew she musn't.

She answered instead, "Only if it's kindly meant, and true."

"What is it to you?" he mumbled. He paused and added, "Besides, I do have a friend . . . a very loyal friend." He reached up and patted the cold scales on Rithel's back, who lay flat on his shoulder. Rithel stared at Fair. His tongue darted in and out. "And I live in a world you'll never be privileged to see, where spirits and visions fill the void of all that I've been robbed of. They give me great comfort. I pity you that you don't have that."

She said, "Robbed?"

"My place in this world, or the place I'm supposed to fill, has been taken from me. It is a painful thing to fill a space in the air, when it's not the space you're meant to fill."

Fair said, "Or *think* you're meant to fill."

"I long for . . . well . . ." He looked at Fair, suddenly angry at having said so much.

Fair waited and watched to see if she could gather the light of his transparency. In a moment, he began to fade. Just his light remained. What she saw horrified her. He was as gray as smoke from an oily fire. But wait. A glimmer of flickering light struggled to shine in his fluttering heart, which was—sadly, she thought—no bigger than his nose.

Fair shook her head and closed her eyes. She'd seen enough. She picked up the other foot. As soon as she finished washing it, Harrold King shoved the bowl at her with his other foot and said, "That's enough."

Water sloshed out of the bowl and soaked her lap. Her peach-colored dress shone for a moment where the water had landed. Somehow his rudeness had no effect on her. She sensed that what pushed the bowl at her was not so much the foot of Harrold King but his loneliness and selfishness. His frustration that he'd been robbed. She touched the Ruby Eye on her forehead and simply wiped up the puddle around her.

Fair stood and turned to find her way out, with her dog at her heels. She heard him shout at her, "Come back to see me one shobbasim from today . . . to wash my feet."

He's going to let me go, she realized. She went over to her dog and patted him on the head. She looked back.

She thought for a moment and figured out when that would be. "On the Secondren Don, your Highness?"

"Of course it's the Secondren Don. Can't you count?" he paused. "Now go home." He wiped his greasy fingers on a cloth and once again consoled himself, "Ahh, my feet."

"I'll be here in one shobbasim," Fair said. "Your feet will get better." She ran off, with Sauveren lumbering right behind her.

Harrold King turned to Fella Doon when she was out of earshot. He said, "Take the maiden and her dog to the caves." He looked up at Pewgen Flype and made a signal with his hand. Pewgen Flype nodded and ran on ahead to make sure he was in the caves by the time she arrived.

Fella Doon's face paled. He turned to face Harrold King. "Yes, your Highness."

Harrold King grunted.

Fella Doon followed Fair. He shuddered at what was to come and what he had to do.

22 : Down in a Cave

ella Doon knew he needed to appear tough. He unlatched the door to the cave and slammed it open with a loud crash. Pewgen Flype looked up casually from a small wooden table as though he were surprised. "Well? What have we got here, Fella Doon?"

"We have one more." He pushed Fair in, somewhat gently.

Fair stumbled into the cavernous room and regained her balance, standing awkwardly and confused. Her nose was filled with the smell of dampness, but not just any dampness. It was mixed with the stench of urine. It was so strong she nearly retched. She shivered. She noticed she was in a rectangular space, with roots poking out of grated metal windows in the ceiling. Torches burned in sconces on thick, wooden beams that supported the center of the room.

When Pewgen Flype saw Fair, a slow smile spread across his face like a grape juice stain on a tablecloth.

Fella Doon disappeared. He soon reappeared with the dog. Sauveren brushed past Fair, who quickly reached out and let his fur run through her fingers. He took his place next to Pewgen Flype, who had, by now, given him a special place to sit next to his table.

Sauveren's warmth was a small comfort to Fair when she felt him brush by. She could still feel the wispy feeling of his fur on her fingertips, almost like a daydream.

Fair noticed movement and stirring on the floor. When her eyes adjusted to the darkness, she saw hundreds of hoomin close to her age lying on thin mats along both sides of the cave.

"They're everywhere," she mumbled.

Wide, staring eyes.

So silent.

So pale.

They must look like me.

Or do I look like them?

Fair had the terrible realization that perhaps she was with all the wee hoomin that had been whisked away from their parents. She felt her knees go weak.

When her eyes adjusted, she saw even more. Red lizards scurried and scrambled along the dark, stone walls. The faintest sound of scratching sandpaper came from them when they moved. The sound was everywhere.

Hoomin and lizards. Dampness. Dark. Not again.

"Everywhere," she mumbled again.

"Silence!" Pewgen Flype yelled.

He belched and scraped his chair back loudly from the small table where he had been feeding himself. His round flat face looked like a very well-fed pumpkin with shining grease around his mouth, but his body was skinny and hunched in a stingy sort of way. He wiped his slippery hands on his sunken chest and and took a torch out of its sconce on the wall behind him. He looked at her from his downcast head.

"Come here then, vermin . . . shriveled pea . . . did you roll off the table and get forgotten? Or no. Weren't you the princess who lived in a golden castle? I almost forgot."

Pewgen brought the torch to the table and sat down again. He pounded his mallet so loudly that Fair jumped in her skin, "Come here, pitiful creature. I'm not going to ask you again."

Fair noticed that the stone floor was uneven, so she skimmed her feet along until she got to the table. Her eyes hadn't fully adjusted to the dim light, and she bumped against it. Pewgen's goblet shook and sloshed wine onto its surface. He looked annoyed, took a bite of meat, and held the torch up to her face. She shivered. The Ruby Eye felt cold on her forehead, as though a piece of ice were being pressed into her skull.

Pewgen Flype stood up from his chair and walked around to the front of the table. He moved the torch from side to side, and up and down. Inspecting her. Sizing up. Glaring.

As Fair and Pewgen Flype stared at each other, Fair noticed he was a grotesquely thin hoomin who stood slightly bent to support the weight of his orange-haired head. His face looked flattened by a well-deserved punch to the face. His eyes were narrowly set, apparently incapable of opening any wider than a narrow, suspicious glance at the world around him.

She looked around in horror at the rows and rows of wee hoomin chained up. They were lying on flat little mats. They were bony. Their hair was dry and dusty. Their dirty stone-colored clothes all looked the same and hung off their angular bodies.

"Why are they all here? Is this a workshop?" she asked.

"Silence!" Pewgen Flype repeated.

He paused and mocked her words. "Workshop? Why . . . we wouldn't make you work here," he said with a lowered, obsequious head. His curling lip filled with what appeared to be disgust and loathing for life, or anything living. "You get all sorts of treats here. And all the food you'd be wanting. A comfortable bed like you ain't never had. A new change of clothes. Now . . . to the middle of the room with you so we can have ourselves a little chat."

Fella Doon was sitting on a stool next to a rough hewn wooden post. He silently stood and walked towards Fair.

"I'll handle this, Fella Doon," said Pewgen Flype.

Fella Doon sat down again. *I'll wait. The time will come,* he told himself.

Pewgen Flype looked around at all the slaves in the room and loudly said, "What we have here is a thief! Do not speak to her. Do not trust her. She is filthy of mind and soul. I would cut out a pound of her flesh myself if I knew it would cure her and make amends for what she stole . . ." then he emphasized and looked around the room at the matternots, ". . . from Harrold King himself!"

A thief? Fair thought wildly. *What's he talking about? A thief? Me? I didn't steal anything.*

He pulled a knife out of his belt. It shone in the dim light.

"But instead, I will cut off this mass of flea-infested hair."

A young hoomin called out, "Don't touch her."

It was Hale.

Pewgen Flype cast him a cruel glance and said, "Come here, Lisper. You're the one I always rely on. You can have a better look this way."

Pewgen Flype tripped him when he walked in front of him. He placed his foot on his stomach. Hale could feel the cold stone beneath his back and he watched in horror as the monster moved the blade of the knife back and forth to make it glint in the dim light.

Pewgen Flype then pulled a fistful of Fair's hair and sawed it off a few inches from her head. He held it above Hale's face and let it drop. The boy hoomin felt an intense sorrow well up inside him. *Who is this matternot? Why is she here? She's different.*

Pewgen Flype took another handful of hair and said to the matternots, "She cannot be cured of her abominable weakness, nor ever restore her good name. By the way . . . thief . . . you have a new name. He grabbed another fistful of hair and cut it off with one more slice. When he was done it was difficult to tell whether Fair was a girl or a boy hoomin.

He gave a push with his foot into Hale's stomach, and Hale felt instantly nauseous. He felt something like an old memory return to him: strength of some kind, as though it ran in his blood.

He felt helpless and full of anger, but he thought he'd take this chance. "Treat me as you will, sir. But leave her alone." He felt the boot go even deeper into his stomach this time.

Pewgen Flype glared at him. "You used to be my favorite."

He sat down and opened a book on his table. He dipped a feather quill into a bottle of ink, then poised his hand to write in it. He looked at Fair, "Now out with it! What's your name? Oh wait. You don't have a name. I'm giving you one."

"But I do have a name. It is . . ."

"Worthless," followed Pewgen Flype. "You have a new name now. The same goes for Lisper." He motioned to Fair with the feather quill. "You are Worthless One."

Then he pointed to Hale, who was getting up from the floor, holding his stomach. "And you are Worthless Two." He wrote down the date, then the words "Worthless One" and "Worthless Two."

He paused and turned to Fella Doon. "Now take this moldy bread to my table of shame. She'll stand on it until bedtime. Chain up Worthless Two here." He nodded to Hale. "Right now." He whirled around, looking annoyed at Fella Doon. "I said, now! What are you waiting for?"

Fella Doon led Hale away.

What's going to happen to me? Fair thought. She looked over at Sauveren. They stared at each other.

When Hale was far enough away, he turned around and squished the now-small figure of Pewgen Flype between his finger and thumb, feeling some relief. "Poofs," he whispered. A faint smile.

Pewgen Flype turned to Fella Doon and said, "Prepare a nice pair of chains to go around those skinny little ankles of hers. They're so small and boney you could probably yank them both through one of the links and end up at her neck."

Fella Doon clicked his heels. "Yes, sir!"

"Oh," added Pewgen Flype with a curl of his lip, "and I think there's a nice little bed for Worthless One, over in that corner there." He hissed "Worthless" as though a dry wind were shivering and searching through his teeth for a place to go: around corners, through empty streets, and finally ending up nowhere in particular.

Fella Doon went to a wooden box and rummaged around with a lot of noise to find a pair of chains for Fair. Somewhere far across the room, Fair could hear Hale being chained up. She tried to memorize where the sound came from.

Fair stood on the table of shame through the entire afternoon into evening. Her knees buckled at times. The matternots sat in a group on the cold stone floor and listened to Pewgen Flype give them their lessons. He pulled Sauveren along as he paced. Fair was on the table right behind him.

"Worthless One here needs to know the way things are. So we're going to teach her that. Now answer me, 'What is good and right?'" Fair was on the table behind him.

They chorused, "Anything that you say is good and right."

"Good. That is right." He gave a yank on the rope and Sauveren yelped. "And if you don't think something is good or right that I tell you, what do you do?"

"We do what you say is good and right."

"Why?" He kicked the dog. Fair weakly pressed her lips together. *Stop it*, she silently willed. *He's my dog*, she thought.

"Because it is good and right to do so."

"And what are the best questions to ask me?"

"No questions are the best questions," they said in one voice.

"That's right," he said, with a well-aimed spit at Sauveren's face. "No questions are good enough for Pewgen Flype. You just do what you're told."

Fair's weak voice came from behind, "But what if I don't understand?"

Pewgen spun around and shrieked, "Was that a question?"

Fair said, "Yes. It was."

"And do you know what happens to naughty matternots who ask questions?"

"No sir," Fair swayed with the feeling that swept through her of wanting to sleep . . . just sleep.

"Hold out your hands, Worthless One."

Fair held out her hands.

"Not like that, you idiot. Palms up." He pulled a switch out from under his belt.

Fair stole a quick glance at Sauveren. His eyes looked sad. She held her hands with the palms up.

Pewgen Flype whipped them with the switch. She felt the pain of fire. She closed her eyes. She saw the burn sear into her skin.

Over.

And over.

Little Sparrow, she heard. *Ow . . . my father. He'll . . . ow . . . put his arm around me . . . ow . . . and hold me close. He's out there . . . ow . . . somewhere.*

Hurry, she told herself. *Remember.* She tried to imagine her father's face as the switch branded her hands like a hot pipe, but nothing came. She felt helpless. *But I can't. Must be something I can . . . ow . . . do. Alright then. Something I can remember. The field of flowers. The grassy path. The Door of Reunion. Have to . . .*

She pinched her eyes shut as tightly as she could and pressed her lips together, as though they would stay stuck forever. But it didn't help the pain go away. Finally, she couldn't bear it any longer. The memories wouldn't stay. No more came. All she felt was fire. Rising up. Burning as though her hair would burst into flame from the heat.

"No!" She cried out.

Sauveren barked.

Pewgen Flype gave him such a hard kick that the dog grunted and lay down.

"Are you telling me what to do, thief?" He whirled back on Fair and kept his switch poised in mid-air, ready for another whack.

She could hardly speak. "No sir."

"You're a liar. And do you know what happens to liars who tell Pewgen Flype what to do?"

Her head rolled back as the words "No sir" left her mouth. Her knees began to buckle. She forced herself to stand straight. Using the muscles in her neck to force her head upright took every bit of concentration she possessed. She gritted her teeth. Again she felt the sharp stinging on her hands. *Mother. Oh mother.*

The wee hoomin cringed as Pewgen Flype whipped her hands, over and over with the switch, until the pink stripes turned to red and began to bleed. He finally stopped and calmly turned around.

"There now. And what actions are good actions?" he asked.

One of the boy hoomin took his eyes off Pewgen Flype and snuck a glance at Fair. Pewgen Flype noticed the boy hoomin staring at her. He slammed the switch down on the ground in front of the boy with frightening speed.

"Keep your eyes on me. Now, as I was saying. What are good actions?"

"Doing what we're told," they chimed.

He added, "And looking at this pathetic excuse for a hoomin behind me is not a good action. Do you understand?" Everybody nodded, including the boy hoomin. He forced himself to look at Pewgen Flype.

"And finally, life . . . ," he said it slowly with ups and downs in his voice, as though they were supposed to finish the sentence.

". . . is never fair," they finished.

"Was it fair that this thief got a thrashing?"

The room was silent.

Soon, heads began to shake, "No."

"That's right. But did she deserve it?"

All heads nodded.

"Why?" He paused, then answered his own question, "Because she broke the rules. And don't forget it!" He whipped the switch into his other palm. "*Never forget it! Rules are rules! And now to other matters.*"

He continued to lecture. Every once in awhile, he turned around to observe Fair where she stood on the table. As the day wore on, Fair's eyes began to roll back into her head. A day had never demanded so much of her. Ever. She began to sway like water, lapping on the shores of Lakinren Bae.

A daydream.

Firelight.

Her father's voice.

A story around the hearth: ". . . the Ballen Nor swims in the bottom of the Bae. He is old as the ages, wise as the sages, and larger than three boats . . ."

I'm falling. Floating, she thought. *Let me go under.*

The stone walls in the room began to swirl around her like gray water pulling her down. Her eyes opened and shut in slow motion. She saw the sea of faces in front of her begin to surge and pull back, surge and pull back. The pain in her hands felt far away, as though it weren't even a part of her. In fact, she felt as though she had left her body. Such a relief.

A flit of light dashed in front of her and disappeared. It came back again and hovered in front of her. She knit her eyebrows together and tried to focus. A thought formed itself in her mind. *A tiny hoomin with wings. Did you all see that?* Then it was gone. "Lovely," Fair mumbled. She surrendered all her mortal forces.

Pewgen Flype shouted, "Fella Doon! Enough. Catch her, before I have another death on my hands to make excuses about to Harrold King. She'll walk to her bed."

Fella Doon ran up to the table and caught her, just as she passed out. He put Fair over his shoulder like a sack of potatoes. An orange-haired wee hoomin appeared at his side.

"Permission to speak to a matternot, sir," said Fella Doon.

"Permission granted," said Flype.

"Permission for a matternot to help?"

Pewgen nodded. Fella Doon turned to the orange-haired wee hoomin and said, "You'll help me here and get her settled in her bed, now."

The wee hoomin nodded. Fella Doon put Fair down and gave her a jiggle. She came to and wobbled a bit. He turned to Pewgen Flype and asked, "Permission for a bit of supper to revive the wee hoomin?"

"She's a thief. When she wakes up in the morning she'll eat—if she wakes up at all. That kind of death needs no explanation." Pewgen Flype then pointed with the mallet to the corner. "Over there with her."

Fella Doon and the wee hoomin gently led Fair to the corner, near the door. He quietly told her to stand with her feet a little bit apart so he could put iron bands, he was sorry, around her ankles. He let her know they would feel cold, and sometimes they would hurt when she walked.

He looked up at Fair. "But don't be afraid. We don't want you to come to no harm." She nodded. He coughed and took a quick look over towards Pewgen Flype, who was stuffing his face with a big forkful of mutton.

He added, "Don't ever talk to me. Sometimes you'll think I'm mean, but I need that rulemaker to think I am."

Fair just stood there, silently. She fluttered her fingers near his nose as a sign. Fella Doon smiled to himself, because he realized she understood.

Once chained up, Fair plopped down on her thin pokey mattress. She felt lonely. Afraid.

Her mother.

She was a distant nothingness.

Her father.

Did she even have one any longer?

The cool air of the caves hit the back of her neck. In her numb and muffled loneliness, she reached up and felt for the hair that had once been there. She was shocked to discover small remnants of stubble. She heard someone sniff next to her.

A weak voice asked, "Why did you steal?" It was the same girl who had helped her to her bed. Her rust-colored hair puffed out around her head like dry, soft weeds.

"I didn't steal anything."

"Not nothing?"

Fair began to speak, then thought better of it. She answered instead, "Nothing."

"Then why did Pew say you are a thief?"

"Pew who?" Fair asked.

"Stinky pew pew. That's who. Pewgen Flype."

Fair smiled weakly.

"I washed Harrold King's feet. I did something for him. That's all."

"So that's what a thief is. We shouldn't do things like that, then, I suppose. It's bad. Trouble follows," said the girl. She turned to face the sound of a pair of ankle bands clinking. Pewgen Flype was unlocking them.

He was glaring at Fella Doon, daring him to stay make a noise.

Fella Doon sat on his stool and told himself, *The right moment will come. The right moment will come.*

Fair realized her new friend didn't know what a thief was, and followed, "I don't think you understand. But who are you?"

The girl said, "What do you mean?"

"I mean," said Fair, "do you have a name? When someone talks to you, do they use a special word that says who you are?"

"I'm not anything. Just empty. That's all," she said.

Fair felt the Ruby Eye grow warm. Memories of Rall Kindaria filled her mind, and she saw this girl standing next to her in the great battle. Fair looked more closely at the girl, then she saw Sauveren in her place for just an instant. This time she didn't shake her head or think she was going mad.

She said, "I know that you are a great warrior. There is nothing to be afraid of. Ever."

"A great warrior? Me?"

"Yes."

The girl reached out and touched the Ruby Eye on Fair's forehead. "If you say so . . . that's beautiful."

The two were silent for a while, then the girl said, "Wait . . . A long, long time ago, I used to be called something else. " She searched in her mind for a long time then said, "Ffff . . . um . . . Fee . . . Fidavine. Yes, that's it. Fidavine Belle. And next to me this one was called . . . uh . . ." She was unable to finish because she was quickly interrupted.

"Don't speak it. I don't have a name. I don't want a whipping."

Fidavine Belle looked scared and said, "Right. I ain't told you my name, either. Forget it, like. Down here we are called matternots . . . the girl ones and the boy ones. Except you. You get called Worthless One, I guess. Maybe that means you're special."

"But why are you called matternots?" Fair asked.

Fidavine Belle looked over again at the wee hoomin who was now being dragged by Pewgen Flype into the barred opening behind his table. It's the same place where Sauveren had first been locked up.

Fair said, "What's he doing?"

Fidavine Belle turned to Fair and said, "You'll find out when it's your turn."

Fair didn't quite understand and decided to ask the question that had been on her mind since she had arrived. "Don't you ever think of escaping?"

"Icksapeen? What do you mean?"

"No. Escaping," Fair said more clearly. "Running away. Never coming back here."

Fidavine Belle rolled over and said, "Where else is there to be 'sides here?"

"Home," Fair said.

"I don't know what you mean," Fidavine Belle said with such finality that it ended the conversation.

That night, once everyone was in bed, a loud droning racket, along with the sounds of sleep, filled the echoing cave. How could anyone sleep through that noise? Fair put her hand to the Ruby Eye. She tried to remember the words that were born with it when it grew up out of the moss.

> *Purity of heart, strength of mind,*
> *They who seek shall also find . . .*

She tried to remember the rest, but only the last words came,

Look to me and through me and all will be clear.

"Look through me," she muttered. She searched back and forth along the rows and rows of matternots on her side of the cave. It was so dark she couldn't see much, so she imagined looking through the Ruby Eye.

When she did so, her vision became clearer. She could see through the darkness. What she saw had a faint red glow to it. She noticed that the floor along the opposite wall was lined with rows of boys. There was Pewgen Flype's table. She thought about watching to see his transparency appear as she gathered light, then changed her mind. There was no need. She knew.

She looked in the middle of the room and saw the table she had stood on. Her side of the room was filled with rows and rows of girl hoomin. So many of them.

She looked where she had heard the sound of Hale being chained up and was surprised to see him sitting up, staring at her. She gave a small, careful wave and he waved back. *He saw me.*

She saw the matternots around her and the rags they wore for clothes. She saw the lizards and the darkness. She saw the barred opening of the cage but couldn't see past it, for an inky blackness lay in front of it, around it, and even went into the stone. The lizards had all gathered around the opening of the cage. Fair realized the sound came from them rattling all in one place.

What Fair saw around the mouth of the cave amazed her—dozens of glowing tiny winged hoomin floated inside the stone and outside the opening. Or so she thought. Their hair was long and whitish-gold. In fact, they were whitish-gold from head to toe, and any detail in their faces, hair and flowing robes was of a deeper golden hue. What Fair saw of their color, however, was a luminous, delicious pink. They fought the lizards viciously, holding shields and swords in their hands. They wore wrist wrappings and necklaces of the same sort of moss blossoms Miss Tilly supposedly kept hidden in her pockets.

Fair muttered, "The Impissh Nissen!" They were similar to the ones she had seen earlier, but slightly different in color.

Soon, the cage door creaked. The lizards exploded from the cage, slithering in all directions over all the sleeping wee hoomin, up walls, and along the rafters. Fair saw the girl hoomin walk out of the cage and stumble back to her bed.

Fella Doon locked her up with the clinking and clanging of chains, then went to his stool to keep watch. He held his head in his hands. Tufts of hair poked out between his fingers. He seemed angry.

Fair looked at the girl hoomin again. There was something different about her now. There was a faint, golden cape tied around her neck. It covered her completely and shimmered like pure gold. Fair wondered how long it had been there. She gently shook her new friend, "Wake up." Fidavine Belle ignored her and rolled up into a little ball.

Fair heard the quiet grating of sandpaper and tried to see where it came from. There, on the wall above her she noticed a red lizard. Its ribs heaved in and out. The closer she looked, the more she could see something like steam coming out of its mouth. She felt a sudden chill. She realized that the stone in front of the lizard was being covered in a layer of frost that grew thicker with every breath. She saw little spots of frost forming wherever the lizards had planted themselves. Over the course of a few minutes, Fair watched the spots spread and grow into icicles. All she—or any hoomin had—was a very thin wool blanket. She pulled it up to her chin and prepared herself for a long cold night on her thin straw-filled bed. She looked over at Sauveren, who sat next to Pewgen Flype at his table.

Sauveren, you're so close, she thought. *So close.*

The last thing Fair remembered was the girl hoomin whimpering while the Impissh Nissen floated like fireflies above her, offering words of comfort. One Impissh Nissen in particular held the girl's earlobe and whispered, *"Dro ei li swihllah* . . . I am so sorry. I am so sorry. Just know you are not alone. It's not your fault. You haven't done anything wrong."

The wee hoomin didn't seem to hear a thing, but the golden cape wrapped itself around her. She felt calmed by it without knowing what it was that soothed her. She soon calmed down and slept.

Fair shivered, wondering what was so wrong. *Something is so, so wrong,* she thought.

As soon as Pewgen Flype left the room to head for bed, Sauveren quietly left his station. He padded over to Fair, circled around her and lay down. He took a deep breath and sighed, then lay down his head.

Fair felt the warmth of his breath wash over her. She felt the warmth of his companionship seep into the depth of her fatigue, and she melted. *Sauveren. He's here.* She felt a deep, profound comfort flow through her. They were together again. He would keep her warm. She hadn't expected it to be like this when she found him. Not more cold and darkness. She snuggled underneath him as far as she could until she felt the blanket of his fur surround her.

An opening formed in her mind as the numbness evaporated for a moment. She wanted to tell him everything she had seen that day, but she knew she musn't. She was too tired to talk anyway. She felt her stomach rumble with hunger and wondered how the boy was doing on the other side of the cave.

Then something occurred to her. *His name. The way he spoke. It couldn't be.* She tried to imagine her brother as a little boy. His name was Hale. He would be older now. The face looked different. His hair was darker, but the way he said his "s's" was similar.

Tomorrow, I'll look at his neck, to see if there's a freckle. She dug her fingers into Sauveren's fur and had one last thought, "I've got to get out of here. I have to find Selador."

Then she closed her eyes and slept.

23 : Lessons to Learn

lang! Clang! Fair jumped awake at the sound of a bell. Fella Doon was ringing it. The grates in the roof still showed a night sky, twinkling with stars. Sauveren sat next to Pewgen Flype's table.

The room had grown frosty through the night. Bluish-white icicles hung from the rafters and stone above, thanks to the lizards.

Fella Doon shouted, "Rise and shine mongrels! Rise and shine!"

A clanking of chains filled the cave with a deafening sound. The main chain was pulled at the end of each row of matternots. Each chain moved like an angry snake out the ceiling rings, then down and out of ankle chains, out of the next ceiling ring, then down again, swinging and clanging until all the wee hoomin were free.

The matternots bolted up from their floor mats. They shuffled across the cold floor and lined up in front of two long tables that flanked both sides of the door. Basins were on the tables. The girl hoomin stood in three lines on one side, the boy hoomin on the other.

Ice had formed over the water in the basins, and the first hoomin in line poked and stabbed with their hands to break the ice off the top. They picked out the pieces, splashed water on their faces, and gave their hands a rinse. The water was brown and dirty. It hadn't been changed for days.

Fair watched, and wondered. Fidavine Belle came back, remembering her new friend. "Come with me, Worthless One. It's time to wash up and stand in line for inspection."

Fair said, "My ankles are burning, Fidavine Belle." They were surrounded with dark pink spots that had begun to swell.

"Please don't call me by my name," she whispered. She pointed at Fair's legs, "That's fleas. Your ankles'll get used to it . . . they go for every bit of my legs. Least you're just ankles. Don't scratch." Fair shuddered, rubbed her ankles viciously, and stood up, "What do I do?"

"Follow me. Quick now."

Pewgen followed the two of them with his eyes.

They shuffled to the end of their line. There were three lines for each table, and it took some time before Fair and Fidavine Belle had their turn. Fair stiffened at the cold that hit her face when she splashed the dirty water onto it.

"Now wash your hands."

"Where's the soap?"

"There isn't any. Just dig under your nails, like, to get out any dirt." Fidavine Belle took a close look at Fair's hands and said, "You don't have any dirt there, yet. You're done. Now wipe your hands on your dress."

Fair wiped her hands, then used the cloth to wipe her face. She felt the Ruby Eye as she did so. She took a deep breath and thought of Sauveren. Then Hale. She looked over at Pewgen Flype. He was feeding a couple of lizards some crumbs from his pocket.

Soon, his voice cut through the air, "Atten . . . tion!"

All the matternots shuffled into two, long lines that faced each other. Pewgen Flype strutted up to one end of the line and looked up and down the rows, studying them through narrowed eyes, tapping his switch against his open palm.

"Now then, what have we got here? . . . Stand up straight and look as presentable as you can . . . you're too far apart . . . I want each one of you to take not one, but two, steps in, so I can see you better . . . ehp! That's too far. Back up a bit!" Fair thought he was trying to sound like Harrold King. The wee hoomin backed up slightly. He began to eye one wee hoomin at a time, starting with Fair's row.

"Chin up!" he lifted a wee hoomin's chin with the butt of his switch.

Fidavine Belle whispered to Fair, "He's my brother." He was the one who had been watching Fair on the table of punishment the day before.

"Not that high!" Fidavine Belle's brother lowered his head a bit.

"Teeth?" Her brother opened his mouth wide and showed his teeth.

"Hands?" The boy held up his hands and Pewgen Flype inspected them top and bottom.

Next, he came to Hale. He stepped on the boy's foot and ground in his heel. Hale winced. When Pewgen Flype took his jaw in his hands and turned his head from side to side to look in his ears, Fair saw a long brown freckle. *There it is! My brother. He's alive. Cael and Thelras promised.* Fair wanted to run over and grab him and tell him who she was. But, then again, maybe he knew.

A hot feeling flushed over Fair's face. *All those years I was in the cellar alone. At least I could have been here. It's not right.* Fair looked around at all the matternots. *I was alone. I'm sure my mother meant well,* she told herself. All the same, Fair felt a deep disappointment. She could have been with her brother.

Pewgen Flype finished up his tedious inspection on the boy's side, then started with the girls. He came to Fidavine Belle. She looked straight ahead and stood tall.

"You have a new friend, I see."

"I don't know what you mean, sir."

"You are not to talk to her. She is deceitful, dishonest, a liar, and can't be trusted. Do you understand me?"

Fidavine Belle remained silent, because she refused to agree. He took her silence as a "yes, sir," and said, "Very well then. Teeth?"

Fidavine Belle opened her mouth wide to show a row of darkening, decaying teeth.

"Hands?"

She held out her hands and held her breath. She had not washed her own hands because she was so busy helping Fair.

"What is this? Look at the dirt under your nails! You should be ashamed of yourself! Turn them over!"

Pewgen Flype began to whip them mercilessly until Fair cried out, "Stop it! I won't have it!" She kept telling herself, *Do what is right, let consequence follow.*

He whirled on her and said, "What did you say?"

Fair stood up taller and said, "I said stop it, Pewgen Flype."

He turned back to Fidavine Belle and said, "You have broken the rules and developed loyalty with another dog-loving matternot. Look what has happened because of your weakness. Your loyalty is to me! Down to your underclothes."

Fidavine Belle's eyes grew round, and she gulped. "What do you mean, sir?"

"You heard me. Take off your dress and stand before us all in your underclothes." He pointed to a spot in the middle of both rows. "There."

Fidavine Belle lifted her chin, and her nostrils flared slightly. She walked deliberately to the spot and stood. *I'm a great warrior*, she told herself. *I have nothing to fear.*

Fair quietly moved one foot forward, sliding it along the stone floor. She put her weight on it and moved the next foot. Before Pewgen Flype realized what was happening, Fair reached out and took Fidavine Belle's hand.

Fair silently stood beside her and began to take off the dress she had been given to wear. Fidavine Belle looked at Fair in disbelief, then did the same. Soon, the two of them stood in front of Pewgen Flype in their gray, sleeveless undershirts and baggy bloomers, flaunting his power. Hale felt a lump in his throat that was hard to swallow. His fists tightened up. Fair heard the words from the Scrolls of Truth echo in her mind:

There is great strength in quietly allowing another's foolishness to reveal itself.

Pewgen Flype stood there with his mouth open for a moment. Then, he spoke through his clenched jaw, "Difficult to live with. Flawed. Both of you." He glared at them for a long while. The cogs in his dried brain were whirring, "You'll build walls. Day after day, shoomin after shoomin." This was the hardest work any of the matternots had to do, because it meant they had to lift stone after stone from morning to night, day after day. The hottest weather of the year was coming.

He turned to the row of matternots and said, "These two pitiful creatures that stand before you in all their nakedness are unclean. Unclean! Do you see how dirty they are? You must not touch them, or you will inherit their impurity. Do you see? They are flea-bitten . . . filthy of soul!" Fair thought he sounded a lot like Harrold King.

Then, turning to Fair and Fidavine Belle he said, "Listen to me. You have *nothing*! You *are* nothing! The clothes you wear . . . where do they come from? From me. The food you eat . . . where do you get it? . . . from me! Without me you are *nothing*! I can take it all away in a moment." He snapped his fingers and turned his back on them to walk away.

Fair stood there shivering.

She spoke up, "I have everything, sir."

Pewgen Flype whirled around.

"You have nothing, Worthless One!"

She continued to speak with a kind of defiance in her voice that surprised her. "I am loved. I have a family. I know where I come from. And I have a dog that loves me." She looked at Sauveren, then snuck a glance at her brother. She didn't know where her father was yet, or if he was alive, but she had known love as a child from her parents, and her mother had been there for her all those years. Pewgen Flype's words were only words. And they were false.

"Not any more you don't. The dog is mine."

"At least I have known love and kindness."

"You will never know it again, you wretch."

The memory of Rall Kindaria tickled at Fair's brain and left her with just a feeling. It was just a feeling, but it was a sustaining feeling. A sense in her heart that she was cherished, even as she stood there in her rough and oversized underclothes.

"I will always have it, as will every wee hoomin here. But you, sir, have a mean heart. And so it is you, Pewgen Flype, who have nothing. You won't be able to do anything to stop my brother and me from escaping."

Fair held her breath, even though she was furious.

"Me? A mean heart?" Pewgen Flype raised his arm to give Fair a switching, then the light of realization flickered in his mind and he stopped. "Your brother? What do you mean?" He lifted his arm again, ready to strike. Sauveren put himself in between the two of them. Pewgen Flype said, "Out of my way, dog." He gave Sauveren a whip with his switch, then cocked his arm back for another swing. He would deal with Fair next.

"Stop it!" yelled Hale.

He looked at Fair and she looked at him.

He remembered.

Fair was still holding her breath. She felt her hand begin to tingle and in a moment the feeling went straight to her first finger. She folded her arms and pretended—while she silently pointed her finger at Pewgen Flype—that she could move him with a flick of her finger. She swung her finger sideways and upwards. It worked.

Pewgen Flype swung around to face Hale. He found himself lifted off the ground a few inches, then back down again. It was just a slight movement, but just enough that he was startled into wondering if he had hopped in a moment of fury, without knowing it.

Hale said, "I'm her brother."

Fair looked down at her finger. No one had noticed.

Fella Doon quickly spoke up, "Permission to speak, sir."

Pewgen Flype was out of breath with rage and his face was red. He huffed, "Permission granted. You may speak no more than one sentence." His eyes bored in on Hale.

"I ask that I never be put on wall detail with them two, filthy matternots . . . not them, or their friends."

Pewgen Flype said, "Are you telling me what to do, Fella Doon?"

"No sir. I wouldn't never presume . . ."

"Then I'm sure you won't mind that I'm assigning you to wall detail as of tomorrow. You'll finish up your duties in the quarry today."

Fella Doon pretended to be disappointed and said, "But sir . . ." At that moment, he resolved to do everything he could to help Fair and Hale escape.

Pewgen Flype ground his jaw at the rebuttal, and with an awful smile and turn of his head, he said, "Alone. You'll have no other Protectors to help you with the impossible task. No more discussion. I have work to do. And you'll take those four brats with you."

He was referring to Fair, Hale, Fidavine Belle, and her brother. He rubbed his hands over each other in a circling motion as though he were slowly washing them. He went to the next wee hoomin in line and said, "Teeth?"

That night, Fair stayed awake until the sounds of sleep echoed in the cave. She had a plan.

24 : Fair Holds Her Breath

 ewgen Flype slept with his head on the table. During the night, Fair practiced her newfound ability. She spent hours and hours holding her breath and using her finger to move things around while everyone slept.

She had torn off a piece of her clothing and tied it around her fingertip to keep anyone from seeing the glow of her fingerlight.

First, with a flick of her finger, she lifted Sauveren's ear and left it there, hovering as though it had heard a sound. Next, she worked and worked until she was able to cover Fidavine Belle with her blanket, which had slipped off.

Then, she tried something bigger: Pewgen Flype. With a lot of breath holding and gradual lifting, Fair managed to lift him, his chair, his footrest and his table into the air while he snored, with his head resting on his arms. She left him floating just a few feet from the ceiling of the cave. Now all she had to do was wait.

She slept and woke in fits and starts but managed to stay awake just as everyone was stirring. When the matternots noticed Pewgen Flype's precarious state, they began to whisper and point. Looks of glee appeared on their faces and they sat up, waiting to see what would happen.

Fair motioned to a few matternots that they'd better lie down, and they passed the message along. They all began to lie down in a wave of movement. They watched as though they were asleep. Hale coughed rather loudly, hoping to wake up Pewgen Flype.

Pewgen Flype snorted.

He sat up in his chair. It stayed firmly in place, hovering in the air. He rubbed his eyes and stretched. Fair held her breath and kept her finger poised, ready for action. He rubbed his hands on his face and smacked his lips, then turned and took a step before realizing that things weren't exactly as they should be.

When he was mid-step, he realized he was falling and made a quick, twisted grope for the table to catch himself. Fair made a subtle flick of her finger, and he froze in mid-air, a few feet above the floor. She made a little swipe so his face could loosen, and he yelled, "What are you all lying there for, you fools? Get me down from here!"

The matternots stared at him with one eye closed. They just lay there and waited.

Fair lay quietly on her thin mat. She slowly moved her finger and lifted his legs until it looked like he was sitting. She let him down slowly. His eyes searched the air wildly, but he couldn't even turn his neck to see why, or how, or who was doing this to him. Then, when he was just a few inches above the ground she let go. He fell with a plop.

The matternots lay as still as they could. Their shoulders shook with suppressed giggles, and Fella Doon watched in round-eyed disbelief. He looked around the room to find some sort of clue, but found nothing.

Pewgen Flype shot up and dusted himself off. He was not going to admit humiliation, so he said, "To the quarry, ever last one of you. There will not be an inspection today."

The matternots were unchained. They filed out of the cave into the tunnel, while the table, chair, and foot stool hung in mid-air behind them.

25 : A Taste of Misery

ella Doon had quarry duty. A low door stood open at the far end of the cave. Fair and Hale bent and walked through the door stiffly, chained at the ankles. They were in line with the rest of the matternots in their group, lined up two-by-two.

They wound their way along a tunnel that slanted slightly upwards. Soon, Fair saw a pinpoint of light ahead of her. As they got closer, it grew bigger. When she walked out of the tunnel, she was hit by the blinding rays of early morning. *Daylight feels different with chains on*, she thought. The air felt warmish against her skin, but somehow it offered little relief.

"Grab your tools," Fella Doon said, rather harshly. "Get to it. You know what to do."

Pewgen Flype stood right behind him. He nodded with exaggerated satisfaction, trying to look important after his brush with humiliation a few minutes earlier. He turned on his heel and disappeared into the tunnel, leaving Fella Doon in charge.

When Fella Doon heard the door close far down the tunnel he looked at the matternots and smiled. "What happened in there?"

The matternots burst into laughter and he held up his hands to silence them. It didn't work. He let them have the first laugh they had known in nine years.

Soon, they began to talk amongst themselves, trying to figure out how it must have happened. Fair heard one of the matternots say, "I don't care how it happened. I just hope I get to see it again."

Fella Doon sent them all to do their work, knowing it had to be done, *or else*. In an instant, Fair and Hale were swept along with all the other matternots who clanked and clattered off in separate directions, up and down the quarry pit. Fair watched closely as Hale began to hammer away at a wall of stone in front of him. Behind, the quarry trail dropped sharply off. They took a moment to look at each other. Faint recognition. Smiles of distant memories. Aching inside. Confused.

There were quite a few trails above and beneath them, since the trail spiraled around the pit. A pool of water filled the bottom, due to rain and seeping cracks of water that ended up there.

Fidavine Belle took charge of Fair and gently led her to a stone wall not far from the cave opening. She handed Fair a hammer and chisel.

"What am I supposed to do?" Fair asked. The tools felt heavy in her hands.

"Nothing. Fella Doon won't mind. Just be ready to act busy in case Pewgen Flype shows up."

"I will."

"And thanks, Worthless One. For what you did."
She patted a jagged stone ledge. You can sit and lean
against the wall." She looked over at Fella Doon, who
was surveying the scene, and he nodded in approval.

"You would have done the same thing," Fair said.
"Stinky Pew Pew." She giggled, then she faked a stern
look. "You broke the rules, Worthless One. Back in the
caves." She looked at Fidavine Belle and said, "They
aren't real rules. They're only rules that Stinky Pew made
up."

Fidavine Belle said, "Then you don't love him."

"What do you mean?" Fair asked.

"Love means doing everything he tells you to do."

Words from the Scrolls of Truth echoed in Fair's
mind:

If you push aside what matters to you to please another
who is hurtful towards you, that is not love.
It only reveals the lack of love you have
for yourself.
Do not let your lack be visible:
Speak up. Stand up. Stand tall.
Soon your void will be filled with who you are:
a powerful and strong light that shines.

What matters to you, matters—
because you matter.
Do not let yourself be treated as less than you are.

Fair then felt a rush of words flow into her mind. She was surprised at how clearly formed they were, but she knew the source from whence they came: Her mother had spoken them many times during Fair's dark years in the cellar.

She echoed those words for her friend. "Fidavine Belle, when someone hurts you on purpose, that's not love. It's wrong. If you keep letting them do it, that's not love either. It's wrong as well, because you're letting that someone be less than they really are. They end up despising you for your weakness, then they convince themselves they're right to treat you so poorly."

Fair could tell Fidavine Belle had no idea what she was talking about, so she said, "Owls eat mice because they are small and weak. You're all acting like mice in the caves." Fair thought about Harrold King and Pewgen Flype. *Owls*, she thought.

Fidavine Belle said, "But everything Pewgen Flype says is true."

Fair shuddered when she realized her friend had grown to love the creature that preyed upon her weakness. She wanted to say more. She wanted to tell her friend she was just punishing *herself* by acting small. Instead she spoke with finality, "You're lying to yourself."

Fidavine Belle looked shocked. "But I don't lie. I'd be punished if I did."

"Not even to yourself? Haven't any of you ever said no to Pew Pew? Haven't you ever stood up because he was wrong?"

"He's never wrong."

Fair said, "Keeping you away from your mother and father is wrong. Don't you miss having a warm bed and parents who love you?"

Fidavine Belle looked Fair in the eyes. She could hardly speak. She trembled out the words, "Very much." She looked over at Fella Doon, who was looking up at the sky, beyond the rough-hewn walls of the quarry. He stiffened. He quickly motioned for Fair to get to work, but it was too late.

Harrold King was peering down at them.

He hollered, "My surprise inspection has been rewarded, I see." His voice echoed amidst the clanging of chisels against stone. He had been helped down into a lying position by one of his Protectors, and he lay sprawled like a beached whale on the grassy edge so he could peek down. Rithel sat on Harrold King's forearm, looking down at the matternots.

"Fella Doon?"

"Yes, your Highness?"

"You have a slacker on your hands. Throw her into the pool. It might wake her up a bit. I need every last matternot if I am to find the best possible stone for my statue."

Hale stopped hammering and pricked his ears. Was he talking about Worthless One? He tried to remember her real name. He didn't turn around, but stayed on alert and started hammering again, with long pauses in between.

"Begging your pardon, your royal eminency, but she . . ."

"I know who she is. Do it anyway."

"Very well."

The matternots continued to hammer and chisel into the stone, as if nothing were happening. Their capacity for feeling, concern, or consequence had not been nurtured by the love of a kind parent for more than nine years. Fidavine Belle and her brother were the few exceptions who still felt. Who still cared. The numbness hadn't taken them over, for some reason or other.

Fella Doon took eternally long steps towards Fair and grasped her by the shoulders. He whispered, "Do you know how to swim?"

"I don't know," she said, without moving her lips. Fella Doon felt faint. That means "no," he realized.

He turned his back to Harrold King and tilted his head down so Harrold King couldn't see what he was about to tell Fair. "If you can swim, swim to your left. The trail ends there. Climb onto it. The walls are too steep everywhere else. I can't do anything else to help you. Things will get much nastier if I do."

"Left?"

"Left." She rubbed her eyes. They were bothering her.

Fidavine Belle took the tools from Fair's trembling hands. She felt him grab ahold of her shoulders, and before Fair knew what had happened, she felt herself sailing through the air. She took a deep breath. Cold hit her feet and sliced through every inch of her skin right up to her head. It pulled at her eyelids. It hurt her stomach. Cold. That's all she felt right then. There was no tingle in her finger. *Iron rings around my ankles. I can't lift. I can't move them. My arms. Yes. Move them. Reach for the sky.*

She thought of the butterfly she had seen when she got out of Gibber Will's wagon. How strange. She moved her arms so hard that the muscles in her shoulders burned. It seemed like she would never breathe again.

Harrold King lay on his belly and watched her struggle, clearly entertained. Then he grunted with dissatisfaction.

Suddenly, there were arms around her, pulling her up. Just like the quicksand.

Up.

Up.

Gasp!

Air!

Am I breathing? Or is this water? Something is holding me up. Holding up my chin. Her eyes searched the air blindly. Who had done this?

"We're almotht there."

It was Hale. Hearty and strong Hale with the lisp. She was glad he was born the healthy one. It mattered right then, at that very breath in time.

As they climbed onto the rocky patch where the trail disappeared into the water, Fair said, "Your ankle rings. They're so heavy. How did you swim?"

"You're my thither."

"Now get back to work, you lazy brats," Harrold King shouted to Fair and Hale. "That should keep you awake." He grunted and rolled over. He reached out his hand to be pulled up. Then he was gone.

Fair and Hale shivered the rest of the morning, while they hammered and chiseled in different parts of the quarry. The stabbing pain of hunger that seized their stomachs gave way to a hollow ache and then a feeling of no hunger at all. Just weakness and fuzzy thoughts. Their thirst was quenched by the ladlefuls of vinegar that the carrier brought by.

"I feel like we've been here for years," Fair said to Fidavine Belle. "I don't even know what we're doing this for."

"Harrold King wants a statue made to look like him," Fidavine Belle said. "He's having a big celebration in honor of himself once the warm weather begins to cool at the end of the Longlightren Dons."

Fair said, "I see." Inside she thought, *I hope I find Selador before the Blood Moon rises.* She worked alongside the other matternots for the rest of the day.

Finally, Pewgen Flype appeared. He blew a whistle and everyone lined up to return to the cave. Fair heard a splash. What was that? She turned around.

Hale had jumped back in to the pool.

Does Liver need to tell about the Ballen Nor, Cael?

Yes. I believe he does.
It may prove to be useful information at some point.

26 : Lisper Leaps

ale jumped into the quarry pool. "What in the Graves?" muttered Pewgen Flype. He turned to Fella Doon and snarled, "You make sure he makes it back to the cave— if he ever comes up." Then he turned and took charge of the matternots himself, "All in!" he shouted.

The matternots began their slow mechanical entrance into the tunnel. They dropped their tools in wooden boxes and headed into the darkness. The sound of clanging ankle chains grew quieter as they disappeared into the tunnel.

Soon, all was silent.

Fella Doon stood alone now.

He looked into the water. It had grown still.

The sun had dipped below the edge of the quarry, long ago. By now the circle of sky above him showed pink. The air was quite cool.

Fella Doon's heart was still. He held his breath.

Hale was under water for far too long.

Minutes passed.

Then the pool exploded as Hale shot out of the water, whipped his hair, and gasped, in one quick movement. He swam to the bottom of the trail, where it sloped into the water.

Fella Doon sighed deeply.

Hale wound his way up the trail that spiraled around the carved-out quarry. He passed Fella Doon, dripping in the timeless gray light between day and night.

Fella Doon whispered, "You found it, didn't you."

Hale nodded. When he dove into the water to save Fair he had seen the opening to an underwater tunnel. When he went back to find it, he swam up the tunnel and found a place where he could breathe. It echoed when he called out.

"That's where he lives, isn't it?" Hale asked. He had often thought of his father's story about a creature that swam in the depths of Lakinren Bae, large enough to swallow a boat.

Fella Doon said, "I'd always heard he had an underwater home."

They were talking about the Ballen Nor.

27 : The Right Way to Build a Wall

fter that miserable day in the quarry, Fair and Hale spent the brother. By now, they were entire Longlightren Dons building walls in the heat with the help of Fidavine Belle and her coming to a close. The air felt cooler.

Hale spent sunup to sundown, day after day stacking stones that had been chiseled out of the quarry. Fair stirred pots of mortar to put between the stones. She became quite skilled at plopping and smoothing mortar onto the stones, then scraping off the extra, once stones were placed on top. She was too weak to do anything else, at first. Fella Doon let her dog stay right with her.

Hale kept an eye on her from where he positioned the heavy, rectangular stones onto the mortar. It was backbreaking work.

For a time that seemed endless the bony matternots stacked and scraped, measured and lined stones. Fella Doon worked right beside them.

On their very first day working together, Fella Doon saw a dark hairy figure running through the yellowing field of tall grass off to his right.

"What, ho! Come here!" he called.

The hoomin didn't hear Fella Doon (or else he ignored him) and kept running. He ran past the next day and the day after that. No matter how loudly Fella Doon called, the hoomin kept running.

Fella Doon noticed that not far from the path there was a bush that the hoomin ran past every day. The following day he planted himself behind the bush and listened. Soon, he heard footsteps crashing through the tall grass, then the sound of breathing. He leapt out and went sailing sideways until he slammed into the stranger. Fella Doon hit him so hard it knocked the wind out of the hoomin, but he held on and they both went down, landing with a thud in the grass.

The hoomin put up a fight, and the two of them rolled over and over in the grass, until Fella Doon got him pinned beneath his chest. He grasped the stranger's shoulders with both hands and had himself a good look. Fella Doon recognized him from that day at Clock Tower Square.

It was the Woolly.

"Where are you going, hoomin? Every day it's like you've got some fire to put out."

The Woolly answered, "I prepare the way. Prepare the way, I do."

Fella Doon looked at him quizzically, grabbed his shoulders more tightly and yanked him up. "Up with you, hoomin. I want you to see somethin'." He wasn't being unkind. He was just stronger than he realized, and the Woolly was big enough not to mind.

He pushed the Woolly over to the wall and said, "Have yourself a good look at them wee hoomin. They're starving and it's my job to see they build this wall, as much as I hate it." He spit on the ground. "This is a fire *I* want to put out. I can't stand to see 'em suffer so." The matternots looked over at him with careful glances. They were already surprised to see him working beside them. And now this! They didn't know what to make of him. He was nothing like Pewgen Flype.

Far down the wall, Fair and Fidavine Belle carved out the mortar in a newly laid section. Sauveren slept in the grass nearby. She saw the Woolly and felt her heart leap within her. He wasn't a monkey any more.

Fella Doon pointed at them. First the Woolly saw Sauveren and said, "Belong to Fair he does. Yours he is now?"

"The dog's here with her." Fella Doon pointed at Fair. She looked like a boy with her short hair.

The Woolly's jaw dropped, "Fair she's not. A boy hoomin Fair is not."

Fella Doon said, "It doesn't much matter to Pewgen Flype what she is. He chopped off her hair."

The Woolly looked at her more closely, and a sparkle of recognition danced in his flaming eyes. He winked at her clumsily to let her know he knew her. When Fair saw the wink, her heart leapt within her.

She saw that she was seen. She knew that she was known. She loved that she was loved, if even for a sunny moment. In the depths of her body's hunger, the transparent part of her felt washed with a river of endless serenity—the part that knew things far beyond what she could touch and feel.

The Woolly clenched his fists. "Down in the caves she is?"

Fella Doon followed, "They don't get much to eat, and it ain't right. Would you much mind finding food for these wee hoomin?" He focused on the Woolly's eyes to see if he understood. "Get some folks to gather what they can to send along, you know . . . . They ain't eaten well for years. And something to scrub their teeth. Like I said, if you don't much mind."

The Woolly took off running without saying a word. He was there the next day with a basket of food and a couple of jugs of fizzy milk. Fella Doon called the matternots over. When the Woolly set the food down he emptied his pockets and dropped the wiggling contents on top of the food in the basket.

"Grubs and bugs," he muttered. "Make you strong they will."

Fella Doon looked down at the pile of meat and rolls heaped in the basket and saw chumpish, wriggling grubs and all sorts of bugs squirming and writhing in a panicked attempt to hide from the sunshine.

From then on, the Woolly came day after day, shobbasim after shobbasim with the same supply of food . . . and bugs.

"Look under the rocks," he would say. And he'd be off.

The wee hoomin ate everything in the basket, including the grubs, and they guzzled the thick fizzy milk, careful to share. They scrubbed their teeth with the chewed and softened ends of sticks—just like the Woolly showed them—until their teeth looked clean. Soon they began to fill out, and they began to laugh and talk with each other while they worked. They learned how to look under rocks to find more grubs in the roots. They got to the point when they didn't even feel the pangs of hunger for days at a time.

Fair grew stronger, too.

As the days went on, she found herself breathing more easily, more confidently. One day she lay back in the grass and stared at the sky. Clouds drifted above her like the whispers of her cellar dreams, and she thrilled to know that these ones were real. Right now, she was warm. Right now, she could smell the scent of life growing beneath her in the grass. Right now, she could see the color of a blue sky and the changing shapes of clouds.

A new feeling was born in her soul just then. She felt it crawl gently through her limbs and spread far beyond her body, tugging at the garment of her soul's farthest edges. This feeling, this something that stretched her wide, unraveled the hems of her soul. She felt the threads weave themselves into everything known and unknown in the world around her, seen and unseen. She saw her beginning as a child of light, woven into the fabric of time.

And on this tapestry of her soul, she saw her life stitched out in perfect purpose, connected to all that was and ever would be. She saw where she hoped to go when her body was laid beneath the soil.

She belonged—even if her life was difficult—like a flower belongs to its thorny stem. Her soul was planted in eternity. Its roots reached deep from suffering. She was a blossom unfolding.

Her heart had been broken.

Open.

This was a good thing.

And she knew it.

She began to hum the melody from her father's music box. With the melodies—she and her mother had counted three tunes that overlapped each other—words began to form in her mind. Soon she began to sing. Quietly.

I descend from, I descend from, I descend from royalty.
I descend from, I descend from royalty.

Hale and the two other hoomin heard her and stopped their stacking and scraping. They'd never heard that sort of sound come out of someone's throat. What was it? Fair and her mother used to hum two of the overlapping melodies together, but since there were only two of them, they were never able to hear the third part.

She saw her brother looking at her. "Come here, Hale. I need you to do something for me."

He knew Fella Doon wouldn't mind if he stopped working for a second, so he wandered over and sat down near his sister. "What is it?"

"Listen to this, then see if you can do it with me." It's just like walking up six steps with your voice, then jumping down them again. She sang another line, another melody:

> I . . . dee . . . scend . . . from . . .
> I . . . dee . . . scend from royalty.

"Now see if you can do it with me." The two of them went over and over the melody until Hale knew it by heart. "How about you sing your part and I'll sing another. I'll start. Then, when I wave at you, do your part three times. We'll both be singing different things, but that's the way it's supposed to work."

"Alright."

After Hale joined in with Fair, his eyes went wide with surprise. He'd never heard anything so beautiful.

Fair had an idea. There were more than just two of them now. In a matter of minutes, she had taught the third melody to Fidavine Belle and her brother. Fella Doon had learned Hale's part.

Before they all put their parts together Fair said, "If you want to know what the words mean, you have to know where I got them. I want to tell you a story." They settled themselves into the grass while she told them about going to Rall Kindaria and what she had seen there.

Then they sang. They sang until the sun began to fall low in the sky.

I descend from, I descend from,
I descend from royalty, royalty.

When they returned to the caves, they all stayed as silent as a grave. They didn't want to lose this privileged work.

One day, while everyone sat in a circle eating their midden meal and grubs, Fidavine Belle's brother said to Hale, "You said she's your sister, and that you have a family, Worthless Two. What's a family? Does that mean you were rich?"

Hale chewed a mouthful of bread that he had just ripped off with his teeth and muttered, "Mmm . . . family. It's a . . . mmm," he swallowed the lump and realized the boy must not remember his parents. He looked at Fella Doon as though he didn't know what to say.

Fella Doon jumped in. "It means they are very rich."

All heads turned to Fair and Hale with longing and admiration in their eyes.

Fella Doon continued, "It's when you have at least one hoomin who loves you very much, who would do anything for you to make sure you're happy."

Fidavine Belle said, "Like you, Fella Doon? Are you my sister?"

Fella Doon smiled. He was taken aback and swallowed a lump in his throat. He'd never thought of it that way. He sniffed and cleared his throat. "Like me," he smiled, "Only I'm not your sister. I'm your brother, because I was born a boy hoomin." He touched the red scarf under his shirt.

Fidavine Belle concluded, "So I'm your sister. We're a family, then. So we're rich, too." She and her brother felt small shy smiles form on their faces.

The boy said, "I didn't know I was rich," as if it were as normal as anything in the world. He stuffed a piece of meat in his mouth. "Fella Doon? . . ." he chewed and smacked. "Where's this wall going?"

"Nowhere," Fella Doon answered. And everyone smiled, because they knew that a wall going nowhere could take forever to build.

On their way back to the caves, Fella Doon announced to his small group, "Tomorrow, things are going to be somewhat different. We'll be having an early start, we will." He took Fair and Hale aside and said, "There's something you need to know."

28 : Something Worth Seeing

A hand jostled Fair's shoulder. She stirred awake with a shiver. She looked through the metal bars of the square opening in the roof of the cave. It was still dark. Fella Doon whispered, "Up you go, Fair. Gotta get going."

The words were fuzzy in her mind. She was confused. She kept her voice low. "But the bell didn't ring. I don't understand."

"You will."

Won't Pewgen Flype ask questions? she thought.

Soon, Fair, Fella Doon and the rest of their small group were trudging through dew-drenched grass towards the wall. Steam escaped from their mouths as they walked along. The nights were growing cooler. Sauveren tagged along behind, licking the wet grass as he went.

Hale spoke through the starry blue of early morning silence. "How come Pewgen Flype let us go so early?"

Fella Doon said, "As far as he's concerned, the more we work, the better. I just told him I wanted to get an early start. Fact is, today is the Joust and Dangle. It's a fight worth watching . . . with good reason."

Fair stopped walking. She said, "The Joust and Dangle? Who's going to be fighting today?" She thought about Tooli, and about what Harrold King had told her concerning her grandfather. She kept the story to herself.

Fella Doon said, "You'll see soon enough. We're going to see it for ourselves."

Hale protested, "But won't we get in high trouble if we go?"

"Never you mind, Lisper. We won't be seen. The Woolly has packed us a wee picnic. Left it in a spot in the woods, he did, right on the edge of the water. Ain't no one going to know we're there but us . . . and the Woolly. And he's silent as the grave."

Fair touched the Ruby Eye on her forehead. It was all so new and hard to digest in her mind. Her years of isolation seemed so far away.

She was having adventures.

The wee hoomin looked at each other, not knowing quite what to make of the news. It sounded exciting, but such a departure from rules and routine was frightening at the same time.

They walked far beyond Osden Shorn, then backtracked through the woods over roots and brambles, until they were close to shore. Fair could see the glimmer of moonlight dancing on the surface of Lakinren Bae. She could hear the water lapping at its edge. Fella Doon led the group into a small clearing and announced, "Here's the spot. Once the sun comes up we'll have a perfect view of the jousting boats and the temple."

Fair noticed that the Woolly had formed a low wall of branches and leaves at the edge of the opening, providing good cover for them.

Fella Doon rummaged around, lifting branches, until he found a cloth bundle. He pulled it out and said, "Let's eat!" The small company ate in silence while the sun peeked over the mountains of High Grave.

The air began to grow warmer as the sun rose. Sauveren pricked his ears when he heard laughter in the distance. At the sound, everyone crept to the wall of branches and peeked over it. Hoomin were arriving one by one, in small groups, and families. They began to spread out on the lawn between Osden Shorn and the woods.

Hale asked, "Who's fighting?"

"One unlucky loser. Such a sorry thing, really. It's the King brothers what's fightin' today. Shame."

Fair wanted to ask about Tooli, but instead she asked, "What was the Joust and Dangle like when you were our age?"

Fella Doon laughed and said, "They were a lot different when I was a young hoomin. Cloven Grave was still ruled by the tribe of Grinnam. It was that way for generations until . . ." He stopped and looked as though he were trying decide what to say and when.

"Until what?" all the matternots echoed.

He cleared his throat and took off his cap. "I believe you asked me about my favorite Joust and Dangle."

Fair gulped and nodded, "Something like that."

"Well then, where was I?" Fella Doon's face changed from furrowed and dubious to the joy of a remembered time. He laughed. "They were much more fun back then, because the winner got to ride on the shoulders of his oarsmen and be paraded through the feast that was always held out on the lawn." He pointed: "There by the side of the boat house." He laughed again.

"What's so funny, Fella Doon?"

"I'm not sure I should tell you." He looked up at Fair and winked.

"Aw, come on. You have to tell us now."

"Well . . . your father and I . . . ahem . . . brought along a packet of dried pepper balls, the really hot ones as big as a baby tooth. Fact is, just one will make a pot of soup spicy hot. We snuck into the boathouse long before the Joust and Dangle was gonna start. We knew ain't no one would be in the boat house just then, because Bander Zothiker—that's your grandfather—said they usually had themselves a Rules Review up in the hall before the Jousters squished into their armor."

Fella Doon changed subjects for a minute and asked, "Have you ever seen the boat house, Fair?" She shook her head. She was thinking about her grandfather, partly.

"Well, it's a cave underneath the castle. Almost as wide as the building itself—the narrow end anyhow. You can hear your voice echo when you're inside. It's all drippy and stony. It's pretty nice when it's hot outside. The light reflects off the water and dances on the stone ceiling. Quite a show.

"There's stairs that lead up from the a stone floor at the back of it . . . never did find out where they went. Bander Zothiker never let us go up 'em."

"So then what?" Fidavine Belle said.

Well, we smashed the packet with our hands to turn the pepper balls into powder, then we sprinkled the powder on the floor of the boat we hoped would lose. You could hardly see it—the powder. Back then, the oarsmen rowed in bare feet so they could get a better grip on the bottom of the boat. They have to pull hard on those oars to go as fast as they do."

Fair said, "My mother told me they still row in bare feet."

Fella Doon nodded and continued, "So, we snuck out of the boat house and got back to the road in time to come in with everyone else. We looked like we was arriving with baskets of food and picnic blankets to watch the jousting."

"What happened?" pressed Fair.

"Well, each jousting crew was rowed out to their awaiting boats that was lined up a good—oh, I'd say five hundred hoomin-lengths from each other—ready to slice past by just a hair so their jousters could have a good jab at one another. They stepped in the boats. The scullers was sitting next to each other, two by two. The armored jouster was standing at the front of the long narrow boat with his lance. Our enemy jouster looked as proud as a hoomin ever could."

Fella Doon stood up to demonstrate. "His chest was thrust out like *this*, and his big rump poked out like *that*, while he held on to his lance, aimed for action."

The matternots laughed.

Fella Doon sat down again. "The jouster acted like he had just conquered a mountain. Only the joust hadn't even started. He didn't know what was comin'."

He looked at Fair and Hale. "When your great-grandfather dropped the red scarf off his balcony above the boat house, the two jousting boats shot into action. The scullers was pulling and drawing the oars in and out of the water like liquid lightning.

"The hoomin all around us was cheering wildly, and it was pure joy to watch.

"It hadn't been more than ten furious dips in the water before we could see the scullers on our enemy's boat was doin' little dancing jigs with their feet. Their oars was going every which way, because they was going mad with the burning in their feet. We could see their mouths making all sorts of shapes like they was yelling, 'What in the . . . !' So, none of them noticed when the green boat approached."

Hale laughed, amazed. "Don't stop, Fella Doon!"

"Well, the jouster could feel somethin' was wrong, so he turned around to have a look-see through the narrow slits in his armored mask. This meant his back was turned to the approaching boat. Before he knew it, he was knocked into the water because the other jouster got him in the back. The inner oarsmen didn't have their oars pulled up, so they got thrown into the water when the oncoming boat rode over their oars.

"The sauvetage boat got there right away to haul the jouster up. . . . He was dangling deep in the water by a line from his bob that was floatin' in the water—that's part of the humiliation of losing. When they pulled him up he was sputtering and swearing a slew of words most of us ain't never heard before, or since. The half empty boat came to a clumsy stop, since it was missin' half its oarsmen.

"Everyone on shore was dead silent. Pretty soon they began to chuckle, then to *hee hee*, and then finally, the entire crowd erupted in an big cheer. It was brilliant."

Fair teased, "I didn't think you were capable of such heartless torture, Fella Doon."

He got a sneaky look on his face and quietly said, "You ain't gonna guess who the pompous jouster was on our doomed boat."

Fair had no idea, so she shrugged her shoulders. Fella Doon laughed and said, "I'll give you a clue. He come from a *neighboring* town. Quite a strapping young hoomin. Big jowly cheeks. Even then."

Fair's eyes grew wide and she said, "Harrold King?"

"The very one," winked Fella Doon.

Today's match had a much different tone than the one Fella Doon had described. The usual large crowd was there on the lawn, waiting for the Joust and Dangle to begin; however, Harrold King permitted no food or blankets to sit on, like in old times.

Hoomin who had been there quite some time shifted from one foot to the other as they stood and talked. Every once in a while they looked out towards the lake to see if anything was happening. There was only one jousting boat.

Greetings Lookwell. I'm calling on you and your
friends to speak for your Hearing Lost host.
Are you ready?

Yes, Liver. Did you see what happened
back at the tree?
I could hardly breathe, my heart was so aflutter.

Yes, I saw. What will be, will be.
For now, I need you to recount the events
of the Joust and Dangle, if you will.

Yes, but . . .

Now, now Lookwell . . .

Yes, I know.
Focus.
Of course, of course.

29 : The Joust and Dangle

n the boat house, two Protectors made last-minute patches in a spot on Tooli's boat. They spoke quickly, since they knew Harrold King was impatient for the Joust and Dangle to begin.

One of them said, "This is going to be a good one. Tooli and Axum have had it out for each other since they were little. This isn't going to be a picnic."

The other one said, "Out for each other? I'd say it's been pretty one-sided."

This was true. The two brothers were as different as fire and water. Axum was the fiery one. Tooli was the water. He was the first-born twin, and Axum resented him for it.

One of the Protectors ran his fingers around a splintered hole in the side of the hull and said, "Where in the blazes do you think it came from? I checked the boat last night and it was fine."

The other said, "All I can say is I'm glad Axum is riding on the other boat. He'd be ornery for a shoomin about having a bum boat." He paused and added with a laugh, "You heard about his father all those years back, I'm sure."

The largest one of the two Protectors chuckled. "Who don't know! Wish I'd been there to see it." He smeared a blob of sticky pitch on a small sheet of wood and said, "Let's get this last bit glued down and held fast." He pressed the wood patch into place. The pitch smelled like pine.

Cat tongues of water lapped at the stone wall that formed three sides of the open cave. The two Protectors lowered the boat, first making sure all the oars were there. They hopped in, gave a loud birdie sort of whistle through their fingers and shoved off.

A bigger, more maneuverable conveyance boat met them at the mouth of the cave. Tooli King sat at the prow, holding his helmet on his lap. They tied their long, skinny boat to that one, and hopped on. They slapped Tooli on the back in a friendly way. He was trying not to smile.

Inside he thought to himself, *Axum's so desperate, it's almost funny.* He turned around and gave a wide smile. "Truboo?" Everyone on the boat understood the way he spoke. One hoomin pointed and mouthed, "A bit of trouble: hole."

Tooli looked at the sleek boat trailing behind them. That was the boat he'd be riding on. He craned his neck to have a look at the patch and winked. "Hmmm. I wondah how *dat* got dere." Tooli knew what his brother was capable of doing to win, and it didn't bother him in the least.

"Ledd's go!" he hollered, pounding the sides of the big boat with his palm. The oarsmen on his boat gave a holler and began to row. At the sight of the two boats emerging from the cave the crowd gave a cheer.

While the boat Protectors grew busy repairing the damaged jousting boat, Axum grew more and more agitated in his conveyance boat. He'd had plenty of time to get ready. He'd had his father send Tooli away to do the menial work of collecting payment at the gate. This was supposed to put Tooli at a disadvantage since he wouldn't have time to prepare mentally.

Axum slammed his armored helmet down on his sheath-protected legs. He was sweaty and hot from being in the sun so long. "Come on! This is infuriating. What in the Graves is taking them so long?" He growled, "Tooli is going down." His eyes had narrowed to slits, and his upper lip rose to meet his nose in a bitter sneer.

Axum's jaw was wide and square. His face had a remarkable toughness to it. His eyes were black and piercing, and his nose was remarkably large. His mouth was straight and his lips had sharp edges. The words that came out of his mouth had a similarly sharp razor edge to them as they slid past the portals of their tough and fleshy guardians.

The crowd grew silent as the conveyance boats pulled up alongside the ready and waiting jousting boats. The oarsmen hopped in, then waited. They turned their gaze towards the balcony.

Each brother was rowed as close as possible to the edge of his perch at the front of the jousting boat. Axum and Tooli each clanked and lumbered aboard their boats and stood at the ready on the prow. They eyed each other through the narrow slits of their masks.

Tooli always thought the Joust and Dangle was an idiotic game. He wondered as he stood there just who had thought up the idea of having someone stand on the narrow prow of a boat in a suit of heavy armor with the risk of being jousted overboard, only to dangle far beneath the lake's surface by a rope around his foot.

He laughed and said in muffled tones, "Dis is doopid!" He knew that although he was smaller than his brother, he was quick and strong. He also believed he was fighting for a cause that filled him with strength beyond his own. Tooli knew if Axum took the throne, Axum would be meaner than their father was, and Tooli couldn't let that happen.

In preparation for this moment, over the course of several months he had practiced holding his breath for longer and longer periods of time. He could hold his breath for a greater amount of time than any cook or servant he talked into competing with him.

The rower behind him looked past Tooli for a good look at Axum's boat. It was far away on the water's horizon. He tapped Tooli on his armor to get him to turn around. "He's out for blood, Master Tooli. I don't have a good feeling about this." To make sure Tooli understood, he slid his finger across this throat.

Tooli said, "Ah know. Ah be carefoo." He would be careful.

On the other side, Axum eyed his brother's boat. He stood like a statue. From the servant's gossip, Tooli knew their father had been pressuring Axum the past few days about the Joust and Dangle. Harrold King was afraid his rule might be coming to an end, due to the prophecy.

Axum's voice echoed through his helmet, "Tooli's been the thorn in my side since we were in our mother's belly. He was not born to rule. I was." There was silence behind him.

"Right?" he bellowed through his mask.

"Right, Master Axum," echoed a few, reluctant voices.

"When I say, 'row,' you row like your life depends on it. Is that understood?"

"Yes, Master Axum."

He said it as though he actually meant it and would do something about it if they failed.

Harrold King stepped out on the balcony, and a sudden hush came over the crowd. Both brothers put on their helmets and slid their face masks down with a metallic clang. He clapped his hands together in punctuated rhythm.

Clap clap—clap clap clap!

The crowd returned the royal clap with the same *Clap clap—clap clap clap!* It was one of the few ways he could get the hoomin of Cloven Grave to applaud in his presence.

Harrold King's mouth boomed, "Good citizens of Cloven Grave." He held his hands behind him, which made his belly pop out. One of his Protectors placed a megaphone up to Harrold King's mouth. "Before we begin today's Joust and Dangle, hear the following law set forth in the Cries Unia."

A hoomin in a colorful robe and tall satin headdress walked up to the megaphone and unrolled a scroll. He read, "According to a recent law by the court of Cloven Grave, the victor will stand in line as the successor to his father's throne, regardless of birth position. At the moment of victory he is to be given continued deference and respect. Any citizen guilty of any lack thereof shall be brought before the court and ordered to wear a mouth muzzle. This shall be posted hereafter on the Cries Unia so there is no room for misunderstanding."

He rolled up the scroll, bowed, and stepped back. Harrold King stepped forward. He held up a bright red scarf. He let it fall off the balcony into the water below. Time drifted in slow motion as the scarf danced through the air to its watery appointment.

30 : Winners and Losers

arrold King dropped the red scarf from the balcony. It floated down through the air like a bright red leaf, enjoying its approaching mirror image in the still water below. It landed upon its reflection in a soft, petal-like caress.

That was the signal.

"Down!" shouted Axum. "Don!" bellowed Tooli.

At the command, the oarsmen lowered their oars and began to row with such furious strength that their shining muscles ripped and bulged with the effort. The caller in the back of each craft rhythmically called, "Pull! Pull! Pull!"

Both boats neared each other with astonishing speed.

Axum and Tooli prepared themselves as best they could with a firm stance upon the prow of their narrow crafts. They eyed one another through their masks and adjusted the aim of their long jousts as they zoomed towards each other.

When they were four boat lengths away, the caller at the back of each boat shouted, "Pull in!" The inner oarsmen pulled their oars in with quick precision so that the boats could slide right past each other immediately.

Each joust was aimed for the other's chest.

The boats were a hair's length apart.

Perhaps it was due to all the wrestling Tooli enjoyed out in the fields, or perhaps it was due to an inspired impulse, but he stooped to one knee as he gave a thrust with his joust, landing a perfect jab to Axum's chest.

Axum's joust made a futile pierce into the air where Tooli had stood.

Axum went sailing overboard. The line around his ankle followed him like a hungry worm with a belly ache. A floating bob was attached to the end of it from which Axum would dangle. The bob disappeared from sight as it went under the water then popped back up instantly, as though it were its loyal and royal duty.

Instantly, an enormously wide sauvetage boat shot into action. It went right to the bob. A few hoomin grabbed it out of the water and latched it to a crane of sorts. The jousting boats glided to a stop, far distant from the dangling loser.

A group of hoomin stood at the ready. Their white-knuckled hands gripped the handle attached to the gear that would raise the line—and Axum—from the water.

As soon as one of the hoomin gave the signal with a drop of his arm, the hoomin holding the crank flew into action, cranking it as though their lives were at stake if they failed.

Harrold King had made it clear that if they made any error or caused the dangler any undue delay, they would find themselves taken to the middle of Lakinren Bae, dropped over the edge of the boat by a line and bob—and no one would retrieve their lifeless bodies until sunset.

Axum hung upside down far beneath the water's surface. He removed his helmet and let it drop. His hair loosened and swished in the murky water like sea grass. His eyes were shut tight.

Instead of holding his breath to await his rescue, he yelled like a wee hoomin who had found a sweetie taken from his mouth by another wee hoomin. Bubbles erupted from his open mouth like a school of shining white fish, darting past his chest, then his legs, finally popping on the water's surface next to the bob.

He had not figured on losing.

Tooli ordered his crew to turn his boat around. Concern was written across the lines of his face as he searched the waters depths beneath the bob. He asked them to row as near to the sauvetage boat as possible to make sure his brother was alright.

With an expectant crowd and two boatloads of hoomin holding their breath, the crane gave a jump. The line jerked taut and a loose-faced and unconscious Axum rose from the water like an overplayed fish. Water poured out of his armor.

They wheeled the crane around and the crew lowered his body onto the deck to revive him. Hopefully. From shore, the awaiting crowd watched for one of the crew to raise the flag. They sat in silence.

There on the deck, the crew loosened his armor then slipped it off Axum's limbs. They turned him over onto his belly and began to push on his back. A gush of water came out of his mouth and they all grew still.

From where Tooli stood on the prow of his boat, he began to realize what had happened. He gripped his helmet against his chest. His jaw clenched and his lips pressed against his teeth. "No. It can't be. Oh please," he whispered.

There was a barely perceptible movement in the water followed by a gust of wind as though the water had heard his heartfelt wish.

Axum's eyelids fluttered and he gave a weak cough.

One of the hoomin hollered, "He's come right!"

The crew exploded in relief and rushed to raise the flag, and call over to Tooli, who gave a barely visible smile. He dropped his head to his chest and seemed barely conscious of anything except his own relieved grief.

Axum had been born with a strong constitution. It took no time at all to revive him after that. When his eyes opened completely a hoomin rolled him over onto his back and said, "Master Axum, you had a good blow."

Axum stared at the hoomin like he was ready to kill him, then shoved him out of the way and convulsed to his feet like a cat. He looked around and saw Tooli standing on the prow of the jousting boat not five feet from the edge of the sauvetage boat's stern. He bent his knees, gripped his fists at the sides of his waist, gave a yell and took off at a drunken run. He leaped over the water and pounded his full weight into Tooli, who looked up just in time to see his brother come sailing through the air right towards him. He filled his lungs with as much air as he could. Then he felt Axum slam into his ribs.

The two of them plunged through the water's surface. Axum immediately lost the grip on his brother, for the weight of Tooli's armor was going in one direction and one direction only. Down.

Axum kicked against the water in the desperate urge for air. The line burned his arm as it followed Tooli with painful speed.

Both crews were filled with disbelief and dismay. They all hoped that Tooli would come off victor. Everyone knew Harrold King wanted Axum to follow in his own footsteps. But he was the younger brother, and Tooli was in his way.

Axum popped to the surface just as the bob slammed into the water and went under. With a flick of his wild, wet hair he sputtered the words, "There. Served him right." He grabbed a hold of the ladder on the edge of the sauvetage boat and began to climb.

The crew had been frozen by the unexpected turn of events. At seeing Axum, they scurried and fell over each other in an attempt to grab Tooli's bob and get it notched into place on the crane's line.

Once done, the hoomin began to pull against the handle, setting the gear to turning. The line grew taught and they began to pull with ardor and hope.

Axum sat on the edge of the boat and dangled his feet in the water. He lazily mumbled, "Hurry, hoomin. Pull. Pull."

They were angry at his nonchalance and pulled all the harder.

Suddenly the crane jumped and the line gave a good tight snap. Just as suddenly the line drew slack and it whipped up like an angry snake, writhing and flipping. Its jagged mouth was the end of a partially severed line. Axum slipped a knife into its sheath on his thigh.

"God of the Graves!" several of them shouted.

Axum yawned. "Save him. Save him please." He looked over the edge of the sauvetage boat into the water's depths, then he lay back and stared at the blue sky.

Two hoomin jumped in. Soon they came up coughing and spewing water out of their mouths. Their shouts spoke of frustrated and heartfelt futility.

In the depths of Lakinren Bae, Tooli King dropped like a stone. His attempt to fight his way up to the surface by kicking and pulling with his cupped hands had proved fruitless against the weight of his armor.

Within seconds, the water around him grew darker and murkier. As Tooli looked up, he saw the glowing surface of the water shrink to darkness. The pain of daggers stabbed his ears.

At that moment, he felt a silence quieter than he had ever known. In that silence was a single thought, closer to him than deafness. *I am part of something much greater than myself.* The silence deepened into his soul until it came out the other side, enveloping him completely. It was so peaceful to him that the whisper of a smile formed upon his face.

Soon, his barrel-chested reserve of air diminished. A small string of pearl-like bubbles emerged through his slightly parted lips. His eyes began to roll back as his mouth formed a shape.

With one, final bubble escaping, he weakly spoke the word, "Fair." Then, his body slammed into something hard. Something that moved. Something that closed its mouth around him. It spoke to his fainting mind, "Do not be afraid."

Well done, Dimbelly. Your job is complete.
I shall speak from fair's throat once again.

I am so glad, because I think I'm about to cry.

31 : An Unexpected Outcome

ella Doon slumped down onto the ground in their hiding place in the woodßs. His eyes glazed over. Tooli was gone.

Fair and the three other matternots appeared equally stunned by the turn of events.

They sat in silence for a long, long time. Fair imagined the dark, falling helplessness Tooli must have felt. An ember of anger burned into her chest and she crawled over to Fella Doon.

"Why did you bring us here to see this? Why?"

Fella Doon grabbed her fists. She had been pounding him in the chest without knowing it. "I'm so sorry. I didn't know it was going to end like this. I just wanted you to know."

"Know what?"

"Harrold King did the same thing to your grandfather when he was king."

Fair pulled back from him and settled down. "I know. He told me."

Fella Doon looked surprised.

Hale looked shocked. "Our grandfather? Why him?" Fella Doon told them the story of their heritage and how their grandfather had been king when Harrold King took over Cloven Grave.

Hale looked thoughtful. "So . . . so that means our father was next in line?"

"Your father was next in line."

Fair got a curious expression on her face. "Is that why . . . my last name. I mean, why my mother didn't tell me . . ."

"Yes."

"Why hasn't anyone ever told me?"

Fella Doon took a sudden interest in his hands, cleaning dirt from under his nails while he took time to think.

Fair couldn't believe what she'd heard. She said, "If our grandfather hadn't died after Harrold King came from Low Grave to rule, then our father would have been . . ."

"King," Hale finished.

Fair remembered the ancestors of her dream—how they were wearing crowns—and she understood.

Fella Doon looked at the matternots with grave seriousness and said, "You ain't to never to speak about this. There's lots of ears in Cloven Grave . . ."

A sudden image came into Fair's mind: a memory of her father bringing a basket of apples into the kitchen when she and her brother were small.

She tried to piece it all together in her mind. It didn't make sense. A hoomin of royal blood, humbly harvesting apples in the orchard and turning them over to Harrold King, who wasn't supposed to be there. Her father must have stood in line at another building—along with everyone else—to receive whatever was doled out to keep the family fed and clothed.

A respect for her father filled her soul that made her proud to be his daughter. Her heart pounded as she wondered to herself what happened to him. She felt a tightening in her chest as she thought of Harrold King. She bit her tongue and looked out at the water again, thinking of what she had just seen. Tooli was gone. He was the first boy hoomin she had spoken to in nine years. *He was almost my friend*, she thought.

Facing the truth about her family was something she hadn't wanted to do again. Not at a moment like this. She sat back on her heels and put her face in the cradle of her palms. She realized for the first time that her life was in serious danger. "How terribly dreadful. We've got to find a way to escape." Hale admitted he was thinking the same thing.

Fella Doon said, "The right moment will come, and it might be sooner than you think. But it's not now. Keep that turtle of patience with you a bit longer."

Hale said, "Why not now? We could just run away when it gets dark tonight."

"And Harrold King would make sure I'd never see my family again." Fella Doon looked out at the Jousting boats. They were being pulled back to shore. "I couldn't let that happen to them." Everyone in the hiding place knew Fair had to find Selador. They knew Fella Doon would do anything to help her escape—as long as his family wasn't left in the lurch.

Fair knew from experience that patience was something she was good at. She laid her head back on Sauveren's chest and said, "I can be a perfect turtle. It's the only way to get where I'm going."

Fella Doon tousled the mop of chopped hair on her head as he looked at the ground. He knew what she was thinking and said, "You'll find Selador. I know it."

On the balcony, Harrold King held up his hands and silenced the booing crowd. "The victory goes to my honored son, Axum King. Give him the deference and respect that you so willingly give me. You may go home now." He smiled and turned his back to them.

A few hoomin tore up clumps of soil and grass. They looked frustrated, as though they wanted to throw them but knew they couldn't—or shouldn't.

Fella Doon's small group stayed hidden until dusk, then headed back to the caves the same way they had come early that morning. On their way back, Fella Doon took Fair aside and said, "I need to warn you. It's your turn in the cage tonight."

Fair froze.

32 : A Small Discovery

 hat night, Fair lay on her mat while the mud of heavy dread filled her stomach. She missed her mother more than ever and wished she were there to protect her, or that Hale was close by so they could talk like they used to.

Or that Sauveren didn't have to stay at his post next to Pewgen Flype's desk right then. She tried holding her breath, but she couldn't concentrate enough to feel any sort of tingling in her finger.

Hale had told her earlier that day just how many matternots were in the caves. He said, "You remember that anthill we found once, and we took a stick and poked into it? . . . all those tunnels?"

She nodded and said, "There were as many ants as stars in the sky, almost."

"That's what it's like down here, Fair," Hale said. "Matternots that could fill the sky if they were stars."

It was hard for her to imagine being in an ant tunnel, let alone a matternot star in the company of countless other matternot stars spreading across the sky. *So many matternots. So much suffering,* she thought.

Someone touched her. It was Fella Doon. He was at her side, unlocking the bands around her ankles. Fair pulled her feet out of the bands and rubbed her legs.

He whispered, "The door is open. This is your chance. Call your dog to you when I nod my head. Don't listen to anything I say after that. When your dog comes, run. Just run. Go the way I told you and you should be able to get out of here."

When Fella Doon told her about the plan the day before, Fair hadn't thought of Hale, but now she wasn't sure she could leave without him. "Can my brother come, too?"

"No. He'll have to find his own way."

Fair felt incredibly sad inside but knew he was right.

Fella Doon looked over at Pewgen Flype, who was unlocking the cage. Fella Doon nodded to Fair.

She whistled as quietly as she could.

Sauveren's ears pricked and he looked back at Pewgen Flype. He quietly walked over to Fair.

Fella Doon said, "Up with you, you filthy rat!"

Pewgen Flype looked over his shoulder at Fella Doon and Fair, then turned back to the lock and key.

Fella Doon held her face in his hands and looked into her eyes. "Go. Now." He pretended to roughly pull her towards the center of the room. Fair yanked her arm free and took off running. Sauveren was right beside her and she took ahold of his collar.

"Through the door, Sauveren," she whispered. "Fast!" She kept hold of the collar, flung one leg over, and held on. She had grown much stronger from so much sunshine, food, and building that wall. His bouncing hurt her eyes.

Sauveren ran with Fair as though he were flying. She heard shouts behind them of, "Worthless One is getting away!"

Pewgen Flype turned around and said, "What's going on?"

Fella Doon yelled, "Get back here!"

Once in the hall, Fair told herself, *Long hall, turn left, then right and right again. Big doors to the outside.*

She guided Sauveren through winding corridors, until he came upon two closed doors in a long hallway. A dead end. *This isn't the way it was supposed to be,* Fair thought. She turned Sauveren around to find another way, just as a painting slid aside on the wall nearby. A door slid open behind where the painting had been.

Harrold King lumbered out, leaning on his scepter. His hair was wet. He had been in the Chamber of Mirrors.

"You!" he screamed, looking at Fair. "How did you get here?"

"I don't know where here is," Fair answered. She only knew she needed to get away, and she hoped they'd find a way out of Osden Shorn unseen.

He wrapped his meaty hand around one of Sauveren's ears as though it were a mouse he'd caught and squished. "Then you won't know how you got back to your nice little bed. What were you doing? Running away?" he said, and slowly pulled the girl and her dog back towards the caves.

"Yes, your Royal Emminency. I was running away."

After some time of swallowing the spit of disgust and rage Harrold King said, "At least you're an honest liar: a liar I'm going to keep right where you can't run away." He was thoughtful for a few minutes of pulling. Fair's head hurt. She said, "You don't need to drag me. I'm not going anywhere."

Harrold King let go. "Not anymore you're not. I've decided: I like to drink the juice from my vineyards and you will make it. All by yourself," he emphasized. "You are going to squish my grapes from now on. And sometimes the squishers just *woops!* slip under and don't come up if I leave them there long enough. Besides, I'm having a very big party next shobbasim—we'll need more than ever. My, my, you have a lot of work to do."

He repeated himself again, "All by yourself. And you'll have your very own special Protector to keep watch. I'll be able to see you from the throne room any time I want to have a peek at how my drink is coming along. . . . You'll like that, won't you?" He finished with a tone that indicated that she had better like it, or else.

Fair didn't answer.

Harrold King led Sauveren and Fair up and down hallways with a great deal of grunting, panting, and waddling until she didn't know where she was. Sauveren followed right behind.

"I didn't know you could walk, your Majesty."

"I take this one little walk every day," he huffed. He took her back to the cave himself and flung the door open with a smashing of wood.

"Pewgen Flype!" he yelled, clutching his chest, breathless with his great effort of the day.

Pewgen Flype ran up and bowed with his palms on his thighs. "Supreme Lawgiver," he groveled.

"What's the meaning of letting these dogs get loose?" asked Harrold King.

"Sir, she . . ."

"You are removed from your post as of this moment. You shall keep watch in the courtyard of the wine press. You are now in charge of one matternot, and one matternot only. No more. No less. Or is this too much for you?"

"Oh, no sir, most respected king. Who is it?" He cast a glance at Fair.

Harrold King pushed her towards Pewgen Flype and said, "Need you ask?"

A long, slow grin spread across Pewgen Flype's face and he said, "I'll do my best."

Fair sucked in a lungful of hope mixed with sadness. She wasn't going to have to stay in the caves any longer. But as she looked around at the matternots she wished they didn't have to stay behind. She looked for her brother and caught his eye. She mouthed, "Tell them the story."

He looked at her mouth and shrugged his shoulders, showing he hadn't understood. Fair tried one more time, "Tell them . . ."

Harrold King looked at Fair and said, "Do you have something you'd like to tell all of us here?" She shook her head. He said, "No, really. I'd like to hear it."

"I was just saying, 'Tell them the story.'"

"What story? You're as crazy as the Woolly."

Fair hummed a few notes from the tune to her father's music box. The tune she had put words to while working on the wall. She snuck glances at Hale, the boy, and Fidavine Belle. They looked at each other with knowing glances.

Harrold King rolled his eyes at her humming and said, "Oh, and Pewgen . . ."

Pewgen looked at Harrold King. "She'll sleep in the courtyard. She is not to associate with the other matternots. I hear she has a friend. You're a failure to have allowed such fraternizing. You'll report to me after even meal where you can wash my feet, then return to the cave."

Fair breathed a sigh of relief.

"What about Worthless One?" Pewgen Flype indicated with his head.

"The night watch will be in charge of her, until you return to your post every morning."

Pewgen gritted his teeth and kicked his heels together, *kak, kak*. "Understood."

Harrold King turned to leave. "Oh, and Pewgen, don't let her rest until the juice is up to her thighs. Now get me out of here, Flype. You will tend to my feet. They are on fire."

Pewgen Flype grabbed Fair by the wrist and looked around the cave. "Fella Doon! You're in charge until I return!"

"Sir!" Fella Doon said with the sound of a hard-stomached Protector. He kicked his heels together, *kak! kak!* as Pewgen Flype disappeared out the door with Fair and Harrold King.

Fair knew Hale would be alright with Fella Doon in charge, but Hale feared for his sister. He felt helpless in being able to stop it all.

As soon as Harrold King and Pewgen Flype were out the door with Fair in tow, Fella Doon turned to Hale and said, "Lisper, you're in charge until I get back."

"But where are you . . ."

Fella Doon ignored his young friend. He unlocked the door that led to the quarry and disappeared. Several hours passed and soon his head poked through the door. He had someone with him.

It was the Woolly. He had pulled a cartload of food and jugs of milk from Lamb's Tavern behind him.

The wee hoomin gave a loud shout and Fella Doon immediately shushed them. "Not too loud, or we'll be found out."

Hale said, "But what about all the other wee hoomin in the other chambers?"

"Not to worry my good fellow. Not to worry."

At that, he turned and snapped his fingers at the door to the quarry tunnel, and in paraded all of the tavern's cooks and helpers with what seemed like an endless supply of food.

While the food was passed out and the wee hoomin were busy feasting and gorging, the Woolly filled a mug with fizzy milk and toasted, "Drinkwater bound!" The matternots smiled. Some of them remembered the long forgotten words and echoed, "Drinkwater bound!"

He whispered to Fella Doon, "Sneak 'em out and hide 'em."

"With so many, there's no place to hide 'em without being found out. We wouldn't want 'em to take a punishing when they got dragged back, now would we?"

The Woolly shook his head. By even meal, every last trace was gone that anything out of the ordinary had happened that afternoon.

33 : Treading Grapes

 ewgen Flype gently let Fair down into a round, wooden vat filled with plump, purple grapes.

He looked over his shoulder to make sure he wasn't in any trouble. Harrold King had ordered that she be treated carefully—the same Harrold King that had her thrown into the quarry pool.

There, up in a window, Fair could see his silhouette. Watching her. It felt creepy.

Harrold King told him, "I want my wine to be clean. You shall not whip her, beat her or do anything to draw blood. *She* must be clean in order that the grapes and juice be clean. If you whip her, you shall receive not one, but two whippings yourself. If you beat her, you shall receive not two, but three beatings. And if you draw blood, you shall be stoned."

A sneer of delight passed over Pewgen Flype's face.

The day was bright. Fair had spent the Longlightren Dons building walls. They had come to a close by now, and the days were growing shorter. There was a crispness in the air that turned Fair's breath into steam every time she breathed. A gentle mist rose from the grapes.

Pewgen Flype wore a long burgundy wool cape to stay warm. "There's a rope hanging down in front of you. That's so's you can hang from it when you're too weak to stand up. The Harrold didn't say nothing about me having to feed you."

Fair leaned against the side of the vat and held on to the rim. She turned and said, "I'm going to escape, Pewgen Flype. You can't stop me."

"Oh, Can't I now?"

"No. You can't."

"What. Do you think your dog is going to save you? Only the Harrold has that kind of power. But . . . oh . . . I forgot," he mocked, "Harrold King *put* you here!" He laughed hard at his own joke, and steam came out of his mouth.

Fair grabbed ahold of the rope. The grapes felt lumpy and strange under her feet, around her ankles, and legs. She pulled the rope against her chest and pressed her cheek against it. She looked into the grapes as if she were trying to read a book, unable to make out the letters. *I'm not supposed to be here. This isn't the way it's supposed to be*, she thought. She squeezed her eyes shut and realized they still hurt from her fall on the platform of punishment.

Pewgen Flype found a stool against one of the many pillars that formed the squarish shape of the three-sided courtyard. The open side was fenced with a brick wall and black iron gate that looked out on the vineyards beyond. The pillars around the edge of the courtyard held up rafters that formed a covered walkway, and there were several doors that led into various parts of Osden Shorn.

"Lift your feet!" he shouted to Fair from where he sat. "Is it that hard?" He looked at Sauveren, patted his knees with his hands, and said, "Come here, dog."

Sauveren padded over to Pewgen Flype and sat down. His tongue hung out the side of his mouth, and he stared at him. Pewgen unlatched the clasp from his cape.

"Leave him alone," Fair said.

"Listen to that worm. She thinks you're better than Harrold King himself." He tied a blanket around the dog's neck. A Protector strode across the courtyard and Pewgen Flype shouted, "Hey, come lookee here! Look at this dog! Who does he remind you of?"

The Protector walked over and spit on the dog. "That one's for the Harrold," then he gave him a kick. Fair heard Sauveren grunt when the foot met his ribs. Pewgen Flype made the dog stand on his hind legs. "Let's dance," he laughed.

"Stop it!" she said. She felt helpless as she watched them make fun of her dog. Her friend. Her companion and protector all those years.

"Lift your feet!" Pewgen answered.

She began to lift one knee, then the other. These were the first steps of thousands she would soon take. Steps that took her nowhere but the very same spot. From a window high above, the shape of Harrold King loomed like a black eye . . . still watching.

In the next few chapters of the story,
Fair won't always be present,
and so I, Liver, cannot tell the story.
I have called upon several other Secret Speakers
to tell what they see from the throats of their hosts.

34 : Final Preparations

hat afternoon in the sculptor's studio, the statue of Harrold King neared completion. Harrold King was carried on his platform into the chalky-white air of the room to make final inspections.

He took a severely critical look at the statue and said to the sculptor, "Well, it's better work than I thought you were capable of, but still not as good as it could have been. It will have to do."

The sculptor stuck out his tongue. Harrold King was behind his back. He pulled a few more faces and kept working.

"You don't deserve payment for your work, hoomin. It's inferior. But, as I said, it will have to do . . . deliver it to the throne room this afternoon. The banquet begins at Fifthren Hour. Sharp."

Not long after, Harrold King sat on his throne as a constant stream of hoomin came and went into the great hall. They bore platters of food, piles of fruits and nuts, towers of cakes and pastries, and candelabras.

"Where is the wine?"

"It's coming, your eminent and royal highness," answered a tall bearded hoomin with sunken cheeks.

"And the maiden . . . is she still treading, Salloroc?" Harrold King hoped that Fair would weary herself from tromping, and if she fell, why then, what a pity she wouldn't be able to get up. If he couldn't snatch the Ruby Eye from her while she was living, perhaps he could retrieve it from her lifeless frame when he couldn't be shocked. Rithel had assured him that her friends, Gibber Will, Azanamer, and the Woolly had returned to their homes and habitats after the castle disappeared around them and that they had no idea what had happened to her.

"Yes, your Majesty. She's still treading. She can barely lift her knees."

To himself he thought, *Good. She'll be dead by morning and the throne will still be mine.* He asked Salloroc, "How high is the juice?"

"Up to her thighs. Shall I have it drained out for tonight's banquet?"

"What for? We have plenty . . . and where is my son?"

Salloroc groveled, "He went hunting this morning, and I've sent out my hoomin to look for him. He hasn't returned."

"Well, he had better be here. He's unveiling my statue after dessert."

A queue of purple-robed hoomin strode through the doors at the back of the hall. Harrold King said, "Ahh. Here comes the choir . . ." He cleared his throat and ordered, "Come here. I want to hear you sing. You shall make a sound that is sublime, heavenly and beautiful. If it is not, you will be sent out on the jousting boats immediately. I have no patience for imperfection."

They stood before him, and he laced his fingers across his belly. He cleared his throat some more and said, "Now. Sing me something peaceful."

The choir arranged themselves and waited for the conductor to begin.

Harrold King folded his arms, closed his eyes and said, "Well? I'm waiting."

The choir began to sing a song that sounded like water flowing between grassy banks, almost like a lullaby.

35 : Something Peaceful

ewgen Flype stood in the courtyard, looking at the sky. The night watch walked up to him and said, "Fella Doon is waiting for you to give him the report."

"Why not the Harrold?"

The Protector said, "He's having his big party. Full up with revelry."

"That's tonight? I don't know which day is which out here."

Pewgen Flype looked up and saw no trace of Harrold King at the window. He gave Fair a smack on the back of the head before he left. She held onto the rope, nearly unconscious with fatigue. She didn't even notice the swat. She could barely lift her legs, but they were moving enough to convince the Protectors that she was getting the job done.

On the other side of Osden Shorn a long line of carriages from faraway lands pulled up to the large front doors. Finely dressed hoomin emerged from their interiors, looking as important and wealthy as they could. Harrold King had spared no expense for this banquet, and the invitations they carried were painted in gold ink on black paper. His red wax seal stuck to the bottom of the page which held down a ribbon of woven gold thread.

As they entered, their names were announced by a Protector who wore a black cap with a white plume. It took nearly an hour for everyone to be announced. Harrold King was nowhere to be seen.

Once everyone was seated and looking around for him, a dozen hoomin stepped forward at the head of the hall on both sides of the throne. They put long horns to their lips and began to blow. It was the same *Brah, brah, brah-brah-brah* heard through Cloven Grave every morning, and the sound now announced the entrance of Harrold King.

Fair lifted her head and listened.

The back doors opened. Salloroc stepped through the door and solemnly spoke, "All arise!" All present stood in a loud *whoosh*.

Harrold King was carried in on his velvet platform. He looked from side to side and waved at nobody in particular. His servants were dressed in shiny red silks and golden shoes. Their heads were covered in turbans made from yards and yards of shiny bands woven over and over until they looked like beehives made of gold.

The room burst into applause as Harrold King was carried to his throne. Once seated, he held up his hands, but the applause continued.

He said, "Please, please . . . don't . . . stop." He laughed.

Once he was thoroughly stuffed with a sense monstrous humility he called out a little more loudly,

"Thank you! Thank you! Please be seated!" He looked at the center of the hall. A large mysterious shape filled the space there. It was covered by white canvas.

All sat down.

"Let the feasting begin!" He took the first bite and everyone followed.

Salloroc left his place by the entrance and crossed the hall while everyone ate and laughed, toasted one another, and gorged themselves on turkey legs and mutton, chewy breads, and wine. He leaned into Harrold King's ear. Harrold King became annoyed. "What is it?"

"Another tree writing, your Highness." Salloroc held out a scroll of paper.

"Not now."

"You'll regret it if you don't read it now."

Harrold King grunted and bit into a turkey leg. "I don't want to read it. Tell me what it says."

Salloroc gulped and read, "To His Majesty Harrold King."

"Go on . . ."

Soon the temple walls shall rumble.
The false king soon shall kneel most humble
To the one true ruler, the one true king
For whom Cloven Grave his praises sing.

Harrold King said, "Pay it no mind. The tree writings, my dreams . . . they mean nothing to me any more. Look at all this!" He swept the candle-lit room with the turkey leg in his hand.

As the air cooled outside, Fair stirred slightly when she heard a faint but heavenly sound fill the air. Inside, the choir had begun to sing. Inside, the room glowed with candlelight. The space felt almost sacred. The music was so holy that tears glistened in the torchlight as they streaked down her grape-stained cheeks.

36 : A Guard Stands Watch

he sun was just beginning to set. Fair continued with her lonely business of treading grapes.

Rows of soft reds, oranges, and pale yellows sat above the horizon. The sky wore different colored robes and waited like an audience for the moon to appear.

As the sounds of the choir faded a nearly full moon began to peek over the hillsides of Cloven Grave. The air in the courtyard took on a bluish hue, almost as though it had been left alone, far from anything warm, or kind, or beautiful.

Pewgen Flype had left, and now the night Protector leaned with his back against a pillar. His dusty boots were stretched out in front of him with his legs crossed. He hadn't bothered to check how deep the juice was getting in the vat. He seemed content to just sit where he was. Mostly.

Just then, an idea seemed to pop into the Protector's head, because he kicked his heel against the earth and stood up from his stool in the corner, taking a glance at the wine vat and the girl situated in dead center. He yawned, gave a good stretch and looked at Sauveren, who lay near his feet. Sauveren's legs twitched while he dreamt.

To make sure the dog was sleeping he whispered, "Whatcha chasing, big fella?" Sauveren made no move to show he had heard him.

The Protector watched Fair's knees bob up and down as she held onto the rope suspended from a beam. He was satisfied she was just going to keep doing more of the same.

Her eyes were closed.

He said to the sleeping dog, "The maiden don't never cause me no trouble."

With a slightly sneaky look, he studied the courtyard and a smile formed on his face. He crossed his arms over his belly and stroked his stubby beard with one hand.

He strode with a pretended air of importance over to the cast-iron gate. He casually peeked through it to find any sign of movement out of the corner of his eyes. Seeing no one, he turned back and strode just as importantly across the courtyard again—looking serious just in case he needed to look busy and guardish. He strode past the vat where Fair quietly squished grapes in between her toes, then past his station at the stool. He kept going. He calmly walked through an open doorway glowing with orange light that led into one of the many hallways of Osden Shorn.

When the Protector's footsteps grew silent, Sauveren opened his eyes and seemed to take an interest in watching Fair.

Taking a torch off its sconce on the stone wall in the hallway, the Protector looked behind him one last time. Seeing no one, he gave a shiver of glee and licked his lips. He then slipped like a whisper down a spiraling staircase to the left. As he wound his way down, the light and shadow of his solitary journey cast dancing shadows on the smooth curve of the walls.

At the base of the stairs, he held the torch up this way and that. Then satisfied that he knew where he was, he found a room that smelled of wood, and dust, and dirt.

"Here we are, me poor taste buds," he said. He found a dry torch in its place on a wall and lit it with the torch in his hand. He lit a few more. Before him and stretching for what seemed like ages. The spreading light of the torches revealed a long wall of dusty bottles lying on their sides on carved wooden shelves held up by carved wooden poles painted to look like candlesticks in what was now a faded peeling gold. He held the torchlight close to get a better look.

He stood up straight and said, "And now as to what I come for," he chortled. "I'm just as deserving as the Harrold himself, and I work a grunt of a lot harder than his Big Jiggleness."

He walked down the long, narrow winery until he got to the end of it. He slipped a dusty bottle out of its curved holding on the shelf and held the torch up to it.

"I'm sorry Harrold, sir," he smiled. "I just couldn't help meeself!" His shoulders shook with stifled laughter.

"I didn't think you'd miss it! I . . . I only had meeself a little sippie poo . . . Well, yes, one of the best and oldest ones of the lot, but I swear I didn't know no better! Jess slap me hands as a punishment."

His eyes glinted in the torchlight as he uncorked the lid with his brown teeth and had a taste. "Oh this is a good one!" he said with relish. "Slap me hands!" He pushed the cork back in the bottle and paused.

"Maybe just a bit more. I . . . ," he uncorked the bottle again and took another sip, ". . . really . . . ," he took another, ". . . am sorry." He began to guzzle. And before he knew it he had guzzled down the whole bottle and wiped his mouth on his sleeve.

When he finished, his eyes were round as though he had just realized something very important—and frightening—(which indeed he had). He hadn't meant to drink it all.

He belched loudly and said, "Oh my!" He wobbled a bit and slurred, "We'll just put this little boddle back in its spot and get up to my station to watch the little maiden. Quick like." He put the cork back in the bottle and clumsily slipped it into its spot. "There y'are, little lady."

Once at his stool he plopped himself down and called out to Fair, "Squeesh em, now. I khant letchew shtop till yer dunn, yuh noh. Eet needs to be up to yer hed, now. Step, step!" He had no idea what he was talking about.

By now, the pallor on Fair's cheeks was pale as chalk. She looked up as though she thought she had heard something. Then the words seemed to register in her mind.

She quietly said, "It's up to . . . my thighs . . . sir." But her words seemed to echo hollowly in the courtyard. Then she began to whimper, "Please, sir . . . let me . . . stop."

Sauveren opened one eye, and his eyebrow moved up as he looked over at the Protector. He closed it again and began to snore. The Protector fought to stay awake, but finally closed one eye. He tried hard to watch Fair with the other. It finally gave up and closed. Soon, the Protector was snoring more loudly than the dog. Sauveren immediately opened his eyes again. His tail began to thump the dusty ground beneath it.

Fair had been treading grapes since sunrise without having had a bite to eat all day, except what she could grab from the vat here and there. As she held onto the rope suspended from the wooden beam, she continued to lift one knee then the other, over and over. Over and over.

What went on in her mind throughout the day is hard to tell, for her mind was more tired than her body. Her delirious thoughts, if they could be seen, looked more like dry leaves shifting in the wind beneath a solitary tree on a lonesome hillside—first one being blown about and swirling briefly in the air, then another. One leaf did seem to get blown about more than the others, however. As it danced in the air Fair weakly whispered, as she licked her dry lips with long pauses between her words, "Sau . . . veren . . . Help . . . me." Her slender fingers absently felt for the Ruby Eye on her forehead. She lifted her knees up and down.

Not long after the Protector had dozed off, another one entered the courtyard and lit a torch on each of the stone pillars. The pillars held up a sort of covered hallway. He looked over at the feet of the sleeping Protector and assumed he was awake at his post, then he disappeared into the covered hallway and in through a door. To someone looking in on the scene, the place looked quite inviting in a cozy sort of way.

Without warning, one of Fair's knees gave way. She let go of the rope and blindly reached into the air to grab a hold of the side of the vat. But she reached out in the wrong direction. She fell to her knees. Her hand splatted onto the surface of the cold, lumpy liquid that surrounded her fallen figure and she found herself grabbing nothing but juice. Her nose was met by the deep, sweet fragrance of grapes. She knelt, lowered her head and stuck out her tongue to taste the meal that had been all around her the entire day. At the first taste she began to drink like a wild animal, unable to stop herself. She didn't even notice that no one was there to stop her.

While she ravenously drank and gulped what fruit she could, her dress grew wet and heavy just beneath the surface. After she had her fill of grapes and juice, Fair began to crawl. She kept her chin up so she could breathe, because the juice came right up to her neck as she moved straight ahead. She could feel the grapes brushing past her arms and making way for her with a soothing, sloshing sound. Her weary mind told her that if she kept crawling she would find the side of the vat so she could pull herself up again.

"I . . . am so . . . so tired," she whimpered. Memories and faces began to flutter around in her head.

"Mother," she cried out. The cry was no louder than the chirp of a bird. "Father . . . Hale."

She began to crawl along the bottom of the vat, trying hard to keep her head tilted up. She crawled straight ahead. She made it to the walls of the vat. She weakly clawed at the rough wood and eventually pulled herself up. She hung over the edge for a moment. With great and slow effort, she forced herself to stand, sure the Protector was going to reprimand her if she took too long.

She said, "I'm sorry. I . . . I didn't mean . . . to fall."

She was too delirious to realize that he would have done something by now. And so, she obediently turned around and took a step to begin pressing grapes again, feeling for the rope.

Everything looked dark.

The torches aren't burning in their sconces, she thought distantly. But they were burning.

At the first lift of her knee, she felt strength slip from her like a cloth pulled out of her soul. As though time itself had slowed down, Fair fell clumsily sideways, moving in a long, very slow dream. At that moment everything that followed seemed to take hours instead of the duration of a breath.

As Fair's body slowly fell, her head turned to the side and flopped around, limply. First one hip, then her shoulder, disappeared into the dark universe of the world she had waded in for so long. One of her arms hung limply as it slipped into the sleepy nectar. Fair felt the soothing embrace of the grapes that willingly moved aside to let her slide in among them. It all felt so welcome to her, and she felt a comforting peace come over her, as she let go of all the effort she had willed herself to put forth for so many hours. So many days.

A small, single thought swirled into Fair's mind as her cheek slid into the cool liquid slumber beneath her. It was another dry leaf that danced beneath that lonesome tree on that lonesome hillside. The leaf thought was the remembrance of a face. Fair felt a yearning to call out for help, for the face—those eyes—

that looked at her with such love. And they were above her dark liquid world. She wouldn't find it there.

She turned her face sideways before it went under. She pushed her chin up to speak one last time. The Ruby Eye began to glow. Its warmth spread through Fair like fire. And then, her small hand emerged from beneath the surface of what she knew would soon be her grave. She touched the Ruby Eye in a desperate effort and cried out in barely a whisper, "Help me, Sauveren!" The words bubbled and disappeared as her mouth went under.

The light of the torches glowed orange and warm and made the gently swaying grape juice shimmer like polished bubbled glass.

37 : Fair Disappears

he courtyard lay still for what seemed like hours, yet only a breath had passed.

Sauveren flew from his curled up resting place like a tree trunk hurled across a garden in a violent storm and landed to the side of the vat, where all now lay silent and still.

He stood up on his hind legs and hung his paws over the edge of the vat. He began to make little whimpering dog sounds. He solemnly licked his chops and watched the stillness before him.

Soon, a small glow of orange-red light began to grow within the vat. The dark, red-colored juice appeared to mound and boil, bubble and surge, and a voice resounded in the air. It seemed to belong to no one, for no one else was there. The voice was slow and deep, thunderous yet calm,

> *Purity of heart. Strength of mind.*
> *She who seeks shall also find.*
> *Eyes to see. Ears to hear.*
> *Look through me and to me*
> *And all will be clear.*

From the depths of the grapes and vines, a dark bubble emerged. Upon closer inspection, it appeared to be the back of Fair's shoulders. She began to rise up out of the vat like a mist. She was limp as a rag doll. The red liquid beneath her seemed to have taken on a life of its own, pushing upwards, pressing against the gentle burden that lay above it.

Soon, she lay draped over a melodious red fountain that formed a column beneath her. Fair's short hair lay against her cheeks, and grape juice cascaded off it like a waterfall. Juice dripped off her dress, the ends of her fingers, and toes.

Sauveren panted with that eternal smile on his face. His tongue peeked out just beneath his nose. He waited as the column moved closer and closer to him. It finally let Fair down gently until she was very close by.

He grabbed the shoulder of her dress with his teeth and pulled her as close to the edge of the vat as he could, using his paw to pull one of her arms over the edge. Then he gave another, firmer tug up and out, so that Fair's chest rested on the edge of the vat. He sat down on his haunches and looked up at this maiden he loved. The Ruby Eye glowed like an ember and shone on her face with the faintest light.

She hung there. Limp. A drop of grape juice hung from her eyelashes then fell onto Sauveren's nose. His pink tongue darted out and licked it clean. He chomped the air a bit.

Fair's shoulders suddenly jumped as a cough erupted, and she sucked in a lungful of air. She wearily opened her eyes. She didn't see anything, but was too tired to notice. If she had been able to see, she would have observed two black sparkling eyes staring up at her, a shining black nose, and a pink, panting tongue. Her dog gave a small bark.

"Sauveren." She slowly smiled.

"Here I am."

He spoke.

"You're here . . . ," she sighed, not even comprehending that her dog had spoken.

Back in the hall, the guests applauded wildly. Never had they heard such music. Such purity. Such peace coming from a choir of voices. Harrold King sat at his place at table, licking his fingers, exulting in the loud praise and exclamations being shouted by his guests. He felt as though it were he himself who had performed. He reached up and clapped his hands, and a servant appeared at his side.

"Dessert," Harrold King said, "Bring it out." The servant bowed and scurried away, backwards.

Harrold King turned to Salloroc and fumed, "Axum is still not here. I want him here to do the unveiling, right after dessert!"

"Yes, your royal eminency, I know. But he's nowhere to be found," Salloroc said, his voice cracking. He looked nervously around for a way to escape from his uncomfortable position, knowing there would not be one.

"Find him!" Harrold King commanded in a stifled breath, as he looked around at his guests and nodded with a smile.

Salloroc took a deep breath and began to blink rapidly. He gulped. "But what if he is not found?" He gulped again. "Your Highness."

Harrold King began to search the crowd of feasting guests as though he were searching for an answer. An idea seemed to strike him and his eyes lit up.

"The maiden . . . bring me the maiden!" he gloated.

"What . . . what maiden?" Salloroc questioned.

"You idiot. *The* maiden. That Zothiker!" His nostrils flared as he cocked his head to one side and smiled at his guests. He gave them all a delicate laugh then said between smiling teeth, "She is out there now, treading grapes. Go get her. Now. Drag her in if you have to. She's a weak, pathetic thing." He puffed out his chest, quite pleased at this new turn of events—due in fact, to his own brilliance.

He said, "Just think, a Zothiker to unveil my statue. How funny!" He rubbed his padded palms together. "A Zothiker!"

Salloroc stood at a doorway of the hall with two Protectors and gave them instructions. His long, bearded head and hollow, carved cheeks were tilted to the side. They leaned in so they could hear. One was tall and thin, the other one short and squatty. Soon they nodded and disappeared through a doorway.

They headed down the hall leading to the winepress courtyard. Their shadows grew and shrunk as they walked down the torchlit hallway.

"So what do we need to do?" one of them said. "Pour a bucket of cold water on the creature to clean her off?"

"Yeah. The Harrold don't want any grape juice traipsed all over his floors."

"She'll still be drippy from the water," the first one reasoned.

"That, I don't think he'll mind. You know—a bit of sport."

Back at the winepress Sauveren whispered, "I'm going to pull you out."

Fair said, "Who . . . are . . . you? I want my dog." She tried to whistle, but no sound came out.

"Just listen to me and all will be well," Sauveren assured her. "Now hold on with your arms and I'll reach down and gently grab one of your legs. No questions now."

"No questions . . . are the best . . . questions," she whispered automatically.

Sauveren said, "All questions are good. Just not right now. Now let's get you out of this vat."

"But the Protector . . . ," Fair protested. "He's . . ."

"Drunk," finished Sauveren.

Before she knew what was happening, Sauveren was up on his hind legs, pulling up on her thigh with the soft flesh of his muzzle. Soon, half of her hung inside the vat, and the other half hung out. Sauveren placed himself alongside the vat and quietly, but urgently said, "Now let yourself slide down onto my back. I will carry you."

Fair groped with her hand. "It's dark. I can't find you." A distant memory of the touch of Sauveren's muzzle when he was a puppy played in her mind. She had just felt it again.

Fair sleepily smiled and let herself drop, bit by bit until she realized with the pats and searching fingers of her free hand that she was lying on the back of her own dog.

"There you are, Sauveren." *My dog. He's here*, she thought.

She soon lay on his back like a weary rider headed for the comforts of home after a long, difficult trip. Speaking into the air she said, "Not the caves. I just want to rest. Sleep."

"Just reach into the pouch under my neck, Fair," he whispered, as he began to walk towards the iron gate.

She raised her head. The realization that her dog had spoken began to dawn on her.

"Wait. You're . . ."

"Sauveren?" he paused. "Yes. We have no time to lose . . . the pouch . . . find it."

"I can't see . . ."

"I know," Sauveren said. "I will be your eyes." The damage done when Fair fell on the platform of punishment had finally taken its toll.

Soon, he could feel Fair's gentle fingers fishing around in the fur beneath his neck. "A little further," he added.

"I've . . . got . . . it," she quietly triumphed. "You," she paused. "You can speak."

He ignored her and continued, "Good. Now, reach inside and you'll find a key."

She found the key.

"Now pull it out." He situated himself against the gate underneath the lock and said, "Reach away from my shoulder with the key in your hand, and you will feel cold iron bars. This is a gate."

She let go of the key and said, "I'm not leaving without Hale."

"If you stay you will die, Fair. Lisper will be alright."

"How do I know?" she whimpered.

"Just trust me. Follow your heart."

Her searching fingers found the key again and she grabbed it firmly. She knew what she had to do.

Sauveren said, "Now let your hand slide up the bars until you feel something wide and flat. This is the lock.

You will need to figure out how to put the key where it belongs so that you can twist it and open the gate."

Fair mumbled, "But how did you get the key?" Her eyes closed as she poked and prodded at the face of the lock, making a small, clinking sound.

"A sleeping Protector doesn't know when his keys are gone missing," he answered.

"There!" Fair perked up. "I've found it!"

"Now put the key in and give it a turn," Sauveren instructed.

The two Protectors strode through the doorway into the courtyard and looked at the vat. It was empty.

"Where is she?" the bigger Protector said.

"Maybe she's gone back down into the caves for a crumb . . ."

The other Protector pointed. "Over there, I ain't sure what I'm seeing, but it don't seem right." He pulled his bully stick out from his belt and said, "Hold on there, youse! How'd you get in here?" He took off at a run.

At the sound of the approaching Protector's shouts and footsteps, Fair's hand began to shake. She fumbled to find where to put the key in the lock.

"A little higher, Fair," Sauveren directed. The dark metal key clinked and scratched, poked and prodded until Sauveren said, "There!" Fair quickly thrust the key into its hole and turned it.

Sauveren calmly said, "Trust me, Fair. Hold onto me like you'll never let go."

"Give me strength," she whimpered.

He turned his head quickly around to look at her and said, "So let it be spoken. So let it be done."

Fair felt a surge of sweetness and force course through her veins. She swallowed and sunk her fingers into the fur under his neck. She grabbed fistfuls of it as Sauveren pushed the gate with his nose and flung it wide.

The bigger Protector turned around and kicked the sleeping Protector's foot. "Whatcha doing hoomin . . . they're getting away!" He gave a loud snort and raised his head, only to lower it again and keep sleeping.

The confused Protectors now took off at a run, and by the time they both got to the gate, Sauveren and Fair had disappeared into the night. Their galloping shadow appeared to float vaguely in the moonlight.

"Crikes! What do we do?" groaned the shorter, stocky Protector. "If we take chase, we ain't gonna catch the little beggar on that beast, and the Harrold will have our hides for not bringing her back."

"He'll clobber us for not chasing after them, too," the other one reasoned. "It stinks either way."

"Yeah, but I ain't gonna keep him waiting when he's so plum proud about that immortal life stone statue of his'n that he plans to show off tonight. I'll unveil it meeself if needs be."

"There ain't gonna be no unveiling tonight," the taller Protector solemnly said. "I ain't told you, but that maiden we was supposed to get just now . . . she's a Zothiker."

The other Protector's' eyes grew bigger and rounder as the growing realization took shape in his mind. "I ain't heard that name spoken since I was a wee hoomin. I thought they was all . . ." He made a slicing motion with his finger across his neck. "You know."

"Guess not."

With that, the two of them began to slowly walk with dread caution back to the Grand Hall. After a few heavy steps, the new terror of just how much this disappearance would threaten Harrold King—and them—sunk in, and they took off at a run.

"You tell him," one of the voices shouted, echoing in the long hall.

"No. You."

38 : A Small Detour

auveren ran with Fair on his back. Their only route of escape was the front gate. The only way to get to the front gate was alongside the castle wall. "But what about everyone down in the caves, Sauveren?" said Fair.

"I know. But you and I have a journey to take, Little Sparrow."

Fair wondered how he knew to call her that, then realized he had been paying attention all along, even when she was a small girl on her father's lap. When he would hold her close and whisper that name.

"But we . . . I won't . . ." she couldn't seem to find her words. Then she said, "I mean, I won't leave unless they can come, too."

Sauveren stopped running and turned around. He said, "You have a good heart. There is a way." He ran back the way they had just come, and he sniffed along the western wall until he came to a spot where it looked as though ivy grew out onto the ground. He pawed at the mass of viney shadows, revealing an opening in the wall. There was no door or gate, so they easily slipped through. He turned around and pulled the vines back into place with his paw.

"Still, now Fair. We are in a tunnel. Lie flat against my back so you don't hit your head."

The space grew lower and lower, and soon Fair could sense that the roof of the tunnel was just above her head. Sauveren began to lower himself and creep on all fours.

Soon, the space began to get a bit larger. Fair could smell the stink of the caves wafting up the tunnel. She said, "I don't like this place." They were nearing Pewgen Flype's cage.

"It's safe as long as I am with you."

They came to the barred door, and Sauveren blew on the latch. It unlocked with a flurry of powdery light and they entered the room.

Pewgen Flype fell over backwards in his chair at the sound. He did a series of flops and twists, until he was able to see where the sound came from. Hale saw Fair and Sauveren. He pulled at the chains around his ankles.

Pewgen Flype put his whistle to his mouth and was ready to blow when Sauveren said, "The tongue is undone. So let it be spoken, so let it be done." His voice was strong and powerful, yet quiet and comforting.

Pewgen Flype dropped the whistle. His eyes grew round as marbles. "What the . . . ?" he began. Then his mouth started to make strange shapes. He seemed to be trying to chew something or spit something out. It was hard to tell. Then he began to cough as though he were going to gag. His tongue dropped out of his mouth, plopped on the stone floor like a toad, and just sat there. Completely still.

He was so shocked that he put his chair back upright and sat in it, not quite sure what to do. He laced his fingers together and put them on his lap. Terrified.

"It is done," said Sauveren.

A little smile started to form on Fair's mouth. She hardly dared speak. "Did you stop him?"

"In a manner of speaking."

Fair took courage, "Send . . . send the lizards away, Sauveren. I mean, if you can. You can do that sort of thing, can't you?" The sound of grating sandpaper grew so loud that it was almost deafening. The lizards banded together and dared Sauveren to send them away.

"Yes, when it's a good wish." Then, with that same powerful, yet quiet voice, he said, "Lizards be gone, never more to return. So let it be spoken, so let it be done."

Sauveren began to growl as he paced the floor. A long, deep breath like a canyon wind began to blow out of his mouth. With it a pure, white light filled with flecks of gold began to swirl and glide along the floor, up walls and posts, and along the ceiling rafters. It spread into the other chambers and down to the next level. The lizards darted their tongues out frantically at the golden flecks that floated around them. Like a swarm of red ants, they began to scurry towards the square openings in the ceiling and crawl out. As the dark swarm of lizards grew smaller and smaller around the openings. The sound of sandpaper grew fainter and fainter until it was gone altogether.

Meanwhile, the matternots in the cave sat chained by their ankles, watching this whole scene in wonder and disbelief. Hale could hardly stand being chained up.

Fidavine Belle's brother spoke up and said in a rush of words that came out in one disbelieving breath, "What are you doing? You're going to get a whipping, Fair . . . and your dog . . . he can breathe gold and silver."

Fidavine Belle added, "All . . . all the lizards ran away! . . . and Pewgen Flype's tongue . . . it was disgusting!"

Everyone looked over in Pewgen Flype's direction. He had fainted from the shock and fallen to the floor.

Fair held onto the fur between Sauveren's shoulders. She turned her head here and there to listen to Fidavine Belle and her brother.

She said, "He can? . . . They did? . . ." and felt a smile spread across her face that was so big it felt strange. Hale began to pull at his hair and laugh. Fidavine Belle and her brother followed, and soon all the matternots were laughing.

39 : The Chase Begins

y now, the two Protectors were almost at Harrold King's throne room. The choir was still singing, singing every song they knew, in fact. Harrold King was waiting for Fair to come unveil the statue and it was taking much longer than expected. The room was warm and dark; the throngs of guests glowed in the candlelight.

The Protectors ran into the hall with their hands on their bully sticks shouting, "She's escaped! The Zothiker's gone!"

The choir stopped. The hall grew silent and all eyes were fixed on Harrold King. Everyone looked so immovable and still that the place looked like a painting.

"She what? . . . How?" he growled, breaking the silence. "Where?"

"Out the vineyard gate," the large Protector shouted, out of breath, "With that big dog."

Harrold King's beady eyes darted back and forth as though he were listening to something whispering in his ear. He shouted, "Several Protectors at the front gate. Several more to the O'Nelli Gate. Patrol the roads and woods . . ." No one moved. "Organize the troops!" he yelled to Salloroc. "After them . . . Now!"

Sauveren stood stock-still. He pricked his ears and listened. He could hear the thudding of horse hooves, followed by footsteps rushing past the opening of the tunnel.

"What is it?" Fair said and patted him on the head.

"It has begun."

"What has begun?"

"The beginning and the end."

Fair's head moved around in such a way that it looked like she was drawing circles with her chin. It was the way she had learned to see in the darkness all those years in the cellar. With her ears. Her senses. The feel of things. "You're speaking in riddles, Sauveren."

"The end of one era and the beginning of the next. It's time to go."

Fair felt a confusing sadness. Hale read her mind.

"Go. We'll be alright," shouted Hale.

Fair said to him, "Tell them."

"I already did."

In a chorus, the matternots all said, "Go, Worthless One!"

"Quiet," whispered Sauveren. "They might hear you."

Once all was quiet, Fidavine Belle's brother asked, "But how will you escape? They're outside and surrounding the place by now. "I mean, you're running away, aren't you?"

"Yes," Fair said. Then she said to her dog, "But not without my friends."

"There is a way," said Sauveren. He headed for the door near Fair's old sleeping mat. He lifted a paw and pressed down on the latch. Before he and Fair walked out the door, he turned and said, "Do you trust me, Lisper?"

"Of courth," he lisped.

"It is your job to lead."

"I don't understand."

"You will. You'll be in disguise until tomorrow at midden meal."

Hale looked confused. Sauveren said, "My sheep you are, my sheep must run. So let it be spoken, so let it be done."

Hale still looked confused. "What do you mean?"

He hardly had time to finish his words before a dark, brownish-black fur of sorts began to grow on his face, arms and legs. White wool poked out from his neck and back.

"What the . . . there's . . . faahr." He tried to say "fur, " but it came out as more of a baa sound. Hale's hands and feet shrank and hardened into black hooves. The chains slipped right off his feet. His clothes disappeared completely.

"Lisper . . . ," Fidavine Belle's brother said. "Lisper's a sheep! That's impaaahh-ssible." He felt his throat and looked at his feet. It was happening to him—and all the matternots.

Sauveren said, "Wait until you can feel the rain falling through the ceiling windows."

"Wait for whaaaht?" said Fidavine Belle's brother.

"Lisper will know what it means. Good-bye."

Fair held on to Sauveren's neck. He walked over to the door and Fair heard it creak open.

"Why are you going right into the middle of Osden Shorn when everybody is looking for us?" Fair asked.

"Because this is the last place they would look."

"But how will we stay here without being found?" Fair was worried.

"I have a plan."

Fair and her dog left the cave and a season of her life behind.

Osden Shorn was completely empty of Protectors and servants. Sauveren took Fair right into the heart of the place. In the central hall there was a staircase that led downwards. This is where the two of them quietly padded down the long stone steps. On the other side of the wall Harrold King and his guests waited in anticipation for Fair's capture and return.

"Where are we going?" Fair whispered.

"To Drinkwater," Sauveren said. He spoke in a reverent hush.

Of course, she thought. "The Door of Reunion?"

"Yes."

Fair thought about all the time she had spent in the caves of Osden Shorn. If she hadn't been there, she wouldn't have found Sauveren, and they wouldn't be going to find the Door of Reunion. She said, "This was all part of the bargain, wasn't it."

"*The* bargain. Yes."

Soon Fair felt Sauveren slow down. She heard a click. A latch released. A door creaked open. A cool breeze hit her face and she was met by the sound of lapping water. They began to bump and jostle down a flight of steep stairs. She reached out and felt an uneven stone wall on her left. It was wet from seeping water. She could feel cool air hitting the other side of her face.

"Where are we?" she puzzled.

"In the boat house," he whispered. The sound of their quiet voices bounced and echoed around the enormous cave. The moonlight reflected off the water on Lakinren Bae and filled the room with a soft, bluish-white light.

"I . . . I can row if you need me to," Fair offered quietly. "I know how to do that." She thought of the smelly bog where she had rowed with her father and Hale, even though she was very small.

"That won't be necessary."

They reached the carved-out floor at the back of the cave. Sauveren approached the steps that led down to the water, where a boat bobbed near the bottom of the steps. The faint sound of someone snoring echoed in the cave.

He took one step down. Then another. Two more steps to go. He ignored the boat off to their right and kept walking.

40 : Water All Around

air lay flat against Sauveren's back and held on as tightly as she could. The Ruby Eye on her forehead glistened in the moonlight.

"Sauveren? I hear water lapping on every side of me." Behind her, she could hear the boat clunking against the stone wall near the steps.

"Are you afraid?" said Sauveren.

"Yes."

"If I told you that no one will find you between here and Drinkwater, would you feel safe?"

She shivered. "Yes."

Sauveren said, "Look."

"But I can't see."

"Yes you can."

Fair heard the words in her mind, "Look to me and through me and all will be clear." Her Ruby Eye. *Of course.* She touched it and remembered her first night in the caves of Osden Shorn and how she had been able to see through the darkness. She wanted to see again.

Fair took a breath and sat up. She touched the Ruby Eye. It grew warm and soon Fair was able to see through it.

She saw water in front. Water on each side of her. Water behind.

She looked down at Sauveren's paws. They were completely dry. Only his toenails got wet, leaving the smallest drops behind with each step.

The air was pierced with the sound of the hunter's trumpets. Fair flung her head up to listen.

"They're for me, aren't they?" Fair concluded.

"They're looking for you."

"I don't want to go back, Sauveren. The caves are a horrible place. She felt overcome with the recent memory of her long, long imprisonment and began to fear that she would never know anything else. She began to sink into the water.

"Sauveren!" she cried. Her arms reached into the night air as she flailed to stay above water. Her head went under and bubbles popped to the surface. Her head bobbed up again and she fought to keep it up.

Sauveren calmly lay down on the water. Fair grabbed a fistful of fur and held on.

He said, "Fear is a terrible thing. If you believe that I can save you from drowning and from anything else that threatens you, then you will be alright. Keep your thoughts on that one thing. Forget the rest."

"That one thing," Fair repeated. She held on and put her cheek against Sauveren's ribs. She nodded and swallowed a big mouthful of lake water. She could feel the layer of dried grape juice on her skin and clothes wash away.

Fair made her way onto Sauveren's back once again. The silhouette of girl and dog walking on the moonlit, misty ripples was a peaceful sight compared to the shouting and branch-breaking search taking place for them all over Cloven Grave.

The Protectors were everywhere: at the front gate, scouring the edges of the vineyard walls, her cottage, along the road, and in the woods.

As Fair jostled from side to side she had time to let her mind wander. "I want to go home first, Sauveren." She had hardly allowed herself to think about her mother during all that time away. It was too painful. But she had dreamt of her, of her father, and brother. Dreams were fine, because they were so real. It was as if she was truly with them again. To think about them in the day was a mockery of the truth that she was not with them, no matter how badly she wished it were different.

But now, the caves of Osden Shorn were behind her. Sauveren would make sure she never had to go back.

"Will you take me home, Sauveren? I just want my bed and . . . ," her voice quivered, "to see my family."

"I understand, Fair. But we're Drinkwater bound. You made a bargain."

She hardly heard him. She was tired and hungry. "Please? *Then* we'll go."

"Your home is not safe right now, Fair. Protectors are everywhere, and they are waiting for you in your cottage."

"I'm so hungry." The echo of her mother's voice curled through her mind like wisps of fog.

"Fair, if you ever need to come home in dangerous times, go to the chicken coop."

Fair said, "I'd like to go to the chicken coop. It is almost like home."

"That is a much safer choice. Since you wish it, and it is a good wish, I will do your bidding."

The two of them walked for a long time, staying in the shadows of the trees along the shoreline of Lakinren Bae. Soon Fair said, "I can smell the Sinky Down . . . that stinky bog. We must be close."

41 : Mother Hen

auveren approached the shore with Fair on his back. He stepped on land. He carefully wove his way through the woods until they stood in the shadows on the edge of the round lawn at the back of Fair's cottage.

Fair looked through the Ruby Eye and saw Protectors walking around inside her cottage in lamplight. She couldn't see her mother and realized she had probably hidden in the cellar.

Fair felt a pang of guilt shoot through her again. She felt badly for not going home, but she knew it had to be this way. They stood there on the edge of the woods near the lawn and watched the yellow windows of the cottage.

Inside, one of the Protectors said, "You'd think she'd be here by now if they was going to come this way at all."

Another one said, "We'll wait here till we get orders to do somefin' else." Three or four Protectors stood at the windows, doing a poor job of trying not to be seen, watching to see if they could see any sign of Fair.

"This place ain't been lived in fer shoomin it seems. Ain't any sign of food in them cupboards," one Protector said. He walked into the hall and wiped his hands against each other. Lariel had been hiding in the cellar since Fair left. She understood what would happen when her brother, the Protector, told Harrold King where they lived.

A cold drop of water hit Fair on the head, then another. Soon, a soft but steady stream of raindrops was falling on Fair and Sauveren. The rain sounded like a soft breeze blowing.

Sauveren headed for the chicken coop on the far side of the garden shed. It was a three-sided wall with a slanted roof that opened onto a little fenced yard of dirt. The open side of the coop faced the lake, well-hidden from view of the cottage.

He lay down. Fair got off and snuggled up to him. The earth was dusty and dry. Fair warmed up next to his fur and heard the sound of hens rustling awake in their nests.

"There should be lots of eggs here, Sauveren. I'm good at eating bugs and grubs, so I don't care if they're not cooked." Fair tried to convince herself. She gulped at the thought of eating raw eggs.

She looked through the Ruby Eye into the nests that lined the wooden boxes around the lower border of the coop. She crouched and searched for eggs underneath the hens, moving from nest to nest.

"Not a one, Sauveren! I don't understand . . . . Why, someone's been gathering the eggs. Look, fresh footsteps." She gasped. "What if the Protectors . . ."

"They won't come this way, Fair. Those are your mother's footsteps." She felt relieved. Her mother was eating well, even if it was raw eggs, or cold boiled ones at best. She smiled at this reassurance and placed her fingers on one of the footprints.

Fair came to the last box. She felt underneath the hen's belly. It was warm and soft. She smiled when her fingertips felt something smooth and hard, roundish and warm, and another one next to it.

"Two eggs. That'll do." She pulled them out, and the hen ran off, fluttering her wings. She saw something out of place underneath the nesting box. "Hold on, what's this?" She looked more closely through the Ruby Eye. It was a small old box with a curved top. When she opened the latch and lifted the lid, she could barely make out the shape of something round. It was a wrist wrapping made of moss blossoms from Miss Tilly.

Fair's mother had hidden the box with the hope that Fair might come back. If her daughter quietly returned—even if for a moment—the wrist wrapping would be her way of letting Fair know she cared, and it also let her know her daughter had been there if she found the box empty.

"Mother," Fair smiled in a sad sort of way. "How did she know?" Fair shook the little bracelet and its bells made a small, tinkling sound. She ran her fingers around the moss blossoms it was made with. She wrapped it around her wrist, then put the box back where she found it. She sat down to enjoy her little meal, along with the feeling of being loved by her mother—even if from afar.

She carefully cracked an egg and opened it above her mouth, poised to catch the slimy meal. She managed to gulp, then tried it with the second egg.

"That wasn't so bad," she grimaced. She stuck out her tongue and shuddered. Thoughts filled her mind of all the time she spent in the caves of Osden Shorn.

Building the wall.

Treading grapes.

Eating grubs and insects.

All the hard work.

The meanness.

Pewgen Flype's words.

The feeling, "You are unclean!" came from nowhere and dropped like a heavy stone in her heart. It was the kind of feeling that has no words because it is so painful.

The image of Pewgen Flype came into her mind. The thought of him and of all she had suffered made her feel worthless and small.

She had been brave when she stood next to Fidavine Belle during that morning inspection many shoomin ago, but now that seed of thought—*you are unclean and filthy of soul*—sprouted a leaf. She lay down in the dirt and curled up. There was something else that caused her to ache right down to her bones.

"What's troubling you?"

"Nothing."

"Nothing?"

Fair's voice caught and she choked out the words, "The grassy path . . . it wasn't what I thought it was." She began to shake. "It wasn't safe . . . or easy."

"But it brought you to me, didn't it?"

Fair gave a small nod. "And I'm sure my father's still out there somewhere. And Selador, too." She sniffed. She heard something knocking on the side of the chicken coop. She jumped, then froze.

"Sauveren?" she whispered, almost unable to breathe, "What's that sound?"

"It's an oak leaf beating against the side of the wall."

"I thought . . . ," she began, then kept quiet.

The wind blew up gently from the lake and with it brought the sound of the water, lapping the shore. Fair's mind was so full of the fright and terror that she had lived, and what could happen again to her if she got caught, that even the smallest sounds felt like a threat of danger. Pewgen Flype.

"Someone's coming," she jumped.

Sauveren sat with his head on his paws and watched her. "It is just the waves on the shore. You're safe here, Fair."

He paused and watched her a bit longer. "Come over and get warm." Once she snuggled up to him he said, "Much you have suffered, much you have seen. Your heart is now pure, your body now clean."

Fair felt something wash through her that was fresh and clear. It filled her up and stayed there. She looked through her Ruby Eye and saw a mother hen standing in the middle of the rain. She had run out of the coop when Fair and Sauveren crept in, and now she stood with her wings spread out while rain dripped off the bottom edges of her wings. Several peeping chicks huddled under her wings for shelter. Moonlight sprayed through the light rain and created a glow around the hen and her chicks.

Sauveren said, "You have suffered and I have wept to see it."

Fair felt for his muzzle, then used her fingers to search her way upwards. Sauveren closed his eyes to let her touch them. She felt hardened tears in the inside corners of his eyes.

He said, "Those are the tears I have wept for you. They will always be there. If you take them away, they will just reappear. So you'll always remember."

Fair said, "When I was little, my parents used to sing me to sleep. I know I'm sort of old for it, but can, can you sing me a . . . well, a lullaby?"

At that admission she began to sob. All the pain and loneliness she had silently borne in the caves of Osden Shorn broke through her soul like water bursting from a shattered jar. "I want my mother! I want my father!" Her mournful cry echoed through the hillsides, sounding like a wounded creature.

In Fair's cottage a Protector pricked his ears. "Did you hear that?"

"What?"

"That sound. Like a cry."

A few of the Protectors grew silent and listened.

"There it is again."

One of them said, "Yeah, I hear that sort of thing in the woods outside my cottage. Animals."

Sauveren began to sing,

> *Sleep, wee hoomin in my bosom,*
> *Warm and cozy you may rest.*
> *Loving arms are round you tightly.*
> *Endless love is in my breast.*
> *Not a thing shall mar your resting,*
> *Nor a hoomin do you harm.*
> *Be at rest, my wee, wee hoomin.*
> *Sleep, wee hoomin, on my arm.*

Fair began to breathe softly and steadily. She was already asleep. Sauveren continued to sing,

> *Sleep in peace tonight, my beauty.*
> *Sweetly sleep my work of art.*
> *Why have you just started smiling,*
> *Smiling gently in your heart?*
> *Could it be some Nissen is smiling*
> *Down on you in joyful rest?*
> *With you smiling back and sleeping,*
> *Slumbering sweetly on my breast?*
> *Fret you not, 'tis but an oak leaf*

Beating, beating at the door.
Fret you not, a lonely wavelet's
Murmuring, murmuring on the shore.
Sleep, wee hoomin, here there's nothing,
Nothing that can frighten you.
Smile in peace upon my bosom.
Dream of nearby Nissen true.

Far away, back at Osden Shorn, Hale felt raindrops land on his black nose. He walked clumsily on four hooves to the opening of the cage, and the rest of the sheep filed into a line behind him. Soon, the flock filed one by one into the cage, up the tunnel, and out into the rainy night. Pewgen Flype still lay unconscious on the floor.

Chains lay on empty mats all around him.

42 : A Way Prepared

ery early the next morning, pink fingers of light spread out like an open hand beyond the tall, jagged mountains of High Grave. Soon, the sun rose up over the edge of Mount Rilmorrey. It cast a lemon-yellow haze that hung like a net in the misty morning air.

Fair slept in the comfort of Sauveren's protection. He opened his eyes at the sound of approaching footsteps and pricked his ears. He didn't want to wake Fair, and so he stayed as still as possible, while searching with just his eyes to find out where the sound came from. His eyebrows rose and dipped as he looked from side to side.

A foot lifted over the low fence of the courtyard and stepped onto the dirt. It was filthy and bare, and the lower part of the leg was uncovered, because the pant leg above it was torn. It was hairy and wild.

In a moment, the next foot appeared and a face thrust itself into the chicken shed. The figure squatted on his heels and stared at Fair, running his fingers through his tangled beard.

"Welcome back, Woolly," Sauveren whispered.

Fair opened her eyes and blinked into the dark world of her blindness. "Get away from me."

"It's alright. Pewgen Flype isn't here. We've escaped," said Sauveren.

Fair sat upright. Her memories of the night before came back to her and she smiled weakly. "I'm safe." She turned and wrapped her arms around Sauveren.

"Grubs and bugs," said the Woolly. He spilled a handful of squirming, bulging bugs the color of peeled potatoes onto the ground. He said, "Eat 'em."

"The Woolly, is that you?"

"Grubs and bugs," he answered.

"Come here. Let me feel your face." The Woolly came over towards Fair and took her hand. He placed it on his forehead. Fair let her fingers slide over the contours of his eyes, his nose, and cheeks. She asked him what she'd wanted to know since the day she saw him at the wall. "How did you get changed back?" When her hands came to his beard, she said, "And what about Azanamer and Gibber Will? Are they . . . "

"Rock and rabbit no more," said the Woolly.

"Anything is possible, Fair," Sauveren said.

Fair understood. It was Sauveren. He undid the spell.

Fair felt like her whole journey along the grassy path had been an illusion. It was all part of bringing her right to the place she was. Right then. And she laughed. She also realized she felt starved. She groped and felt for her moving morning meal and popped the grubs into her mouth a few at a time.

"Thank you," she said with a final gulp. "I'm so thirsty. I wish I had a little something."

"I have prepared the way," the Woolly said. He handed her a flask of fizzy milk.

Fair drank. She thought of the flames she had seen in his eyes long ago at Lamb's Tavern. "What do you mean?"

"They're coming," the Woolly said, as though he were talking about nothing in particular.

Fair choked on her words. "Who's coming?"

"It's time to run," said Sauveren.

"To the drink," the Woolly said. He reached into a pocket and pulled out a sky blue strip of torn cloth. Azanamer had taken it from the inside hem of her skirt and given it to him. He put it in Fair's hands and said, "Tie this around your eyes. Protect you from branches."

Fair tied it around her eyes and fashioned a knot at the back of her head.

What he didn't say was that morning—very early— he had been seen on Cloven Grave road by a group of Protectors. They were returning to Osden Shorn after a fruitless search for Fair. It was still dark when he walked past them. He was going in the opposite direction.

"Where are you headed, hoomin?" one of them asked.

"Drinkwater," said the Woolly.

"We ain't thirsty," said one of the Protectors.

"Naw, I bet it's a code, like he's talking about a place. Like maybe he's gonna be taking the maiden and her dog there. I seen 'em together before. They're friends, like."

"Him and the dog? I ain't so sure."

"Me neither, but there's an old hoomin who knows about this sort of thing." The Protectors took off at a fast pace for Osden Shorn. That's when the Woolly ran straight for the chicken coop as though he knew where Fair—or Sauveren—would be.

Sauveren said, "Hop on my back, Fair."

She was silent for a moment, listening to something deep inside. She thought of how much she liked her home and family—or what she had once had. As she slipped on to Sauveren's back she said, "I miss Mother and Father so much."

"I know."

She patted the fur in between his shoulders. Her voice shuddered and she could feel her chin quivering, "Choose what is right let consequence follow . . . that's our family way."

"It's been that way since long before you were born."

"Follow your heart, come joy or come sorrow," she finished.

"To Drinkwater. Come joy or come . . . sorrow."

"To Drinkwater," Fair echoed. "What will we do when we get there?"

"Get you something to drink. Then, in due time we'll look for Selador's Gate—and that Selador of yours that you're supposed to find."

Fair gulped, "It's finally time, then."

"Yes."

"More grassy path to follow," said the Woolly. "Made this part just for you, I did."

Leaving the little dusty red treasure box behind in the chicken shed, they silently followed the Woolly through a path in the woods. He had carved it out over the previous shoomin. The bells on Sauveren's collar tinkled in the morning stillness.

43 : The Great Void

arrold King paced the floor of the Throne Room. He tottered from side to side, rubbing his hands together. "Read it to me again," he said to Salloroc. Pewgen Flype stood off to one side. Silent.

Salloroc read,

> *Soon the temple walls shall rumble.*
> *The false king soon shall kneel most humble*
> *before the one true ruler, the one true king*
> *to whom Cloven Grave his praises sing.*

"A bunch of nonsense!" snorted Harrold King. He turned a ring on his finger. "I don't believe a word of it!" He growled with enough hesitancy that Salloroc forced himself to look at him out of the corner of his eye. Harrold King's face was pale.

"Once she is in my possession I will not deal with her as kindly as I have done so far. There is only one solution for a Zothiker. I should have done it long ago."

Salloroc wanted to remind him that he couldn't touch her. Then Harrold King said, "I have a plan."

Rithel scurried out from under the crown and said, "We need to act quickly. The Harvestaren moon is growing full."

"So what?"

"Surely you remember hearing about the night of Blood Moon. After that it will be too late. Just trust me. Tell me your plan."

"Harrold King said, "No. This one is of my own making. All yours have failed. Intentionally, I believe." His shoulders slumped. Rithel knew right then that Harrold King understood he had only been his pawn.

Harrold King appeared stolid outwardly, but something in his eyes revealed he'd been crushed by the fact he'd been used. He looked as though he had lost his place in the world. Rithel's tongue darted out in satisfaction.

Earlier that morning Harrold King had Pewgen Flype drag the shepherd, Wollan Sash in from the pasture where he had been tending sheep. It was the same shepherd Gibber Will had passed long ago when he drove Fair to Lamb's Tavern on her day of maidenhood. Pewgen Flype didn't notice that Wollan Sash's flock had grown tremendously.

Wollan Sash stood in front of Harrold King, who said, "Drinkwater. I am told you have been there." He fished, hoping Wollan Sash would assume he knew it was a place, if indeed it was.

Wollan Sash stood silent.

"Come here, old hoomin," Harrold King ordered.

Wollan Sash walked up to Harrold King.

"If you value your life, you will show me exactly how my army is to get there."

"I am not worried about the value of my life," Wollan Sash calmly said. "You can't do anything to change its worth."

Harrold King thrust a feather pen at him and said, "Over to that table with you. Draw."

Wollan Sash walked with the ease of a hoomin familiar with the movement of the earth. He glided over to the table and sat down. He muttered, "The Planter Era is about to begin. The Fallow Era is doomed." He dipped the tip of the feather in a bottle of ink. He began to draw a map.

"What did you say, old hoomin?" snipped Harrold King.

"I am an old hoomin," he answered.

The double doors crashed open at the far end of the hall. Axum strode in and yelled, "What happened? Everybody's leaving!"

Harrold King ignored his son.

"I said Father, where is everybody?"

"You ask me *now*? Where were you last night? You were supposed to be here to unveil my statue. What kind of son are you?"

Axum walked up to the canvas that covered his father's statue. "If that's what you wanted me for, then you shall have it!" Axum grabbed one corner and gave it a heavy yank. He looked at his father with a chin of defiance. Harrold King stared at the statue and it appeared to gaze back at him, mocking who he was and why he was in Cloven Grave. He rubbed his hands nervously together.

Harrold King said, "Where were you?"

"Out hunting. I lost track of time." This was completely untrue. He had been in the boat house, sleeping soundly in the boat, bobbing near the steps.

While his father spoke, Axum narrowed his eyes and sized up the situation. He looked at Salloroc, then Wollan Sash. "What are these hoomin doing here? I want them gone."

"You'd be a fool to do such a thing if you were in my place. A matternot has gone missing from the caves."

"And?" Axum said, as though to imply his father was making no point whatsoever.

"And she is a Zothiker. The one that was on the platform of punishment the other day."

Axum's face grew pale. He spoke quickly. "Where? Do you have any idea where she might be?" He walked up to Wollan Sash at the table and looked down at the beginnings of what would be a map, "That looks like the Quorum Range."

Wollan Sash said, "Mount Rilmorrey, sire, to be more exact. You'll have to get through the Searing Ruwens on the Southwarsten side. Many a hoomin has died trying . . . now if you don't mind, I'm needing to get back to my sheep."

The Searing Ruwens were flames that shot up from the earth at the mouth of the Quorum Range. There was no other entrance, and many hoomin had died over the years trying to get past their unpredictable explosions.

Axum ignored him and said, "Salloroc, get my dogs. All of them. And enough provisions for two days."

Pewgen Flype didn't dare mention anything about Fair having a brother in the caves, since the caves were now empty. He motioned to Harrold King that he'd like to be part of the army. Harrold King nodded.

Wollan Sash stayed silent. He knew it would be much longer than two days before they returned to Osden Shorn, because once they got past the volcanic flames of the Searing Ruwens—if they succeeded, that is—they would have to travel through three more passes before getting to the pool of Rilmorrey. It was a steep and arduous journey.

Harrold King said suspiciously, "Your dogs won't be any good for the hunt if you just took them out."

"Let me worry about my dogs, Father," Axum snapped. He turned to face Salloroc. "Salloroc? My dogs."

"He's under *my* bidding, Axum. I will order someone else to get your dogs. *You* will be under Salloroc's orders." He pounded his throne with his fist. "For a young hoomin in his fifteenth year, you need to remember your place."

Axum ignored his father's last remark. "And what do we do when we find the Zothiker, Father?"

Harrold King looked at Salloroc and nodded.

Salloroc's voice was like steel. "Kill her."

Men on horses, hounds, and a restless young Axum all paced and pawed in the courtyard of Osden Shorn. They waited for the signal. A line of Protectors stood on the balcony overlooking Lakinren Bae with trumpets held to their lips. At once, they all began to blast the hunting call:

Brah, brah, brahhhhh!

The sound of baying hounds exploded into the air followed by the sound of hundreds of horses' hooves scrambling on cobblestone. Soon, dogs and horses thundered out of the gate at Osden Shorn, heading in the direction of Mount Rilmorrey, deep in the heart of the Quorum Range.

The folded map bulged from Salloroc's chest, beneath his jacket.

Pewgen Flype followed him with the rest of the army. *What a welcome change from the caves,* he thought.

Axum was shoulder to shoulder with Salloroc. Their horses' muscles rippled and shone in the early morning light. They were followed by a small army of Protectors on horses.

Once they were far from Osden Shorn, Axum whirled his horse around without saying a word.

"Where are you going?" Salloroc yelled after him.

Axum said, "It's not your concern."

⤙❊⤚

Fair could hear the sound of trumpets blaring and fear caught at her throat. "Do you hear that, Sauveren?

"Yes."

"But what if they catch us?"

"The path we're taking is a new one. No one has ever been on this trail except the Woolly. He made it."

The Woolly said, "Prepare the way I did."

Fair began to breathe more easily and asked, "Can you tell me where Drinkwater is?"

"In the mountains."

"You mean High Grave?" Fair asked incredulously. She had often stared at their jagged height from her mother's window, on nights when the moon was full.

"We will see it today, Fair."

Soon the Woolly said, "Wait for you there." He took off through the woods, leaving Sauveren and Fair alone on the path.

Sauveren said, "Hold on with all your might, Fair. No looking this time."

No looking? That's odd, she thought. But she trusted Sauveren. "Alright," she said. She lay down on

⤙ 410 ⤚

Sauveren's back and sunk her fingers deep into the fur on his shoulders. Her cheek lay flat against his furry back.

"Ready?"

Fair checked to make sure the blindfold was in place. She wanted to peek through the Ruby Eye, but she didn't. "Ready." She pressed her lips together.

Sauveren sat back slightly on his hind legs.

He appeared to explode forward.

He ran with the speed of wind.

The two of them sped effortlessly through the narrow, winding path that looked out over Lakinren Bae. The sound of the bushes and branches on both sides of them whirred in Fair's ears. She felt them whip at her face, and she realized why the Woolly had given her the blindfold. The steam from Sauveren's breath puffed out and trailed behind them like long tufts of cotton.

The wooded path began to rise and leave the lake farther and farther below. The shoreline soon turned into steep cliffs, for they were approaching the jagged mountain range of High Grave.

Fair took a deep breath in and said, "What is that smell?" Her nose was pink from the cool air.

"Pine trees, Fair. They grow in the mountains," he huffed. They glided at lightning speed through a place where the path curved. By now, they were surrounded on both sides by pine trees. All at once, a treeless vista opened to Sauveren's view. The glistening lake of

Lakinren Bae was on their left. Before them the path rose slightly and disappeared.

Into nothing.

As they got closer and closer to the end of the path, Sauveren could see a cliff on the other side of the void. Far beneath them a small silver thread of river wound its way into Lakinren Bae. The chasm was too far to leap across. The drop down to the river was too far to fall without smashing on the rocks.

Fair could hear the faint sound of rushing water, far below.

"What is that sound, Sauveren?"

"You've got keen ears. It's a river." He said nothing more but continued to run straight for the chasm.

Soon, his front paws landed on the end of the path and sent a rock tumbling and crashing to the river below. It broke off roots and small trees that clung to the side of the cliff.

Fair was oblivious to the danger that lay just before them. She continued to hold on tightly, with her cheek pressed deep into her dog's fur.

Sauveren's front legs reached out into the space before them, his hind paws pushed off the edge of the cliff. They were in midair.

Sauveren flew high above the river and began to drop.

"Whoa, Sauveren. This is a bumpy ride."

"Up we go," he simply said.

The two of them rose with a surge of power into the air and flew over the cliff on the other side, high above the treetops.

Sauveren's front legs remained stretched out as though he were positioned for a very, very long leap. His back legs looked as though they were still in the act of the final push from the edge of the chasm.

Fair said, "That's better. It's smoother now."

"Yes," he smiled. "This part is smoother. Just hold on tight." She gripped her fingers deeper into his fur.

"You've never run so soft-like," Fair said.

Far below and behind them, Sauveren could see a small train of dust rising outside the village of Cloven Grave. He curved off in that direction. Soon, he and Fair were directly above the rising dust.

Far beneath them, the army of Protectors had cut through the village of Cloven Grave and were now heading for the distant foothills of High Grave. Their elbows bounced against their ribs as the horses beneath them pounded the earth with their hooves. They had bows slung over their chests and quivers full of arrows on their backs.

Salloroc said, "If they'd a come this way, there's no way to know it. Last night's rain smoothed everything out. Now it's all just dust over hard dirt."

Another Protector said, "The Woolly's mad . . . dingy like . . . but he knows enough to spill the beans if he knows somefin'."

Meanwhile, the Woolly crashed up the mountainside like a monkey racing at lightning speed. He tore through branches, scrambled and clambered up cliffs. He reached for vines and climbed like he weren't hoomin at all. His toes gripped like claws onto rocks and into the clefts in the cliffs. His hands grabbed onto branches and vines like they had glue on them.

Spittle dripped from his mouth and mixed in with his beard that he had tied into a knot. He kept muttering, "Risen low, risen low. To rise you go below."

44 : Drinkwater Bound

auveren veered away from the army and left it far behind. He and Fair soared at breakneck speed towards the Quorum Range.

"The wind sure has picked up, Sauveren," Fair said.

"In a way," he said. He could feel that she had a tight hold of him and knew she was safe as long as she did so.

It didn't take them long to fly over the foothills. Sauveren could see the pass leading into the mountains. The Searing Ruwens erupted with flashes of fire and steam. He knew it would take all day for the army to reach that spot. This was good, for there was much to be done.

He took Fair high above an enormous, bowl-shaped mountain range. Each mountain looked as if it was an arrow that had shot up through the soil with the hope of striking sky. Their sides were relatively straight. Each mountain touched the one next to it halfway down, forming the jagged rim of an irregularly-shaped bowl. Years and years of erosion filled up this jagged bowl with smooth pathways.

In the distance, two of the peaks thrust upwards, slightly below Mount Rilmorrey. A waterfall fell between them. It wound its way to the base of the foothills, taking many winds and turns out to Lakinren Bae. This was the river he and Fair had sailed over when the ground dropped away into the gorge.

This is where he headed.

It wasn't long before he and Fair arrived above a waterfall that fell between the twin peaks. A light blue pool shimmered at its base. A wide green meadow grew to one side.

"I see the Pool of Rilmorrey, Fair."

"The Pool of Rilmorrey?" she asked. "What is it?"

"It will be called Drinkwater once we get there."

Her jaw dropped. "And then we'll look for Selador's Gate?"

"In due time." Fair felt slightly impatient, but she knew she needed his help. She took in a deep breath of resignation. "Alright."

He flew lower and lower until he could see an old path opening up beneath them. He landed on it in full stride and kept running.

"It's sort of bumpy here, isn't it?" Fair said. She wrapped her arms more tightly around him. "And I can hear water now."

"Yes, we're almost there." The path was quite high above the pool.

Soon, Fair felt the cool spray of water flutter against her face. She took a deep breath in.

"Let me tell you what is going to happen here, Fair. We have come to a waterfall that pours into the Pool of

Rilmorrey. The cliffs on this side of the fall are too steep to get there."

"How will we find our way down?" asked Fair.

"Behind the waterfall. It's much easier on the other side. Are you ready to come?"

"I'm not sure," she said.

"You have shown me that you will look to me through a broken heart."

She didn't answer.

He said, "The Ruby Eye. You can see through it if your heart is humble. Your heart is humble."

"It is? Is that why . . ."

"You are ready," he said. "Climb on my back."

"No, I think I can do this part myself, as long as you're here," she said.

"Then just follow the sound of my voice. If the time comes that you cannot hear me, you may need to look through your broken heart. Doubt not. Fear not," he said.

My broken heart, she thought. Fair stayed silent and pondered. *All those years my heart was breaking wasn't such a bad thing.* She turned her head this way and that to pick up any sound. She heard him leave and followed his footsteps, using her mouselike ears to see with. After just a few footsteps, she decided to use the Ruby Eye.

The closer they got to the waterfall, the more difficult it became to hear Sauveren. The sound was deafening. The water fell from so high up that when Fair looked, she couldn't even see the beginning.

She followed the lumbering shape of her dog to the edge of the waterfall. Then she saw Sauveren disappear. Where did he go? She couldn't move another step.

The words came to her mind, "Doubt not. Fear not." It was Sauveren's voice.

She put one foot forward, then the next, repeating the action. Water spray drenched her. She was dripping when she got to the edge of the waterfall. She could no longer see because the Ruby Eye was covered with water droplets. She felt the ground with her feet. All those years in darkness had helped her to feel what she couldn't see with her eyes. She felt the path curve to the right ever so slightly. She kept moving.

Soon, her head swirled with the sound of an echoing chamber of sorts. She heard water rushing past on her left.

"I'm behind the waterfall," she said.

"You are," said Sauveren. "Now, come to where I am."

She dried off the Ruby Eye and looked. He was another ten paces or so ahead of her. She could see the light of day through the rushing water. The space behind it danced with waving light and shadow. The mist tickled her face.

"It's so beautiful! I could stay in here forever." She took small nervous steps up to her dog. She reached out and put her hand on his wet back to steady herself.

"That's far enough," Sauveren said. "When you hear me say the word *bound* take a deep breath in—and hold it."

She nodded.

"Now climb on and take hold of my collar." She held on tight and he cried, "You are Drinkwater *bound*!"

Fair felt a yank on her arms. She took in the deepest breath she could and held it. She felt something slam down on her back. It was so painful it nearly knocked the air out of her. It took her a moment to realize that they had jumped straight into the falling water. She felt herself roll and tumble with Sauveren as they dropped through the frothy, deafening thunder.

She felt air all around her.

Then nothing but water.

Then air again.

She felt like she would fall forever. From a distance their shapes tumbled and tossed, in and out of the watery foam on their way down.

"Take another breath, Fair!"

She filled her lungs.

Fair felt herself plunged deep into a wet world where she knew she musn't breathe. It was the pool. The collar slipped out of her fingers. Sauveren was gone, and she felt pain in her ears. She could feel the waterfall pound down on her back. Then she felt something grab her hair. Sauveren had it in his mouth. He used his webbed feet to kick and swim as hard as he could to rip away from the water that pummeled them relentlessly down.

Fair fumbled around with her hands until she found Sauveren's neck. She grabbed a hold of his collar again. They popped to the surface, *gasp!* She gulped the air as though she had never taken a breath in her life. She craned her neck to keep her head above water.

"We made it, didn't we?" She gulped a huge mouthful of water and coughed.

"Yes," Sauveren gasped.

"I wish I could have seen that . . . it, it must have been amazing." Her face was drenched with water.

"Yes, it was. Well done, Fair," said Sauveren. "Now let me take you to shore." He left watery footprints behind them as he walked onto a trail, with Fair on his back.

As they walked along Fair felt her face grow warm. "My face is getting hot, Sauveren."

"We're at the fires."

"The fires? But aren't we looking for Selador's Gate?"

"I believe, somehow, we're getting closer to finding it. But first, I must say this: you have drunk from the waters of life, and now you must go through the Embers of Espritan to breathe the air. You'll need to walk."

"Can I look?" she asked.

"Of course."

She looked through the Ruby Eye and saw a glowing path in front of them. Steam rose from the embers, and fire burned on both sides. She got off and stood next to Sauveren.

"Will it hurt?"

"On the contrary."

They were almost at the path. He took his first step onto the embers and said, "I give you the Cape of Thelras, so that you will never be alone . . . Look."

Fair watched through the Ruby Eye as he began to walk between flames that reached at them from both sides of the path. Hot coals glowed beneath his paws. As he moved forward, sparks and small flames rose from the coals and converged above her. They came together and formed a cape of burning orange sparks. She saw it curve and spread like a falling leaf, and place itself gently on her back. She felt a wave of comfort surround and fill her as it clasped itself around her neck.

"The cape. I've seen this," she exulted. It was the same sort she had seen appear for brief moments on the hoomin, in the caves of Osden Shorn.

This thought filled Fair with a contentment she had never known, even with her family, even in her memories and daydreams. Every fear she had ever known melted away. She laid her cheek against her dog's shoulder. She felt a tear slide down her nose. She knew everything would be alright. Come joy or come sorrow.

"Are you still thirsty, Fair?"

She lay sleepily and quietly muttered, "Just hungry."

"Hungry? Ahh." He seemed to think for a moment.

Fair slowly sat up on his back and something dawned on her: This was the first time in recent memory that she didn't feel consumed by thirst. She looked through the Ruby Eye. Sauveren was walking towards a meadow that opened up before them. There was a single tree in the center of it. It bore beautiful white glowing fruit.

"We have come to the Pastures of Prepahr." Sauveren took her to the tree and said, "Pick anything you like."

The branches were so heavy with fruit that they surrounded her. She spied a perfect one, close by. She needed both hands to pick the fruit because it was so large. She used both hands to twist it off the branch. She took a bite.

As the juice slid down her small throat, it filled Fair's mind with memories of Sauveren's eyes looking back at her. When she imagined he was with her along the grassy path. When he seemed to appear in front of her. She knew what she had seen in his eyes. But what was the *word* for it? What *was* the word?

The feeling inside Fair's soul right then was so expansive and clear, that she decided it would take many, many words to describe what she had seen, and felt, and known.

Sauveren said, "There is only one word for it, Fair. It will come to you. And now, we must move on."

Fair felt a rush of hope combined with the finality of knowing. She said, "We're getting closer to finding Selador's Gate. I can feel it."

At that moment one of Salloroc's hoomin shouted, "I can see the Searing Ruwens!" He pulled the telescope away from his eye and closed it, "We should be there by nightfall."

"Let's stop and rest the horses," ordered Salloroc. "Fair won't be going anywhere in the dark."

Pewgen Flype pulled back on his horse's reins and waited.

45 : The First Howl

auveren walked away from the tree in the Pastures of Prepahr. Fair took another bite of the fruit in her hand.

Sauveren found a path that traversed its way to the top of the waterfall. He took Fair behind it once again and came out the other side.

They plodded the rest of the afternoon and early evening, deep into the heart of the Quorum Range. Fair could hear the hush of Sauveren's paws echo off the steep walls around them.

The air grew cool when the sun went down. Fair looked up through the Ruby Eye and saw that the mountains on both sides were so sheer she could only see a long, narrow slice of dark blue.

When the moon rose at the low end of the sliver Fair felt her skin crawl.

It was large.

Round.

And blood red.

She knew they had only one more day, if Thelras had been right. The Woolly had talked about the night of Blood Moon. The temple walls of Osden Shorn. A new king. Three days of blackness.

"Sauveren, the moon is red. I'm frightened."

"This is all as it should be, Fair. It is part of the plan."

She wrapped her arms tightly around his neck and snuggled her cheek deep into his fur. Soon she noticed a worn-looking fence along the path. On the other side of it she saw gnarled fruit trees on a downward sloping hill. She saw an old gate.

Sauveren said, "We have come to the Orchard of Agesmeneth, Fair. I'm going inside for a moment. Will you wait here?"

"But you can't. I'm out of shackles. You know, payment for passing."

"Not to worry. I will make the payment this time." He paused. "Will you be alright?"

Fair wanted to ask what he would use for payment, but she simply said, "Darkness doesn't bother me, Sauveren." An owl hooted in the distance and she gulped. "Not really."

"There are different kinds of darkness," he said. "Some you see, and some you feel. You have gathered much light, so you should be fine."

Fair thought of Rithel, Harrold King, and Pewgen Flype. She wiggled her finger and realized she hadn't used her fingerlight since leaving the caves. She hadn't needed to with her dog nearby.

Sauveren lay down. Fair slipped off. She was used to being cold in the caves, so this evening air was nothing to her, even though it made her shiver. This was a different kind of cold. She sat down and leaned her back against a tree at the side of the path. She pulled her knees up to her chin and settled down to wait.

Sauveren walked up to her and licked her cheek. She put her small hand on his black wet nose and said, "I'll be here when you come back."

He looked at her with that look that she had seen so often. She smiled.

That look: what was the word for it?

Then he walked slowly over to the gate and pushed it open with his nose. She heard it creak open and closed.

While she lay there waiting, an invisible blanket of suffocation seemed to come over her. She could hardly breathe. She felt as though she was going to be crushed into the earth. She tried to hold her breath but only felt strangled. No fingerlight. Nothing.

She heard her mother's voice, "Light banishes that which is dark." She tried hard to think of the Impissh Nissen. The Cape of Thelras. Sunshine. Nothing seemed to help.

She thought about Rall Kindaria. Selador. As soon as she thought about him, the stranglehold let go and the heaviness departed, leaving her feeling very sleepy.

She yawned, "Different kinds of darkness," and fell into a slumber.

She was jolted awake by a cry that pierced the night, as if someone, or something, was hurting her dog. The sound brought bumps to Fair's flesh. She scurried over to the fence and looked frantically into the orchard. Her whitened knuckles gripped the fence. In the distance, two mountains formed a canyon. The Blood Moon floated there: round, full, and ominous.

Fair saw Sauveren sitting on his haunches in front of the moon. He was crying to the sky in a long sad sound. *No one's hurting him. He's alone*, Fair thought. *How strange.* But she felt no relief.

She couldn't tell if he was singing, crying, or speaking a language she'd never heard. No hoomin in the valley of the Graves had ever heard such a sound.

It was the first howl.

Sauveren's anguished song flowed through the air like like searching rivers of blood. It wound through the windows of every cottage, seeped into the caves of Osden Shorn, and dripped into the hollow of every animal's den. Creatures pricked their ears and licked their young.

Stones cracked and released their long-held secrets. The soil in Cloven Grave shifted and whispered unspeakable tales. Trees began to sway violently as the traveling whisper spread from one leaf to the next; yet, there was no wind. Clouds parted as the howl rose above the moon and echoed among the stars.

Some of the hoomin sat up in their beds when the cry woke them. Some went to their windows and looked out, surprised to see a red-colored moon. A few dreamily remembered the Woolly had mentioned something about it. Soon they were all asleep again.

While Sauveren howled, trails of mist rose from the hearts of the sleeping hoomin, lifting them ever so slightly above their beds, then down again. It rose from the soil itself and drifted down from worlds beyond. The mists slipped quietly out of the windows, sliding along orchards and fields.

Like small white streams, they began to converge into a wide lacelike river and rise in the air, mixing with the descending mists from worlds beyond. The ghostly stream headed in the direction of Mount Rilmorrey.

The mists carried with them every sorrow, every pain, every wrong and every evil known that each hoomin would ever think, feel, or do. When they reached the height of the mount, they began to screech and howl. It looked as though Rithel himself were searching for something—something to fling down. But it was not Rithel's doing.

Soon, the screeching mist rose high into the ink-filled night like a snake about to strike. It dove straight for Sauveren and bit into his heart. The rest of its ghostly body followed, striking him over and over, until the end of the screeching tail slipped inside with one final jab. He fell to his side, panting for breath.

The weight and force of the mists pressed him into the rock, leaving the shape of his body forever marked upon the stone.

The immediate silence was astounding.

Fair had seen her own mist rise to join the rest and felt herself lifted and let down again. She held the fence even more tightly and saw a flicker of light in Sauveren's side.

It began to grow and overtake the dog until his fur looked white. The light condensed upon itself as though it were gathering strength, then exploded with such force that it knocked Fair onto her back. It spread to every nook and cranny of Cloven Grave and beyond.

Into the soil.

The trees.

The twinkling stars.

The sleeping dew.

It showered every living soul with sparkles of light that drifted onto their sleeping frames. It melted through their skin, filtering right down to their bones. They were forever changed while they slept.

When Fair regained her strength, she sat up. *What was that light? What happened?* she thought. Sauveren lay motionless on the rock. She wanted to open the gate and run to him, but felt she shouldn't.

In the moonlight Fair saw something glint off Sauveren's fur. His whole coat was shining wet. Somehow, it was something she didn't want to see. She heard him whimper.

She held her knees for hours. Shivering. Wondering. Soon she heard the gate creak open and closed. She heard the heavy padding of Sauveren's footsteps, then his weary voice.

"Are you awake, Fair?"

"I saw . . . ," she began. She wanted to tell him about everything she'd seen. But he stopped her.

His words came slowly. "I'm tired. Let's sleep."

Fair wanted answers, but she knew he needed rest. She reached out for him to snuggle close. When she laid her cheek against his fur she realized it was wet in a thick sort of way.

She pulled back. "Sauveren?"

He was silent.

"You're sticky and wet."

He whispered hoarsely, "The Laws of Memory are no more. You are washed clean."

She pulled her hands away. Bewildered. Uncomfortable. Washed clean? Whatever did he mean? She absently licked the side of her mouth and tasted blood. With amazement and deep sadness Fair realized he was covered in it. *That's why his coat shone in the moonlight*, she thought. She wrapped her arms around herself then realized it was all over her now.

Sauveren said, "And now, it's time for you to find Selador's Gate."

Fair was surprised that she felt no relief. What happened in the orchard had been so unexpected. She thought about the bargain she had made with Cael and Thelras in Rall Kindaria.

She had her dog with her.

She had found her brother.

But she still hadn't found her father.

She didn't dare guess whether or not she might find him for fear that she had misunderstood. Perhaps he had been sent out on a Joust and Dangle.

Then it hit her.

"You've known where it is all along. So why did Thelras ask me to go looking for it?"

Speaking seemed to take all the strength out of him. "To be a witness that it happened, Fair."

"That what happened?"

He paused, knowingly. "Would anyone believe it otherwise?"

Fair thought of the Blood Moon.

The converging mists.

The howling.

He spoke haltingly. "We'll go in the morning. Now, let's rest."

Fair's heart sank. "Father," she whispered. She felt betrayed, but at the same time she had a feeling that her quest had nothing to do with actually finding the gate at all. It was what happened along the way.

They fell asleep next to the orchard that night. The full Blood Moon watched over the old gnarled apple trees, showering everything in rosy mist and beauty.

It wasn't long before Fair felt the warmth of the rising sun. She slowly woke up. She shook Sauveren and said, "It's morning."

He stood and stretched his front and back legs. He yawned. She heard the faint sound of a horn's blast. Dog's barking. She felt her way over to Sauveren and said, "They're coming."

"I know. This time you'll need to ride. We need to move fast." Fair hopped on. They ran until the sun was high. The heat made Fair feel faint from thirst and hunger.

"Are we almost there?" Fair quietly asked. She licked her dry lips. She could smell the rich sweetness of the air rising from the damp undergrowth around them. It was all she could do to even speak. Her strength was giving out. Sauveren kept tripping on roots and stones on the winding, mountainous trail. Fair had to hold on tightly.

Soon, she felt as though her head were turning around in circles.

"Sauveren!" she hoarsely whispered through cracked lips.

"I think I'm . . . ," she started to say. Then she slid off his back and collapsed on the ground.

Sauveren nudged her shoulder with his soft wet nose. "Just a little further, now. Can you smell the water?" He felt weak himself, but knew they had to press on.

Fair lay on the path. She could feel the soil under her cheek. She nodded. She licked her lips, but it didn't help to soothe the cracks that exposed such soft, pink flesh inside them. She could taste blood. Her own.

Sure enough, when the direction of the gentle breeze was just right, the fragrance of water filled Fair's senses. She seemed to gather strength when she smelled it. She reached out for Sauveren. Finding a hold she sunk her fingers deep into his coat. With his black wavy hair poking through her fingers in a tight grip, she tried to pull herself up.

"Just need to get," she paused, "my legs," she took a breath, "under me." She just couldn't do it, no matter how she pulled this way and that. No strength.

"Sauveren . . . I, I can't go any further." She heard the sound of the dogs. Another horn blast. The sounds were much louder now. "I'm sorry."

Just then, a pheasant shot up from the bushes next to them. Loud and explosive. Fair gripped Sauveren's coat even harder. "That's not them is it," she said—not so much a question as a statement.

"No, we still have time, but be quick about it if you can. Try to pull yourself up one more time. Lie across my back."

Fair tried and tried. She grew more and more frantic with every passing moment. *They're getting closer. I can hear them,* she thought.

An explosion of breaking branches struck Fair's ears. Something or someone came out of the bushes and grabbed Fair's wrist.

She screamed.

Her old habit returned: she cocked her head to see with her mousey ears through the darkness. Her blank eyes looked up to the sky she could not see. She was silently pleading for help. She twisted her head again to see with her other ear. The hand still held her wrist.

"What have we here?" said a voice.

Fair smelled a familiar fragrance. A sweet fragrance. Her voice sounded dry.

"Is that you, Azanamer?"

"Yes."

"They're after us . . . Harrold King's Protectors."

Azanamer pulled a rope from the deep recesses of her dress. She said, "They may be Protectors, but they are no warriors. They feel nothing but fear and they act upon it, and it alone. Now we shall see who the true warrior is. I'm going to tie you on so you can't fall off. It might hurt."

"Can you hurry?"

Azanamer quickly laid Fair upon Sauveren's back. "Spread your arms wide, Fair. Slide your hands down along Sauveren's legs." Azanamer flung the rope over Fair's shoulder and quickly lashed Fair's stretched-out arms to Sauveren's side. Then she lashed Fair's waist and legs to his back.

Azanamer said, "All done. Now you must drink." She uncorked a flask. "Here's a bit of apple cider."

"But I can't drink like this, Grandmother."

Sauveren said, "I'll stand up and put my front paws on this tree." In one graceful movement, he was upright.

Azanamer held a leather pouch to Fair's lips and squeezed it. "There now. Have a sip, Fair."

Cool, sweet apple cider slid over her tongue. She let out a small cry when the liquid made her swallow. Her dry throat felt pinched at having to rub against itself. Fair made small slurping sounds. She was able to get several good swallows. Whatever didn't go in her mouth dribbled down her chin onto Sauveren's fur.

Fair croaked, "I, I was so thirsty. Thank you." Her tongue felt big, as thought it was filling her head.

"Your turn," Azanamer said to Sauveren. "This will revive you." She put the flask to his mouth, and he drank thirstily then stopped when he saw a flash of red through the branches and leaves far below them. It was Salloroc's cap.

The Protectors were now several switchbacks below them. He and Fair still had several minutes of advantage. The army still had to go in the opposite direction to get up the last part of the pass into the flats.

Azanamer gave Sauveren a slap on the rump and whispered, "Now go. You don't have much time."

Without a sound, Sauveren sailed sideways from his hoomin-like stance against the tree. He glided up the trail, ducking branches and leaping over roots with no effort. Fair felt tied on snugly, so she relaxed her cheek against his fur while he ran.

It was the first time in days that she had been able to truly rest. The smallest whisper of a smile graced her lips. It felt to her as though she were riding upon an enormous furry pillow that floated beneath her. It came as a delightful surprise after so many hours, days, and shoomin of following the grassy path. Toiling in the caves. Building the wall. Going without sleep. Having a heart heavy with care.

With the scent of apple cider rising from his damp fur and filling her lungs, Fair actually fell asleep—there upon the back of the creature who loved her—there upon the back of the creature who ran with graceful speed up the zig-zagging mountain trail, far from the hot pursuit of their would-be captors.

Please take a moment to speak
for your host, Dimple Bum.

But of course.

46 : The Shepherd

ollan Sash led his flock of sheep down Cloven Grave Road. He was headed in the direction of the Quorum Range.

One sheep led the rest. It was Hale. All morning one thought had circulated in his mind: Free. At last. As he traipsed along on his new, cloven hooves he looked up at the sun.

It was reaching its zenith and would soon be as high as it would get for the day. At midden meal, all the matternots would change from sheep, back to their original selves. I have to move quickly, he thought.

"Wohhh-laaahn," he bleated.

"Yes, Lisper?"

"Howwww much lonnnger until mihhhden meeeeeal?"

"We should be at Azanamer's cottage in time. But we've got to hurry."

"Buuut I neeehhd tooo gehhht hohhhme," Hale said, "I neeeed to gehhht somethinnnng." Hale had daydreams of his own that had kept him company during his imprisonment in the caves of Osden Shorn. He remembered his father saying two things: "This sword will help usher in the new era." The other had to do with their large family clock. His father always said, "There's a lot of family history in this clock."

Wollan said, "You must hurry. It won't be long before you're walking on two legs again."

A group of Protectors galloped past the flock of temporary sheep. Hale knew how serious his decision was.

"Yehhhs. I can hurreee."

"Then go. Your cottage is just ahead, behind the red gate. It's not far. Come find us when you've finished doing what it is you need to do. You can do it. You must." He then repeated the final words of the legend of the Planter Era. "Open the door and lance the bull, amidst his anguished cries."

Hale realized Wollan Sash knew exactly what he was going to do.

Wollan Sash came to a trail that led into the woods to his right. He stood at the opening and shooed the sheep into the woods that led to Azanamer's cottage, one by one.

As Hale took off down the road, Wollan Sash called out after him, "Can you find the trail head when you come back to find us?"

Hale took note of the exact location. "Yehhhhsss."

It seemed to take forever for the long line of sheep to disappear into the woods. When the last one slipped into the shadows, Wollan Sash took a step into the opening and was enveloped in darkness.

Hale arrived at the red gate. He scurried around to the back of his cottage. He noisily clambered up the steps of the back porch. The place felt distantly familiar to him. He felt a rush of being home at last. He noticed a couple of Protectors rummaging about near the edge of the chicken coop.

"Dummmmmb hooves," he muttered. *They make so much noise.*

One of them looked up and said, "Somebody's sheep got loose. Look! The beast is on the porch."

Hale nudged open the back door and carefully stepped inside. No one was about. He knew he didn't have much time. He went into his parent's bedroom and tried to get a hoof underneath a floorboard. It was nearly impossible. He pushed and pounded clumsily. He stopped every once in awhile to look out a window to make sure he was safe. He clip-clopped to the back of the cottage and noticed that the two Protectors were headed back his way.

While he stood on his hind legs, he noticed his hooves felt funny. In an instant he was gripping the windowsill. He felt a slight breeze on his face and realized that the wool was no longer there. He felt himself grow taller and ducked just as one of the Protectors looked in his direction.

"Oh help," he whispered. He looked down and was relieved to see that he was not only dressed, but he was covered with a cape. Boots were on his feet, and a silver helmet had appeared at his side. A belt held his pants up, adorned with a silver buckle that looked like a dog's paw. *Sauveren*, he thought. *You're with me even now.*

He crawled over to the fireplace and quickly stood up to grab the sword that hung above the mantle. It was gone. *Oh no!* He crawled to his parents' bedroom where he easily lifted the floorboard. From the shadows he pulled out a horn that he and Fair had blown on their birthday, long ago. He looped the red cord over his head and across his chest. It hung near his waist.

He heard the back door open as one of the Protectors said, "I don't care if there's a sheep in here. Whatchoo worrying for if it poops in the place or not? The place is empty. Let's get back for midden meal."

"Just a quick look," said the other.

Hale ran into the pantry, lifted the cellar door, and climbed down. He let the door down quietly, while he held onto the rug, so it would cover the cracks. He stayed where he was until he could no longer hear the sound of footsteps.

"Who's there?" a voice said. It was a woman's voice.

I know that voice, Hale thought. His own daydreams all blended into one. He whispered, "Mother?"

Lariel struck a match and lit a candle. She came to the bottom of the stairs and said, "I knew you'd come back."

Hale ran down the stairs and wrapped his arms around his mother. He had grown so much in nine years. He was surprised at how small she seemed. He pulled back and looked at her. "The sword isn't above the fireplace any more."

"I know. It's time," she said.

She ran over to Fair's low lumpy bed and reached underneath the damp mattress. She pulled out a sword that was still in a well-oiled, leather sheath. The hilt had a single stone set into both sides of it: a ruby-red moss blossom in the shape of a broken heart. The two stones were identical to the one Thelras took from Harrold King's scepter and placed into Fair's forehead. Lariel pulled out a belt and handed it to Hale.

He said, "I know this heart, Mother."

She thrust the sword at him and said, "Yes. Now go. We'll meet again."

Hale put on the belt. He took the sword and kissed his mother on the cheek. "Until then, Mother." He grabbed his helmet.

Soon he was creeping through the woods as silently as he could, stopping at the sound of Protectors, then quickly slipping through the shadows when they were long gone.

It seemed like an eternity before he got to the trail. He found it smooth and free of roots. He took off at a run. Soon, he stumbled into a clearing.

Azanamer's cottage stood there surrounded by a grassy meadow. No one was about. He walked to her back door and heard a low whistle behind him. He looked towards the edge of the woods. He saw low bulky shadows. It had to be the matternots. He ran over and found Wollan Sash among them.

Wollan looked at the sword and the horn. He said nothing.

Hale looked into Wollan Sash's eyes. "I have something I need to do." he said. He wasn't sure exactly what it was, but he knew the answer would come to him at the right moment.

"You did well, son. You did well. You'll wait until sunrise?" said Wollan Sash.

"Yes."

47 : Trapped

ootprints, sir . . . coming out of the orchard," announced one of the Protectors. Pewgen Flype pointed.

"I'm not stupid. I see them," said Salloroc. He looked down at Sauveren's paw prints that led into and out of the gate.

The Protector said, "What I don't understand is how we didn't see any footprints until now. They had to get past the Searing Ruwens."

Salloroc shook his head. "I don't understand it either," he said. He had lost two hoomin in the Searing Ruwens. That was all. Before they left Osden Shorn, he forced Wollan Sash to reveal how to get past the unpredictable, explosive flames.

"There are always two explosions close together then nothing. Then three more will come. After that, we had enough time to get five or six sheep through. Then the same pattern started all over. We never lost a one."

"We're not talking about sheep, Wollan. We're talking about my hoomin, curse you."

"About the same then, sir. Five or six."

Salloroc took his hoomin in two groups and they made it. Mostly. He reached up and nervously patted the small bulge in his pocket. Harrold King had sent Rithel along. He poked his head out for a look around and a wicked smile formed on his face.

Rithel hissed. "Not muchhh longer."

Salloroc ordered his Protectors, "At a gallop. I want to stop them before they get to the Pool of Rilmorrey. The water might slow the horses down too much. Off with you!"

The hoomin dug their heels into their horses' sides. The horses lunged forward, tearing against the bits in their mouths. Their manes whipped like black scarves in a fierce gale.

Sauveren and Fair needed to go between two sets of mountains before they reached the safety of Drinkwater again. They had already made it through the first. Salloroc and his hoomin were quickly gaining.

I can hear them! I can hear them! Fair whispered to herself. She trusted that Sauveren would keep her safe, but it was hard to fight back the doubt that when the time came, he might not be able to protect himself. Or her. "Do you think they have bows and arrows?" she said.

"Yes."

"What do you think they will do to us?"

"You don't want to know."

"I'll pray for your strength."

"I need it," he puffed. He didn't dare say, but his muscles were weakening by the minute. The night before had drained him of any strength he possessed. Now he was running out of sheer loyalty to the burden on his back.

There was a small bend in the trail, and Sauveren knew that when the bend reversed and curved like an "s" in the opposite direction they would be close to the waterfall.

"I can really smell water now, Sauveren. We're going to make it. I know it." Fair allowed herself a weak smile. She nestled her cheek back into his fur.

Pewgen Flype pointed. One of the Protectors followed the direction of his finger. He shouted, "I've spotted them, sir!" He had spotted Sauveren just before he ran around the bend in the trail. He looked like a black streak.

"Push on! We have no time to lose. Harder now. Prepare your weapons. Orders are to finish the job."

Salloroc slipped his own bow over his neck in one swift and easy movement while he shouted commands. He reached over his shoulder. He pulled an arrow out of the quiver on his back. Rithel watched from Salloroc's pocket. The lizard's eyes glinted. The dogs began barking as though they were being strangled. They were eager to find their prey. Salloroc dug in his heels and sped ahead of his small army.

For a moment, all that could be heard was the reverberating echo of hooves, hounds, and the heavy breathing of hoomin on the hunt.

He rounded the second bend and saw Sauveren running towards a waterfall. Trapped. The side of Salloroc's mouth curled up in a mean smile. The maiden was tied to her dog. This was too easy. He shouted at Fair, "Tell your dog to stop or I'll make you stop!"

Sauveren turned around to face the approaching army. They pulled up on their reins. The horses' front legs pawed the air. The dogs ran on ahead, eager to finish tracking their prey.

Salloroc approached.

Sauveren edged backwards the closer Salloroc came. Fair could hear the roaring of the waterfall behind them. She shivered uncontrollably; yet, she wasn't cold in the least.

"Oh, Sauveren."

"I know."

Salloroc called off the dogs and they reluctantly obeyed. He called over his shoulder, "Stay back. I've got a job to do . . . in the name of his Majesty Harrold King." He turned back to face Fair and her dog. He narrowed his gaze onto the girl. Then he looked squarely at the dog beneath her.

Sauveren said, "Not here, Salloroc."

Salloroc stepped back. The voice was too deep to be the maiden's. He stared at the dog in disbelief. He had seen its mouth move. It couldn't have been.

Salloroc looked around him, then back at Sauveren. "Who spoke?"

"Is it such a surprise?" Sauveren asked.

There is was again. His mouth moved. Fair could feel Salloroc's gaze. It penetrated through her and her dog. She heard him say something about a bedeviled dog. The tone of his voice sounded unpredictable. She heard the sound of a bow being pulled taut.

Salloroc deftly slipped the arrow into place and pulled back.

"For his Majesty!" he yelled. He released his grip. The arrow shot out with frightening speed with a whirring sound.

48 : A Job to Do

 ale woke up while the sky was still dark. He had no idea why he had gone back for the sword.

And now, he had no idea what he was going to do with it once he got to Osden Shorn.

He just felt propelled by an urge beyond himself. He ran through the woods and snuck through the front gate of the temple. He found his way to the tunnel leading back down to Pewgen Flype's cage and crawled down. The stench was unbearable, and so familiar.

He pushed open the cage door. All was quiet by then, since the Protectors had ended their search inside the temple. Soon, he found himself running down hallways. Looking. Listening. He stopped when he heard voices. They were arguing. A settled feeling came over him, and he understood that this is what he had come for.

The sound seemed to come from the other side of a pair of double doors blocking a long hallway. Hale opened the doors. He looked around and noticed that the voices seemed to be coming from behind a painting of Harrold King. It hung on the wall to his left. He snuck up to it.

"You're nothing but a weak, pathetic excuse for a father. And you are certainly no king."

"Stop it, Axum. I never knew what it was like to have so much power, but these mirrors . . . they," he paused. "They have ruined me. Stay away from that room. It was beautiful when I first found it, but I had an evil wish in my heart when I came to Cloven Grave. The Chamber of Mirrors has turned that wish into monstrous proportions." He patted the spot on his shoulder where Rithel often sat. "And as for that, that crawly thing . . . it never lets me alone. I'm a cruel hoomin."

"Yes. And you've taught me well. Now it's my turn." Axum laughed. "I can't believe you've kept this such a secret for so long."

"The mirrors will be destroyed long before you ever get to the throne. I'll make sure you never know their power," said Harrold King.

"What makes you think I'll have to wait so long?" said Axum.

Hale heard a struggle and soon the painting of Harrold King split open with a loud crack and tore down the middle. Splinters shot out from behind the painting and Hale thrust the sword in front of him to protect himself.

Harrold King charged out from behind the torn and distorted painting of himself. He came towards Hale like a raging bull. His face was contorted with anguish. He cried, "Protectors! Help me!"

Hale didn't have time to pull the sword back. Harrold King fell right onto the end of it. The sword seemed to have found its mark.

Harrold King stopped when the sword pierced his chest. He looked at Hale with round bewildered eyes. He fell to his knees with a loud thud. He rolled onto his back on the cold stone floor. He looked up at Hale and gurgled, "It was you all along."

"No sir," Hale answered. "It was the dog."

"Dog?" he mumbled. A trickle of blood formed a trail out of the corner of his mouth. His eyes began to register what Hale meant and he said with emphasis, "*That* ugly thing?" He began to laugh. He couldn't stop laughing, but soon his laugh grew weaker and weaker until he breathed a final sigh and closed his mouth. The final bit of air that left his nostrils made a high-pitched whistle. Axum stood at the doorway, dumbfounded. "I didn't know my father could whistle through his nose."

"Yes. And he's probably dead, Axum. Or are you that heartless, not to have noticed?"

Axum's face brightened. Then he looked at the sword in Hale's hands. He recognized the heart in the hilt of it. "Where did you get that sword? It's mine!"

"Take it," said Hale.

Axum reached for the sword. His hands passed right through it. "You!" he screamed. "What sort of trick is this?"

Hale was stunned. He'd seen what happened and it didn't seem real. "It's no trick. Here. You can have it." He felt sick that he may have killed someone with it. He looked behind him at the elevator shaft.

Axum was too afraid to try to grab the sword again. "The mirrors," he said. He brightened and stepped over his father's body. He ran for the spiral staircase that led down to the Chamber of Mirrors.

After Axum left, Hale knelt down beside Harrold King. He looked at him for a long time. He tried to understand how this hoomin could have made his life so miserable for so long.

What was it about words that exerted such power? Words out of his lips, now silenced and still, had kept Hale in the caves of Osden Shorn for most of his life. He felt sorry for the bulk that lay in front of him. He reached out to put his hand over the hoomin's mouth to be sure he was dead. He'd seen Pewgen Flype do it many times. He couldn't feel the warmth of Harrold King's breath.

Hale hesitated before leaving him lying there. But he knew that would have to be dealt with later. He ran up and down hallways until he found the balcony overlooking Lakinren Bae. He blew into the horn as long and loudly as he could.

Back in the hallway, Harrold King's finger twitched ever so slightly.

49 : Escape

auveren reared up on his hind legs. He turned around and lunged into the trail behind the waterfall, just as the arrow whizzed past. Fair was still tied to his back.

The Protectors hardly had time to think. They released a volley of arrows into the frothing white water.

Salloroc shouted, "They'll never survive! The water will crush them." He smugly rode up to the edge of the waterfall and cursed. There was a path.

"The trail goes behind it. They went behind the fall! Move ahead."

Salloroc and his hoomin inched their way into the deafening hollow behind the falls. The horses were skittish and needed coaxing to move along. Once they came out the other side, Salloroc noticed that the trail wound down in a series of switchbacks. It led to a grassy meadow that grew next to a large pool. By now, Sauveren was nearing the bottom of the trail.

"Drinkwater, my good hoomin," he surveyed the scene. "This is Drinkwater."

The Protectors sat on their horses and surveyed the scene below. Deep down, Salloroc had to admit that this place was magnificent.

"Let's go," said Salloroc.

"Drinkwater Bound!" they shouted and raised their bows into the air.

The hoomin nudged their horses down the path until they could launch into a stone-flying, dirt-kicking fury. Salloroc kept the corner of his eye trained on the dog. He was headed for the meadow. Beyond it two of the steep mountainous rises lead into a dead end. Part of a sheer black granite wall glistened there and appeared to smolder in the sunlight.

"We've got them both," he gloated, "There's no way out. Send the dogs on ahead."

Commands. Shouting. The dogs burst through the horses' rippling legs and shot ahead, barking and yelping. For an instant the trail was a mass of explosion: rising dust, prodding legs and kicking hooves.

⤛ ❦ ⤜

Fair and Sauveren plunged into the pool once again. When they came up, she could hear the dogs barking behind them. She wondered if she would ever see Sauveren again after this moment. She wondered if she would make it alive. They were near the edge of the pool by now.

I've got to ask now, she thought. "Sauveren? Do you think . . . ," she hesitated.

"Just ask."

"Can you make me see, Sauveren?"

"Such great faith. We don't have much time. I'm going to ask you to scoop up some mud. Do you think you can do that if I kneel down?"

"I'll try."

He quickly knelt. "Now. Grab what mud you can."

"A little lower. I don't feel anything."

He got as low as he could to the ground. Her fingers brushed against wet earth. She squished a handful of mud.

"There. I've got some."

"Just hold onto it. We don't have time for anything else."

"If you say so."

He ran through the glowing Embers of Espritan. Fair felt the warmth of the flames on both sides of her as they passed through. He crossed the meadow and headed for the grassy corridor between the two steep mountains. Beyond, he could see vines hanging down the shining black wall. Just in front of them lay an old weathered sheep's gate. It looked like a ramp with sturdy fences on both sides. Just wide enough to allow one sheep through at a time. It sloped upwards and ended in a narrow platform. Sheep would have walked straight along it, one by one, into the waiting wagon.

Sauveren ran to the gate with Fair still on his back. He was just running up its slope when he heard a shout.

50 : The Final Moment

alloroc arrived far in advance of his hoomin and watched the dog run with Fair up the sheep's gate. "Ready!" he shouted.

They'll never escape, he said to himself with a crooked smile.

The army galloped into view of the sheep's gate. They pulled back on their horses' reins. It hadn't taken them long to load their arrows. The hounds ran to the base of the gate and barked at Sauveren, shoulder to shoulder. The Protectors stretched out their arms and cocked the other arm back. They placed their cheeks near the sinew that held the notch of the arrow.

"Release!" Salloroc shouted.

Sauveren leaped off the edge of the platform at the end of the gate. As he landed on the grass, he and Fair could hear the whiz of arrows shoot over their heads. The tips struck the stone wall further beyond. He kept running.

Fair knew they were trapped. She could feel it. She could hear the echo of the arrows around her and could tell they were at a dead end. Curtains of ivy covered the sheer black granite wall behind them. Every leaf held its breath in perfect paralysis.

"Cael and Thelras help us," she uttered. The dogs had begun to surround them.

As Sauveren slowed to a stop he spoke, "It's time. We're almost there."

Fair could hear the sound of the hoomin and horses in the background. A glimmer of hope passed through her heart. "Selador's Gate you mean?"

He panted, "We just went through it."

She had heard the wood beneath Sauveren's paws as he ran up the sheep's gate. "What, you mean the ramp?"

"Yes. There's just one more . . . thing."

Fair realized he must be talking about the Door of Reunion. She could hear the sound of horses in the background. Her entire life distilled itself into a powerful picture. A story. She imagined just then that it was woven into her luminamen and that she'd been staring at her life for nine years without knowing it.

"Why did I need to come here, if I'm not going with you?"

"To be a witness that it happened, Fair."

"A witness?"

"Would anyone believe it otherwise?"

Fair thought of the Blood Moon. The converging mists. The howling. What was about to happen?

"But what if we don't survive?" she asked, "Then what?"

"Your Secret Speaker will write the story of the Great Deliverance in the Eternal Book of Time. His name is Liver. He will tell this story.

Fair heard another voice, "Turn around, mongrel." It was Salloroc. He rode next to them on his horse. "So this is the Zothiker weasel, and her talking dog, a fine combination. You haven't made this job very easy, and I can't say I like you for it."

He spit on Sauveren and gave him a kick in the ribs. "You've had quite a burden on your back. She was just a bad dream: one of the Harrold's bad dreams, and I'm going to make sure she never sits on that throne. We're going to make your load a little lighter on you now."

Salloroc turned back to his hoomin, whom he had ordered to stay a ways back.

"Call off the dogs." They had been pacing and circling. Waiting. One of the Protectors called off the dogs. They stopped barking and reluctantly loped away.

Salloroc sneered, "Where do you run when you cannot hide?"

"I do not need to hide," answered Sauveren. "You don't want the maiden. You have come for me."

"You?" Salloroc laughed. He clenched his jaw. He narrowed his eyes. "You lie!"

In one movement he reached back in his quiver for an arrow and positioned it for a deadly aim at Fair. Sauveren reared up on his hind legs, completely hiding Fair from view. His chest was completely exposed.

Salloroc had aimed for Fair, but the arrow hit Sauveren instead. When it pierced his heart his body twisted and fell limply against the wall behind him. He and Fair slid like clay down the black granite wall.

They lay in a crumpled heap.

Completely still.

There was a faint cracking sound. A lightning bolt shot into the corridor. It smashed the platform at the end of the sheep's gate. The air exploded with echoing cacophony. Pewgen Flype looked at the destruction and went pale. He looked up to see black clouds rolling and boiling across the sky. His jaw dropped in fear.

"Get up, you fools!" Salloroc yelled. He had barely noticed the lightning and thunder. A few drops began to fall from the sky. They softly pelted the ground.

Salloroc walked up to the dog and stepped on him with his boot. He gave him a push with his foot. Sauveren and Fair were limp. Her face was pale.

"The arrow reached its mark," he said to himself. Then, more loudly he said, "Sound the horn! And Pewgen Flype, come untie the poor wretch."

One of the Protectors gave a loud blast through his horn.

Brah, brah—brah-brah-brah!

Pewgen Flype untied Fair. Her body rolled off her dog. One of her arms flung loosely out to her side and revealed a bright red patch of blood spread across her chest. He looked down at Fair, then to Sauveren.

He felt something like fire sear his eyes. He didn't know what made them burn and so he rubbed them. They were wet. He thought of the caves. His tongue. While he stared at her, he saw something he hadn't ever noticed before: This maiden looked so innocent. He looked away and cried to himself silently, *"What have I done? I've been a fool."*

Rithel climbed out of Salloroc's pocket and stared at the scene. He was breathless with excitement. He looked at Salloroc and said, "You did well, Salloroc. You did well." He gave a loud shriek and transformed himself into a dark, smoky flame. He shot out of Salloroc's pocket and out of the grotto, leaving a smudge of gray smoke behind him. Salloroc watched Rithel leave and scratched his head.

One of the Protectors asked, "Do you want me to take her down on my horse, Salloroc?"

"Leave them both here. Harrold King just wants to know we finished the job." He shouted. "Our work is done. Back on your horses!"

All the Protectors returned to their horses, but Pewgen Flype stayed behind. When he found himself alone with the two bodies, he covered them both with the vines that spread onto the ground from the black stone wall. As he did this, he felt the boulders of cruelty fall off his shoulders and shatter on the ground around him.

He found a stick and wrote three words in the soil, "Please forgive me." He turned, found his horse, and rode away.

⚶

The sound of horses, dogs and hoomin was long gone. The silence of soil and stone seeped out of the mountain and made itself heard. A solitary leaf settled itself in a vine above the two figures. It began to whisper. A breeze blew into the grotto.

In an instant, the leaves turned from green to deep orange. Thousands of them.

They began to flutter.

Then they took flight—one by one—until the air was filled—with butterflies.

The shifting orange swarm covered Sauveren like a blanket and wrapped itself around him like a cocoon. It rose and slowly turned until Sauveren appeared to be floating upright. Nothing could be seen of him; yet, he was there.

Within the swarm, a small golden light began to spin around his paws. The faster it spun, the brighter it grew. It rose higher and higher until Sauveren was completely surrounded by light. Life seemed to fill and solidify his once-limp limbs.

Like a thread being unraveled, the light began to return to normal where it began. The swarm of butterflies let Sauveren back down to the ground and left him standing on all fours. Alive.

He reached down and loosened Fair's fingers with his paws. The clay-like mud was still soft and wet. He pulled at it with his paws until the clump fell onto the ground. He clawed it into two pieces and patted it into two cakes of clay. He picked them up with his mouth and placed them on her eyes. He nudged them into place with his black, shining nose.

"Fair," he spoke.

She didn't move.

"Sight once gone is now returned. So let it be spoken, so let it be done."

Fair groaned and moved ever so slightly.

"My eyes . . . so cold. So heavy. Am I dead?"

Sauveren reached down and took the mud off her eyes. He said, "I am here." He stroked her hair. It immediately began to lengthen, curl and grow, until it returned to its original length. It spread on the ground around her head like a brown halo.

Fair's eyelids felt cool and moist. She opened them and saw Sauveren looking down on her.

"I can . . ."

"See," he said, and licked her cheek. She rolled to her side and wept as she held his feet.

"My eyes," she said. She felt the gentle pull of her hair as she rolled over. Astonished, she searched with her fingers on her head and then let them follow along the curling strands that spread out around her.

Sauveren and Fair looked at each other in silence for a moment. He lay down and let her cuddle up close to his chest. "It's time for me to go where you cannot come," he said.

She begged, "But can't I come?"

"You and your brother still have things to do."

She wrapped her arms around his back and squeezed her eyes closed. She felt like she was going to choke on her tears.

"But will you come back?" Her chin quivered.

"I will come again. Will you wait for me?"

She pressed her face into his fur and nodded. Her shoulders shook. Through muffled tears she said, "I'll keep whistling for you. Like a bird."

"And I'll come into your heart whenever you call. And now, may I have the key?"

She had no idea what he meant. "The key?"

"You've had it with you for a long time."

Sauveren rose and headed for the endlessly high, black wall. He used his paw to push aside the vines until he found what he was looking for. He held the curtain of leaves open to show Fair the shape of a broken heart, carved into the jet black stone.

Fair understood. She said, "Let me do it."

No sooner had she spoken the words, when something warm and smooth appeared in her hand. She quickly closed her fingers around the something before it fell out. Fair felt her forehead. It was smooth again. The Ruby Eye was gone. She walked to the heart-shaped hole in the wall, and a searching, living root appeared to be waiting to have its moss blossom returned. She opened her hand and put the two halves of the Ruby eye, *click, click,* into place. Impissh Nissen floated nearby, watching. She looked at Sauveren, who nodded.

Imperceptibly, the wall began to move. First it appeared as a crack in the stone. A blinding light struggled for escape behind it, as though it had been trapped. The crack widened with the sound of small bells, revealing the shape of a door. Fair gasped when she realized it was the Door of Reunion. She said, "But you were supposed to open it. Not me. I didn't mean to . . ."

He quietly said, "I opened it back in the orchard," then stepped over the threshold into the depths of the mountain behind him.

Fair sat down and watched Sauveren go with her arms clasped around her knees. Although it hurt to look, she forced herself to stare at what she saw.

He was immediately engulfed by butterflies, then by a glowing, white hot brilliance. She could barely make out the shape of his silhouette, but he appeared to stand up on his hind legs and walk. In a moment, he stopped and turned around to face her.

Near the top of the orange swarm, some of the butterflies moved aside to reveal what lay behind them. Fair saw a pair of eyes looking at her.

Glinting.

Clear.

Those eyes, she said to herself. She knew she had known it deep inside for some time.

"Selador," she whispered.

"Be at peace, Fair, and know that I am." He paused. "Emerge."

While Fair watched his brilliant silhouette disappear behind the curtain of butterflies, she muttered, "I know what the one word is."

The door slid closed with a heavy, solid sound.

The curtains of ivy began to tremble and sway. Soon the traveling whisper blew through the hillsides of Cloven Grave and the trees gusted to and fro in excited gossip. The glory of the day was whispered by the leaves, who heard it from the branches, who heard it from the roots, who heard it from the dirt and stones around them.

51 : Home Again

air woke up to the sound of a horse whinny. As she came to, she realized in a very sleepy way that her head was bouncing on something that smelled like the mountains. She tried to force her eyes to blink in an effort to wake up.

The Woolly had found Fair at the base of the Door of Reunion. He couldn't tell if she were asleep or dead. He carried her through the Quorum Range, past the Searing Ruwens and over to Gibber Will's wagon.

Azanamer sat in the back of the wagon on a pile of pine needles with Wollan Sash. The Woolly gently laid the maiden down between them. Then he ran off.

Harrold King's entire army had gathered at the base of the mountains to welcome the hero home. They silently stood at attention in their kilts and tall fur hats. Their swords were drawn to let her pass beneath them. The entire village of Cloven Grave lined the road. They stood with heads bowed as the wagon rode by. They stood in silence, not sure whether they were witnessing a funeral procession or the return of the maiden who brought them the miracle.

"She's awake," said Azanamer. She sat calmly, like a stone, in the back of Gibber Will's wagon. She dabbed Fair's forehead with a damp cloth.

When Azanamer spoke, Gibber Will turned around on his perch at the front of the wagon. He wiggled his nose with a sniff. He saw Fair looking around, trying to figure out where she was. He stood up and gave a wave to the villagers, "She's awake! Just in time to be comin' home, she is."

Fair furrowed her brow and looked around. She was too sore to sit up so she rolled over slightly and noticed that she was lying on a fragrant bed of pine needles.

"It would have been a painful ride without them," said Azanamer.

"Thank you." Fair paused in an effort to remember. "But how did you . . . how did I get here?"

"The Woolly carried you down," said Wollan Sash.

Gibber Will said, "I brought the wagon as far as the Searing Ruwens."

"You've had quite a fever," Azanamer smiled. She dabbed Fair's forehead with the cloth. "Here, have a sip of this." She put a flask up to Fair's lips. Fair took a few small gulps.

"That's enough. I'm not too thirsty."

"What? You, not thirsty?" smiled Azanamer.

Just then, Fair heard what sounded like a herd of cows moaning ahead of the wagon. It was the sound of bagpipes warming up. Soon, majestic music filled the air.

Azanamer helped her up when she saw movement on both sides of the road. Something was coming out of the woods. Fair heard voices join the bagpipe tune. It was so familiar to her. One by one, she saw matternots step out of the woods like soldiers. They were singing the song she had taught her friends that warm afternoon while building the wall that went nowhere. The girls and boys wore boots and woolen capes, large silver belt buckles in the shape of a dog's paw. They held silver helmets at their sides.

A cheer erupted from the villagers on both sides of the road. The sound spread until every last hoomin and wee hoomin was shouting, "She's awake! She's awake!"

Some of the parents ran up and down, scouring the matternots' faces, looking to see if they might recognize their long-lost wee hoomin. Soon, the villagers congregated around Gibber Will's wagon.

Then, someone called out, "No more Harrold King! To the new queen. Hail Fair!"

Everyone began to cheer, "Hail Fair!"

She asked Gibber Will to stop the wagon. She stood up and said, "But I am not the miracle you've been waiting for."

No one was really quite sure what she was talking about. Of course she was. Harrold King was gone. Fair had everything to do with it. Surely. She—and her brother that drew his sword and blew that horn. Maybe it was her brother. Where was he?

Far down Cloven Grave Road, Fair spied a flutter of color. She pointed at it and said, "There is your miracle."

Everyone looked. A swarm of butterflies came towards them. Golden light sprayed out through gaps between their fluttering wings. When they got close to the wagon, they all flew away, and the hoomin folk of Cloven Grave looked in wonder. It was Fair's dog. He was walking towards them.

A dog?

The new king? But how?

Soon, the sky above them began to change. It looked as though it were lowering. Coming closer. The villagers looked up and stared. The sky was filled end to end with shimmering, wee hoomin of Light who were looking at Sauveren, singing.

The villagers looked at him in wonder and confusion. One by one, they knelt and bowed their heads. He walked past them all silently and was overtaken once again by the butterflies. The same golden light the villagers had seen began to spray out between their wings.

Soon the light was gone, and the butterflies flew away in different directions. The children of Light had disappeared.

The road was just a dry and dusty place.

The sky was just a sky.

He was gone.

Fair said, "Cloven Grave is not our real home." She looked up at the clouds. The bagpipers started up once more, and the villagers cheered. Gibber Will flicked the reins to take Fair to her cottage, several cansees away.

As the wagon approached the cottage, Fella Doon bolted up excitedly. He had been sitting on the porch wringing his hands with worry. He knocked on the door and shouted, "They've come back! They've come back!"

Hale burst out of the door and ran up to the wagon.

Gibber Will pulled up on the reins. "Woah, now."

In the space of a wing's beat, Fella Doon was at the back of the wagon, "Do you know, I can come and go anytime I fancy, now that . . . well, now that the Harrold's gone. It's a wonder the likes of which I ain't known for the longest time. I'm glad you're all in one piece."

"Me too," said Fair.

Fair's voice! Hale ran to the back of the wagon and saw his sister lying on a bed of pine needles. His hands gripped the rough-sawn wood. He seemed as though he would leap inside the box.

Fair looked at him. Hale saw something different in her eyes. He stared at her hair, unable to believe what he saw. He waved at her, almost not daring to believe what he hoped was true.

She gave a small wave back.

"You can . . ."

"See," she finished. "Each one of your faces. Sauveren opened the Door of Reunion, but he's not Sauveren at all. He's Selador."

"The one you were supposed to find?" Hale asked. Then he said incredulously, "He, he was with you all along!"

She looked at him and nodded. "I heard you blew our horn to send a signal that the Law of Memory was gone forever."

"It's true," Hale nodded, "All the horn blowers stationed at posts along the route to Mount Rilmorrey sent my signal up the mountain. It met the signal of the horns that had been blown from the Pool of Rilmorrey, when they thought you were dead.

"Everyone in Cloven Grave cheered when they figured out that Harrold King was dead—even the Protectors all the way up on the mountain. You should have seen how black the sky was. It stayed that way for three days. The air was so heavy we couldn't even light a fire to see by."

"How dreadful," Fair said, "And were you really a sheep?"

"The Protectors didn't even know it was me."

"Really?" Fair asked. "You could walk right past them?"

"Honest. Fidavine Belle and her brother, too. All of the matternots."

Fella Doon said with a crack in his voice, "I ain't never told you, but Fidavine Belle and the boy . . . they're my own flesh and blood. They're home again, thanks to you. I don't need no red scarf now."

A feeling of calm drifted onto the company of friends gathered around the wagon. Meanwhile the leaves in the surrounding trees hung as still and expectant as though they couldn't stand the suspense any longer.

"It was Sauveren, you know," Fair said. "All along."

Hale said, "I'm sorry he's gone." He squeezed Fair's hand.

She smiled weakly. "He's not gone. We'll see him every time we look for what someone needs, then do it."

Fair looked at Gibber Will and Azanamer. "Do you remember . . . when I helped Miss Tilly? . . . Sauveren was her all along, even though he wasn't really her . . . but I could see him in her face," she said excitedly. "And when I spoke to Tooli King and gave him courage . . . and that white-eyed old woman in the woods . . . it was Sauveren."

Fella Doon looked apologetically at everyone, as though Fair was a bit delirious. "We're just glad you're alright, Fair. It's easy to imagine things some times."

"But it's real," said Fair. "It's real when you look through a broken heart. You see things."

She looked at Gibber Will and her eyes widened. "You were a scared rabbit, Gibber Will."

He wiggled his ears and nose dramatically. "Me a rabbit? That's a good one."

"And you were so brave, even though you didn't know it." Gibber Will looked around at everyone and smiled proudly.

"And Azanamer, you were an unfeeling stone, but you really could feel, even though you didn't think you could." Azanamer smiled knowingly.

"And the Woolly . . . ." Fair looked around. ". . . where is he? He was a crazy monkey . . . but he was the wisest one of all. And I saw Sauveren's face in each one of them. He was always with me."

Azanamer smoothed back a bit of Fair's hair with her gnarled hand and smiled. "You have learned to look."

Hale said, "You might want to come inside now, Fair. I have something to show you."

Hale took Fair inside the cottage. Their friends stayed outside. Fair and Hale saw the Woolly sitting on a chair near a crackling fire. He was holding something wrapped in red cloth on his lap.

Their mother was cutting his snarled hair with a pair of black scissors. His ears appeared. Then his neck. Soon, she began to shave off his beard. Long, matted tufts fell away, revealing his cheeks and chin. When the last furry piece dropped onto his lap, a mouse scurried out of the pile.

Fair looked at the Woolly and caught her breath. *It couldn't be.* She watched him thoughtfully brush the remnants of his beard off the cloth-covered shape. As he unwrapped it, Fair saw a box with a painted mountain scene on top. He lifted the lid on its hinges. Music began to play. Just then, an iridescent, blue butterfly flitted out an open window.

The Woolly spoke slowly, "Little Sparrow." He smiled at her and opened his arms wide.

Epilogue

ael's hand is reaching for me. He's pulling me out of the Eternal Book of Time. I have been comfortably nestled in its cover so the story could be written in its pages for you to read.

Report to me, Liver . . . to both of us.

Here is my report: I have told the story of The Great Deliverance, Thelras and Cael. I have fulfilled my purpose.

Well done, Liver. You have been faithful. Do you have anything else you would like to say? You have only a few moments to speak.

Yes. I have a request.

What is it?

The Scrolls of Truth. What will happen to them? The matternots need to know everything.

You are wise, Liver. We have heard the silent cries of the wounded. The Scrolls of Truth are safe and the matternots will know everything. They will emerge. And now, are you ready?

I am ready. *Both of them are reaching for me.* Take me, and throw me into the stars where I will shatter into a million different pieces of light and join all that has been, is, and ever will be . . . .

Your hands . . .

                     they are so

gentle.

          And the stars . . .

                         they are

          so

                              pure.

Shake thyself from the dust; arise, sit on thy throne
. . . loose thyself from the chains of thy neck,
O captive daughter of Zion.

ISAIAH FIFTY-TWO
VERSE TWO

Père O mon Père, je te remercie.

Je lave les pieds de ton fils avec mes larmes.

Axum King: [Axm] Harrold and Sophrea King's youngest son, the brother of Tooli.

Azanamer: [Ah-zuh-NAHHmr] An elderly woman who people whisper comes from the Night People (who live in the pastures of prepahr in Mount Rilmorrey). People call her grandmother. She is known for her gift to heal and give comfort and has skin the color of freshly turned soil.

Cael: [Kale] Father of Selador, Rithel and the children of Light. Known as Father King of Light. Rules with Thelras, Mother Queen of Light.

Fella Doon: One of Harrold King's lead guards. He is called upon to perform many tasks.

Hale O'Nelli: Fair's twin brother.

Harrold King: A wicked and evil man who began to rule in Cloven Grave—uninvited. He makes everyone bring everything they make or grow to him once a shoomin for the Rendering. Then he gives it back to them in much smaller portions and keeps the rest for himself. He has 400 guards to protect him.

Impissh Nissen: Small, spritely creatures that cultivate jewels in the moss that grows in the woods. Legend has it that they can grow and shrink in size, and they have been given the responsibility to protect and guard the souls of the hoomin. They are only visible to those who are ready to see them.

Lariel O'Nelli: Tharin and Hale's mother.

Pewgen Flype: [Pewgn FLYpe] A greasy, pumpkin-faced captain. He wants to prove to Harrold King that he can follow the rules to perfection. But he tries so hard that he breaks rules to do it.

Rithel: [Rhymes with last two syllables of "off<u>icial</u>"] He is the brother of Selador.

Sauveren: [SO-vruhn] He is Fair O'Nelli's enormous and faithful dog. He stayed with her in the cellar for nine years.

Selador: [SELL-uh-dor] He is the brother of Rithel in the realm of Airen Or. Son of Cael, father king of Light, and Thelras, Mother Queen of Light.

Fair O'Nelli: The main character in *Secret Speakers*. She spent nine years of her young life living in a cellar.

Thelras: Mother of Selador, Rithel and the children of Light. Known as Mother Queen of Light. Rules with Cael, Father King of Light.

The Woolly: A strange fellow with a long, black and tangled beard, who roams the fields and woods of Cloven Grave in his bare feet. He wears tattered clothing and eats only honey milk and the bugs and grubs he finds beneath rocks and rotting logs. He is known for making no sense, and riddles.

Tilly Mote: She takes care of all the little children in the village of Cloven Grave. She refuses—or is unable—to speak to grownups. She is known and loved for all the moss blossom trinkets that she carries in the very large pockets of her apron. She claims that many of them come from the Impissh Nissen, the creatures that plant and grow jewels in the moss that grow in the woods.

Tooli King: Harrold and Sophrea King's oldest son. He has a younger twin brother, Axum.

AUTHOR'S NOTE

 Warning: This is not the usual Author's Note.

If someone told me, "It's time for you to make an accounting of your life. You have one day left to live before you return to your Creator. But there's only one problem: you won't be allowed to see or speak with anyone between now and then."—what would I do?

I would ask for some paper. I would write two letters. Since letters get lost, I would slip them in this book you hold in your hands. That way they'd be around for a long time.

"Alright, but you only have one hour to write."

Hence, an Author's Note that reads like this one. I admit it's risky and unusual for a work of fiction.

LETTER NUMBER ONE

To my children and your children's children,
(This letter is private, just for them.)

LETTER NUMBER TWO

February 14, 2010
Dear cherished reader,

Since I only have a moment to share my last words with you, I want to tell you a story about how *Secret Speakers* came to be, then leave you with a challenge. Years ago, the matternots in the Caves of Osden Shorn appeared so vividly in my mind, and the scenes wrote themselves so quickly, that my fingers could hardly keep up during the three days I secluded myself in a room at Zermatt, in Midway. Yes, I was writing fiction, but at the same time I realized (in a way I am only beginning to understand) that I was writing about a global problem that has been around for ages. I was also writing about values that need to be absorbed into our cultural consciousness.

Odd as it sounds, there were times I wept as I wrote, overcome with a sense of the suffering that so many quiet souls endure. May I simply say, I see you. I love you. It is for you I chose to keep the title of *Secret Speakers* during a time I considered changing it. You matter. Your life matters.

Fair O'Nelli is fictional, but if you felt anything for her, grew to value her as a character, and value her life and her strength, then you felt my passion in writing her story.

If you have a desire to understand the lives of real children and women who go through real challenges like Fair's, I want to ask you to read *Half the Sky*, by Nicholas Kristof and Sheryl WuDunn. As you do, you will understand my hope-filled vision that you, as a reader, can make a difference in the world in small, simple ways that will give deeper meaning to the purpose of your own life, as well as create life-changing opportunities for girls and women. You will also understand my challenge.

One night, while I lay in bed after reading the accounts of real girls and women in *Half the Sky* whose lives have been marked by oppression *and* opportunity, I felt as if countless voices were crying out from the dust to me. It is difficult to describe, because it felt—and still feels—so real. It was a magnificent moment. Their stories validated the gut-wrenching feelings that haunted me during the twelve years I worked on *Secret Speakers* (which began as a non-fiction book). The stories of our sisters in *Half the Sky* confirmed to me my long-time passion to write an underground novel that could be read on many levels, especially between the lines; a novel that could possibly give birth to a new cultural philanthropy in our nations.

Students learn best through story. Stories make us feel. Ideally, when we learn and feel, we understand. When we understand, we are given a choice to value that understanding, then act with the power to achieve something good, born from that desire. Or we can do nothing.

As a student of life, after reading *Secret Speakers*, I hope some of you will give value to the lives of those whose opportunities for improving their circumstances can be bettered through education, reading, and the Arts.

Children need love and kindness from those who care for them: mothers and fathers, teachers, aunts, and uncles; yet, often they don't get it. Is it possible that children can experience love and kindness and discover untapped skills through a book like *Secret Speakers*? I might be wrong, but I hope so.

Feisty Fair O'Nelli forged ahead on her own in many ways; yet, she couldn't have survived without the influence of the two strong women in her life or without the education she received at her mother's knee during her years in the cellar. My feeling about her story is that it has always been floating around. She is every child who suffers. She is every child who needs kindness.

We write what we know since we are each the literal center of our own perceptual universe. What did I know? Enough to know I needed to get on my knees and ask for constant inspiration while writing. I was also influenced.

I graduated with a BA in English with an emphasis in Creative Writing. My collegiate-born fascination with Dante's poem, the *Divine Comedy*, had a strong influence on me. I was also influenced by an ancient poem written on tablets telling of *Inanna's Descent to the Underworld*, by the *Bible*, and by *The Wizard of Oz*. I was also influenced by stories about my childhood hero, Harriet Tubman.

These influences, along with my life-long love of symbolism, allegory, languages (both dead and alive), the Christian teachings of my faith, and this journey called life, have all gone into what I know. Finally, a research trip to visit the Highlands and meet the people of my ancestral Scotland influenced me tremendously in describing Cloven Grave.

Here is my challenge to you: Strive to help another live to her full potential. Be kind. One place you can start is Care.org.

I offer this book to you with all my heart, with gratitude for life and the gift of love. We all have heart songs to sing that are born of pain and sorrow, joy and gladness, love and loss. *Secret Speakers* is my song.

-*Karey Shane*

P.S. I plan to live to 100 if my Nana and Aunt Liberty Lula are any indication of the genes I was born with. I have *years* of sequels and literary possibilities ahead of me. This book is just the beginning.

⟫ ACKNOWLEDGMENTS ⟪
The Short List

First, I'd like to thank those who helped *Secret Speakers* see the light of day. Without your help, it would still lie gasping in a pile on my desk.

Thanks go to Vanessa Carlisle for being the best consulting editor I could ever hope to find. Your insight helped shape the many decisions I made for the story.

Thanks go to Sadie Parker for your outstanding work on the final edit. Thanks also go to Pops (Lanny Britsch), and Linda Hunter Adams.

Thanks go to good-hearted Rick Frishman and Dan Poynter, for all you taught me about self-publishing.

Thanks to Brendon Burchard for teaching me the importance of creating events that bring people together. Because of your influence, the global *Read & Rate It* event came to be.

Thanks to Kathleen Horning for your input during the book discussion guide process.

Thanks to Katherine Farmer for introducing me to the works of Charles Pierce, de Saussure, and Kohlberg.

Thanks go to my uncle, Bill Swinyard, for educating me on the joys and nightmares of Photoshop.

Thanks to Simon Vance and Kenny Hodges for bringing the story to life as a phenomenal audio book. The first person to order it was a mother for her blind daughter.

Thanks to David Jones for bringing the Luminamen to life on my website. I knew it was possible! You proved it.

Finally, to Otis Chandler and the team at Goodreads: Elizabeth Khuri Chandler, Jessica Donaghy, Michael Economy, and Ken-ichi Ueda, I offer a humble thank you. I could not have found my cherished *Secret Speakers* family this early on and in such a fun way without your incredible social media site for those who love to read. You gave me a second home during a challenging time when I was surrounded by walls for days on end.

✑ ACKNOWLEDGMENTS ✑
The Long List

There are many cherished people I wish to thank for influencing my life so that I could write the book I always dreamed of. I didn't know what shape it would take, but your part in my life brought me to the point where it became impossible *not* to write it. Throughout the years, and nearly every day, someone has appeared in my life to teach me something wonderful and new about how to live out my life, this God-granted gift.

I've been blessed with the opportunity to live in many places and travel to faraway lands, but the first person that deserves profound thanks is my angel mother, Shirley, who has shown much strength and courage throughout my life. I watched her cheerfully press forward after my father died. She taught us five small children to pull weeds, cook, do our chores, and sing our way out of sorrow. I would not be here if it weren't for her. Obvious, but not so obvious.

Next, come my sisters, Gwennie and Lisa. They are my best friends. Special thanks goes to my twin sister for being the best cheerleader of *Secret Speakers* on this planet. She's lived and breathed its many incarnations with me for more years than I dare admit. And special thanks to my brothers, Phil and Jeff, for being so wonderful in your spheres of influence. I appreciate you.

Deep appreciation goes to the late Shirley Collins, my Honors English teacher at Skyline High School. One day she said that everyone in the class moving on to AP English would do very well, except for . . . then she said my name. Argh matey. The whole class looked at me and I tried to shrink in my chair. Then she added that I had a gift for creative writing, as shown by my paper on Faulkner's *As I Lay Dying*. I knew right then that I wanted to and could be a writer.

Secret Speakers would not be what it is without the love and support from friends in New Orleans, Montréal, and Richmond, Vermont, as well as friends from my youth.

Thanks go to Fran Pomerantz, for your dear friendship, soul-nurturing food, and for opening your home and heart to our family over the years. Thank you, Jane Barlowe, for walking in the woods with me, and for literally helping me find my footing. Thank you, Jean Bressor, for your good laugh and for bringing out my own hidden laughter when I thought I'd never laugh again. Thank you, Diane Mariano, for your hugs, for massaging out that knot in my back that brought me to my knees all those years ago with Marcia Levison guiding you over the phone. No one matches your Halloween parties. Thank you, Jean Campbell, for being a kind friend and a home away from home. Such love in friendship shared with each one of you has sustained me all these years more than you'll ever know.

Thank you to those at the Richmond Free Library for so many years of good books, for reading to my children—and for all the times you folks looked away when I didn't have the change to pay for my terribly overdue books!

Thanks to the Jack and Kim Kane family for opening your home and your hearts to my family. The same goes for you Elsie Maurice and Dan. And thanks to the Bryant Gile family of girls, with a fond wave to the late Judy Gile. And I can't forget to thank Sally Pitt, Vicki Williamson, Sarah Paulson, and Lauren Cundari for your guiding friendship over the years.

Thank you to my friends in New Orleans, wherever you are. It saddens me not to be able to find where you are since Katrina hit. Some of the houses we lived in don't exist any more when I look on Google Earth. If any of you read this: Michelle and Wally Landry (and your adorable girls), Bianca Medina Woodson, Jocelyn and Lee Williams, and Carmen Bagneiras, please let me know you're well. I'd love to hear from you. And Marianne Galvin, hello wherever you are, dear friend.

To Terry Tustain, my cherished friend from my years in Montréal, thank you for always cheering me on in my writing efforts, for all those years you opened the next issue of

Mothering magazine, wondering if that would be the issue where you'd find something I'd written.

A deep thanks goes to you, Fatima and Jay Glowa, for our memorable holidays together with my children. Thank you, too, to Corinne Gehmlich, for your wonderful friendship.

How can I thank you, Steve and Sabrina Lindsley, for your goodness? And Diane Terry, thank you for literally going the extra mile in Chicago and being an anchor for my soul. Lori and Scott Featherstone, thanks to your and your boys for watching over Grandma Shirley for so many years. Ben, a special wave to you. Bananas and peanut butter. Cheers!

Secret Speakers would not have been written without the appearance of four noble beings in my life: President Dieter F. Uchtdorf and his adorably fun wife, Harriet, as well as Joachim and Trudy Schenk. Sie sind mein Engel. Sie gaben mir die Hoffnung. Danke. And thank you D. Todd Christofferson for your personal challenge to me years ago. I believe I've begun to meet that challenge with *Secret Speakers*.

Thank you, Dr. Lucinda Bateman and all those at the clinic who helped me have a better quality of life the past two years: Ali, Kristen and Laurie.

Most recently thanks go to Rogan Taylor and your technicians, and the amazing Marv Roberson for giving me hope that I will be restored to health and strength through physical therapy.

To my children, Quinn and Dwight, your ideas helped me in writing *Secret Speakers* (and designing the cover) more than you know. Sadie, I want to thank you once again for your superb editing work.

I'll never forget you, Quinn, taking notes by car light, while we brainstormed about the story during that heavy snowstorm from Boston to Vermont on our way back from Thanksgiving at the Plimoth Plantation.

Thanks especially go to you, Patrick, for helping me discover strength I didn't know I had.

I began by thanking my mother. To sandwich this all, I now wish to thank my beloved children for being so courageous. You are precious to me. I ultimately wrote this book for you. It may be a long time before you read this, but my love flows between the lines of each and every page. It is there for you, regardless. Life isn't always what we would wish or hope it to be, but I know that love—in its divine, peace-giving splendor—fills in all the holes if we allow it. All of them.

And finally, I thank God for the beautiful trials of my life that have brought me to my knees. Because of them I have come to know that love is the only thing that matters. Because of them I know that we are each known and loved by God and that we're on his time, not ours. Because of them I have come to know that hope is a force to reckon with. Because of them I know that compassion is the great eraser and that we are all brothers and sisters. Because of them I know that pressing forward is always the best choice, come what may.

And because of them, I know that Christ takes our burdens from us as soon as we're willing to give them up. May God bless you and hold you in the palm of his hand. Always.

Secret Speakers: Read & Rate It Event

The (possibly) first-ever online global
early review for readers, by readers.

I want to personally thank each person who read *Secret Speakers* online during the global *Secret Speakers: Read & Rate It* event on Goodreads and Facebook, beginning December 25, 2008. Over 700 people signed up, which was amazing to me. I have to admit, I doubted that anyone would brave reading a 500-page manuscript online. It's difficult to read something that long on a bright screen. And yet, many of these heroic readers (almost all whom I have yet to meet) did just that. They hail from Australia, Iran, and North America.

And now, to speak to each one of you on the list: thank you for providing feedback that helped shape the story. *Secret Speakers* wouldn't be what it is without you. Because of you, I put in two chapters that I'd taken out (the Joust and Dangle scenes, if you're wondering, including Tooli's fate). When I asked you to compare it in terms of likeability to *Harry Potter* and *Twilight*, I was shocked that you asked me to add "better than" to the poll. If I'm ever in your city, I hope I have the honor of meeting you. Just let me know who you are. Be prepared for a big hug.

Kacey

P.S. The list of readers is on the following page. To the many not listed who read the e-manuscript (who chose not to do the Goodreads.com review), thank you. If I've missed anyone, I'm sorry!

~ Read & Rate It List ~

Jillian Aasen
Jewel Adams
John Allen
Nicole Anderson
Kara Bankhead
Melia Benjamin
Linda Bennion
Cheryl Bishop
Ronda K. Braunberger
Shirley Britsch
Lanny Britsch
Stephanie Brooks
Susan Cochrun
April Daniels
Cecily Davis
Dawn Delgado
L. Sue Durkin
Kathy Evans
Rebecca Everhart
Keyanah Fearrington
Sarah Flinders
Aspen Garfield
Madison Elise Goerend
Alexa Guerra
Weldon Hathaway
Letitia Harmon
Julie Jacobs
Shelby Jardine

Kevan Jensen
Anastasia Jespersen
Tamara T. Jordan
Lisa Justus
Wendy Leneham-Cohen
Clare LoCoco
Beth Ann Mayberry
Ancel McIntosh
Sheryl Mehary
Sheila K. Miller
LuAnn Morgan
Novin Nabavi
Kathy O'Marra
Helen Kiaya Pemberton
Elaine Raterman
Hollie Robb
Steve Rothwell
Jeff Shane
Hilda Soares
Gwendolyn Soper
Shannon Soper
Robin Sullivan
Rhonda Thye
Tianna
Victoria Valdes
Michelle Wasserbaech
Sherry White
Hannah Wilson

A portion from the sale of each copy of *Secret Speakers* goes to
the Humanitarian General Fund.

WANT TO HELP SPREAD THE WORD?

Here's exactly what you can do to help:

5 ideas for peeps who tweet on Twitter:

1. **Tweet and RT #SecretSpeakers when you finish a chapter.** Comment on it. Be sure to use the # sign in front of SecretSpeakers (the 'ole hashtag-aroonie)

2. **Send your peeps to SecretSpeakers.com** to make their own name star. Tell them how incredibly cool it is—that is if you agree

3. **Be sure to include @KareyShane.** I want to know my Secret Speakers family!

4. HERE's a FUN ONE:
Go to Pollpigeon.com. Search "Is Secret Speakers better than Twilight?" VOTE! It shows up on twitter

5. Get creative and let me know about it :)

We are fam-i-lee . . .

DID YOU KNOW . . .
Secret Speakers is self-published?
It's true. I'm the author, Karey Shane. Will you please read this page? Thanks!

WANT TO HELP SPREAD THE WORD?

A **fast and easy** CHECKLIST of exactly what you can do:

AMAZON: Tag it . . . Listmania!

1. **Go to Amazon.com** to tag this book. Here's how:
2. **Search "Secret Speakers and the Search for Selador's Gate."** A window will open.
3. Now **tap your 't' key twice**.
4. **A window will pop up that lets you 'tag'** *Secret Speakers*. **Important: You're allowed three tags.** I highly recommend these ones, wink, wink:

YOUNG ADULT, FANTASY, GIFT IDEA

1. **Now for Part Two: Listmania!**
2. Stay on the *Secret Speakers* page. See that **box that says Listmania! off to the left**?
3. Click on it to **create your own list.** Use these words pretty please:

young adult fantasy, ya fantasy, teen fantasy, paranormal, paranormal fantasy, adversity, human rights, humanitarian, gift book, gift idea

4. Click on **Add a Product.**
5. Finally, **type in "Secret Speakers and the Search for Selador's Gate."** That's it! Thank you.

DID YOU KNOW . . .
Secret Speakers is self-published?
It's true. I'm the author, Karey Shane.
Would you please read this page
(and the two pages before this one)? Thank you.